CHAOS AND CREATION

THE ORIGINS OF CYLLA

CHAOS AND CREATION SERIES
BOOK ONE

HARLEIGH ROSE KNIGHT

TRIGGER WARNING

This book may discuss topics that are not suitable for everyone and may be difficult for some readers. This book includes: mentions of parental neglect, emotional abuse, infant death, dismemberment, physical abuse, panic attacks, and attempted sexual assault.
This is a story about deities with loose inspiration from mythology. If topics of violence and death are too much for you, put the book aside and take care of your mental health first.

To my children. Thank you for encouraging me to be a mother and follow my dreams at the same time.
I love you, my world.

AUTHOR NOTES

This book started in a very different place than it is today. I started with Ruri, named something completely different, and she was going on a journey to discover that she was a sleeping god. Things evolved over a year. She is still going on a journey to step into godhood, but I had too many things that I wanted to do, and I just knew that I needed to back the story up because some things in the story just wouldn't feel the same if I didn't.

I wanted a story about diverse kinds of love. Romantic partners are usually center stage, but the love between best friends or siblings is just as big and strong. I hope that while reading, you find someone inside of the pages to connect with.

I hope that you see all of the different examples of love. I hope that some part sticks with you when you close the pages.

CYLLA
OURANOS
OREST
BRONTIDE
SEPHTIS
DAXO
BRISA
MIDORI
SELMOR

ELOWEN
ASHBELL
YR
ENDIS
EREBUS
ELD
MOIRA

CHAPTER ONE
THE AWAKENING OF DEATH

The Teachings of Starlight

I was once only a glow of starlight. I knew my glow was bright, but it mattered not. There was no one to admire the shine or care for the glimmer, surrounded by silence and darkness. I started to dim out until a strange feeling of hope warmed me. I envisioned children and a world—landscapes of all colors and water deep. I clung to the feeling.

CAYM

Light started to fill the edges of my eyes. Darkness was the only thing I knew—quiet, endless darkness. The light that peeked through the endless abyss was a shock. It startled me, and I took a breath. I pulled in until my chest ached from being too full.

"Thamm, please," A voice pleaded from somewhere that I could not see. "If you would just hold still, I can grab it."

More light entered my darkness, and shapes outlined in a blurred ring began to form.

"It's not as easy as you make it out to be!" A second voice yelled.

The blur became two clear figures the more I blinked. A man with tanned skin and long grey hair held up another with short golden hair. They looked as if they were copied from each other. So similar, but one had a beard as long and grey as the hair on his head.

Why was I seeing them?

My sight became as constant as my breath. The man in grey tossed the blonde over a stone slab to the other side. I was sure he would be tangled in the abundance of vines that covered every surface of the slab. The blonde man's body made a thud when it hit the other side.

I floated in nothing and nowhere. Able to see the two men, but they were unaware of my presence. They were surrounded by a glowing color. I glided closer from my position above them. They walked along the ground, but I floated above them.

My lungs stopped aching, and my eyes stopped burning. Then, I was only curious.

I watched the blonde steal a golden peach from a tree. He plucked it with fear in his eyes. When it was in his hand, and nothing occurred, he looked at it with pride. He gave me a strange feeling. The bright red color around him told of ego and anger. He felt wrong, as if he weren't supposed to be—not just in the location, but at all. He made me feel uneasy and untrusting.

Another tree grew, but the tree was in my realm. It grew taller, brighter than the trees they plucked from. The emotions that it fed me when I touched it were so much stronger than the aura of the man. I had nearly forgotten he was there at all.

I felt a heartbeat from the tree but nothing else. It did not move nor speak. I wanted to stay with it. To sit with the tree and remain. The tree was my first glimpse of warmth. Of comfort. The tree was silent and unmoving but still somehow nurturing. I wanted to care for it, to embrace it. I wanted to thank it. For what, I did not know.

It did not matter what I wanted nor how I silently pleaded. I was pulled unwillingly back to the men.

A petal from the tree landed in my palm before I was pulled too far, and when it did, a shock filled me. An unknown force pulled me against my will after the men so quickly that I thought I might split in two. As if to tell me I was tethered to them.

I was covered in a buzz of sensations that set my skin on fire. When I stopped in front of the man in grey, my body was covered in emerald streaks of lightning. I stood so close to the man that if I moved, I would have touched him. Yet he still did not see me.

A transparent wall, a veil, separated us. He had no idea of my presence, but I somehow knew all of his movements.

When the burning of my skin stopped, it sparked something in me—something that held memory. I was the God of Death. I was in the veil that held the dead from the living. It was wrong. I shouldn't be where I was. No matter how I tried, my mind was too cloudy to give me the information I was pushing it for. I felt outside of myself.

I felt as though I knew exactly who I was and that I should not be dead, and yet I knew nothing of any concept outside of darkness. My temples throbbed, and tingles radiated up my feet.

The man on the other side of the veil stopped in front of a red-headed woman. She leaned on the frame with a frown.

"Next time, I'm going to feed you to Emon instead of offering you shelter." She said.

"Who will keep you company then?" He smiled back at her.

Her words rolled with sarcasm, "Like Emon, I'd finally have some peace."

She felt the same to me as the golden-haired man—strangely empty and uncomfortable. She made my heart beat irregularly. Something about her eyes sank my stomach. They were crimson in a way that should have been beautiful but ended up being only unnerving. She was surrounded by an orange glow that reeked of ambition.

"You'd miss me too much." The man replied.

"You'd miss me, too!" the blonde yelled. "Like you missed throwing me in the right direction. Or, like, you missed climbing over the wall with me, and you definitely missed helping me recover the item we went to the garden for!" His cheeks were flushed.

The blonde held up the golden peach for everyone to see, and the woman shifted uncomfortably.

She felt fake to me. She felt as though she should be where I was standing, and I knew that I should have been where she was standing. We were on the wrong side of the veil.

"You stole from the Sunlight Garden!" She yelled and pointed.

"Lower your voice," the blonde urged.

The man cut the fruit in half and separated the peach from its seed. He tossed the peach to the ground and closed both of his palms around the seed. Whispered words that I could not understand hummed low, and my body screamed in agony in response.

The seed glowed with a green light and started shaking, but so did I. My body felt as if it lasted for an eternity. When it finally stopped, silence hung in the air.

"Very impressive." The woman mocked, "You two can leave now."

"I can't believe I held up a heavyweight like you for a three-second light show. You said that you'd figured it out this time." The man frowned.

I looked up at the three of them, still unaware of my presence, from my hands and knees. The pain had stopped, and I welcomed the moment of relief while I watched droplets leave my head and hit the ground. It took every bit of strength I had to resist whatever was happening.

I lifted one leg and rested my hand on my knee. I needed a moment to pull in a few more breaths before standing all the way. I was beginning to feel heavier than I knew how to hold up. As if I was being shoved out of the veil and into their realm before I was ready.

I did not get the chance to adjust before I was pulled by a force that I could not see. I was pulled against a smooth nothingness until I was back in front of the tree.

How? I did not know.

A branch from the tree, still in the veil with me, lowered itself and shoved me with such force that the veil in front of us started to rip, and I was inside of the peach seed. I screamed, and I clawed at the rough brown surface surrounding me on all sides.

I was frantic. My cheeks felt hot and my chest tight. My hands shook, and my nails ripped with the force of my clawing.

It did nothing. I pulled in hot air that I had already recycled too many times.

My efforts had done nothing to any part of the walls that began to shrink in on me.

"Let me out!" My voice was raspy, and I did not recognize it.

My legs kicked at the seed, then again. I lost track of how many times I tried to escape. The seed cracked after what felt like an eternity. A slice down the center that begged me to leave. I gave it what it pleaded for because I wanted it the most.

I hardly felt real before, but I was truly detached from my own mind. I wanted out.

I need the fresh air, the freedom that the crack offered. I needed light.

I kicked and clawed at the crack. I shook and struggled until the seed shattered away from me. All three of the beings that I watched, what had to be only moments ago, looked at me for the first time.

"Stars be damned." The man in grey gasped.

The woman held a hand over her eyes and shifted away. I moved my eyes between the three; It looked like I had brought an ill reaction to them.

"I can tell you didn't prepare for this because you have no clothing for him to wear. So, did you at least pick a name for him?" she asked.

"I'll be naming him Caym." The man answered.

His voice had a different kind of tone lining it. A tone that made me feel like I was on the same plane of existence. He sounded happy when he spoke to the man, but anytime the woman spoke to him, his voice turned bitter. It must have been normal because she only had a kind tone when talking to the grey beard.

"Do you have any clothing we can use, Helia?" The blonde asked.

"Of course, my dear brother. I'm always here to ensure my thoughts pick up where yours end." Her eyes rolled backward.

She leaned halfway inside of her doorway. It was too large for her, and she looked oddly small inside of it. A screen still covered half of the entrance as if she had something to hide. It was decorated with the same kind of tree I saw before coming here: pastel hues on a sunset background with small black birds flying across the sky. When she leaned back out, she came with a gown surely too big for her. She tossed it to the blonde before crossing her arms.

"You should wear the gown and allow him to wear your clothing. It's what any decent parent would do, after all.

Seeing your son shamed so quickly after his first breath?" She lifted her hand to her chest and gasped. Something about the action felt purposely fake.

Son? I was no son of his. I was, who was I again? I knew who I was just a moment ago. I seemed to have forgotten. I was forgetting as quickly as I was thinking. I knew many things a moment ago that I couldn't recall. It all seemed to begin by seeing the inside of a seed.

I just recalled a tree, but I could no longer recall its look.

The blonde and Helia fought with each other. I could hardly understand them. They did their best to yell louder than the other, but I did learn his name was Kyrell. There were enough words and insults hurled that I also understood he was the God of Life. A god who was terrible at his duties but finally caught a break with me.

The graybeard backed himself out of the room. He seemed to take advantage of the two being distracted.

"Kyrell," I shifted my head, "The strange-looking thing with the unmanaged fuzz dangling from its face seems to be escaping. Would you like me to kill it?"

"Kill?" Helia shrieked.

The man's jaw dropped open, "Strange looking?" he rubbed his face. "Kyrell, when you help me make my child, I want less of whatever you put in him for this to happen."

"The man's observation is spot on, and though the only deity sad from the loss of Thann would be Helia, I still don't want to have to explain a situation I don't even understand to Yumi. The same Yumi that sent me to see why my Emon was so worked up. She felt a creation event occur and wanted me to check on that first, but I was sure they'd be the same event, and it looks like I was right, huh." The girl clicked her tongue in annoyance.

Helia took a step back and pushed the screen closed behind her without a single word.

"Astra," Thann praised, with arms open. "I was just about to head your way."

"Stop," Astra lifted her ash-tinted hand. "Yumi will want answers, and unless you want me to tell her you've brought a strange man here after stealing from the sunlight garden myself, I suggest you get to walking."

She was different from the other three somehow. It wasn't in the way she looked—she did look different from them—but it was more than that. She sounded harsh in her tone, but she was soft in her presence—somehow full of light. She felt like peace. I saw a flicker of pink surround her.

Kyrell looked less courteous and spoke with clenched teeth, "If someone needs to explain anything to Yumi, I'll do so myself."

"You may want to pull the stick out of your rectum before entering her throne room. You may also want to consider a way to cover his lower parts." She pointed down.

She turned on her heels and left my line of sight. Things sounded as if they brought me into a situation that I didn't want to be a part of.

Did he need help with the stick that she mentioned? Why would he have put it up there? Had they planned to acknowledge me? Did they bring me to life for nothing?

"We should-"

Kyrell cut him off. "I'll go, but it will be the last time I have to answer to someone like Astra. She thought she was so much better than I could be because she was the first to fulfill her duties. She always looked down on me because she could use her powers first. I only need to start building a kingdom in Cylla and leave this petty realm filled with lesser deities." Kyrell gave a look of disgust to Helia's doorway.

If there was a lesser deity, it had to be him. I didn't sense much of anything from him.

He stomped out of the room as though his feet were too heavy for him to control correctly. He did not look back at me on his way. I wish he would have stayed so I could have gotten more answers. He talked of lesser deities, but from what I sensed at arrival, there weren't many deities at all.

Was I wrong? His soul was tinted in color when I was in the other realm. Though, maybe I was wrong. Its color faded from my memory. I knew it had been there, hadn't it?

Where was I when I saw it?

Only Thann was left with me, "May I have some of the clothing now?"

He shook his head, "You can't have any of mine. You're far too big. Mine wouldn't look right on you. It's not that I don't want to share. You're just too tall, and I'm-"

"Short with a little mush in the middle," I answered.

"No reason to be rude." He mumbled.

I left the room that we occupied. Maybe Yumi would have more for me, whereas Kyrell did not seem to care. He called me a son but seemed quick to leave me. My mind was foggy, and I didn't remember everything I knew I needed to, but I knew he didn't seem like a father figure to me.

"You're going to get lost!" Thann called.

"I will be fine," I answered.

"Yeah, well, you're already going the wrong way." He grabbed me and took me to the other corridor.

He guided me down another hallway that felt longer than it needed to be. My legs listened effortlessly, but my mind was already tired of the walk. It was a beautiful sight, but it didn't feel warm. White was the base of everything. It felt so easy to blemish.

"Where are we?" I asked.

"Semper, the realm of the Gods." He answered.

"Why is everything white?" I questioned again. "It's blinding."

"Yumi taught us it symbolizes the purity of the deities." He answered.

Purity? What kind of place was I in?

Thann pushed the door open and motioned me inside. He did it so quickly that I understood he was done with my questions. Kyrell already stood in the room. He looked even further displeased than he had before.

"Kyrell." Yumi's voice, like silk, sounded before I could fully enter. "Astra said you were the reason that Emon was out of the Sunlight Garden and worked up?" The silver of her crown was nearly blinding. "I heard you finally lived up to being the God of Life."

Kyrell nodded; his teeth still clearly held tightly together.

"He looks strong." Yumi smiled.

She looked me in the eyes. She didn't look for their color or shape. She looked for a window inside of me. She gazed so deep that I felt her fingertips inside of my mind. What there may have been to find, I hardly knew.

Astra turned her head to Yumi, her huff of breath loud enough to turn all heads toward her except Yumi's. Kyrell's eyes left Astra quickly and met Yumi's. He followed her gaze and realized what she stared at. He moved to me with speed, grabbed me by the arm, and pulled me forward. He held his chin high when we stopped.

"I created the first descendant of any of your children." He announced.

"Wouldn't using his name be a better way to introduce him?" Astra remarked.

Yumi stood; she used one hand to lift her skirt just enough for the tips of her feet to be visible. Her peach skin was soft in color and texture, but her rounded eyes pulled all of the attention. They were large compared to the rest of her features and chestnut brown in color. She took the space between us too slowly, and I felt a tinge of impatience at her speed.

"You look just like Kyrell!" Her hands rested on my forearms; It appeared I was too tall for her to reach anything else. She used her grip to jerk me down to her level. "You are perfect!" Her voice rose to a higher pitch when she pinched my cheeks between her fingers.

My face cried for help with every pull and tug she gave to my cheeks.

"I believe your observations are incorrect." I tried to say through her grip. "Kyrell's looks are comparable to a god done well enough to survive life but nothing to chisel into stone. I couldn't have gotten my jawline from him."

"Was that you trying to joke?" Astra asked, her lips turned down.

Yumi gave a small laugh, "He is a little sore on the eyes, isn't he? What is your name?"

"Caym," Kyrell gritted out.

"That is a perfect name," Yumi answered. "You should have brought him here sooner. He's missing something silver and white for our family colors, but that can wait, I suppose.

"You aren't going to punish him?" Astra seethed.

"First, I'm going to clothe our newest member," Yumi said, waving a hand over me.

Fabric grew around my body. All white in color with hints of silver trimming. A plain top, then a vest. Pants soft enough I wanted to keep touching them, then an overcoat.

"Next, I'll ask you what there is to punish. We should be celebrating! This day reminds me of when you all were born." Yumi still smiled up at me.

"Astra's eyebrows lifted, "Will everyone be celebrated for stealing what you've said isn't theirs? You tasked me with protecting the Sunlight Garden and laid it into law that no one is to steal the golden fruits or touch the Tree of Life. Caym comes from a golden peach!"

The more Astra spoke, the less her voice sounded concerned with punishment of her own.

"If I hand out golden fruit, will everyone bring me such a prized gift?" Yumi's hands still gripped me with gentleness, but her tone was becoming increasingly annoyed with the girl.

"What do you want, Caym? Anything at all. I'll give it to you as a gift."

"A realm," Kyrell interjected. "We want a realm to build up as a home for the dead."

"What a great idea!" Yumi cheered. "I will need to check that your abilities are compatible with such a task. I also need to speak to Kyrell alone. Everyone else may leave."

She let go of me and walked to a fabric screen sitting in the room. It was positioned to create a pretend wall. The screen was silver like the rest of the room. Still, the silver wasn't enough to break up the white, and the room was overwhelmingly bright for it. She stopped before we could reach the other side of the fabric wall and pulled me back down to her.

She lifted her pointer finger, and it emitted a glow of soft light. She pressed it to my forehead before I could ask any questions.

"He is the God of Death. It seems you knew exactly what he needed from the start, Kyrell." She took her finger off my forehead.

I thought it was best to learn more before I engaged with Yumi. There seemed to be a lot more going on than I could see yet, and Yumi felt somehow familiar. I knew it was impossible to know any of them, but when I looked at her, I saw something I couldn't put my finger on. Others occasionally showed a blur of color, but she did not.

I watched Yumi, the Goddess of Starlight, pull a blossom from her dress pocket. She motioned me to come back down to her, and I listened. She plucked a strand of my black hair and ruffled the rest with her other hand. She still looked at me with light in her eyes and a smile on her face.

She wrapped the strand of hair around the blossom and blew it into the air. They didn't have the chance to fall to the ground before Yumi snapped a finger; it grew into a layer of vines up the wall. They sat beside another set of vines filled with roses, crimson in color, that showed the image in ripples of a realm I somehow knew to be named Cylla. It felt familiar, like she did.

The second set of vines she grew sprouted emerald orchids and the ripples inside of it showed a blank canvas of the brightest green grass.

"Come," Yumi motioned to all of us.

The image on the other side was no different than the ripples showed. It was ready to be formed. Yumi still smiled, but it began to unnerve me. It was her eyes that took on a more serious note to them. They could not resist holding the words she didn't speak. She was displeased by something.

"Caym seems to have been born with markings on his skin," Yumi said, more to Kyrell than I. "I don't want to cause any alarm, but I'm sure you can see how it's abnormal. I want it to be understood that I'm laying strict rules for the time being. He is not to enter the Sunlight Garden, and he is absolutely not allowed anywhere near or to touch the Tree of Life. Is it clear?"

Kyrell nodded.

"It's only until I can be sure he won't bring any harm, you understand." She said.

"He should stay in Merripen and attend to his duties, harm or not," Kyrell said.

"Don't be ridiculous-"

They kept talking, but I had no interest in listening. I had not been truly invited to listen to a conversation yet. It was all about me, but none of it to me. I lowered myself to the ground and ran a hand over the grass. I was eager to start something. Eager to meet other gods that did not have a hidden agenda. When I touched the grass, however, it started to die beneath me. I tried again in another spot, and it, too, died.

"Yumi," I called back. "It's dying."

She walked over to me and put a hand on my shoulder. "You are death. Things are happening as they should be."

"But how will I grow anything here? How will I build a realm?" I shook my head.

"By allowing it all to die," she cupped my face in her hands. "The dead will live here; it does seem right for everything else here to be in the same form. Don't worry, my boy; it is all as it should be. Your father can bring life to what needs it if you only ask him."

"You and I will become close," Kyrell said.

The thought made me uncomfortable. I wasn't fond of him. I didn't know if I ever would be. My mind was fogged, but I still knew his presence was wrong.

"You can make this realm anything you'd like, Caym. I will bless you as the God of Death and leave you in charge of it. Kyrell will teach you, and if you should need me, you may find me exactly where we just met." She reached her hand up and gave me another pinch.

She left, and so did Kyrell. I did not expect to be tossed to the side so quickly. I went back to taking in the scenery. It went on as far as I could see. I tried to touch a flower, and it slowly withered away again. Kyrell didn't have the time to teach me anything. Maybe someone else would.

I hesitated, at first, to walk through the portal alone. When I worked up the courage to do so, it worked the same as it did with Yumi. I was half-heartedly convinced by Kyrell's attitude that he would have locked me in. Deities were still in the room, which I also hadn't expected.

"A blessed item? We are blessed items."

I leaned around the screen that sat in front of the vines just enough to see with an eye. It was Thann; he pulled a knife out of his pocket and flung it open. Before I could react, he used it to slice off his pointer finger at the first knuckle and toss it to Kyrell. "Use it."

Kyrell hardly caught it; his face grimaced. "I admire the

commitment, but don't you dare say a word to me about it if this doesn't work, you disgusting fuc-"

Thann hushed him before he could finish his words and hurried him along.

What were they doing?

It only took a moment before the finger hit the ground and grew a girl. She sat in front of the two, dazed and confused. Another creation so soon after my own seemed careless.

I didn't know much, but I was sure that I needed to stay on guard and become a silent observer. In the brief time I was present, I could see that trust in the realm was slim and ambition was high.

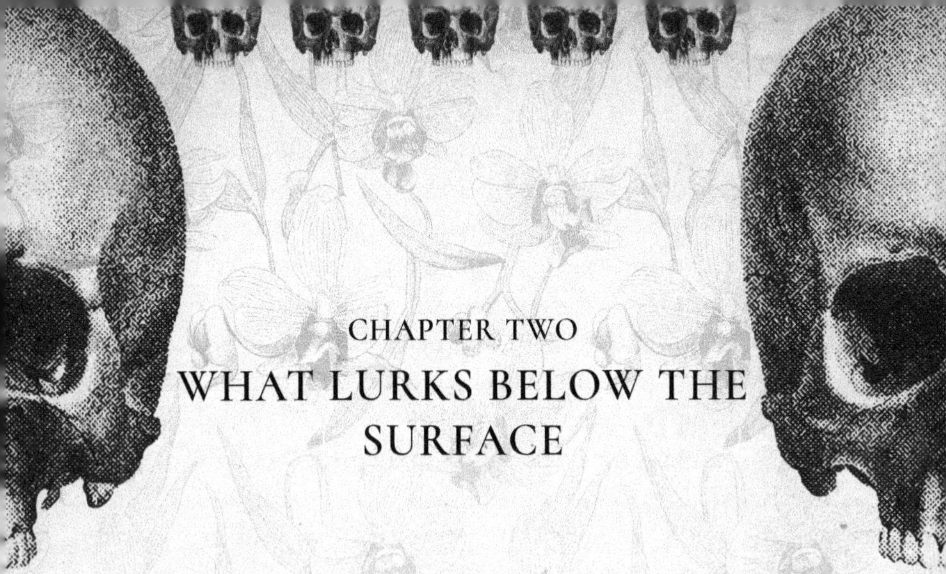

CHAPTER TWO

WHAT LURKS BELOW THE SURFACE

The Teachings of Starlight

I thought my hopes were strong enough to finally manifest into something solid, something I could touch, so I tried. I tried with every piece of whatever I was. The wants and hopes I had spent so long in silence dreaming of must have been more substantial than even I understood because after only a tiny amount of time, there I was. A sparkling star filled with light, now a woman with two feet, legs, hands, and a face. I had sparked creation with my own mind.

CAYM

It had been a long three years since my creation, and I was handed the blank canvas of Merripen. My time in Semper was quiet and largely spent alone. Not because I wanted it that way and not because of a lack of effort on the part of others. They were all too interested in me.

Kyrell's primary pursuit was to keep everyone out. I thought the realm was to be mine and that I was to be something important.

I tended to the realm's every need; I hurt my body to build it, but I rode waves of confusion when I had to listen to Kyrell claim all the rewards. It's not that I wanted everything that Kyrell wanted. Our goals were not aligned. I only wanted to be rewarded one more time and be in a position to ask Yumi for anything at all again. I only wanted to be rewarded so that I may ask for my freedom.

Yumi told me I was free to roam as I pleased, that my only rule was to keep away from the Sunlight Garden, and I would, but Kyrell did not agree. Not since the moment she said it. She was all too happy to forget her words. If I had them in a more solidified way, they may become usable.

I've learned that what happened in the dark had a hard time seeing light. Any mark he left on my body, he healed himself. Kyrell silently dubbed himself my true maker and, as such, my master.

I watched the sun disappear behind the orange sky, and the two moons that replaced it rise sixty-four times since the last time I was able to sneak out of the vines and see anything beyond my small patch of light. Every rise brought me closer to the only question I had left.

Why am I listening to him?

I learned that I was to be considered the next generation of deities, and they were the creator and primordial deities. They were the Gods of rebirth, life, time, space, and fate. Yumi was the Goddess of Starlight and in control of everything—words, actions, and anything in between. She ruled it all. It was only in the title because of all the things I could say for sure—it was that no one feared her, truly.

Today, I sat by the vines and watched black mountains against the horizon of the orange-tinted skyline, so sharp they looked as if they could have been teeth. I was certain that if many did realize the vines between realms carried voices, they did not care. I often sat with them to feel company and listened to conversations each of the residents had when they thought privacy surrounded them. I held many secrets close.

At the very least, Kyrell couldn't have known. If he had, he would have also taken the vines from me. His refusal to let me leave at first felt protective, the attitude of a loving father. After endless discussions of what it would take for me to leave, he found reason after reason why the answer would always remain no; I stopped asking. I stopped considering him acting as a father.

I would come close to the decision to leave, and then I would hear plans of scheming from the throne room and decide against it. I was confident in my physical strength; I was not confident that I was equipped to deal with endless attempts on my life or being thrust into their games.

Maybe that was the excuse I used to make myself feel better for not trying. Maybe Kyrell was right, and loneliness was what I deserved.

I tilted more towards frustration today; I may also say sadness. I was left to wait for a visit to plead with Kyrell to grow new plant life where I could not. I tried endlessly, but anytime I tried to tend to it, it died. My touch seemed to carry only the ability to take life from everything. I wouldn't admit it out loud, but I silently tested it on Kyrell. It wasn't that I wanted to kill him, per se. I wouldn't have mourned it if he had died, but I needed to know if I was safe to touch anything or anyone at all.

Kyrell showed no sign of pain or deterioration. He only thought I was trying to be sentimental. It was another moment I realized he was not like a father. My touch disgusted him. Only my accomplishments that were in line with his demands were worth pride.

My life ran on small rewards behind Kyrell's back. As such, I treated life like every detail needed to be absorbed. The vines gave me the ability to learn what Kyrell would never teach me. The Gods that had been created were blessed with basic abilities, mostly centered around creation specifics. I could terraform land and fill craters with water. Raise mountains and build structures with no end in sight. So could most others, according to Yumi. It was one of her many lies.

Astra, the Goddess of Space, was beyond skilled. I listened through the vines of the planets Astra made and the complaints of how she could also form new stars. Kyrell flickered. I was his best achievement, and he never sparked enough to repeat it. Minna never attempted; I was sure it was because she had no ability at all. Thann, the God of Rebirth, was a mystery to me. He was with Helia or silent.

Helia, the Goddess of Time, spent more effort on other hobbies. She never stopped making me feel uncomfortable.

They all seemed to have a reason why they could not perform.

Sometimes, I reasoned that I was locked away because Kyrell did care. That he was only trying to protect me from a realm filled with deities that could do nothing. A realm where I was sure to have a target on my back because I could do things.

That was harder to believe recently. One of the conversations that I overheard Yumi have through the vines made my desire to leave higher than it had been yet.

Yumi talked of the second realm, Cylla, and I understood its goal was to fill Cylla with mortals. She explained to Helia that they would give us purpose. I understood I was to look after their eternity in Merripen when their time in Cylla ended.

What I did not understand was why Yumi did not tell

anyone outside of Helia that she would die without the mortals. I did not understand why she didn't tell everyone that without Cylla and the prayers the mortals would bring, she wouldn't be strong enough to keep the tree under control. She wasn't telling anyone else much of anything that would dissolve their happiness.

Between her words and the feeling surrounding the other deities, I was beyond curious.

I considered that she had grown weaker after she created so many things or that perhaps she was worried someone would take her place on the throne of Semper. Louder than my thoughts was the pit in my stomach that told me I needed to find solid answers.

I knew with Kyrell in charge of my freedom, I'd have ample time to learn only what I needed to learn and never be given an answer by him.

I also knew I'd never be graced with the company of even the smallest flower. I ached for it. I wanted the souls who stayed with me to have a better eternity than I was cursed to spend. I built up a central area for Merripen that Kyrell knew of, and in a small stance of rebellion, I also built a small home away from all eyes.

I kept my home simple, made of logs that I put together after tying cloth to my hands. It didn't fix the problem I had with my hands, but it gave me enough time to build. I turned all the rot marks that my touch created on the dying wood inward and hid them among each other. The marks were a hidden secret that only I knew. A secret tale of how hard I tried to build something small and beautiful.

I paved walkways with stones and plotted spots for homes in the city center. The city of the dead would be as beautiful as I could make it once I could get an understanding of the curse on my hands.

I noticed that I picked too much skin off my lip with my teeth while I paced back and forth in front of the vines. My ability to stop glances at the vines grew thinner the lower the sun sat in the sky. Yumi was supposed to check my progress. My realm depended on others to first do their duties, so I didn't see the need. I had nothing to show her.

The sun dropped even lower while I thought, and so did I. My shoulders slumped with my desire. Yumi wasn't the only one late. Kyrell was late for his visit, as well. He didn't need to make haste when he knew his prisoner would behave and mind his meaningless title in his empty prison.

What good did I do by not leaving my confines?

I knew no one else would have kept to these rules. It would have been reasonable for me to go and find out what was causing him to be tardy.

I was too indecisive. I always swayed back and forth. I was never able to commit and be satisfied with going or staying.

I fought with myself over the idea. I had two feet waiting for me to use them. I knew how to leave, and there was nothing solid between the vines that truly held me in place. It was only the words of Kyrell that kept my feet still. For what? I was a god, too. I was free, too. Wasn't I? Wasn't I powerful and more than a body to command? Maybe Yumi didn't step in because she wanted me to see that for myself.

I always talked myself onto the tip of a mountain before I reasoned myself down by saying I didn't truly have anyone waiting for me on the other side for it to make a difference. The only changes I would make were the scenery and a fight. I thought myself back onto that ledge, and when I stood to march through the vines, Kyrell appeared before me. The gold on his clothes hit every piece of light left on his way in.

I'd think of the sight at a later time as if it were a message to stay put.

Kyrell's mouth hung open. He was prepared to call for me as if I were a pet.

He didn't consider me a priority. He didn't consider what it was like to be utterly alone with only your thoughts endlessly. He didn't care about the position he left me in every day. I wasn't sure he even saw me as a being like himself.

"You're late," I whispered if only to keep from a yell.

"Late?" Kyrell's eyelids narrowed.

"You come every other day at the peak of sunrise to check on me. It's long past mid-day." My words dripped disappointment.

Kyrell sighed. "I had something to do first. Thann had to show off his plot of land in Cylla. He built a school he named Orest and brought rock golems to life. It's all absurd if you ask me. He thinks he's going to run a school and train mortals. In what? How to be a failure? How to overcompensate with giant creatures? Yumi wanted us all there, so of course, I made an exception for your absence. Astra wanted a fight, and naturally, Minna joined in. I know they're trying to corrupt you. It's all from a place of jealousy. When Minna couldn't contain herself anymore, she vomited. It wasn't just a symptom of envy. It was a result of rage, and she created the goddess of wrath from her bile. How can anyone be trusted that holds so much of an emotion that they spew an entire being from it?" Kyrell shook his head. "No one thought it odd that she just puked up a deity. They all seemed to ignore the fact that Helia helped him to build it all. I heard her discuss using blood to make the golems with my own ears."

My ears rang, and I was the one filled with wrath the more words he spoke. "I want to leave," I said and stood taller.

"Leave?" Kyrell almost shouted. "What do you mean, leave? Did you not hear anything I just said to you? I created you to take care of this place, and you're already ungrateful for everything you have when out there they use their own blood to get ahead!"

I felt my face fall. "I've done everything you've asked me to. I've done it without tricks. The realm is developed and nearly ready for something not even here, so I sit alone in silence. I watch the day go to night and night go to daylight again while you are busy with Gods that I can't speak to, in a realm I cannot visit. Then you gossip to me as if nothing I just said matters to you! You cannot imagine how that feels."

The way he looked at me, the redness that formed on his cheeks. The vein I saw in his neck all spoke of his hypocrisy. He went on about his sister, but he was the one brewing rage the same way. He turned his back to me and slung his hands at my city, sending buildings crashing to the ground. Homes turned to rubble, and wood holding together shops split in half. My city looked as if a disaster had moved through it. He ruined my realm out of anger. I knew he would use it as a reason why I had to stay.

The only thing he was good at was destruction.

He trudged back to where I stood, face still flushed, no longer from anger but exhaustion. I heard his tired sigh before he spoke. Any frustration he held, he released on me.

"If you're lonely, I'll create something to keep you company, but you aren't to leave. You have too much work to do here. You can do better than whatever that was you built. I know you can. You cannot leave, Period. You wouldn't understand the games that are played in Semper even if I let you. Everyone is looking for something to hold over someone's head. Stay here and be safe. Free of any tainting." Kyrell said.

I hardly had any strong emotions of my own to give him. That was who he was, and I was so used to it that even though I knew what he did was wrong, it hardly brought anything out of me. My own anger never made a difference.

"Games are played here, as well. You've prepared me well enough that I may surprise you." I answered simply.

His bare face allowed me to see every small movement that occurred. He didn't have the slightest stubble to cover any of the twitches. I lied to myself; I felt my face heat and realized maybe I had strong emotions for him.

"I won't repeat myself. I won't listen to your disrespectful comments, either." Kyrell took a deep breath and composed himself. "What you don't see is Yumi losing her grip. She keeps having outbursts. She will be her normal passive, reasonable self; the next moment, her frustration leads her to lash out; she isn't far from hurting someone. You no longer know what you'll get with her!"

I stopped his words. "You said you'd create some sort of company for me." I locked eyes with his. The gold in them didn't do a good enough job of hiding that he was an awful God. "It would be best if you didn't discuss such subjects with me. They don't have anything to do with me and may taint me."

"Fine. You're right. I won't fill you in on things that are meaningless to you." Kyrell twisted his neck as if to crack it.

He watched me for a few extra moments, and I saw the displeasure on his face. We didn't challenge each other any further. The event was more to me than our disagreements had been before. It gave me the burst of energy I needed to see clearly.

Maybe I was the only one keeping me locked away.

Kyrell formed a ball of light in both hands; he held the beam that formed between us both and directed it to the ground. He let it linger above the blades of grass before he slammed both fists, red with heat, into the ground. The light dissipated, and from it came a cloud of smoke. The smoke took form in front of me. Its shape was the same as mine in outline, but it had no skin or muscle. Several more formed from the still-waving smoke; before either of us knew it, there were too many to count.

They stood before both of us but gave all their attention to me. They were tall in stature, outlined in waves of smoke. Their faces had the shape of an eyeless skeleton. With two tusks that grew in a curve well under where their chin should have been, pumping hearts were visible in their chest cavity, with no clear answer as to how it was being held in place. The veins that started with the heart and lead, entwined through bone, were the only other sign of Life in them.

"I'll call the Nola," I said.

"Don't make me regret this," Kyrell said. He looked at me like he already did regret his choice. "I still have things to finish before my day ends, so is there anything else?"

I shook my head in response. I had no other words to say to him, and judging by the pace at which he left, he didn't have anything left to say to me. I hardly had the space to think about any of it further when I turned around and saw the Nola already fast at work. They were filling in homes that still needed stone. They healed the grass I killed. They were rebuilding what I had, what Kyrell turned into disaster without my asking.

"That is quite a sight."

I nodded my head. They not only worked quickly but what they built looked immaculate. They had no lessons, were taught nothing, and yet they-

Wait, what?

"Yumi!" I jumped out of my skin.

"They aren't easy on the eyes, but they will make things easier for you." She said. Her orange hair was wrapped in circles on her head. She somehow managed to thread it through her headdress.

I thought so much activity in Merripen would be great, but it made my heartbeat quicker, and my palms sweat from all the noise.

"Both are true." I tried not to sound startled.

"I apologize for being late. We had a gathering in Cylla. Kyrell said you weren't feeling well, but that seems less than true." Her brown eyes looked at me with knowing, yet she never truly intervened.

It was like a new wound when she expected me to play along with her happily. I wasn't granted permission to be upset that she allowed things to go on as if they happened outside of her control. How can someone be both the face of ultimate say and the face of passive ideals at the same time?

"I am not ill." I agreed.

"I can understand how trying to befriend deities so much older than you are, well, it can be intimidating. Juniper, Goddess of Wrath, was also created recently. The two of you could try and develop a friendship." Yumi offered.

Was she delusional? I scraped my lip with my bottom teeth again. I could taste the small bits of blood from the skin I was pulling away, but I still could not stop myself.

"Yumi, may I ask a question?" I paused.

"Of course." She agreed.

"I've noticed some things seem a bit off in Semper," I said.

"Oh?" She urged me to continue.

"I've noticed some of the deities seem to be weaker than the others. By weaker, I mean completely powerless. Astra uses her abilities as if she never knew a time without them. Minna struggles to use hers correctly as if her abilities don't belong to her. It seems-" She stopped me.

"Caym, it's only because yours came to you so naturally that you see things differently. I know you are eager to have Merripen sprawling, and we will get there with plenty of understanding. In the meantime, maybe encourage your father that you are proud of him." Yumi smiled at me.

Her words disgusted me. Every single time that man was called my father, I felt hatred and bile fill my throat. I knew what a father was, and it was not Kyrell. I had knowledge of a place before. A place called the Age of Moonlight, but every time I reached for it, it moved further back. I forgot every time I could remember. I only grasped the words "Age of Moon-light," but I didn't know what it meant.

The smile she held on to never tilted. She never looked at me with disappointment like the God of Life did.

She never faltered. She was hard to believe in. I heard what she said when she thought she was alone. I knew the wavering in her voice when she was another day down with no progress and how she covered it all up in the presence of mixed company. How could anyone trust that?

I gave the Goddess of Starlight a smile and a nod of agreement all the same. It was to be my last act of pleasing for the sake of pleasing. No more for her or Kyrell. There wasn't any justification for it, and I couldn't push myself to explain away their behavior. If Yumi did not see my life as an act of cruelty and wanted to do something for my sake, then I would have to do it myself.

I left her behind. I snapped my fingers and turned myself into a shadow. I formed back into a man in front of my cottage door. So much noise came from inside, and I was terrified of what I could have found. I pushed the door open quickly with one finger so as not to rot it away. Inside were a handful of Nola. They squealed and screamed over my cooking pot. One fanned at flames that were uncontrolled. One stood around them and squealed the loudest. It was clear he lectured them.

The last three grabbed at fruits they skewered with sticks over the flames that were charred beyond recognition.

"What is happening!" I shouted.

They all stopped mid-movement. Not a single hushed squeak made an appearance.

"Nothing to say for yourselves?" I looked around and shook my head. "Where did you even get this stuff?"

A Nola grumbled, and somehow, I understood it.

"You stole it from the garden in Semper? The one with the tree?" I ran a hand over each temple. How did they even leave so quickly? "That one is on fire," I pointed.

A Nola picked the burning one up and ran him outside. He shifted the weather from calm skies to clouded. I watched it in surprise. They were more than I thought they could have been. The Nola called down rain and dumped the other underneath the cloud.

Squeals came from my side, the skeletal limbs crossed in mimicry of my own. Another squeal followed by a higher-pitched shriek.

"Yeah, I agree. Some of them aren't too bright." I answered him.

He held out his thin, lanky fingers, and a black apple was offered to me.

"You go ahead," I answered. "I'll wait for something a little less crunchy."

I snapped my fingers to send the storm clouds away and brighten the sky again. The action brought a light breeze to the area. I let out a deep breath of relief, happy to have things back to quiet.

I was deceived, lied to by the quiet wind. A Nola was in front of me again. The sockets where eyes should have been on the Nola flickered with light before projecting an image in front of me. Helia stood hidden behind a tree. She watched a newly injured Thann cradle the arm he had ripped open on a tree. Though the wound looked disgusting, it would heal.

A branch sat on the ground, covered in the blood that was still flowing from Thann's arm. Helia crept behind them, but they did not notice her. They went through the portal and left her there alone. She knelt down and used her bare fingers to scavenge through the crimson liquid on the ground. She lifted a piece of flesh that had fallen from Thann's arm and sealed it in a jar.

I was disgusted by the sight, but nothing could have prepared me for the sight of her removal of her foot covers to rip her toe open. She snapped and cracked a piece of bone from her foot before she sealed her skin back shut with a thread and needle. Helia combined her bone with Thann's flesh and a blossom from the tree of Life.

My jaw could have hit the dirt when it worked. In front of her stood two women who looked as confused as Helia looked excited.

The Nola's eye sockets went back to normal, and he stood in front of me with a squeal, then a second. He told me that the creation event was complete, and I had no words. It was going to take some adjustments, but if the Nola showed me every major event the gods had a hand in, I would have the biggest advantage against them.

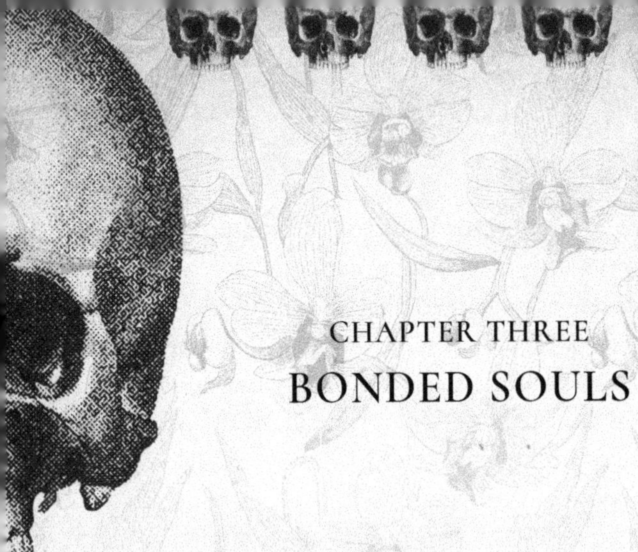

CHAPTER THREE
BONDED SOULS

The Teachings of Starlight

I grew the longest orange hair, and my eyes glowed in matching. It took me several tries to learn how to move my legs correctly. When they finally started listening to my commands, they carried me across a ground that rippled like I knew water would but was still solid and unbreaking. I could see through the ground, but it was empty as far as my sight would carry. The only thing to be seen inside was my reflection. When I turned my sight to the other direction, there was a tree. Tall and light in color. It had the same shimmer I was so used to being covered in myself, but it also bore small, pink blossoms in as many shades. I would imbue it with power to aid me in my journey.

CAYM

Orla, Thann's daughter and the Goddess of Night, paid me a visit after hearing of the newest members of the realm. She was reluctant at first. She claimed she wasn't afraid of Nola, but because of the way she took the smallest steps and the large gap between her and them, I wasn't convinced. They weren't the easiest on the eyes. They were hard on the ears, too, but they were overall harmless.

The air in Merripen was beginning to smell like fresh flowers. It was the sight of my hidden home that brought me the most joy. The Nola had been hard at work gardening. My log home was tucked sweetly in between trees and surrounded by bushes of flowers.

"They won't hurt you." I motioned Orla along, "Just don't ask them for anything to eat."

She dodged them and rushed the steps to my porch. She placed herself in the rocking chair I made for her, which seemed like ages ago.

"You keep saying that, but the way they're looking at me, I don't believe it," Orla said.

One Nola appeared by her side with a glass, and the two of them screamed in unison. Orla lifted her fist to make contact, but the Nola misted its face into shadow, and Orla's hand slipped through.

"Orla, I thought you were supposed to be fearless? You're losing it over a glass?" I shook my head at her.

"It came out of nowhere!" She yelled. "I am not scared of them."

"Good, because we have a lot of gardening to do today. We can help them!" I pointed to the empty side of the cottage.

"Actually, I brought you new paints! It took a little longer this time because everyone wanted a piece of fruit from the Sunlight Garden now that Yumi loosened her grip on it.

Minna knows she can use it to help her make children; she keeps taking the ones I need for the red color." She held up a small wooden container.

"It didn't feel that long to me." I lied. "Now I can finish the picture for the bedroom."

I didn't think she heard me. She kept glancing at the Nola beside her.

"I'm telling you, they're less harmful than Kyrell," I told her.

I held up my hand, and the Nola made contact with its own hand. Both of our palms clapped together, and the Nola held his up for Orla next.

"We're calling it a high five since it's up high and five fingers. Get it?" I lifted my brows at her multiple times.

She clapped her hand against his but did not offer a laugh at my joke.

The Nola pulled Orla up from the rocking chair to the patch of open space and pointed her to the pile of rose bushes that needed to be laid out. It was clear he was giving her orders. Orla looked back at me, and I gave her a thumbs-up. I wasn't used to the situation yet, either. Things became a lot different very quickly for my way of Life.

My existence felt useless and wasted. When the Nola were created, things seemed to move at a pace that made me anxious. I hadn't been alone since their arrival, and if I were to be honest, it was a hard adjustment. One I wasn't expecting. I grew used to the silence, and my jaw hurt from all of the chatter. My nose was stuffed with so many new scents. It was hard to be thrown into such vibrancy and keep my head above it.

I would joke with her out loud and feign disappointment over her not instantly loving the Nola, but the fact was, I understood. There was nothing wrong with them, but their look was shocking. Things felt so locked in idle around us all that the sudden movement shook too many things.

I took a seat in the grass beside them. I had a small window of time that I could help them. We had yet to find a way to fix the issue with my hands, but if I made quick choices, the Nola could heal it fast enough that I didn't feel entirely wasted. I took what I could get because of all the things that went on; being able to feel the leaves under my finger was the best.

"Can I ask you a question?" I tucked roots into the dirt.

"Sure." She said from her own hand shovel.

"Do you remember anything from your creation?" I asked.

She stopped doing any real work and started playing with the dirt instead. She did just enough to look busy but not enough to matter.

"For a few minutes, I knew a lot. It was like I had lived an entire life before this one. It went so fast, and now all I know is that a woman's voice urged me to do something for her. She was almost desperate that I complete the task." Orla sighed, "I don't remember what it was, though."

She looked as if she were lying when she said that she couldn't remember.

"All I remember now is a tree and the feeling that I'm missing something. Something so important. It feels like I'm missing the other half of myself." I smiled, "I thought maybe talking about it would trigger something, but I don't remember any more than I did."

"Me, either." She answered.

She looked at me in silence for a few more moments as if questioning her next words carefully.

"I do keep having dreams." She paused to take in my reaction.

"Of?" I urged.

"A feminine voice. She comes to me every night and asks me to help place a puzzle piece. When I ask her where to find the piece, I can't hear what she says. When I finally heard her speak again, she told me that she had placed something inside of me. That I have to split my heart and soul for it to bond correctly. I don't understand any of it, but I know it feels important. It's all I can think about. She tells me I will be rewarded for splitting my soul, but I don't think I care for a reward. I think I only care about how important it feels to listen to her." Orla was no longer looking at me.

I could not begin to think of a reason someone would need to split their soul. My existence was dealing in souls, and I couldn't understand her or what could be accomplished. She at least sounded honest.

We gardened in silence because I couldn't find the right words to make her feel understood and not out of her mind. The Nola passed around concerned looks, but even they didn't speak. It was clear she had something else to say by how thick things felt between us. I cleared my throat a little too loudly, hoping it would cause the tension to break, but it did not. I tried again, but before I could complete the noise, she sat her shovel down and stared into nothing.

"Can I ask you another question?" She asked, but she still did not look at me.

"Sure," I said.

"Why do you let Kyrell control you? I've seen the way he treats you. Everyone whispers about it. We've seen you in comparison to Kyrell. It just doesn't make any sense. You're treated like a dog, but you never bite back despite having a clear advantage to do so." Orla turned to face me.

"I don't know how to answer that. I've been asking myself the same thing." I said.

"I don't believe you." She said.

"Sometimes I say I'm going to leave. I tell myself it doesn't make sense, and I'm going to go. I never make it far before I ask myself what the point of leaving is. What do I have out there? Is it worth the trouble when I'll come back here to sleep at night all the same? What can I see out there that I can't see in here?" I shook my head.

"You sound just like him right now. It's as if you even have his tone of voice. He really brainwashed you, didn't he?" She got to her feet. "I have to go; I need to meet him today for one last thing so that I can never be involved with him again. You should think about it. If you can come up with your own reason why staying here is better, then stay. If you can't come up with anything that Kyrell didn't tell you first, then can you really say you're here of your own will?" Her eyes lingered on me for a moment before she left.

I watched each step she took away from me. My head pounded to match step for step of her walk. I couldn't argue with her. I didn't want to. I considered her a friend; she had never shown me otherwise. I had to take her words as a form of care, didn't I?

She wasn't saying anything I hadn't thought of already.

Nothing I didn't want to say out loud myself. It was my own constant battle. I could only ever convince myself with Kyrell's words. My own said to leave.

I glanced to my left, and the Nola stood beside me; he did his best not to look directly at me.

"What do you think of me?" I asked.

He gave a shriek of enthusiasm.

I nodded, "I like you, too. If I were to," I rolled my hands in consideration for my next words, "go to war, would you fight for me?"

The sound the Nola gave was a hiss; he kept it going beyond what I thought he could have held his breath for. Every Nola stood beside him; they appeared from nothing and formed squared blocks of perfectly aligned terror. I don't think there could have been a clearer answer. They showed me how quickly they could prepare for a war. They put into sight, instead of words, how fast they could and would defend me.

I felt foolish for a moment. Foolish that I would need such a gesture to stand against someone that I knew inside was not as strong as I was. It didn't change the fact that I did need it. It did give me the confidence to do what I had been longing to do.

I kept my head high while I walked to the vines that held my freedom. My chin tucked for a moment when I reached the rim of the exit. One step, and I would be in another realm. I would be a new deity, a changed god. I would tell him that I was not staying here. I wanted to live; I wanted to find what it was I was missing. I felt my palms start to fill with moisture. Maybe I could do it tomorrow. Maybe-

The Nola shoved me through, and I stumbled forward onto my knee; I stopped myself from going any further down with my opposite palm. There was a fabric and wooden wall that separated the vines from the throne room, and I almost forced it to tumble down.

I got to my feet and brushed my clothing down. I pulled at the ruffles and bunched-up fabric. I would punish that Nola when I got back. I would give him so many duties; he'd be paying me back for seven lifetimes.

A scream ripped from Orla, guttural and deep. A scream that didn't typically come from a scare or a minor situation. It was of pure agony and suffering. It echoed in everything it touched. It was the last pinch I required before I stepped into the other side of the wall and into the throne room. Orla was on her knees. She shook and dripped sweat. My heart sank further than I thought possible. Kyrell stood over her, but she never begged him to stop.

Was that the business she had to finish with him? Was that how she would make her dream a reality? I didn't consider how serious she was when she said the dream drove her to make it a reality.

Kyrell sunk his hand into her chest and pulled it back out. A blue light followed his fingertips. It ran from inside of her to him, and he ripped it in half and shoved what was left back inside. Orla's breath was deep and slow from her new posture on all four limbs. Kyrell split half of her soul with his other hand.

He took his time and looked over every bit of the pulsing flame that came from her as if he enjoyed her pain before he finished the task. The pieces of her he held turned into two daughters that gasped for air the same way she did.

I moved to Orla's side before I was stopped in my tracks, unable to lift my feet any further than they had already carried me. I was left breathless and blank of the thoughts I had been rolling over just a moment ago.

I felt myself crack and lose every piece I once thought I had a grasp on. My heart had an ache to it, and my skin was raised and burning. I was lost. I was lost in the most beautiful emerald eyes I had ever imagined laying my sight on. Lost in the most delicately defined features to ever come into existence. When I found myself, all the cracked pieces came back together. When breath finally entered back into my lungs and, thoughts started to play back in my mind: it was only her that filled me.

She was the piece I was missing. I could feel it in every inch of my body. My soul felt as if it sparked in her presence.

I breathed in the scent that still lingered on her white hair as my oxygen. It was sweet enough; I could smell it from where I stood. My vision only took in the sight of her and the fragments of myself glued back together by the glow that radiated off of her pale skin. I found my saliva hard to swallow down with how dry my throat felt.

I hardly remembered what I had thought or done before I laid eyes on her. The only thing that filled my mind was the need to help her off the ground. To know her name. I had forgotten where I stood until I realized she needed to be covered. I pulled the shirt off of my body and knelt down in front of her. I moved the hair out of her face and pulled the shirt over her head.

"Caym?" Kyrell's voice was as confused as his face.

"I want to name them Ruri and Sage," Orla said.

I only took in Orla's words because I needed that name. The way I would address her, confess to her that I'd help her in whatever way she needed. I needed to finish sorting the long white hairs from her face and ensure her exposed skin wasn't freezing.

"What are you doing here?" Kyrell demanded.

"Kyrell, don't sound so harsh. He's free to come and go." Yumi said.

Kyrell shot Yumi with a side-eyed glance before he ground his teeth together in an audible scrape.

Yumi lifted both hands to hush the room, "Are you alright, Caym?"

I nodded. "As you said, I can come and go as I please. I wanted to help. It was hard to miss all the commotion with my doorway so close."

"See, he's joining us just like everyone else does. There's no need to be so abrasive," Yumi said, looking at Kyrell.

"With your permission, in front of everyone, I'd like to be granted the ability to move freely in Semper," I said.

The conversation was with Yumi, but my eyes couldn't leave Ruri.

"Of course, Caym. You already know that you can." Yumi responded.

Ruri ran the tips of her fingers over my cheeks. They were as soft as they looked. The contact was as electric as I counted on. Every bit of her felt like my other half. She leaned in closer to me and wrapped both of her arms around my neck. She only stopped when her lips were against my ear.

"I thought I'd never see you again," Ruri whispered. "We have to find her. We need her back."

"Who?" I asked, confused. "How do we know each other?"

"Kiss me." She requested.

I became suddenly aware of all the eyes in the room when

my nerves lit me up like the fires of a cooking pot. She gave me no time to react when she put both hands on my shoulders and pulled me into her. Our lips met, and it wasn't only a feeling. Real sparks started to fly between us.

White lighting came from nowhere I could have explained and filled the room. Her skin lit up in the same markings as mine. When both of our bodies glowed in emerald streaks, and the sparks died out, silence followed.

"What was that?" Orla mumbled.

"I do not know," Yumi said. "We should all go back to our quarters now."

"I can assist them back to their rooms." I insisted.

Kyrell's eyes shot in my direction. "You need to get back to Merripen."

"Didn't Yumi tell you he no longer has to stay locked up there?" Astra spoke from the doorway.

Kyrell refused to look at her, "We have things to do there."

"Like what?" Astra asked. She walked the rest of the way into the room. "Caym already made more progress in Merripen than all of us working together in Cylla. Unless you plan to chain him down there to be sure?"

"Kyrell wouldn't do that," Yumi said. "I'm sure Orla can use the extra help. After that, he can get back to Merripen, and his duties will still be waiting."

I didn't ingest anything else he had to say. I snapped my fingers, and Nola appeared. I pointed to the girl with black hair called Sage, and the Nola lifted her as if her weight meant nothing. I lifted Ruri, and he followed me out of the throne room.

On my walk behind Orla, I could not have remarked on any details of the compound. We made it to their quarters without incident, but I only took in the three different shades of green inside Ruri's eyes the entire walk.

Orla pointed me to a side room, and I entered it. I tried to lay Ruri down, but she sat and pressed the pillows instead. I understood that it was a lot to take in at creation.

The Nola entered the room behind me, and Ruri's eyes shot up at him. I was prepared to give her a speech the same way I had to give Orla.

"What is he?" she asked.

"He is a guardian of Merripen," I answered.

"He is the cutest thing I've ever seen." She said.

"You haven't seen much," I remarked.

The Nola did not seem to have the same thought as I did.

"What is his name?" she asked.

I suddenly felt like an awful father, "He doesn't have one."

"I'll call you Jeb!" Ruri said. She scratched at Jeb's chin as if he were a pet.

He seemed to approve, so who was I to stop the two of them?

"Can I ask you something?" I hesitated.

"What?" Ruri looked back at me.

"Who is she? The girl you said we needed to find. What do we need to do to help her? Does she know what these markings are that showed up when you kissed me? Why do yours match mine?" I realized it was a lot to ask, but I needed to know before she could start losing it like the rest of us had.

She looked at me for a long set of heartbeats. "I don't remember anything other than her voice anymore. She sounded so soft. So, inviting. I knew she would be warm and welcoming. She spoke to me, but it's lost now. The more real I feel, the less I can recall." She touched my face again. "I remember you, but it's slipping too quickly. Every memory I play in my head fades away just as quickly."

The sparkle was still in her eyes, but it was glazed with a layer of sadness. I noticed the dark circles under her eyes. She looked exhausted. I was sure it was intensified by the low light in the room. Molded wax sat around the bed she was moving herself deeper into. I still wanted to talk to her about it. I wanted to press her harder before she could forget. I felt like I would drive myself insane with how many more questions were added to my list with no answer.

I felt sick when I thought about having to go back to Merripen and not see her again, but I felt guilty when I watched her drift off to sleep. I stood from the chair made of tightly wound tree roots that sat beside her bed as quietly as I could. My feet didn't betray me; they indeed stayed silent. She knew all the same. Her hand wrapped around my wrist, and it startled me.

"Please, stay." She whispered.

How could I deny her? She held onto me even when I sat back down. I knew I would pay a price for staying and avoiding Merripen and Kyrell, who would no doubt be looking for me, but I would watch over her until then.

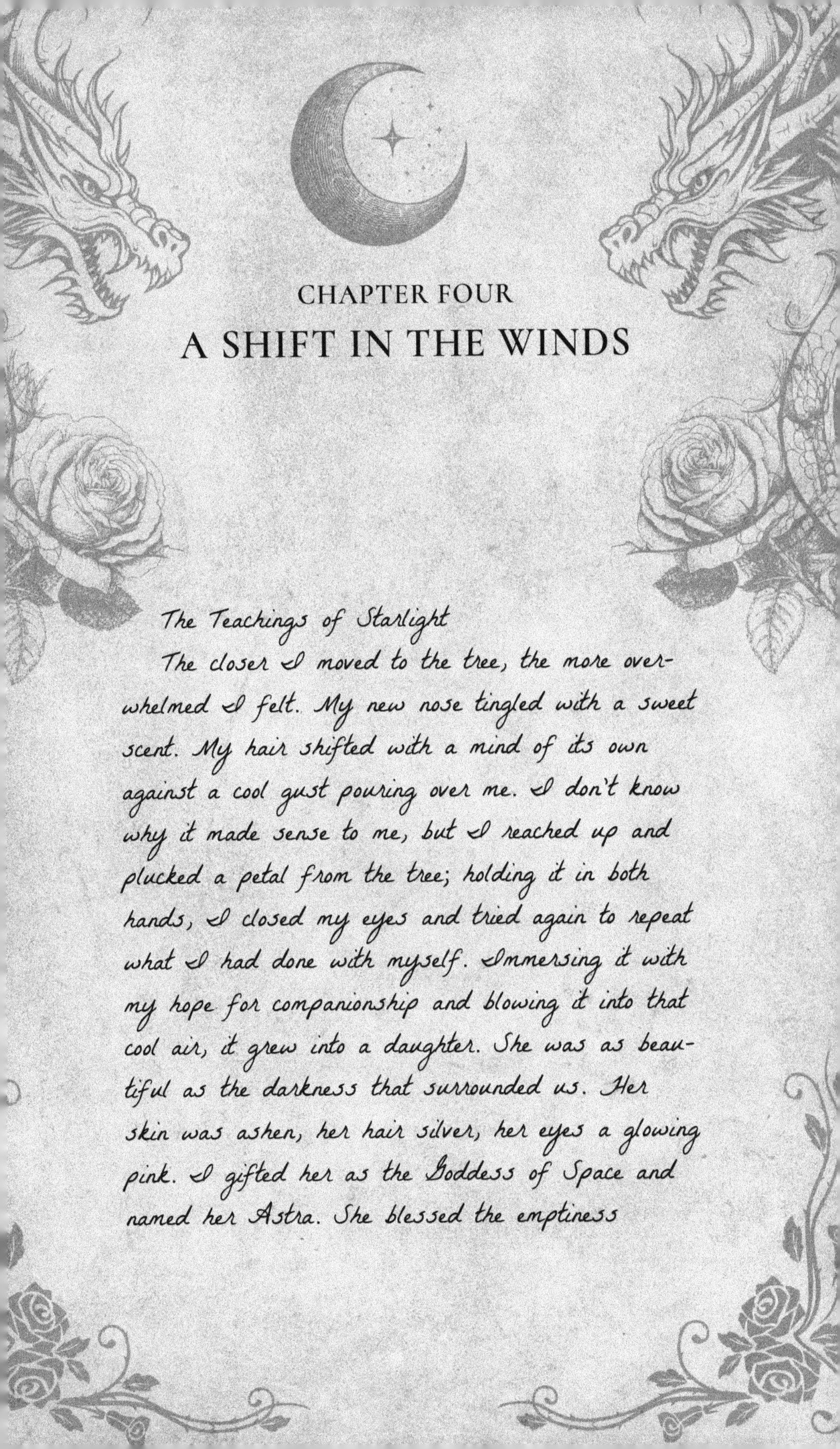

CHAPTER FOUR

A SHIFT IN THE WINDS

The Teachings of Starlight

The closer I moved to the tree, the more over-whelmed I felt. My new nose tingled with a sweet scent. My hair shifted with a mind of its own against a cool gust pouring over me. I don't know why it made sense to me, but I reached up and plucked a petal from the tree; holding it in both hands, I closed my eyes and tried again to repeat what I had done with myself. Immersing it with my hope for companionship and blowing it into that cool air, it grew into a daughter. She was as beau-tiful as the darkness that surrounded us. Her skin was ashen, her hair silver, her eyes a glowing pink. I gifted her as the Goddess of Space and named her Astra. She blessed the emptiness

*around us with planets that lit up the surround-
ings. She made me proud but also worried.*

RURI

Yumi assigned me to a set of quarters far away from the throne room and the entrance to Merripen. It left me far from Orla and my sister as well. Sage, the Goddess of Nature, did not leave the original home we were taken to. I wasn't offered the same choice. No reason was given to me as to why.

The space she granted me was gracious in size. Lavish in decoration but warm only in heat from the fires and filled only with the sound of bushes that rustled against each other outside of the windows. I spent nearly no time there. I shared Sage's bed most nights. Some nights were too long, and so I visited Juniper, the goddess of Wrath. She had a love of tending to plants, and we tended to them together.

I didn't fill my pond in the courtyard with fish. I felt bad for the idea that they'd swim alone, endlessly wondering if their master would arrive to feed them. I closed the doors to my residence, one by one behind me. They were big, too big, and served no real purpose outside of being able to feed conversations with the idea of how much one could accomplish with so little but imagination.

It seemed to be a theme I was having a hard time understanding. I kept hearing of how Yumi created everything with only a little imagination and a dream. Thann created an entire school in Cylla with only a dream and some imagination. My imagination didn't seem to be as good at making things happen without hard work.

I kept my footsteps quiet and quick through the corridors. I wouldn't have minded running into a few deities, but Helia was the one I wanted to avoid. She was unnerving. Her favorite thing was blood; my favorite was being far, far away from the feeling she gave me. Something was wrong with her.

The chamber of starlight held Yumi's sigil of power on the wall and her prized possession, her throne. I didn't need to be told how much she loved the throne. It was built of white oak and silver glimmer. I watched the way her hands would trail the smooth wood when she thought no one was looking. The way she looked at it with such pride. I had hoped she would look at me like that one day. That after some time of proving myself and showing I could do my duties well, she would love me in the same way she loved that throne.

Yumi entered just as silently as I had.

"Sorry that I'm a bit late." Yumi smiled. "Come with me."

She moved to the entrance of the sunlight garden that connected to the Chamber of Starlight, and I followed.

"This is the Sunlight Garden. It holds the Tree of Life, and all of you are connected to it, all of Cylla, as well. I hope that you and I can work together, once you've become more comfortable and settled in, to make Cylla feel like everything we've been dreaming it could be." Yumi finished speaking.

I offered her the same gentle smile she gave me. "I would love to help with anything you need. I want the same thing as you."

"Let me show you what kinds of things you could do," Yumi said, moving deeper into the garden.

I followed her through trees and bushes of flowers. Past a pond that looked so deep that I was afraid to move any closer. Yumi stopped in front of a stone stand and put her palm flat against it until it glowed. When the glow was full and bright, it turned the sky black and opened up a full picture of the night sky with every single star in front of us. Yumi waved them around and scattered them throughout, even to the far corners.

"Come," She motioned me over. "Give it a try."

I was so happy to be asked that I didn't hesitate. I moved to the stone and flung stars in an erratic mess.

"All right. That's enough." Yumi said. Her lip twitched a bit at the side. "I have to finish attending to the rest of my duties, but we will meet again soon." Yumi touched my shoulder and moved on.

I waited until she was out of sight and entered back into the Chamber of Starlight. I slipped through the passageway of realms that held liquid mirror crossroads and my happiness. Inside of Merripen, I could breathe. The air was fresher, clear. The sun was warm on my skin. I felt lighter. The realm had an air nowhere else had.

The most attractive idea around the vines was that they placed you exactly where you wanted to be when you walked through them. I didn't need to walk anywhere; I was already in front of the small log home I wanted to be at. I could tell without going inside that Caym was not there. He would have found me already if he was. Seven seconds was the most I stood at an entrance before his eyes were on me. He could sniff me out with an accuracy that amazed me.

I walked up the stairs to the deck surrounding the front entrance and sat in my rocking chair. I sat in Orla's for all my visits until one day; I found my own sitting beside the table. Afterward, there was a pair always seated in front of the home. I heard two squeaks immediately upon sitting down. One of the little white rabbits kept in Caym's back garden seeking me out. I lifted her onto my lap and grazed my hands across her fur. Sage's creativity was what brought them to life.

The screeches of a Nola came next. He shot up the porch in streaks of lightning and smoke, with its usual ear-piercing squeals. Jeb was with me as much as Caym, maybe more. I kept that to myself so he wouldn't know. There was no reason to tell Jeb that I knew he lurked in the shadows around me. He only meant well, and it gave him confidence when he thought he was a successful, silent protector.

"Hello, Jeb. Where Is Caym?" I asked.

The audio was only a squeal, but it was a language I came to understand with enough practice and attention to detail. I understood he was telling me Kyrell had Caym. I had yet to see the castle myself, but Jeb assured me it was worth the view. They worked on it tirelessly. Caym and I agreed it was too risky to be there. We both knew Kyrell would be less than pleased if he found me here. According to his rules, the realm was forbidden to anyone but the two of them. I stayed here for Caym, so it didn't bother me not to visit. I understood his concern was my safety, but I didn't understand why the rules were different for certain deities.

"Jeb?" I asked. "Since we're alone. Can I ask you a question?"

He lifted his thumb.

"Do you think what we're doing is okay?" I asked.

He tilted his head.

"I was thinking last night. I worry sometimes that Caym is so lonely here; maybe I'm taking advantage of him. Maybe I'm feeding into his desire for companionship only to solve my own. Sometimes-" I had to pause and take another breath before I could finish speaking the words out loud. "Sometimes I think maybe it's not me he loves, but the ability to have conversations. Am I replaceable?"

His squeal made me put both hands over my ears and hold them shut. "I'm sorry, I'm sorry." I pleaded before slowly trying to open my eyes. They opened to meet a man on his knees in front of me. He gripped my chin in his hand. Scrunching my cheeks into my teeth with his fingers.

"Who put such an idea into your head?" Caym asked.

I hadn't noticed him arrive until he was already speaking. Jeb was too loud to have heard someone come up the stairs.

"Minna," I mumbled.

"If any advantage has been taken, It's Minna's doing.

There is no such situation here." He said, letting me go. "She took a chance to try and worm into your thoughts."

His fingers brushed one side of my cheek and pushed hair behind my ear. He repeated the actions on the other side before he pressed his lips against mine. It felt like the contact lasted only such brief seconds. No place in the realm of the gods, mortals, or the dead felt as much like home as he did. He felt like the place I belonged. The place I was born for. I couldn't help but let the words of others get to me. I only wanted what was best for him. I could only hope it wasn't true and he felt as safe as I did.

Caym pulled away from me, but I could still feel his lips move with his words. "Minna lost control of herself over my possession of this realm so drastically that she puked up the Goddess of Wrath. That should tell you she is not someone to let poison pour into your ears. If one hundred goddesses filled this realm, and I was free to choose any one of them that I wanted without consequences, it would still be you. I don't know how or why we're connected yet, but I know we are."

I smiled at him, but I didn't speak. I couldn't have said anything better. We could spend our day going back and forth with poetic words, but I could just as happily get lost in the galaxy behind his eyes. They were filled with flecks of color. It was fitting that his eyes had just as much to say as he did.

Jeb interrupted us, rolling his eyes with a new creation event. I did not fully understand why the Nola kept doing it, but in the event of a life or death, Caym was shown. I assumed in silence it was to give him an insight into how they would be placed at their time of death. If they were to be deemed worthy or if they were ill-intent enough for their souls to be destroyed.

The Nola showed Thann, the god of rebirth and the man they called my grandfather, holding something I couldn't make out. Their voices carried from the projection.

"Please, Thann. Please stop! He's innocent!" Astra shrieked.

"I won't have a god of sin connected to my family line. I won't have a little bastard running around created from things you stole! I won't do it, Astra! I'll teach you both a much-needed lesson in one swoop." Thann yelled but never looked back.

Astra went crashing through the vines behind him, leaving a wreck of petals on the marble ground. She was closer to him and the item he carried than she had been yet. She couldn't keep up with him through her begging and pleading. She offered him deals and her own life in exchange. They were at the bottom of his mountain, near the river that started in his land and ran through the lands Astra claimed for her own. It was the only body of water to run through the ice-covered lands and remain unfrozen.

I felt a lump form in my throat every time she tried to form words. It felt like what we were watching was taking an eternity too long, but the reality was it had only been a few quick moments. Hardly enough to understand what we were seeing. I looked at Caym, and it was clear he didn't have a better grasp than I did. It wasn't until Astra dropped to her knees and let out a scream, unlike anything I had heard before, that Thann turned to look at her, revealing what was in his arms just enough for both of us to see an infant.

I could not believe what was going on. I didn't consider how ruthless they could all be towards each other in the face of disagreement. I had more faith in their ability to control themselves. I felt my heart sink but also race.

I felt useless seeing the images that no one was putting a stop to. I felt rage as well. How was an entire realm letting something so dreadful go on? A realm of the most powerful beings. Ones who called themselves just enough to rule over other races. I didn't waste time considering the consequences of my actions. I called the vines to me, and I went through them and into Cylla.

I could make it in time to stop him from drowning that infant. I knew I could if I only rushed.

When the river was in my sight, I saw that I was wrong about both. I was too late to stop him, and drowning wasn't what he wanted. Piece by piece, he filled the once sparkling blue water with crimson red streaks.

My stomach twisted, and my heart sunk far too low. What had he just done? Where was Yumi?

My mind was too filled and racing too fast for me to catch up. I could only focus on what was directly in front of me. The tears that were flooding from her eyes turned her ash skin pink and her eyes red. I knelt down with her. She only collapsed to the ground in front of my knees. I tried to lift her, but she was unable to assist me. She was little more than dead weight filled with grief. I moved the hair from her face and did my best to wipe away her tears, but they flowed too freely. My efforts meant nothing.

The way she looked at me, with more pain than she could hold, begging me to do something. Pleading in silence to help her undo what had just been done. The thought hit me that maybe I could. Maybe Caym and I could find a way to help her. The infant would go to Merripen, after all. Caym should have him.

Astra's eyes left mine when she saw Yumi. She shouted and gripped the ground beneath her as leverage to hasten her movements. Pulling up dirt with her nails.

"Do something! Please! Help him!" She sobbed, grabbing at the bottom of Yumi's gown.

When Yumi didn't move or spare her even a glance, Thann spoke.

"Let this be the lesson you and everyone else needed. The lesson you've yet to be taught well. If you want to run free and do as you please, there will be consequences. This is the mildest one that I will allow you. What's mine is mine. Don't touch it. You stole hair from Orla to make that God of Sin, and he's back where he should be." Thann held up his palm with the soul glowing in it.

"Mark my words, Thann!" Astra screamed.

I did not hear the rest of their argument. My heartbeat was too loud in my ears. Was he trying to imply he gave out justice? That his actions were fair in nature? Did he truly think that what he had done was for the greater good? That his actions were justice? Did he feel nothing watching Astra?

I was boiling over, spewing out of each side; if he didn't feel anything yet, fine. If these were the moral grounds that he claimed, fine. We could discuss morality. We could talk about what would happen if no one knew their place. We could explore what punishment was.

I stood back on my feet, but my ears were still filled with sobs that I didn't think I'd ever forget. No one would ever unsee the crimson river. I let my fingers relax and pulled water from the river, forming ice crystals and unleashing them at Thann. I used my other hand to send a second wave of them, then a third. I threw them until he was on the ground, held down by them. One through his shoulder, staking him into the dirt. Another through his hand.

"You're right. There will be consequences!" I yelled.

I put the ice away and pulled from the sky instead. He writhed under the ice that was plunged into his skin, but it still brought me no satisfaction.

"Justified punishment should be given for anyone who doesn't know their place, equally, on that we agree. I didn't realize your place was giving or taking life.!" I called out.

I was losing my grip on myself. He opened his mouth to speak between the pain, but It made me more resolute in my steps, and I shot his tongue with a bolt of lightning. I was over the top of him before I knew I had completed the steps that sat between us. I was unleashing an endless wave of blue and purple lightning into his chest. The sky around us hung with dark clouds and lit up bright with each crackle into him. The markings on my skin glowed in response.

"Stop! Not for him, but for yourself. Stop." Caym said.

He put both of his arms around me and pulled me off of Thann. I felt him only briefly before Yumi put chains on my wrists.

"This is only until you calm down," Yumi said. "Besides, you can't fully kill a God unless you destroy their heart. He will slowly heal and be on his feet again if you keep at this."

"What are these?" I shook my wrists.

"Fate chains. They'll ensure you can't use any more power until you're thinking clearly." Yumi answered.

Things went black for me until I opened my eyes again and was seated in the Chamber of Starlight. Thann was seated beside me, but not in chains. His eyes had yet to open, and Helia, the Goddess of Time, sat beside him, crying as if he were the one who died instead of Astra's child.

I felt dizzy and disorientated.

"What happened?" I asked.

"You were given something by Yumi," Caym said from the other side.

"I had to calm you down," Yumi said. "You weren't yourself, and I didn't want you to get hurt."

The longer my eyes were open, the more my vision cleared, and I felt a bit more like myself. "I won't take any of it back."

"I'm not asking you to. I'm only asking that you conduct yourself in a manner proper for who you are." Yumi answered.

"And Thann? What of him?" I demanded.

"I will handle things from here. I assure you something like that won't happen again." She said.

"It shouldn't have happened at all! Where were you? What will your punishment be?" I yelled.

"You will only make things worse for yourself if you don't learn when to stop." She said.

I opened my mouth to speak again, but Caym held his hand over my mouth.

"You won't enjoy the kinds of punishments she gives out. It's common for Astra to receive beatings for her work in the Sunlight Garden. Quiet now." Caym whispered.

Yumi took a deep breath in and let it out slowly. "I ask that you control yourself from here on out. As the ruler, I will see to it that these kinds of things are handled as they should be. Until you can be sure you won't have another outburst, I request you stay in your quarters." Yumi stood and held her head high for the rest of the way out of the chamber of starlight.

"It's Astra's fault he had to act so rashly!" Helia demanded. "He's a kind soul; he only acts to protect his family!"

"From an infant that can hardly hold its own head?" I scoffed. "You're both pathetic."

Caym lifted me up, and the chains on my wrist dropped to the ground. Released by some sort of magic I could not see.

Minna, the Goddess of Fate, entered next and commanded the chains to her hands, where they faded into nothing.

"They're my own making and good for rendering any deity useless." She smiled. "I only followed orders; don't hold it against me," Minna said.

"It doesn't matter if I blame you or not, does it?" I said, leaning further into Caym.

She shook her head, "I suppose it doesn't." She turned to leave but stopped for a moment, looking at Helia in disgust. "That's a nice necklace you have there." She pointed with her head.

"Thanks, it's Thann's teeth I gathered from Cylla," Helia said, stroking it.

There was something wrong with her, and finding out what it was was on my list of things to solve. Against my desire, we followed out behind Minna. Helia stayed with Thann, who was not yet awake. It was a relief when Minna went her own way and didn't speak a word. Today was unusual all the way around, it seemed.

When we arrived at my quarters, Caym placed me on my bed, and I could finally breathe out a true, relaxed breath. He lowered himself to a sitting position at my feet, looked up at me, and waited for what else I had to say.

"I cannot make sense of his actions. I cannot think of one single thing that makes sense of what he did! Can he truly not control his emotions? Can he not share with his family? Why does he not consider her his family? Doesn't Yumi keep saying we're all family? Where was she? How can she allow this? How does she still sit with a smug look after such a thing? If he can get away with these things, where is the line for the rest of us?" I searched his eyes for a read on what he was feeling.

He softened his voice, "I cannot speak to or make sense of Yumi's state of mind. I can assure you that feelings aren't rational. Yours weren't. You shouldn't try to apply logic to sort them out; you'll never find an answer of peace. He could have taken any path or stopped anytime. Same as you. All you can do is know what you will stand for and stick to it. You showed that today. Astra could not force him to become a monster if there wasn't one lurking under his surface, just as no one could have forced you to speak up for her if there wasn't already a good heart beneath your chest." He pointed.

I nodded, but I still couldn't find comfort without an understanding of why.

"He's done what he wanted to. He's just not ready to face the blame for it. Helia made two children using the same methods as Astra, and hers still walks untouched simply because Thann feels differently about the two." I started to spiral into a ramble again, but he stopped me.

"The difference lies in Thann not knowing." He said.

"So, ignorance of a subject is an excuse?" I shook my head.

"Not an excuse," he said, putting both of his hands on my thighs. "It's only surface-level reasoning. You have a good heart, Ruri. It's not a quality worthy of the realm of the gods. You aren't like them. You make a choice and are strict about it because you're sure of it being just. You won't understand them because you're too different from them." He said.

"If I were willing to face the consequences of helping Astra get him back-" he cut me off.

"I would be willing to face any consequence or take any punishment to support what you wanted." He said, unwavering.

I smiled at him, knowing we didn't need to exchange any further words, and he tucked me into rest. I didn't want to say it out loud, but I felt more drained than I ever had before.

CHAPTER FIVE

A WARNING OR A PROMISE

The Teachings of Starlight

The longer I watched The Goddess of Space, and the more I saw her smile. The longer I took in the glow of her aura. My heart pounded, and a sinking filled me. What if we didn't have enough time together? If she was only here for a brief moment? What if we didn't have enough time together and I couldn't take in all her details? A second daughter from a second petal. This time, I had not touched it; I had not blown on any or tried my best to focus my intentions. She grew all the same, and I thought her to be just as magnificent as Astra. This daughter I blessed as the Goddess of Time and named her Helia. The reddest hair surrounded her face, complimenting bright red eyes and pink flushed cheeks.

RURI

I stood, hands behind my back, in silence next to Sage while Yumi read over a report she brought. Sage was tasked with checking the progress of the realm of mortals. Some deities decided they didn't want land in Cylla, and Yumi expressed constant disappointment in them. I couldn't seem to move past my disappointment in her. The question eating at the back of my mind was maybe she didn't step in because she knew she wasn't strong enough to stop Thann.

The idea that the creator, that our ruler was not only weak but lying plagued me.

Sage tried her best to reason with me, to tell me how absurd that notion was. Of course, she was strong enough; she was the creator. The strongest being there is. We didn't need to know all things, she said. I doubted she believed it any more than I did. She sounded like she was trying to convince both of us when she discussed having blind faith. She was only trying to protect me in the same way Caym had. They both wanted me to stay out of trouble and not act on impulse again. I understood it, but understanding and following are different.

Watching the Goddess of Starlight sit on her throne, still graceful in every movement she made. Blinding us all in the Chamber of Starlight from so many refractions of light. It felt unreal. To sense the growing dislike for someone, while still admiring them. To know someone is wrong, and to feel it in your mind, but to also wish in your heart to make them proud of you. It was unsettling to try and process.

"Sage, this says there's been no change in two lands?" Yumi looked up from the reports.

My sister nodded. "Sephtis, the land the Goddess of Pride took is still only sand, as well as Brontide. The land that the Goddess of Envy took. A bit of progress can be noted with a few homes on the mountainside, but of Brontide, nothing grows there."

"What's your opinion?" Yumi asked.

"You would know better than I on how to proceed with them. I look forward to learning from you." Sage answered.

Yumi smiled at her and stood from her throne, closing the distance between us with agonizingly slow steps. She had a talent for showing off. When she reached the both of us, she put a hand on each of our shoulders. "You two make me very proud. One a little more than the other, given certain outbursts. Nonetheless, I consider you both blessings. If you keep doing so well, soon, one of you may take Astra's place by my side."

She spoke with a smile on her face, but my stomach turned at the thought. Sage's face never so much as winced at the comment. She was indeed better at wearing a mask than I was. Neither of us was burdened with responding to her, saved by the grace of Minna, the Goddess of Fate, who stormed her way into the chamber of starlight on her own mission.

"Minna!" Yumi called with joy.

"I've come to show you my newest son, Deimos, God of Dreams, and ask that you give him a job," Minna said.

"A job?" Yumi asked, scrunching her brows.

"Yes." Minna nodded. "If Caym is the keeper of the dead and Thann the god of Rebirth, shouldn't there be a place in-between? A place where souls can be kept while they wait to be reborn? It would lessen the work on poor Caym."

Caym? Since when did she care about him? I had heard she stole the blood of sin from the river and tricked the God of Life into helping her create another deity. I watched her meet with Kyrell on my way to Yumi; she was flooded with tears then. She looked amused.

"What do you think, Deimos?" Yumi asked.

The man stood nearly as tall as Caym. He was striking in the face, but it was because he had two different colored eyes.

One red and one black. The glowing white of his hair matched Yumi's, and it complimented his eyes with the contrast.

Deimos looked up for the first time since he entered the room. "Yes, I'd like to help you. Please allow me this honor."

"Finally, one is worth something," Minna mumbled.

"All right, then. You do make a good point." Yumi said.

Yumi turned to look between my sister and I. I could see the thoughts running through her mind; then she stopped on me.

"I want you to create the realm." She smiled.

"Me?" I pointed at myself. "I wouldn't know how!"

"Consider it the next step in helping the land flourish. It will give me reassurance that we both still hold the same goal." Yumi said as she urged me to the vines.

How was I supposed to create an entire realm in my first year of life? I didn't understand how to even begin considering it.

I lifted both of my hands and flung them at the vines. *Make a portal!* I thought hard about it, but it did nothing. I turned myself to face further away from their eyes. I did not need to read their faces. I walked closer to the vines and thought of creating it. I thought of each vine that needed to grow and what it would look like on the other side. The form started to take shape, but after only a few inches of growth, it withered away again.

She was being cruel, and for what? Was it to teach me a silent lesson?

I tried one more time, and it was only the same: a few inches of vines and then dust. I felt a lump form in my throat, and tears moistened my eyes. I choked it back. I ate the tears and shame, even with its foul taste. If bringing me down a level and humiliating me was her goal, I'd not give her tears in the end. I'd not be a disappointment and a whimpering mess.

Why did she need to humiliate me that way?

I worked up the courage to turn around and admit defeat, but Sage took my hand into hers instead. She didn't speak, nor look at me. She simply closed her eyes and tightened her grip on my fingers. I returned the commitment and closed my eyes.

The air felt warm around us, and my body felt electric. It took only a second, and we snapped our fingers in unison. I opened my eyes, and in front of us stood the new portal. Emerald tulips blossomed around the edges, and I tried to choke down my need to jump and scream.

We both turned around, and Deimos perked up at the sight of its completion. Yumi's mouth was open ever so slightly. It was enough to be clear of her shock but not enough to see inside and consider her in shock.

She pulled herself together and turned back to her business. "We will call it Cosima, the realm of the spirits, and it will be under your command." Yumi smiled at Deimos and took his hand. She burned something into his wrist that I could not see. "This cements things for your ownership. Is there anything else I can give you?"

Deimos looked at Minna and then back to Yumi. He held a serious tone. "There is one more thing." He lifted his tan hand and pointed to Minna. "I want her locked out and unable to enter."

Minna's jaw dropped open, "You ungrateful little shit!" She shrieked.

Yumi looked confused. "I don't understand."

"You don't need to. You asked if I wanted anything else, and that's my only request." Deimos responded, lowering his hand.

"I-" Yumi stuttered. "Okay." She waved a hand over the barrier, which only glowed red momentarily.

Deimos kissed Yumi's cheek and entered the portal to Cosima without another word to the room.

I hardly cared. I was resisting the urge to turn to my sister.

The way Sage was squeezing my hand let me know she was, too.

Yumi's attention was back on the two of us. "Since that was so easy for the two of you, I know what your next task is, Ruri. You can be responsible for making the mortals that will inhabit Cylla. You have the week to report progress to me. I also would like you to meet with me alone later to discuss other plans, too."

She took my hand and cut it with a small, clear knife. It looked like a toy but cut with ease. I groaned under the slice, and she collected my blood in a small jar.

"What are you doing?" My voice shook.

"It's needed to finish the process of realm creation. I will handle the rest; you two may leave." Yumi said, corking the jar.

Sage pulled me out behind her while I still gripped my hand in pain. She was charging us ahead as if we had to fight our way out of the emptiness in front of us. She didn't relent until we were closer to Juniper's quarters than the throne room.

"Thank Starlight, that's over with," Sage grumbled. "Create a realm, create mortals; her demands get more outrageous every time she makes a new one! You're supposed to simply do what the God of Life can't? Sounds lovely!"

She truly was good at masking for Yumi and being exactly what made Yumi comfortable. She slowed her pace, if only a little, but didn't release her grip on my arm. She slammed the wooden doors apart and open, flung me inside Juniper's quarters, and closed the doors behind her.

"Girls!" Juniper, Goddess of Wrath, motioned us in, "Just in time to help me finish potting these plants."

I took a seat at her stone table and took a breath. It was surrounded by her pond, filled with koi fish. She already had tea placed for the three of us, and I didn't hesitate to drink it.

Sage and Juniper sat after me, and Sage wasted no time spilling the news while Juniper passed us flowers to repot.

"Can you believe that?" Sage yelled, "It's like she's setting us up for failure!"

Juniper nodded, "So what are you going to do about it?"

Sage looked back down to her pot and pushed the dirt around. I couldn't help but smirk at the sight. She was always loud and ready to gossip, but her line stopped there.

"I'd rather stay a backdrop," Sage whispered.

Juniper laughed at her, and Sage clicked her tongue in response.

My smile from her faded too quickly. "It is starting to feel more stressful here than it had before," I said.

"I do agree, but I also agree that it's best to stay a backdrop." Juniper's smile also faded.

"I just-" I sighed and sat my plant down, "I just don't understand how it's so easy for everyone to pretend like nothing happened. Helia is dotting on the God of Rebirth. Astra is at risk of losing her position here in Semper. Yumi is out to punish us for existing? Caym is recovering from thirty lashings at the hands of Kyrell, and for what? For what?" I yelled. "Simply because he left Merripen and witnessed what happened?" I sunk back down into my seat and felt my shoulder slump, too. "I just can't get the image of Astra sobbing on the ground out of my head. Why didn't Yumi do something? I want to befriend her, to help her, but I'm afraid I'll not be welcomed or cause her more problems."

Juniper leaned over the table and cupped my face in her hands, "You're a sweet girl, Ruri. I'm sure she would be grateful for a shoulder. What you need to hear is that this situation has nothing to do with you. You couldn't have done more than you did, and you did nothing wrong, okay? You could not have changed anything."

"I know you're right, but my heart doesn't agree," I whispered.

We sat pouring more soil into pots and tucking roots inside their new homes. I lost track of how many we had done or still had to do. I couldn't calm my racing heart. I had more to say, and I was trying my best to resist.

"It's probably not the time, but I heard Minna was caught flirting with Kyrell," Juniper said.

Sage and I glanced at each other from the corner of our eyes, and I fought the urge I had even harder.

"I heard the two of them have been doing more than just flirting." Sage joined in.

"She is not the only one I've heard who has been involved in quite a romantic life." Juniper nudged my arm.

"This is outrageous! How can the two of you gossip right now?" I sat my pot down harder than usual.

Both of them looked at me with disapproval.

"The two of you would rather talk about this than creepy Helia, what she's collecting, and why. Or checking in on Astra? Aren't you even a little interested in Yumi's room? What answers might be there? Everyone is even going as far as to act blind to the fact that Caym and I have the same lightning streaks all over our bodies!" My breath was falling heavy.

"It's not that I don't care," Sage cut Juniper off.

"What are we supposed to do?" Sage sat her plant down beside my own. "Groaning about a problem with no solution is wasted time."

"If we talk, maybe we can find a solution. It would be worth a better try than gossiping!" I crossed my arms.

"Yumi is very interested in you two. I do think it's because of the markings. I think it's why she's been testing you, too." Juniper said.

Sage nodded in agreement but had nothing to add.

"I asked Helia's daughter Crystal about the markings since she's the goddess of love, and she told me not to tell, but she made the two of you mates. Maybe that's what it is!" Juniper said.

"Mates?" I questioned.

She shrugged, "She didn't elaborate."

"Do you know what else I heard?" Sage whispered. "Helia has a secret room she uses to keep Thann's blood in," Juniper said.

"Back to the gossip already?" I glared.

Sage shook her head. "We could find something useful if we went snooping."

I don't know what possessed me to say what I said, "We should go."

"You think?" Sage's eyes lit up.

I nodded.

"Let's go!" Sage stood.

"Juniper?" I asked.

She shook her head, "Count me out. I don't want to be the next addition to the room."

"Before we leave, I want to make you a garden here. Big enough to really grow things in. I want to infuse it with a special kind of magic so we can grow things others can't. You're the only one I can trust to keep it safe and thriving. I know it's selfish of me to offer you a gift and then request something from it, but I want to try and grow the seeds for mortals from it." I said.

Juniper waved. "It sounds like fun to me. I'll see you girls when you're done causing trouble."

Sage grabbed my hand, and the two of us were off, doing our best to keep our footsteps quiet while we ran down the hallways. The two of us had developed a talent for spying in our free time. We knew that we shouldn't have, but we could not resist.

When we entered Helia's chambers, I used my magic to twirl a golden thread around us, soaking the both of us in a layer of invisibility. It was merely a party trick in comparison to other abilities, but it made things easier to go unnoticed.

Deities could see through it if they wanted but hardly did. They never paid much attention.

When we entered the bedroom, we watched Helia take out a wooden stick and put it under the coals, providing passive heat to her room. Once it caught fire and flames grew on the end of it, she opened a screen door to a small room she kept hidden from the outside; the screen looked like part of the wall.

Helia used the flame to guide herself around the corner, and I kept a bit closer out of fear. It didn't take long for us to enter back into an open room. Small walls and low ceilings hid us and the secrets she kept away from the light. The entire compound sat in bright colors, but it was dark and quiet there. She used the flame to light small chunks of wax that sat all around a table. The light filled the room and showed what was laid out all around. Thann. Hairs from his beard lay in one bowl. Nails labeled 'toes' sat in another bowl. Pieces of clothing draped over here and there. There were jars of what looked like blood beside wax. They all had labels with dates.

She sat on a cushion, watching her collection with eyes lit brighter than I had ever seen. Helia reached into her dress and pulled out the newest addition to her collection. I backed up, regretting my choices. I would never let myself go inside bedrooms again. If we were caught, we were sure to end up in jars, too. I glanced at Sage and saw she shared my regret. We both tried to slowly back up, but it wasn't fast enough; voices interrupted us, and her head shot up. My heart wanted to stop for fear of being heard. I used every ounce of willpower to turn and run. I did not want to be locked inside of that room. I was Praying to Starlight that Helia would be too worried to notice us.

A piece of paper with my markings on it caught my eye before we could fully exit, and I didn't think twice. I grabbed it and shoved it inside of my spring green dress.

We only made it out seconds before Helia did. She still had not noticed the two of us.

"Are you all right?" Minna asked Helia.

"I'm fine," Helia answered, bent over, gasping for air. "What do you want?"

Sage and I did our best to hug the walls and remain in the shadows. We still inched our way away from them.

"I need your help," Minna said.

She pulled out a jar of blood and a golden orange from the Sunlight Garden.

"Another one?" Helia said with disgust.

"Until one is as dutiful as Caym," Minna remarked.

"You better beat this one, then." Helia shook her head.

Helia helped Minna combine the items she brought with a few drops of her own blood, and effortlessly, the fruit sprouted. Roots at first, then limbs, and soon a full girl. Minna shook her head in disgust.

"I'll have to try again for my son. Daughters can't be trusted; they look out for themselves. I should know." Minna sighed.

The girl on the ground threw herself back onto the ground with a sigh. She stretched and groaned, ignoring the comments made.

"I don't have much time before I start losing my memory of the Age of Moonlight. So shut up and listen. Some of you are false. When your true counter shows up, you'll lose your abilities and your sanity. It'll be a descent into madness that will kill you unless you find them and kill them first. You'll know the counter because they'll be near useless, and the true God will be unusually strong. He's coming soon, so you need to figure it out." She smiled with satisfaction.

CHAPTER SIX
A NEW FRIEND AND ALLY

The Teachings of Starlight

Watching Helia give us the time I pleaded for and wondering what these dreams could accomplish gave me my third daughter, Minna, whom I blessed as the Goddess of Fate. She stood taller than the other two, with curls of green just as long as her sisters. Green eyes that could light up the rest of the void. This time, I reached down and ran my fingers over the bark of the tree. Grazing the uneven wood, I dug my nails into a piece already slightly lifted. Pulling it off, I crushed it between my palms, sharpness scraping my new delicate skin. I pushed the dusty remains into the ripples beneath my feet, and from the ripples came two sons. Kyrell, the God of Life, glowing in golden attributes and a sharp bare jaw. Thann, God

*of rebirth, was duller in color, swimming in grey
flowing hair from the top of his head to his chin.*

RURI

No matter the position I shifted myself to or how I moved my
leg, I could not stop it from shaking. It could have vibrated me
across the room if I hadn't been placed in a chair heavier than
it needed to be. The wood weighed enough that I could take
comfort in the idea that my shaking was unnoticed by the
others. The moments I could force it to halt, I was filled with
double the anxiousness.

"Why are we going to take it seriously? If I gave you a
warning about a mystery man, would you take it seriously,
too?" Juniper asked.

"You didn't see her; if you did, you wouldn't ask that,"
Sage responded.

It shook hard enough that I could feel all the water I drank
slosh in my stomach. It didn't distract from the ringing in my
ears, and neither did their voices. I didn't know what I stared
at anymore, either. It had become a blur in my unblinking
thoughts.

"How long are we going to discuss all the reasons it can't
be true? I know we can't remember everything from before,
but enough of us know we do remember things. Isn't that
proof enough that something has to be a lie? What if the lie is
who the creator is? What if the real one is coming? Or an
enemy that killed us all once already? What if we ignore it?
Hmm? What if we pretend we never heard anything? We
have already seen what Thann is capable of, haven't we? What
if he is false? Or true? Do you think Helia would hesitate to
find out? He's nearly fully recovered from our earlier issue.
What if Kyrell couldn't do anything useful because he's one,

and his powers are being siphoned by someone?" My breath was falling heavy and loud.

"Ruri, take a breath," Sage said.

Caym moved to lay his hands on my shoulders, and the warmth of the contact sent a rush of calm through me like a wave. It didn't take away any of the thoughts racing around my mind.

"The point is, we can't be like that either, right? We can't just go around killing anyone we suspect because of a new deity's ramblings. We have nothing to prove their anything but ramblings." Juniper said.

"I think we do, don't we?" I looked between them all. "When I was created, I knew enough to kiss Caym for whatever these markings are. Doesn't that count for something?"

"I do think that means something, too," Sage said.

"Good, because on the way out of Helia's, I found this," I slammed the paper on the table where we were all seated. "It says the markings are for a guardian, and they're protected. That it's a soul bond, a kind of promise to protect no matter what, even to death. What is so important that it needs that kind of protection?" I crossed my arms.

"You think it's true, too? All of this puts a lot of trust in Helia's honesty." Sage said.

I opened my mouth to yell, but Juniper spoke first.

"We should gather more information first. Before we do anything, we can't take it back. It's not for their sake. It's for ours. I don't want to see anyone lashed like I watched Caym or Astra receive." Juniper crossed her arms.

My heart skipped a beat when I realized she was crossing them to embrace herself. She was comforting herself in a moment when we were all raising voices against each other. That lump in my throat was back, that one that made me bite my cheek to stop from crying. I stood and embraced her instead. I buried my head into her shoulder and squeezed her tightly.

That look on her face and Sage's need to argue any point I made. It all made me more inclined to work alone. More driven to investigate these things and kept the information close until I had enough facts to form a solution without causing anyone harm.

"You're right; we should take the time to find out more before we do anything that we can't take back. If you think someone is going to hurt you, don't hesitate." I pulled back to look her in the eyes, "You're worth a lashing or two."

She smirked at me and shook her head in response.

"Sage and I have to get the seeds for the mortals planted. I have something I need to do first, and I will meet you all in Cylla." I said.

I turned and tried to look like I wasn't rushing to leave, but I knew it wouldn't have worked. I hardly made it to the double doors before Caym grabbed my hand and spun me around. He gave me a full spin, and when it was finished, he pulled me into his chest. He rested an arm on the small of my back and another on the back of my head. I felt each finger nuzzle into my hair, and it sent my heart skipping every other beat. He leaned me back until his lips were so close to mine that I could feel his breath, his skin moving against mine.

"I can feel your anxiety. I can sense you're being sneaky from a mile away, my love," He whispered.

I sighed, I knew it was foolish to try and hide from him. "I know where Thann is keeping the baby's soul. I plan to take it and give it back to her."

"Is there anything you need from me?" He asked.

"To tell me if what I'm doing is okay," I whispered.

"Yes, what you are doing is okay." He said. "Helping to give her back what is left of her son isn't wrong." He put his hand on my face, "You are a good Goddess. Stop doubting yourself." He kissed my forehead and let me go, nodding his head for me to run for it.

I didn't need to be told a second time. I planned as well as it could be planned. I told Yumi that we would be planting the seeds to grow mortals today and that I would need everyone's help if we were to get it done in a decent amount of time. Yumi sent out the word that everyone was to meet in Cylla and wait for me. I was sure to be alone in Semper for a small enough amount of time to steal the soul from Thann. He was predictable enough in his hiding that it only took me an evening of watching him to find it.

The halls were empty, as I expected. Nothing but the overgrown foliage to be seen. It was worth the sight, only because of the sky. The entire compound was open above the walls that kept us in. Semper sat on a floating rock surrounded by endless skies that were never the same in color. I slipped into Thann's quarters, confident I would be alone. If he decided not to be in Cylla, he would be with Helia. He liked to pretend he wasn't interested in her or the games she played, but he enjoyed it.

I ran my hand along the wall of his bedroom, using the other hand to make things quicker; It felt like I was taking too long already. My palm finally felt the heat I was looking for, and I silently jumped for joy. I took the framed picture beside my palm off its hanging and saw the glow behind it in a small clear box trimmed with silver. I opened it and pulled the necklace I had been keeping out of my pocket. I transferred the glowing orb into the obsidian cage I carved out and left only an illusion in its place. I haven't taken advantage of my magic enough since it was created. Elemental magic was mine to control. It felt like as good a time as any to start.

I put everything back as it was the best I could and rushed my way back out of his area. If he noticed something off, I was confident my illusion would convince him well enough. My friends worried about me, and I loved them for it. I didn't want to see them hurt, but I was willing to accept the consequences of my actions, and, in a dark place, I kept to only myself; I was willing to kill Thann to protect the choice I was making. I was willing to do worse to protect them. It wasn't my place to say what the ultimate right and wrong were, but it was my place to stay true to myself and say that I would do it no matter what. We would both answer for our choices and in the end, I'd make sure of it.

I stopped outside of the sunlight garden. I did consider how she would react to me. All the scenarios I played out went wrong. In the end, I was an attachment to Thann. How I felt about him aside, my mother was his daughter all the same. Sage still spent a lot of her time with Thann, and I would never abandon Sage for her choice to love her family, but I wouldn't blame Astra for her hate. Even if she hated me, at least she would have her son back. I let out the rest of my breath and went inside.

It was bright and lush. It felt as if it had its own sun that couldn't be seen from the outside. Breathtaking and smelled of fresh lavender. The light put the chamber of starlight to shame. Merripen was warm and welcoming, but that felt like home. I lost my train of thought and my reason for being there when the branches of what I could only assume was the Tree of Life came into sight.

"What are you doing here?" Astra said from behind me. "Did Yumi send you to make sure I was working, too?"

She startled me and pulled me back to reality. When I turned to face her, she looked less than pleased to see me.

"No. She doesn't know I'm here." I said.

"Speak fast and get out, then," she answered.

I took a deep breath, "I know you probably consider me an extension of Thann, and so you find it hard to trust me. I would, too. I also know words are useless-"

"You know, I'm a lot older than you are. I've known everyone here for one hundred and three years longer than you, and in that whole time, not a single deity here stood up for me until you beat Thann." She turned around and grabbed a basket of fruit, then motioned me to follow.

"Yumi?" I asked.

"She has a pretty smile and a sweet voice, but you wouldn't believe what's underneath it," Astra said.

She sat the basket down and grabbed a net, fishing it into a pond surrounded by red and orange-leaved trees. She gathered the leaves that had fallen in and sat them in a pile beside the water. When it was done, she emptied the basket inside, and tentacles reached up, one by one, to grab every cut-up slice he could find.

"Emon is still just a baby, too. From the outside, things looks small and unfit, but if you jumped in, it would be like you entered another world." She cracked a half smile. "The water fills nearly the entire underground of the floating island that we live on."

I knew it had to. Even with her speaking of it, I didn't feel any comfort. The idea of what could be lurking in those waters sent chills across my skin.

"Do you go inside often?" I asked.

She nodded, "I do."

She picked the basket back up and continued on. I knew, without her motioning me this time, that I should follow her.

"Has Yumi truly always been this cruel?" I asked.

"I have enough scars on my back to prove her unwavering punishment for things she considered a slip-up. I still feel them burn years after they've been healed. If you had to ask me, I would consider myself lucky. What you did with Thann should have gotten you plenty of your own." She let out a sarcastic laugh, "A dozen times a day, I have to stop what I'm doing and practice my breathing. I start to sweat and shake. I feel the walls of a place that can't move, move anyway, and close in around me. I take deep breaths through my nose." She imitated her words with a deep breath, saying, "One, two, three." She let it out slowly. "I tell myself it's only my mind playing tricks on me, and I'm okay. It hardly makes a difference, though. Do you know what had?

Remembering you calling down a bolt of lightning to Thann's tongue."

I laughed at the genuine joy in her eyes, "It was some of my best work."

"You think I don't trust you, but I assure you that you're the only one I do trust," Astra said.

The sadness in her eyes sent me into a silent spiral. I bit my cheek again to keep myself from touching her or crying my own tears.

"I know you should be planting the seeds in Cylla, and I still have to hang the stars for Yumi, so they shine bright enough for her tonight and collect petals fallen from the Tree of Life, then water it with its special mixture, then report back to her, you see where I'm going with all of this, right? I don't want to keep you; what did you come for?" she asked.

"Can I ask you one more question first?" I bit my cheek again.

"Sure," She nodded.

"Do you think Yumi has any power, or do you think it's the tree?" I asked.

"Sometimes there's more to the tree than we've been told. Sometimes, I know I heard it whisper things to me. Other times, I'm positive the tree is a piece of Yumi she separated from herself. It's hard to explain." She said.

I hadn't considered maybe the tree was another piece of her. Orla separated pieces of herself to create my sister and I. It didn't seem like a stretch of a theory.

I gave her a soft, quick smile. My words wouldn't mean as much as seeing what I had. I grabbed Astra's hand and placed the necklace inside of her palm.

Astra looked down, and her son's soul shined inside. She looked back up at me with eyes already watering, "How did you get this?"

"I've learned a thing or two since being here. I'm sorry I couldn't have brought it sooner or done more for you. I tried to bring him back, but I learned I couldn't do it without his heart. I swam for hours at night looking but-"

"You tried to bring him back?" she asked.

"I'll keep looking," I said.

She wrapped her arms around my shoulders, and although she was absolutely silent, I felt her tears hitting me, and that was when I broke. I couldn't bite hard enough to offset my own tears.

She let go of me and turned me around, "Go! Before someone finds you here." She gave me a push so I couldn't turn back and look at her.

She wiped her face with her arm and then pulled out the stone that Yumi used for the stars. It was different. I heard the stars scream. I knew it was coming from them. I heard them cry and beg for a body.

Astra turned around and motioned for me to leave again, but I stumbled out. I was too in shock. I needed to make vessels and get whatever was in those stars out.

I gave her what she asked for only because I knew I was already late enough. I held my white silk dress up with both hands so that I could run. I was sure I would be questioned for my absence. I ran through the vines to Cylla, and everyone but Astra was waiting.

"Finally!" Minna scoffed.

"I'm sorry to have kept you waiting, but it's not that easy doing someone else's job." I snapped

I grabbed the pouches of seeds I had tied together and passed them around. I was given no direction when Yumi handed the task off to me, so I took many liberties. Every land would have its own unique people and unique elemental magic. Sage, the Goddess of Nature, would help water them with a mixture of her own and ensure the seeds I created would sprout life correctly. It seemed we couldn't do as much apart as we could together.

"They need to be planted seven inches deep, and you need

to pack the soil back on top of them well. Sage will be coming after you are done to add the finishing touches. If you mess up my directions, your land will not sprout mortals." I looked around, but no one seemed to have any questions.

Everyone moved in the directions of the land they claimed, and before I could move to my own. When only my breath filled the silence, Jeb and Caym appeared from the shadows with a demand. I untucked the bags of seeds I kept inside my dress silk and put them in Jeb's palm. Sage and I worked together to create seeds of different fruits and vegetables for the mortals, but Jeb was desperate to help, so we agreed to give him the task. He left happily, and it spread to me.

One thing I was learning well over my first year was the difference in love. I loved Juniper as a best friend or a grumpy mother figure. I loved Sage in a way no one else could ever understand. We were bonded by blood. My love for Jeb was warming; losing him would be like losing a child. My love for Caym sent me into a panic.

My love for him made me feel like I was losing my mind. It made me blank. It stirred a storm in my bones. It kept me equal parts crazy and sane. He made me hot and cold. The love I felt for him made me scared of the depths I'd go. The things I would be willing to do at his request. I had yet to find a line I would draw. He felt like the only piece that could make me whole, and without him, I couldn't exist. He was in every thought I had. Every picture of the future I could dream up. A reminder of him was in every place I looked. If an idea of life without him slipped in, I was sure my heart would stop, too.

I drank up every change in Caym's face when he smirked at my staring. I couldn't stop the smile that crept in when he let it be clear he knew what I was thinking. I took his hand in mine, and we walked. Taking in the scenery on our way to our destination.

"Did you get to see it when it was bare? Before they started forming the lands?" I asked.

Caym shook his head, "Not in the way I would have wanted."

He looked at me as if he had more to say, but I couldn't stop myself from speaking first. "You have such beautiful eyes."

His smirk grew, "Say the word; your children can have them, too."

I connected my palm to his chest, "You can't be allowed to say things like that; we need to go." I laughed.

He took my hand and turned me into a shadow with him and landed us on the other side, in Ashbell. The land I claimed and had hoped he would want to settle in with me one day. I lowered myself to the ground and used my magic to start creating holes in the ground. I sprinkled my seeds in them and topped them with loose soil, patting them down. I stuck a small stick with a crimson flag beside them so Sage would know where to water.

"It will only take a couple of weeks for them all to turn into living, breathing mortals," I said.

"What are they?" Caym asked.

"I call them Seere," I said. "We will have time to learn them when they sprout. For now, I do have a gift for you as well," I offered.

"I like where this is going." He smirked.

I gave him a nudge and shook my head. "Shut your eyes and hug me."

When his arms were around me, I wrapped my tighter. Ensuring there was no space between the two of us. When I could feel his heart beating, I closed my eyes and lit the both of us in a ball of yellow rays.

"I feel hot like you're setting me on fire." He whispered.

I kissed his lips, and the light exploded, causing the blades of grass around us to wave.

"It's a special kind of magic, only for you. It draws from the sun, and it's my protection for you. I worry Kyrell-"

"Nothing will keep me from you," He lifted my chin.

"Please, you two make my teeth hurt and my stomach turn. Spare me, I beg you, and let me take my sister back without any more of this. We still have things to do." Sage begged. Her face scrunched like she had just seen her nightmares come true.

I let my eyes linger on him for just a moment before I smiled and let go. "Come on, let's go home. We have dinner as a family to attend," I mocked.

Sage and I walked through the vines back to the Chamber of Starlight. She looked at me like she had many things to say, but she wasn't speaking. I nudged her with my elbow, and she scrunched her lips together.

"I don't think I should be telling you this; I don't want to be the reason for more fighting." She rubbed her forehead.

I nudged her with my elbow again.

"I overheard Kyrell asking Minna how her books of fate worked. He was trying his best not to sound suspicious, so of course, it was obvious he was suspicious. He was trying to find out if he could alter fate and separate the two of you." Sage said.

I won't do something that would risk your name being tossed in the middle of a fight." I said.

"Have you found anything?" She asked.

"No. I don't know where to begin. I can't ask the girl directly; she likely will only say she's forgotten. I can't go up to Yumi and tell her that I think she's a liar. She has a tight hold on, well, everything. The only book we freely get until she deems otherwise is The Teachings of Starlight, which is good for nothing but her tales of creation and rules of life." I sighed loudly.

I watched her walk ahead of me, and an ache hit my heart. I knew she wanted to help. I also knew her new friendship with the Goddess of Chaos was already affecting her. Sage thought it would be a good idea to get close to her for information, but it quickly spiraled into Sage wanting little to do with anyone outside of her.

I knew I needed to stay out of it. I was trying my best. Sahir was still new, and Sage was longing for friendship, too. I knew we were both trying our best to get a grip on ourselves and decide who we wanted to be. We were learning our boundaries.

Nothing changed how badly I wanted to sit her down and make her see that I would protect and support her the best I could while she figured things out if she would just let me.

I crossed my arms and looked at the empty space by my side. "What do you have to say about it, Jeb?"

The once blank space filled with shadows before forming a whole Nola.

"I know I should be quiet; I should be obedient and satisfied with the idea that Yumi knows more than I do and has her reasons. I don't know how long I can constantly bite my tongue and be that deity." I looked at Jeb.

He squealed and squeaked until he ended with the question, "Why was Yumi's approval so much more important to me than what I knew to be right?"

I had no answer that would have made sense. Maybe I didn't want to hear myself say out loud that I was still holding out hope that she was better than what I knew her to be.

There was just something inside of me that didn't feel real yet. That felt disconnected from the realm. I felt like I didn't belong. Like most of us didn't belong.

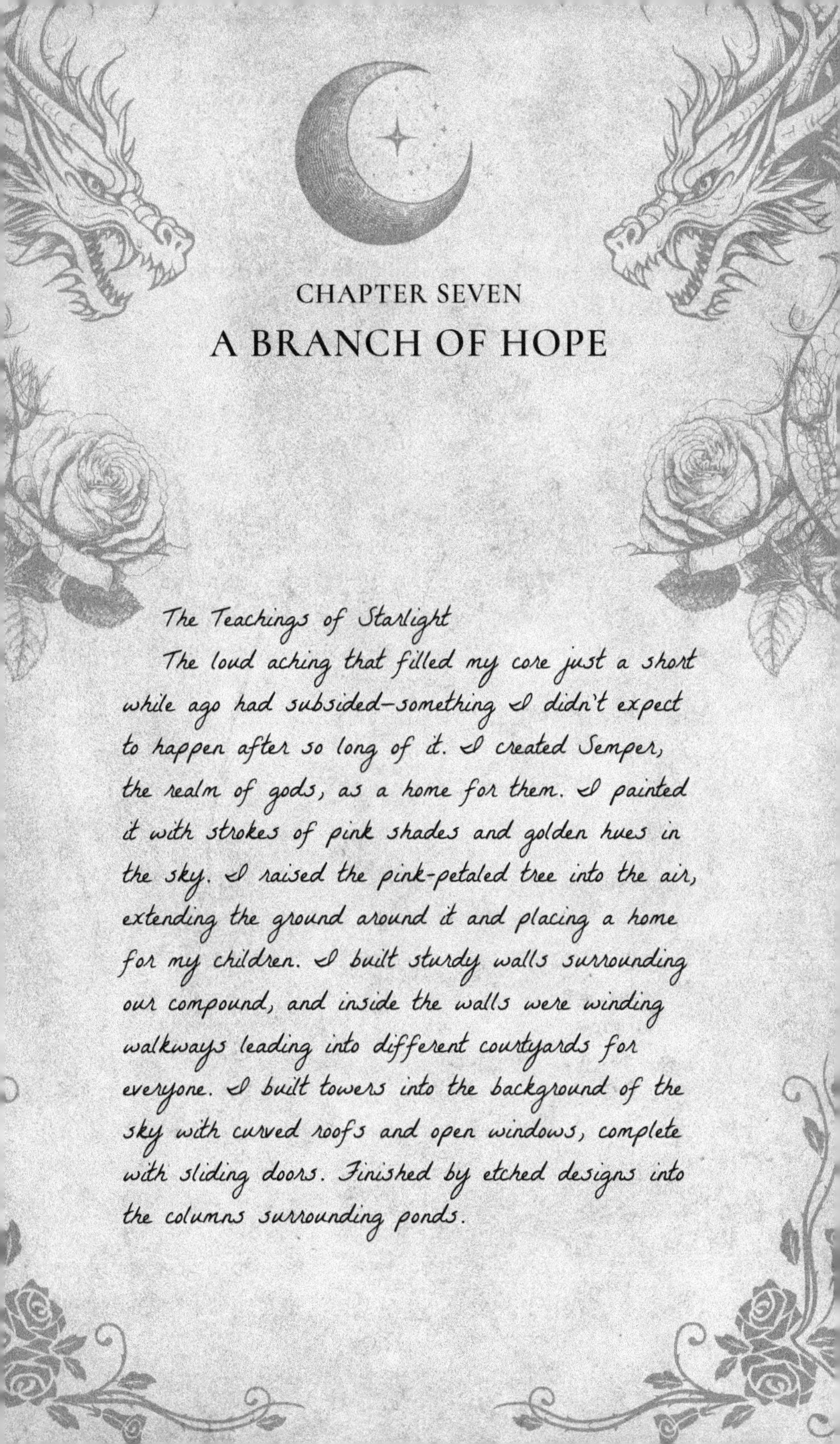

CHAPTER SEVEN

A BRANCH OF HOPE

The Teachings of Starlight

The loud aching that filled my core just a short while ago had subsided—something I didn't expect to happen after so long of it. I created Semper, the realm of gods, as a home for them. I painted it with strokes of pink shades and golden hues in the sky. I raised the pink-petaled tree into the air, extending the ground around it and placing a home for my children. I built sturdy walls surrounding our compound, and inside the walls were winding walkways leading into different courtyards for everyone. I built towers into the background of the sky with curved roofs and open windows, complete with sliding doors. Finished by etched designs into the columns surrounding ponds.

RURI

I took my time to stroll through the halls of Semper. I tried to
move slower by spot-cleaning the stone as I went. I still arrived
at the dinner gathering before anyone I wanted to go inside
with arrived. I wanted someone to ground me in reality before
I went in. I hadn't anticipated how hard it would be to control
my emotions.

Sahir, the Goddess of Chaos, arrived, and I panicked. She
was at the top of who I wanted to avoid. It was in the name;
she was all chaos. I tucked myself behind plants to avoid her.
She didn't glance in my direction when she walked past, which
gave me comfort. When she entered the dining hall, Helia's
daughters, the Goddess of Love and the Goddess of Beauty,
already sat. I felt the atmosphere change from where I stood. I
leaned myself to the doorway just enough to peek inside. The
walls that surrounded the long black table were all white and
decorated with silver framed mirrors and candle sticks. White
was the color Yumi picked for our family. If I thought about it,
it was fitting. White was so easily stained, and it took a lot of
work to keep the stains that occurred clean.

"It feels tense between you two," Sahir spoke.

The two looked at her in unison.

"Creepy," Sahir said. "I guess you must have heard the
news then. It seems you two are taking it harder than I
thought you would."

"What news?" Crystal, goddess of love, demanded.

Sahir lowered her eyebrows and placed a hand on her
chest. "So, you haven't heard?"

"Are you going to tell us or not?" Amaris, the goddess of
beauty, rolled her eyes.

"I don't think you should hear it from me for the first time.
It's not my place." Sahir said, standing up.

Crystal hit the table with both of her hands. "Sit down."

Sahir's face oozed panic, "It's just that word has been

circling that Ruri would only grant magic to one sibling pair, and your mother agreed. She already decided which of you would be granted magic as a gift." Sahir lowered her head.

Is that what she spent her days doing? Thinking of pathetic things to do?

"Ruri wouldn't do that," Amaris crossed her arms.

"Of course," Sahir agreed quietly.

"What makes you so sure?" Crystal demanded, "Is it because you think Helia is sure to pick you?"

Amaris stood, she threw her black iron chair and shouted. Crystal, fingers pointed in her face, nearly knocked over the silver vase of white roses that sat in front of them. Sahir slipped from the chair across the two with a grin on her face and sat between two empty chairs instead. Helia and Minna came in together, and I tucked my head back into the plants as they moved past.

"Do you know what they're fighting about?" Helia asked.

Sahir shook her head, "Anyone's guess is probably right. They don't do much other than this, after all."

Minna laughed; She didn't bother to hold it back.

"What do you think is so funny?" Helia demanded.

"It couldn't be your teaching skills," Sahir remarked.

"Excuse me?" Helia snapped. "Do you think you're any better than them?"

Sahir sat straighter in her chair and set her arms on the table. "It's lovely that you two came today. When I begged Yumi to throw a feast, I didn't see it going so well already. I do have a question, though. What do you remember from the Age of Moonlight? Anything at all? My daddy made sure I wouldn't forget before I could write the important things down. I suggest you be nice to me, or I'll make sure he hurts you first." She tapped her cheek, "Oh, I also heard something about stolen blood and a forest being the origin of some deities. One may be worried if they push too hard; it may come to light and lead to questions about honesty with

Thann, given his reputation of murder." She batted her eyelashes at Helia.

Minna looked at Sahir with furrowed brows, and Sahir's high-pitched voice dropped back down before responding.

I took a break from their conversation to call for Jeb. "Go search Sahir's room and see what you can find of these notes she's talking about!"

He took off in an instant.

"Don't you look at me." Sahir pointed, "You're not my mother, Yumi is. I just wanted to ensure we were all on the same page. Daddy says I can't kill you, but he never said I couldn't hurt you. Now move; you're blocking the space I need for others."

Yumi came in next, and I held my breath harder. I lowered myself further into the wall. Sage followed behind her, and the room quickly filled up before I could interject and question Sahir. Caym was next, but I grabbed him by the arm and pulled him into me before he could get far.

"I wasn't expecting this," he said with a smile wider than the table inside.

"I can feel your excitement pressing against me already," I remarked.

He ran his hand through my hair, gently gripping it before using it to pull my face closer to his.

"We need to talk," I whispered against his lips.

The plants were torn away, and Juniper's face glared into us.

"You're both glowing," she said.

She grabbed Caym by his shirt collar and pulled him through the doorway.

"I did have something I need to talk about," I groaned but followed them inside.

I did my best to straighten my dress before I sat down. I took my seat with a bit more of a rush when Emon glided across the floor with plates stacked atop his tentacles. Yumi did not sit; she held a glass, eyeing everyone with demands of silence.

"When Sahir brought up the idea to gather like this, I knew she was right. Our family has grown lately, and time together is good for us all. After our fun tonight, I'll need everyone to wake up tomorrow with a new outlook. One with determination. It's been too long, and we must get things going in Cylla, no matter what it costs. Pushing yourself past what you think is your limit is how we get better."

Astra, the Goddess of Space, stood before Yumi could finish. Her bloodshot eyes never left Thann, who was seated, being fed every bite of the roasted fruit on his plate by Helia. She scoffed in disgust at the sight before she slammed her hand into the table.

"Astra," Yumi started to speak.

"Don't you dare start a lecture with me!" Astra shot at her.

Kyrell stood next, "I'd recommend taking a second thought before you show this much disrespect."

"Or what, Kyrell?" Astra dripped sarcasm, "Or what? Will you treat me like Caym and make me a prisoner? To late! Will you follow Thann and become a murderer? Try it!" Astra gave him one last look before she left in a rage.

"I'm sorry, but I wonder what the outcome of the meeting over Astra's son was?" Sahir asked.

"Did I not say enough?" Kyrell yelled.

Yumi held a hand to him. "It's all right. It's only fair that everyone should know. We don't keep secrets, after all. Thann apologized and agreed that something like that wouldn't happen again. He will spend time with me until he has a grip on his anger."

I found it hard to keep a grip on myself again. Something about being so close to Kyrell always weighed on me. Just a look at him filled me with fire, but when I heard him speak, it left me one step from falling off a cliff. With the addition of Yumi's outrageous ideals of sufficient and fair punishment nearly sent me off the edge of an invisible cliff. Caym's hand moved to my thigh, and it was the only thing that held the sparks of magic from my fingers.

"Does Thann not still hold his soul?" Sahir questioned. "I don't understand everything yet. Wouldn't he, as the God of Rebirth, have control of it? Caym clearly doesn't have the soul."

Minna cleared her throat overly vocally, "I'd like to interject and toast to Yumi as thanks for so many blessings."

Sahir gave Minna a side-eyed glance and lifted her cup as well.

"Daddy would never allow someone to talk like that," Sahir grumbled, but no one seemed to pay attention to her.

Did I only notice those remarks because I wanted them to be there?

I lifted my own glass but put all of my focus into my breath. Caym left his hand in place but leaned to talk to Morticia, Goddess of Envy, about her land, Sephtis.

Sahir sniffed out her moment and leaned over Sage to speak to me.

"Don't you get jealous of that kind of thing?" Sahir asked.

"Of what?" I narrowed my eyes.

There was an aura about being in Sahir's presence that made me want to turn around and leave, but there was a curiosity behind her voice that instead made me want to stay. I thought for sure that Thann was the tip of my emotions, until I met her. In such a short time, she stirred up so much chaos.

"Are the two of you not together?" Sahir asked.

"You'll have to do much better than this," I said as I gripped my glass.

Sahir's smile grew, "Whatever do you mean."

"If you'd like to bait me into an argument, you'll have to do much better than this, Sahir." I took a drink from my glass and sat it down. I tried my best not to have another outburst.

Sahir nodded and thought about it. "Sage, do you have anyone you like?"

"No." Sage looked at her with confusion.

"Really? A best friend? A favored family member? Anything? Or is Ruri everyone's favorite, and you are simply an extension?" Sahir asked.

I let out a low and slow breath, my heart raced in my chest. The anger that grew inside of me sent a wave through my body. It brought the desire to kill her right where we all stood, no matter the consequence. I tried my best to swallow it back down. To put it in a box and hide it away. I understood that she took her time to see what game she could play with everyone.

"Do you know why you can't bait me like this, Sahir?" I leaned over Sage to finally make eye contact. "You like games; You want to stay behind the scenes and look good. You want to keep an innocent look about you. You're not a mystery to me. You are a copy of Helia, and Thann. I'd rather slice you from throat to belly button right here in front of everyone and watch them play who can put her back together again, instead."

"I like you, Ruri," Sahir said. She laughed loud enough to stop the room again. "You'll be my favorite to play with."

I pushed my chair out and got to my feet. I kept my eyes ahead and left the room without causing a furry scene. While Sahir spoke, I motioned on Caym's thigh with a squeeze not to follow me out.

Jeb pulled me into the veil of the in between with him and handed me a sheet of paper.

Keep the counters alive.
Watch the girls.
Find the guardians and kill them.
Do not touch the tree.
Bond with Yumi.
Stay alive at any cost.

I folded the note back up and handed it to Jeb. He needed to put it back before Sahir knew I had seen it. Her information was not enough. It was nothing compared to the number of questions I had. The notes said not to touch the tree, but I was sure that's what I needed to do. The tree was treated so importantly. Caym wasn't allowed near it, and I was sure it was because of the markings.

I entered the Sunlight Garden and sought out the tree. Standing in front of it, I pressed both hands on its bark. I took a deep breath in and held it, I expected something significant. Nothing happened. I removed my hands, rubbed them together, and placed them back on the bark.

I was pulled inside of the tree, into darkness and all-consuming light. I was shown Cylla burning and a giant viper that murdered everyone who stood in front of him. I was shown Yumi. She stood, surrounded by creatures. The viper turned to a man, and Sahir was beside him. All of Cylla crumbled next.

I was pushed out of the tree and onto the ground. The image of four markings were burned into my eyes. Emerald lighting. Crimson veins. Cobalt blue vines and white tree branches.

The only place I had to try and find answers also fed me nightmares that I couldn't make sense of.

I would be alone for at least a little while longer. Long enough to look at the stars again. I got to my feet and moved deeper inside of the garden and to the star pilar. I worried it wouldn't work without Yumi or Astra to start it, but I was wrong. It answered me as if it had always been mine to call upon. The sky turned black and then lit with hundreds of lights. I reached my hand to one and pulled it to me. The star floated above my palm.

"Hello?" I whispered.

Screams of agony were released. I tossed it back out of fear.

I pulled a second closer and whispered into it.

"Please get me out. Help me!" The voice begged.

I tossed it back, too.

My hands shook, and my thoughts raced. I knew that I had heard voices from them, but the confirmation was horrifying. I couldn't begin to comprehend what it meant if it were true. Did we all come from Yumi's stars?

I pulled another down and shoved it inside of the pocket of my dress before I shut down the star pilar.

I would have to create some sort of vessel strong enough to put the soul inside. I would need to move in secret.

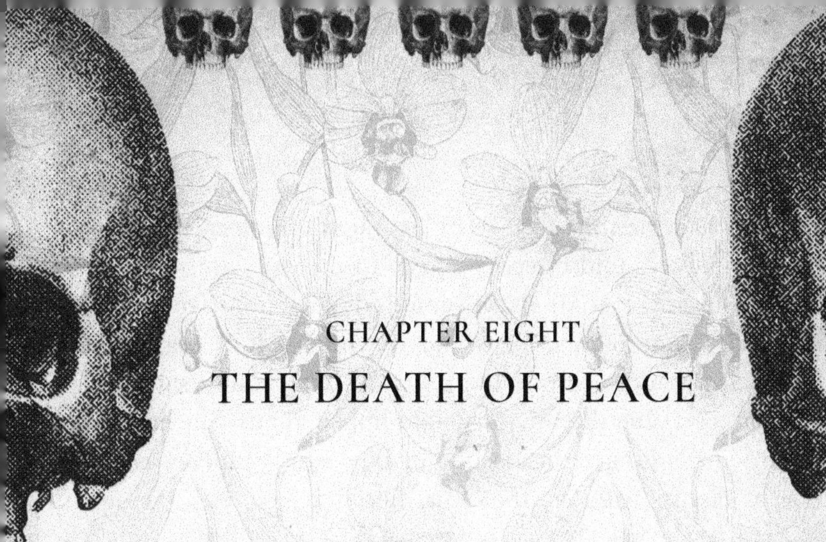

CHAPTER EIGHT

THE DEATH OF PEACE

The Teachings of Starlight

My creations called me Yumi, the Goddess of Starlight, and our joy together was a joy that matched everything I had dreamed of. Our happiness matched every companionship wish I had made before becoming whole. In the first phase of our life together, we would focus our efforts on perfecting a world that would flourish for centuries to come. The word perfection would not be fitting enough to be used as a description in the end— Letters bled down the page to reveal a hidden line; we would burn it and start again if it were anything less than that.

CAYM

I hardly had the time to take in last night's dinner with all of the things I was told I needed to do. Ruri and I came up with a plan to meet so that we could discuss how we would proceed. Yumi offered her little downtime. Ruri was busy ensuring the mortals sprouted properly, but she also started a new project. One she was very tight-lipped about. She created a garden for Juniper inside of her quarters. Juniper was the one to discuss with me that Ruri filled the soil with enough magic that she gave herself a nosebleed.

I wanted to know what she did to push herself hard enough to have physical effects.

I was stuck under Kyrell's thumb, with limited movements. I was left to consider why Kyrell was failing even more miserably than he had been. It was not lost to me that the stronger Ruri got, the more she used her abilities, the harsher Kyrell became. I waited for him again. His only goal since my creation was mortals, and he failed it.

Kyrell would be arriving for more training that I did not ask for. I decided to ask the God of War to visit me first. Kyrell had success with the Nola, but it only made me more suspicious of how he did it. It was as if some other force was granting him abilities in certain instances only.

If I were to be locked away, I would learn to fight. I decided that on my own. I could feel the tension that built in Semper with every additional deity. If the realm were to erupt, I wanted to be ready. I wanted to be able to rely on my hands. They were much easier to grasp than the magic Ruri gave me. When she could help me, it became easier, but between Yumi and Kyrell, the time she spent with me became less and less.

I would have to start finding my own ways to help.

I paced back and forth in front of the vines, hands rested behind my back. Both of the moons that hung over Merripen were gone, and my sun was rising. Golden was every piece of land around me. Merripen went from being empty to lush quickly with the Nola. I offered them their own city but they demanded to remain with everyone that would arrive in the main city, so I obliged.

I stopped my pacing when a voice rose outside of the vines. I moved closer and peered out of the vines. Sahir stood on the other side, with Minna, looking into the vines of Cylla.

"I cannot believe Dysis is still trying so hard to help Ivory build up that pile of sand," Minna said.

"Ivory is doing it on purpose. You know she blames you, right?" Sahir said, still watching the liquid mirror.

"Excuse me?" Minna turned to look at her.

"It's just that I heard her tell Helia it's your fault she couldn't get anything to grow. Helia seemed to think it made sense, too. That you're the sabotaging type, they said." Sahir said casually.

"How does that make sense?" Minna scoffed.

"Helia said something about you being unable to achieve anything for yourself. You failed to make good children, unable to commit to helping in Cylla. You have a poor attitude. They seemed to agree that if they brought it to Yumi's attention, they could convince her to get rid of you. Dysis is there to see if he can find proof that you're involved. They said they were just going to fake the proof to frame you." Sahir said.

Minna watched Sahir in silence, her eyes shifted back and forth as if searching for truth or a lie.

"Do what you will with it; I just thought you should know. It's unbecoming of them to whisper so often behind your back, but to plot like this? I couldn't imagine how that would feel." Sahir said.

Minna moved past her. She grazed her shoulder and entered Cylla. I stepped out of my vines and into the chamber of starlight beside Sahir.

"Have you considered the consequences?" I asked her.

"If you know of any, I'm happy to listen. I bet if I offered Kyrell the ability to lock you inside Merripen or sleep with me, he would be the next pawn on my board. It would help Ruri bend the knee, too." She tapped her chin, pretended to think. "Daddy made plans for you that I am to carry out, but not so soon. I need some time to grow yet. If you force my hand, I'll have no choice but to move things along faster, though. It's your choice." She trailed her eyes down me.

I felt my lips turn down in disgust. "So you're admitting that you plan to hurt me?"

She shrugged as if it meant nothing to her and turned back to the vines. An audible gasp came from her before we could continue to speak. Sahir's hand was over her mouth to hold back her cackles, loud and uncontrolled. In the vines, the sight of Minna as she stood over the lifeless body of Dysis, the God of Peace, was all too clear.

Minna killed him because of Sahir's lies.

"Oh, this is going to be just too easy." Sahir laughed. She ran her hand through the vines to scatter the sight away.

"On second thought, Sahir, it would be best if you were more careful. Maybe I'm not sure what you did yet, but maybe after some time to process what you just did, I could be. Maybe you keep tossing around threats of Kyrell, and maybe I will toss around the threat of making you a member of Merripen. Say I lose my mind, too, and remember, I'm the only one here with an army at my command right now." I tapped my own chin in mockery.

"Caym!" She drew her words out and faced me. "What would your lover say about the way you're talking to me right now? Tsk Tsk. If you ever want a change of pace, my bed is always open to you. Nothing we're doing here will matter soon enough."

"That's enough!" Kyrells voice boomed from the doorway. "Unless you want me to drag you to Yumi, I'd suggest you get away from my son and leave, Sahir."

"No, that's a good idea. We can also let her know how frequently you visit my bed chambers, too." Sahir was still laughing as if none of it mattered to her.

She lifted her velvet dress off the floor and jogged her way out. She never batted an eye at the lies that fell from her lips.

I wanted to follow her. Kyrells eyes on me told me that I was going to be sealed back in Merripen, alone, for a long time.

Kyrell grabbed me by the collar of my shirt and tossed me back through the vines of Merripen and onto the castle steps. It was easy to find joy in being tossed against the bottom and not down the length of the stairs.

The sight of the cathedral-tipped points that sat atop my castle was just as beautiful from the view on the ground.

The blades of grass around me were plucked from the ground with only magic. They shook and then transformed into Gods. For every one of them that I defeated, the next had double the strength. Kyrells gift to me.

"Get up!" He shouted.

I rolled just in time to miss the tip of a blade that landed into the dirt beside my head.

"Do you think getting involved with Sahir will give you a leg up?" He shouted again.

I grabbed a blade from the ground and drove it into the dummy God's chest, and before I could take two breaths, another swung at me.

"Do you think that's how you can earn your freedom? Killing other gods with someone like Sahir?" His shouts became progressively louder, but it didn't make his words any less hypocritical.

I tossed my blade to the ground and marched for Kyrell instead. I had never challenged him in that way, but something inside of me broke as I listened to him.

"I didn't help her kill anyone! I would never help her do such a thing. It's funny to hear you say such things after she let me know how involved you have been with her!" I was still charging for him when he pulled out the fate chains.

It was his promise to me. His promise was that I would be useless with the snap of their claps.

"Caym!" Koa called from the vines. "Don't do anything you'll regret."

Kyrell and I snapped our heads to Koa in unison.

Kyrell dropped the dummy gods back to blades of grass and moved until his finger was in Koa's face. "Get him under control, or I will."

We both watched Kyrell leave before Koa turned back to me with both hands in the air.

"What the hell?" His eyes widened.

I picked my blade back up, only wood, and moved to Koa at a jog's pace. He moved backward to the grass and grabbed a wooden sword from the ground. When I saw he had it gripped, I lunged at him. He blocked me with ease. It was with such ease that I felt ashamed for a moment. He lunged at me in return, and when I lifted the blade to block my face, he hit the wood across my knee.

The contact sent a wave of pain through my body and allowed me to take a breath in and gather my thoughts.

"You need to block more than your pretty face." He said, as he pressed his lips in disappointment.

I decided I would take advantage of him being distracted, critiquing me, and charge him. It was another failed attempt when he hit me on both sides and then used one leg to take both my knees out from under me. I sat on the grass and panted.

"I thought you were supposed to be teaching me; this feels like bullying." I huffed.

"This is me going easy on you. I thought you were supposed to be filling me in on what the hell happened here, not pretending I didn't walk into something." Koa pointed his wooden blade at me.

I waved a hand, still breathing heavily. "I surrender."

"Oh, come on, that was a light hit." Koa mocked.

"I just want five minutes to recover." I pleaded.

"I'll give you one." He said, twirling the sword.

"Sahir lied to Minna. She told Minna that two deities were conspiring behind her back to get her killed by Yumi. Minna killed the god of Peace. I caught her, and Kyrell caught me. He thinks I helped Sahir." I was still out of breath.

"You saw it?" He repeated my words.

"I saw it." I nodded. "She also let me know that she and Kyrell are intimate."

"That's disgusting." Koa shivered.

"You walked in on his punishment for the nothing I did. He was right to punish me; he didn't realize he was punishing me for not stopping Sahir." I said.

"You can't stop her actions. The same as you can't stop Kyrell. They'll do what they want." Koa said.

"What now?" I asked.

"I was going to ask you the same thing," Koa said.

Koa was one of the first people, outside of Astra and Ruri, to make me feel completely comfortable. He took away the feeling of not belonging and grounded me. It only added to my theory that some of the deities here were not truly God's. Koa felt like Ruri—like an old friend I had known all of my life, like someone I could trust with my life.

"So, have you ever been told why you can't go to the Sunlight Garden?" He asked.

"What? No, I assume it's because of the Tree of Life. My touch kills things, so? It makes sense I can't go in." I answered. "Why are you pushing the conversation this way?"

"Did she make the rule before or after she knew that?" he asked. He held out a hand to help me up.

I took it, and he lifted me like I was a babe. "I never thought about it."

"So why do you want this from me?" Koa asked. "What do you need my training for?"

I hesitated for a moment. My next words would shift the direction of our future if I were honest or shift the direction of our friendship if I lied to him.

"I want to find out the truth and get rid of Yumi and the other deities that feel fake," I said.

Koa lunged at me again, with less mercy. I tried my best to keep his aggression blocked, but my arm already shook under the weight he put behind his attacks.

"I have one single memory from the Age of Moonlight. A girl wrapped in blood. Pleading for me to help her while she sits under a tree that looks exactly like the one Yumi guards." Koa said.

Every word made him put more force behind blows, and my arm gave out. I took another hit that threw me off my feet again.

Koa shook his head and held out a hand to pull me up again. "I've thought about it a lot. Why do any of us have these memories if this is our creation? We shouldn't unless this is our reincarnation. I want what you want. I want to stop this feeling of not belonging, of not being whole."

I opened my mouth to speak, but he lifted his sword and swung at me again. "You want to discuss this while you beat me?"

"Of course. I meant it when I said that I've been going easy on you. Let's go." Koa charged.

He didn't let me get to my feet before he moved to me again. I lifted my sword in defense in time to catch him. Our swords connected, and I had a brief, fleeting thought of success before he lifted his foot, laid it on my wooden blade, and shoved it. The back of my head hit the ground, and stars swirled in my vision.

"Maybe I should have asked someone else." I groaned.

"You'll thank me in time," Koa said. He sat next to me.

"So, do you really not have a plan? A group? Or are you just relying on your dashing good looks?"

"We should start with rooms. I'm confident we can find something there. I also think we should decide who we want to start interrogating. We can make it casual, but we need to find out what is remembered and what the theories are. Do any of the originals have these memories, too?" I sat up and rubbed the bump on the back of my head.

"Did you come up with that right now?" Koa asked.

"Yes," I mumbled.

Koa got to his feet and brushed the knees of his pants off before holding his hand out to pull me up for the one-hundredth time. "Maybe if I throw you around a bit more, we can come up with something better." He slapped the sword at my leg in demand.

Ruri and I made a promise to each other, we said we would leave every single thing that is happening behind for just a little while. We said that we would set aside time to spend with just each other, and of course, that meant the Nola would be tagging along in the shadows.

When didn't he?

I was beyond excited. I planned out every detail that was able to be planned. She said she would tell no one for an added layer of privacy. It was all too common for deities to sniff you out and interrupt. I grabbed my basket of carefully packed supplies and snuck through the Vines to Cylla. She was going to meet me at the hot springs we all liked to visit at Orest, Thann's school.

I was sore and exhausted from Koa, which made the hot springs even more tempting.

Ruri hadn't arrived yet, so I took my time setting up everything I had brought with me: a brush, bars of soap, and sliced fruit sticks. I pulled out the blocks of wax we used as lighting and sat them all around the hot spring we would be swimming in, lighting them with magic. The hot spring was inside a grotto. Part of the top was eroded enough to see the sky but not enough to illuminate the entire space.

I stepped back to admire the results of my effort, hands on my sides and a smile of pride on my face. She would love it. Snow covered the entire outside that surrounded us, but no one would have known from the inside. A small waterfall fed enough water onto the ground that flowers bloomed around the edges of the rock.

"Here I come!" She called.

I turned in time to see her run in, in her cherry red slip, and dive into the spring water. The splashing caused all of the candles to flicker out, and I searched the water for any sign of her head. I snapped my fingers over and over until they lit back the way they should have stayed and did my best to wipe calm over my face. She still made me nervous. Not because I thought she'd leave or even judge me. She made me nervous because I always became too lost in her. I could stare at her while she talked for hours without ever getting tired of it. She made me a nervous fool.

Hands were around my ankles and pulled me into the water. I hardly had enough time to suck in air before my head was under the water. It was alright because the moment I was under and opened my eyes, I was met with an enchantress. Her emerald eyes were on me, and a smile moved across her face. Her deep green hair floated in every direction but not over her eyes. She grabbed my face and pulled me into her. Our lips met for what wasn't nearly long enough before she shoved me back and surfaced.

"I thought you would be late," she said as she pushed strands of hair from her face.

"I made sure to plan accordingly," I answered.

I could feel her feet brushing mine under the water.

"Are those for us?" She said and pointed to the edge of the water

"Soaps for your hair and snacks to eat while I do it."

"You're going to do my hair?"

I nodded and twirled my fingers for her to turn around.

"You're spoiling me today." She giggled.

I grabbed a sliced apple and held it in front of her mouth before I started collecting her hair in my hands. It was long enough. I was sure it was heavy but not long enough to be unmanageable.

"It feels strange to think we can speak freely. I'm growing used to having to keep my words to myself." She said.

"I have both of my ears open for anything you want to talk about," I said while I grabbed the bar of soap.

She was silent, lost in thought. She looked like she was deciding where to start.

"We said that we wouldn't—"

"I'll let this one thing slide," I said.

"Have you ever thought about leaving Merripen? I mean, if you weren't with me, would you have already left? I can see the marks on your body that you're trying not to talk about, and they're clearly fresh," She pointed.

"If you are trying to imply that you're the cause of my suffering, you're wrong. With or without you, Kyrell was intent on keeping me locked away, and Yumi was content to let it stay that way. It only became worse because of the markings no one seems to be able to explain." I said.

"Why do you think they keep you in Merripen, but I can roam?"

"The only guess I have is how powerful you are. Yumi sees that she needs you close if she's going to accomplish anything."

"Do you ever regret seeing me when you did? Maybe if you didn't have those markings, you could have been freed by now."

I sat the brush down between two candles and turned her around to face me. Her round eyes were sadder than I had expected to see.

"I would live one hundred more lifetimes in Merripen if it guaranteed me you."

She didn't answer. Instead, she wrapped her arms under my own and tucked herself into my chest.

"Sometimes I think I'm the cause of your pain." She whispered.

I felt my heart crack and my chest ache hearing her words. I fought the swelling of water on the rims of my eyes.

"I was only in pain before you. I haven't felt anything but complete since you."

I held her against me without loosening my grip on her and ran my hands over her still-soaking hair. The heat of the water helped to hide the redness on my face.

"Do you think I'm strong enough to take over something like Semper?" She asked.

Her voice was low, as if she didn't want me to hear her. Was that what she had been planning so secretly?

"Are you asking me this for a reason?"

"Look!" Ruri pointed up, "Speaking of Astra."

Two shooting stars flew across the sky and over the opening above us. It was the perfect addition to the kind of evening I was sure that we would not get again.

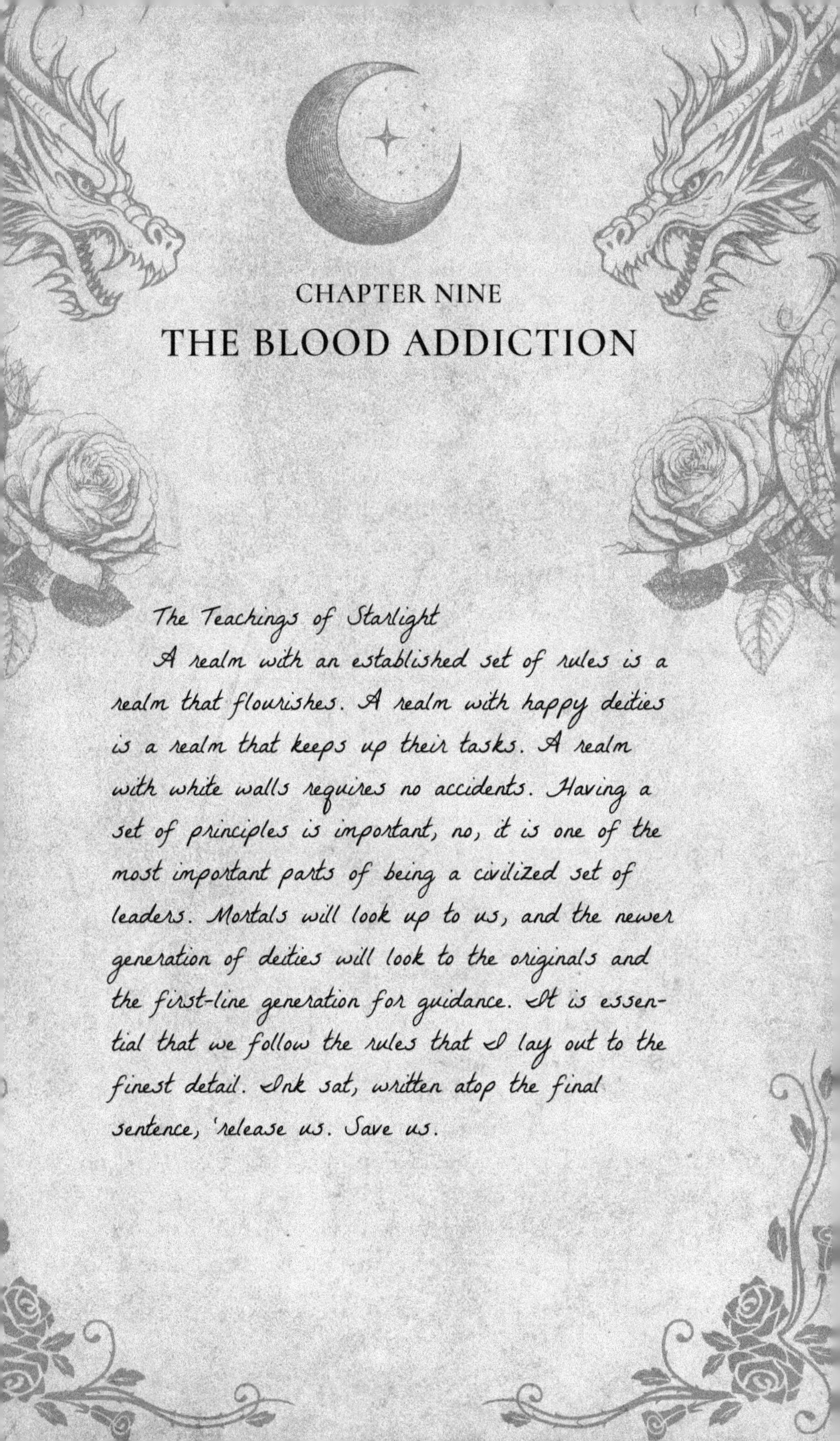

CHAPTER NINE

THE BLOOD ADDICTION

The Teachings of Starlight

A realm with an established set of rules is a realm that flourishes. A realm with happy deities is a realm that keeps up their tasks. A realm with white walls requires no accidents. Having a set of principles is important, no, it is one of the most important parts of being a civilized set of leaders. Mortals will look up to us, and the newer generation of deities will look to the originals and the first-line generation for guidance. It is essential that we follow the rules that I lay out to the finest detail. Ink sat, written atop the final sentence, 'release us. Save us.

RURI

I was exhausted. The kind of exhaustion that a nap wouldn't cure. Sleeping for the day wouldn't become enough, either. I was on my knees for how long; I did not know anymore. Yumi introduced me to the whip, which had only met Astra until today.

She placed me in front of the Tree of Life and gave me sixteen lashings before she left me to reflect on myself.

She demanded that I learn to be grateful and appreciate the kind of life that I had in the realm of the gods. Yumi screamed that if I wasn't going to help the realm, I would only hurt it, and she would fix the problem.

I only asked her why I felt so out of place. I hadn't gotten the chance to fully dive into all of the questions I wanted to ask her. I was sure that, if given the chance, she would hear my words and, in the end, help me feel like my life was my own.

She told me that I was just like my mother and that if I weren't careful, I would pay for it.

It was a strange comment to make. It was the only thing I had been reflecting on while she left me, bleeding, in front of the tree.

My mother was Orla. A Goddess who largely stayed out of sight. The comments didn't make any sense.

Astra was right. The tree whispered to me. The tree was quiet enough that sometimes I considered the idea that I was just losing my mind.

The tree was a she, and she sang to me.

I knew the song she was singing. I did not know why, but it didn't matter. I knew the voice inside of the tree. I did not know how, but it did matter.

I kept reaching my finger out and pressing the bark. When I made contact, the tree showed me the realm burning. Over and over, she showed it to me. I was only shown one other thing: the four different markings.

"Have we learned our lesson yet?" Yumi asked on the way in.

"Yes, ma'am." I had to clear my throat for my words to come out full.

"Good. We have a lot to do today. We need more of the mixture for the tree; you must apply it yourself as well." Yumi grabbed my arm and tried to pull me to my feet.

I had been on my knees for so long that no matter how much force she used, I was not standing yet. I shifted to the side and moved my legs to the side with my hands. They were going to need some time to adjust.

Yumi grabbed the bucket from the table beside the tree and sat it on the ground. She grabbed my hand and pulled my palm to face her. I felt her slice my skin deeper than she had last, and I winced. I didn't open my eyes because I already knew her tiny smirk was on me.

The blood poured into the bucket of water until it was unnoticeable that it had ever been clear. She let go of my hand, and I cradled it.

"We have other things to do." She rushed me along.

I grabbed the bucket with my other hand and poured the mixture onto the roots of the tree. As it always did, it glowed emerald, and although the petals looked brighter every time, the bark wilted. It looked dull and low on life.

I adapted to using illusion magic around Caym to hide the scars I collected on my back and palm. I was going to have to avoid being too close or alone with him for a few days. Illusion or not, today's cut was too deep to pretend.

"Get up already," Yumi ordered as she put the bucket back on the table. Your next task is to create a new form of life. We need some sort of security here. I've heard whispers of deities getting the idea to sneak around. We need to stop it before it can begin."

I nodded, pulling myself up on one knee. My legs started to come back to life, but the higher I stood, the dizzier I felt. I held my stance long enough to count to thirty.

"You have to be stronger than this, Ruri. Honestly, don't you see how pathetic you look? This little bit of punishment has you this frail? Cylla is dying; it's falling apart, and all the work we've been putting into it is going to waste. Whole pieces of land are dying, and instead of putting more effort into your home, are you giving up already?" Yumi shook her head.

I used the table to help pull myself the rest of the way to my feet. "I'm not giving up," I said simply.

Maybe it was her cruel attitude making the land wither away. I shook my head, even though no words left my mouth. No, it's my ungrateful attitude that's not doing enough to help. If I gave more effort, more blood, and more magic, it would thrive no matter what.

I lifted a golden apple and imbued it with magic. I touched it with my finger to see inside; I needed a good look at its root. I imbued it with a second spell and sat it down. I held my hand across Yumi and moved her back with me. After a few moments, it shook and sprouted a man. Dark skin and no hair, he grew large silver wings of feathers.

"Angels to protect what you need," I said to Yumi.

She clapped her hands, and every clap grew another angel until the Sunlight Garden was filled with them.

I saw myself out while she was giving them her full attention. She didn't need anything else from me, not yet. Her tasks and tests were always double what the last one asked of me. I reached up with the handkerchief I kept in the frills of my dress and wiped away blood from my nose. It was happening more frequently.

I only wanted to ensure no one knew about these things outside of Astra.

I walked the halls of our compound until I was inside of the garden I gifted Juniper. I planted dragon flower seeds, and

I wanted to check on one in particular. I placed the soul that was inside of the star I took inside of one. I pressed my finger against the egg, pushed from the inside of the flower petals, and filled it with more magic. It grew bigger until it was fully lifted from the blooming petals, and I plucked it.

I gently tapped on the shell and could hear a tap back from the inside.

How was I to crack the egg?

I bit my cheek and then tapped the shell on a rock that outlined the flower bed. I held my breath until I saw that the egg split ever so slightly up the side, just as I wanted.

I pulled the piece back with my nails until the thick membrane was the only thing between myself and the sandy-colored dragon. Orange and red spikes ran along her little back down to her tail. I turned my nail to the side, punctured the membrane, and sliced it down.

The little dragon rolled out of the sack and stretched. She was still dripping liquid but shook it all off. Her oversized eyes were shades of red and orange, just as her spikes were.

"Ruri!" The dragon yelled.

"I know what I was hoping would happen, but somehow, I'm still in shock that you're speaking to me," I said. "Do you know who I am?"

"Of course I do! You're the creator of seeds, the daughter of creation!" She paused and looked around. "Your mother hid something important for you, but everything is different, " she said.

"What's your name?" I tried to start slow before pouring out my questions.

"Vero. I'm the Goddess of Fall. Your aunt, she——" Vero paused. "She, where are we?"

"We are in Semper," I answered. "Where should you be?"

"You tell me, you created me." She sat, tucking her tail around her body.

"But you were just saying that——"

"Are you going to give me a name?" she asked.

"Vero. I'll call you Vero. Stay here in this garden." I ordered.

I wanted to explode. The control of information was so tight that I had nearly no avenues to explore. The tree only showed me reruns; the stars clearly held souls, but what good was that? For every soul I managed to stuff inside of a dragon, I could get thirty seconds to a minute of puzzle pieces.

I needed to find something to do to relieve stress.

"Ruri! We were looking for you." Juniper said.

"Yeah, I, uh, A dragon hatched, so I was here with her." I stuttered out.

"A dragon!" Juniper squealed.

Caym was behind her. He was in full view when she ran off to meet Vero. I instantly hid my hand behind my back.

"Hey. I brought that piece of obsidian you wanted." He said.

He looked at me as if he already knew I was hiding something. It just meant I needed to try harder.

"Yumi said some pieces of land are not holding up well. That some deities aren't able to do their duties, it's mine to find a solution. I want to create and assign the Goddess of Storms to Cylla. I don't want to use anything that could be tainted." I said.

"Have you considered telling Yum that maybe she puts too much on you?" He asked.

"She doesn't," I said. "Where is Jeb?"

Caym summoned a black mist and reached through, pulling Jeb to us. "Here."

I plucked a hair from Caym's head while I moved closer to Jeb. Caym's hair was long and thick. He didn't seem to notice my movements.

"Just like I told you," I said to Jeb.

I wrapped the stone with Caym's hair and Jeb poured magic from his hands into the stone. The stone went from cold to burning in my palm, and I nearly dropped it to the ground. Jeb kept going anyway, and I filled it with my own streaks of lighting. I formed them from the tips of my fingers directly into the stone. The stone finally tumbled to the ground, and a girl grew after the impact. She drew in breath like she was drowning. The girl's light blue curls looked bright against her dark, glossy skin.

I moved Jeb in front of me, acting as if I wanted to move him out of the girl's space, but I needed something between Caym and me so I could wipe away the blood I felt trickling down my face again.

She was in good hands. There was nothing I could have shown her that they wouldn't do without my words, so I left.

I needed to rest, only a little, while I could.

CHAPTER TEN

MAGIC DOESN'T ALWAYS GO THE WAY IT WAS INTENDED

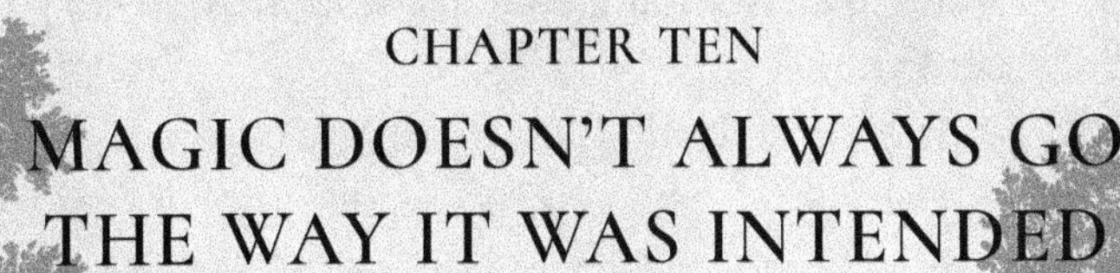

The Teachings of Starlight

The rules for the realm of the Gods are as follows: Starlight is our law; she is not to be questioned. She holds knowledge beyond what the rest of us could begin to understand. She can see the universe in a way we never will. We must not just know but believe that she is making the best choice for all of us. If we start to question her, then we start to unravel and diminish. The Goddess of Starlight is all-knowing and all-powerful. Through her all things—the words shifted themselves on the page—through her, all things suffer.

SAGE

I began to think the biggest reason that Sahir and I got along so well was that I talked significantly less than she did. It was easy for Sahir to make me a backdrop like the rest of Semper did. She still rambled on, and I stopped listening to any of it when she started doing her best to ruin the seeds that had sprouted late. I was in Cylla to check on the seeds that hadn't become mortals yet and do my best to get them to the finish line. It was an easy task that I could have done quickly if she hadn't come with me.

I would be lying if I said Sahir wasn't like a spoiled child. She was, on every level. She gave no second thought to doing what she wanted to do and never considered me or a consequence. We had eternity to work it out together and show her the right path. I just wished she would have gotten it a little better. She stepped on one half-sprouted seed without notice and moved on to rip the leaves off another.

"You all praise Ruri for planting seeds, but soon you'll see that she's not the only one who can do these things. I'm growing life. When I give birth to them, I will make sure you come to watch. I'm going to call them spiders and send them out on your sister." Sahir giggled.

I sighed and bent down to take in the damage she had done. She rambled on and on all day about these nonsense ideas she had, and they never became any more pleasant. Small root systems began to dangle from my fingernails and released drops of water onto the late bloomers. Every drop of water helped them complete their transformation. They would wake up the next day as full mortals.

"I don't know why you're doing this. If they couldn't do it themselves, then they weren't meant to do it at all." Sahir said.

I glanced up at her but didn't give her further acknowledgment.

She crushed another under her foot covers. "Too weak to survive, weak enough to die." She sang in repetition.

A second sprout that was too crushed to regrow. I rubbed both of my temples. "Sahir, you are making things a lot harder for me."

She shrugged, "Too weak to survive, weak enough to die."

She jumped on sprouts in tune with her song.

"Why don't you have your own land, really?" Sahir asked.

"I want to help my mother in Erebus and Ruri in Ashbell," I answered.

"That's pathetic for the Goddess of Nature magic. You could be doing anything at all with all that power." Sahir mocked. "If it's up to Yumi, you won't have a sister much longer anyway."

"What is that supposed to mean?" I stopped and stood back up.

"Yumi has been doing some pretty sadistic things to Ruri in private. I've even been taking some notes." She laughed.

"You're making things up again," I said.

She shrugged. "You believing me won't change what happens in the dark. Yumi's been collecting her blood and putting her through some pretty crazy tests of magic. You can check her palms and back for the proof on your own, ya know. Why do you think she's been sleeping in so much? She's even kept it from Caym."

"How would you know if it was kept so secretive?" I asked.

She pointed to her eyes. "I watch everything."

I didn't answer her. I truly did prefer letting her speak. A part of me didn't want to say too much to anyone. She never cared about anything, but she held every little sneeze as hostage information for later. Sahir was convinced she had some divine protection from her daddy, which we all knew was Kyrell. I had yet to see that he was anything amazing. He was far from good enough to hinge my whole life on as she did.

I left Sahir behind to stomp on the last unstable seedling. I intended to make a gift for Ruri today. Once I was done, maybe I would ask her about Sahir's little rumor. A part of me doubted she would tell me the truth. Even if she had marks on her back or cuts on her hands. She would illusion them away for my view. She thought by lying to me, she was somehow protecting me. The mental hoops she had to jump through to make that make sense to her was more than I could do myself.

I grew my own portals between realms with leaves. They split, and revealed a stone-stepping path to the Chamber of Starlight.

"Where are you going?" Sahir yelled from behind me.

"I have more to do today than entertain you," I called back.

"Of course you don't," Sahir said, following me through the portal. "Your sister is playing with her friends and obsessing over her dragons. Yumi is busy beating Astra for fun. Helia is busy spying on Thann and collecting bits of his blood to play with. I can keep going if you'd like, but I'm sure you get what I'm saying."

"How can you still have so much to gossip about?" I shook my head.

"You seem to know nothing, so I have plenty that's new to you. That makes it easy to keep talking." She stopped talking for only a moment before she jumped with remembrance, "Oh! Did you know Ruri filled Orla's caves with crystals? So many different ones I couldn't even keep up!"

"I did know that," I answered.

"That's something you never say." Sahir mocked.

I stopped at the entrance to the Sunlight Garden; every time I walked near it, all I could focus on was the sticky, sweet mixture of fresh-cut grass and fruit. I took in the golden, larger-than-life pillars that held the draped and stacked roofing. The roof of each building reached higher than needed, but it was a beautiful sight. It would have been the most beautiful place to live out an eternity If the inhabitance were trimmed down a little.

"So, what are we doing here?" Sahir asked, shoving me across the entrance line.

"I wanted to create something for Ruri—something small but powerful—to protect her in case she needs it and to help her with magic in Cylla. She spends a lot of time ensuring the magic flows as it should, and when the mortals are fully thriving, it'll be harder for her to keep up. Not to mention, if what you are saying is true, she will need help against Yumi's assaults." I said.

I originally intended it to be a way for us to pass messages in secret—a small piece of something fun at a time when she and I didn't get much time anymore. We both pulled away, and I knew she thought she was protecting me. She always wants to protect everyone.

"What could you give her that she couldn't give herself?" Sahir laughed.

I didn't open my mouth to press the issue. She was right; I couldn't give her anything she couldn't do for herself. She was strong and smart. She received all of the luck at creation. I was still going to try and make someone happy. My year had two major goals: fix Sahir and find a way to be helpful to someone.

We had to walk past Emon to enter the rest of the way into the garden. He was clearly tired of dealing with the number of visitors because he hardly opened an eye to glance in our direction. He flung a tentacle up and gave a small, half-hearted hiss in our direction before he folded himself back into a sleeping position. He had done his job well enough for today, and I gave him a few pats on the head before we were fully past him.

I grabbed a handful of the seeds and placed them between the golden apples and peaches on the table. It took the smallest swirl of my wrist and a light whisper from my lips before they came to life.

"That was impressive, I guess." Sahir rolled her eyes.

"They need a little more fluff, maybe a lot more," I said and released more vines from my fingers.

They grew wings of the same starlight glimmer that the Goddess of Space always hung in the sky. The wings had no clear definition in shape but enough sparkle to look at for ages. Bright and white, the glimmer was, but their bodies were filled with endless colors and patterns that mimicked the night sky. I was proud of them for a brief time. I couldn't remain that way until I knew she loved them.

"I'm going to call them Fiia of Starlight." I nodded.

"Why don't you ever make me anything!" Sahir whined.

The obvious reason was that she would mistreat it. If she didn't, she would like it for a day or two and then get bored. If both of those options weren't present, then she would just kill it. I never wanted to make anything for her because I knew nothing would be good enough if I did. I could use it as an excuse to make something for myself. I clicked my tongue, lost in thought, and nodded to myself.

"What is wrong with you?" She looked in disgust.

I grabbed another seed and tossed it into the air. When it landed back in my palm, I shot it with a green vine. It sprouted and grew into a small, cream-colored puppy. I moved my hands towards her and positioned the pup face level with Sahir.

"Ew!" She squealed, "It's disgusting! I hate it; get it away from me! Why did you make Ruri something so much nicer?"

I pulled the puppy back to my chest and cracked a smirk. How can she be so predictable?

"Sahir, this is why I don't make you anything," I said and left the garden.

"Why are you always so rude to the only Goddess around here that cares about you?" Sahir shoved me on her walk to catch up to me.

"I could say the same to you," I remarked.

The Fiia fluttered above me, and I ran my fingers through the pup's fur. I did my best to ignore the bratty girl that still followed me. The pup spared no time to nuzzle into the nook of my neck and claim it. I had the feeling Sahir would regret coming with me since the full group was bound to be there, but she didn't see it that way.

I wished they didn't see it that way. I knew I could save her, fix the little screw inside of her that was a bit loose. She just needed someone to understand. I had yet to reach the right channel, but we had time. I was confident that she wasn't going to do anything so crazy she couldn't come back from it.

Ruri spared Sahir no grace in that thought. When I proved her wrong, I would be humble about it. I wouldn't rub it in her face or make her apologize. I would take silent satisfaction in knowing that she had to think I was good for something, right about something, just once.

I entered Juniper's quarters and could hear all the raised voices. Banter and laughter, with a bit of disapproval. A Nola made itself known with a sudden shrill noise, and I jumped. I nearly lost grip of the pup.

"Starlight be damned!" I yelled.

"He really enjoys doing that," Juniper said.

The Nola gave one last squeal of amusement after my shudder, then disappeared in streaks. I ensured he wasn't going to do it again before I joined the gathering around Juniper's tea table.

"I didn't mean to interrupt, but I have a gift," I spoke as I sat down.

"Sage, you're always free to come and go from here as you please," Ruri said.

"We're just discussing things we can't agree on," Juniper said.

"Oh?" I questioned.

"I want to build us a home at the base of the volcano. Orla thinks we should be with her and build a home with the three of us together. Juniper thinks it's too hot for a vacation spot, and Caym made it a game to keep setting Juniper off again." Ruri crossed her arms.

"I enjoy setting her off as well. It's funny to call her the

Goddess of Wrath while she's always crying over something unless you really work her up." I shrugged, "Why don't we just have two homes? Everyone wins."

"What? No, pick a side!" Juniper narrowed her eyes to me.

"The volcano would be a perfect vacation spot," I said.

Juniper threw up her hands and grumbled, "Fine!"

Caym tried his best to cover his mouth and silence his laughter.

"You better stop laughing, boy." Juniper pointed.

I was careful not to touch any of the flowers that were perfectly placed around the walking stones on my way in, and just as cautious about the cups on the stone table. Juniper poured my cup of tea. She still muttered under her breath.

I took a moment while I got into place to take in that Caym changed his colors to crimson. White and silver is what Yumi demanded; Kyrell took the silver out and added gold when Caym arrived. Caym no longer wore Kyrell's colors. He altered his clothing to match Juniper and Ruri. They took the same approach as Kyrell—just enough of a small change to be there, but only in small rebellion. I wanted to bring it up, but I decided to wait and see if they offered me an invitation to join instead.

"So, about that gift." I cleared my throat and motioned them to Ruri. "This is for you. They're called Fiia of Starlight, and I admit, I took the idea from the Nola; they are much prettier."

Ruri reached up and pulled my hands open; she released the rest of the Fiia hidden underneath, and after they were finally done fluttering out, at least one hundred filled the tops of Juniper's flowers.

Ruri took my hand in her own and intertwined our fingers. "Thank you. They are beautiful."

I felt confident and overjoyed until she took her finger to the tip of one's nose, and a spark of magic echoed between them. She gave them a voice to speak. It was a quick reminder that if I did anything, she could do better. She could find a way to one-up anything I created, and she'd never miss a chance to do it. I was shaken from my thoughts by the sound of Sahir. She slapped a Fiia out of the air and turned it to mush on the stone steps under her feet.

My eyes widened in shock, and Ruri got to her feet before I could. I had forgotten she was there; how could I have forgotten she followed me in? There was bound to be a fight that was largely outnumbered. I stumbled off of the stool I was sitting on to place myself in front of Sahir first. I felt the rip of my shoe cover when I did it, but I didn't have time to care. I moved my body in front of hers as a shield.

"Why would you do that?" I growled. "Get out. Don't argue with me, don't linger to spy, get out."

Sahir opened her annoying mouth to speak, but I placed my hand on her lips. "Get out." I gritted my teeth.

She rolled her eyes at me and bit down on the skin of my hand that touched her lips before turning to leave. She was a child, I swear it. Something went wrong during her creation and rotted her brain.

"I'm sorry." I turned around.

"Why are you apologizing for her?" Ruri looked pained.

"I'm not going to let you gang up on her in front of me!" I yelled.

"I don't need a group to accomplish getting rid of her, but I don't for you," Ruri said.

"How kind of you." I rolled my eyes in response.

Ruri sighed and dropped her shoulders. "Why do you want to do this so badly? Why do you want to paint me as your enemy?"

I didn't want to. To have a back-and-forth with her. I turned to leave, but she grabbed my arm to stop me. When I turned back around, she dropped it as quickly.

"Just give me one chance to prove to you she won't

change. That behind your back, she's plotting all the same." Ruri pleaded.

The voice she used reminded me of the months that it was only us and how close we were.

"One chance." I held up a single finger.

I didn't believe she had anything, but for both our sake, maybe it would let us move forward with our paths.

"I give magic to the mortals today; someone has been trying to steal magic, and now is when I enter my plan to find out who it is. Any deity that gets more magic today has been touched by me or has been sneaking around." She said.

Caym took my pup, and Juniper, Ruri, and I left. We made our way to Cylla. Caym wouldn't join because it was too risky. If Kyrell saw him with Ruri, he'd have a price to pay. They did well with using illusion to create a fake Caym to leave in Merripen, but they never pushed it too far.

When we entered the realm of the mortals, It took longer than I expected to get things started. Questions and concerns were being smoothed out for too long. When the talking was finally done, Juniper and I stood back from Ruri.

"All right, all right," Ruri yelled with her hands. "I've heard the demands. I'm not a fairy godmother," She turned and pointed at me, "But I'll do my best." She cracked her knuckles and shook her arms before she glanced back at us again. "Why are you looking at me like that? I might pull a magical muscle if I don't stretch first."

"Ruri," I said. "Get your head in it already!" I pointed.

I wouldn't say a word, but I was using my own magic to push my sight through any illusions she had. I saw the scars on her palm. There were too many to count.

"Okay, okay." Ruri drew her words out.

"Ruri!" Juniper yelled.

Ruri jumped.

"I'm not even that close to you!" Juniper snapped.

Ruri's lips pressed together. "I just had to be sure. I never know with you. Sometimes it's a shout, sometimes it's a vase!"

"Ruri!" I yelled again.

"That's three times you've called my name, but I'm already here." She winked.

I grabbed her by the ear and pulled. "If you don't stop staling."

"Ow, ow! Who's older here? Now I'm too injured to do anything," Ruri cried.

"I'm older. Ruri! By nine seconds!" I yelled back.

Ruri ripped her head away and grabbed at her ear. "Yeah, well, I have Nola."

"Caym has Nola, you mean," I said.

Juniper gave Ruri a look, not just any look, but the look before she snatched her up.

"I didn't need to stretch anyways." Ruri cleared her throat. "Okay, here we go."

Ruri lifted her arms above her head and took a deep breath. She let it out as she lowered her arms. She started a second time, but with her arms, a sphere formed, hovering in front of her stomach. Violet in color, it grew in size the lower her arms hung, and when they couldn't hang any lower, she brought her hands to meet each side of it, triple in size, and pulled her hands away from each other, expanding it again. When it outgrew her in size, she released it, and it erupted in an explosion of heat and color across every piece of land we could lay eyes on.

"Done," Ruri said, brushing her hands together. "Magic granted to the realm."

Juniper and I glanced at each other but didn't move.

"All of the harassment to hurry up, and no, you aren't even going to try anything?" Ruri's eyes pierced the both of us.

Ruri liked to think of herself as a gentle girl. If she could see herself from our eyes, she would see that while she thinks juniper is intimidating, we all consider the darkness behind her eyes intimidating. There was an innocence to her, but it was in experience only. She was innocent of the ways of the world like we all were, but not in the ways of deities. There was no innocence in her demeanor. Only the presence of someone to fear.

Juniper lifted a finger and shot it in the air as a mocking joke, but the outshot a stream of fire, and she flung her neck in Ruri's direction.

"That was the point, Juniper! Why are you looking at me like I committed a crime!" Ruri yelled.

Morticia came through the portal and called Ruri. Her face was green as if she were feeling ill. She stumbled to her knees, and flowers sprouted in every place her fingers touched. It spread quickly; five, ten, or thirty infected flowers appeared around her in seconds. And by the time we counted to ninety-nine infected sprouts, they came together and grew into a girl. The Goddess of Plague had absorbed all the petals and took shape.

"I don't think that was supposed to happen," I said, leaning into Ruri.

Ruri only shook her head in response, eyes widened.

We cut our visit to Cylla short to take the newly created Goddess, Vespera, back to Semper and see if anyone else had been gifted magic or if Ruri's still secret plan had worked out. When we walked through the vines, we were met with a Goddess on all four limbs and Sahir standing over her. Two puddles of bile already lay around the Goddess, and when the third came, it formed a man; before any of us could take in the full sight and process it, I gave Ruri another shove in the back.

Yumi sat in shock, hardly noticing our presence.

I was still wondering how the situation was going to lead me to turn back on Sahir.

Before either of us could speak, Juniper dropped to her knees and started heaving, too. Sahir went down next. I didn't have time to question her before a man was in front of Juniper and a girl was in front of Sahir.

"Oh, you are going to be in big trouble," I whispered to Ruri.

Ruri looked at me, her eyes wider than I thought possible. "How do you know this is my fault?"

The room was filled with the sound of a sick woman until Deimos stumbled through his vines, looking ill, with a man in step behind him.

Deimos sounded as if he were fighting to catch air. "I was dreaming, and then it turned into a nightmare of Yumi being locked away. When I was pulled from the dream, I felt ill." He stopped and looked back at us.

"Let me guess. You got sick, and the bile grew him, right?" I pointed.

Deimos looked at me with relief. "Yes, exactly!"

"It seems to be going around, huh, Ruri," I said, pushing her forward.

Ruri stumbled ahead of the group and gave me a stern glance that promised pain, "I wouldn't put it exactly like that. I was doing what I was supposed to and giving everyone magic."

"And impregnated them instead,' I said.

Ruri closed her eyes and sucked in her cheeks; she was fighting back laughter with every piece of herself. She ran a hand over her face, tugging at the skin. She did her best to pull herself back together. "Sometimes things don't work out perfectly."

"That's an understatement," I said.

"Sage!" Ruri shot back at me.

I lifted my arms, "Don't get mad at me; I didn't knock everyone up!"

"Ruri, Can you stop it?" Yumi finally interjected.

"I can try," Ruri said.

"Do more than try." Yumi gritted. Her face was a smile,

but her voice was one small step away from having an outburst that put Thann to shame.

With her best effort, Ruri attempted to reverse what she had done. She was using so much magic her cheeks flushed. The first time she wiped her face, I thought she was pulling sweat away from the heat. The second time, I noticed it was her nose. She was pulling away blood from her nose in the most silent way she could. A loud storm of steps interrupted us all and pulled our eyes to the doorway. I watched Ruri draw a lock and throw it upward, doing her best to gasp for air in silence.

"You are an evil, disgusting piece of garbage, and you don't deserve the position you have!" Astra screamed with a finger pointed at Yumi, "Did you think I wouldn't find out? Did you think I would've kept silent? Or believed that you didn't know the blood of my son was used to create Deimos?"

"Astra," Yumi's voice had a stutter to it, and her lips fell in a way I had not seen before.

"You better have something good to say or some kind of real action to take; otherwise, I'm going to."

Yumi cut the Goddess of Space off. "Enough!" She screamed, moving her feet. "I said this matter was over!" Yumi was still screaming while her feet carried her closer to Astra. "I asked you, for the sake of the family, not to hold grudges. I want to know who brought this up to you again?"

My heart pounded in my chest at Yumi's reaction. The air grew thicker around us, and the crowded room glanced around at each other, with every single face in fear and confusion about how things could escalate.

Astra looked at Sahir, then back to Yumi. "It doesn't matter. You won't do anything to your pet."

Yumi's hand hit Astra's face faster than anyone in the room could process.

"don't you ever talk that way again!" Yumi's voice was rough and low. "I won't tolerate it. I treat you all equally."

"What are you going to do, Yumi?" Make me apologize?" Astra said, holding a hand to her cheek. "Or will you whip me again? Maybe you'll have another outburst that you can't explain and then apologize later. Just tell me, is it true?"

The newly created Goddess of truth spoke before Yumi could. "Yes."

Astra dropped to her knees. "Did she know for sure?"

"Yes," The Goddess said again.

"Is she lying about more than just that?" Astra whimpered.

She opened her newly formed mouth to speak again, but Yumi shoved her hand into the girl's mouth and took her tongue and jawbone in one pull.

"I said enough!" Yumi's voice shook.

The girl's body hit the floor with a thud, and crimson liquid spilled, staining the white floor on all sides. Yumi dropped the part that she still held and left the throne room without another word. Every deity in the room stood equally frozen, and all faces read disbelief equally except one.

"I'm not cleaning that up," Sahir said with laughter.

No one else moved; we were all too stunned to speak. That kind of escalation was hard to process.

"I, I only meant to make whoever was stealing magic fall asleep," Ruri whispered.

CHAPTER ELEVEN

WHAT LURKS INSIDE THE CAVE MOUTH

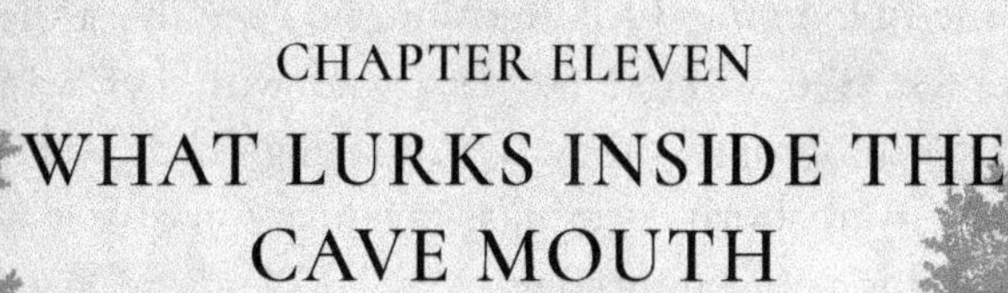

The Teachings of Starlight

The rules for the realm of the Gods are as follows: If words against Starlight are heard, they must be reported. Lies and hatred spread like a sickness. As a follower of Starlight, you must be able to hold those who speak hatred, those who say we are false, accountable. If you are caught with someone who says our teachings are false and you do not hand them over, you will also be tried and punished accordingly. There is no rehabilitation inside of perfection.

The bottom of the page was ripped with remnants of moss and bark as if a tree branch ran across it.

SAGE

Orla was waiting for me at the entrance to Erebus's main cave. I hadn't been inside since the mortals for the land of shadow had finished blooming. Orla told me she gave them their first task: homes. She wanted me to come with her while she checked on the progress they were making. They weren't like deities. We were born as adults, needing some time to ease into life and for our knowledge to settle. We didn't need to be taught a lot. We learned how to interact with each other as time went on.

The mortals were significantly different. They needed to be taught everything from wiping their asses to how to build a fire. Orla thought it was endearing. She found it fulfilling to spend all of her time teaching them. I found it pathetically frustrating. Some of them needed to be told the same thing over and over again. Still, even after three or four times, they didn't get it. My mother seemed to have unending patience. I was excited to see inside of the caves, but nothing more.

The area surrounding the caves was bare. There were hardly any trees or patches of grass in sight. The entrance to the main cave was carved out by hand. The Dwarfs of Erebus had carved into the rock the image of a stone dragon; it stood ready to pounce on anyone who may enter uninvited. They carved it from the likeness of their own dragon. He was the first to hatch from his flower. There were several other dragons whose eggs were emerging from their flowers, but only he hatched. Usha took after the land he lived in. Stone in color and texture, and not particularly big in size, but he was just a babe inside. Docile and sweet. He pounced around at our arrival like a puppy. One that could shake the ground around him.

Usha followed the two of us inside, and I was met with my first glance at what Orla called Dwarves. Small men and women with beards. At first, I thought they were children. Orla nudged me as a hint to stop staring. I tried to pull my eyes away and take in the scenery around me. A light blue glow was emitted from every mushroom around us. The air around us was filled with moisture and the sound of dripping from cave rocks.

"Sometimes," Orla turned to me and crossed her arms. "What you see on the surface is just a small piece of a bigger picture. What's underneath can be a whole world you never thought existed."

"Mom, stop trying to sound wise," I said.

She clicked her tongue at me in disapproval and moved further inside. A Vinna dropped from a mushroom placed above her and wrapped its arms around her neck. Oversized wings like leather that were part of its arms made an off-putting sound every time they slapped together during movements. I had been told about them and how Ruri helped Orla make them to be protectors of the caves. They weren't as cute as I was expecting. I would have added fur. Ruri gave them a spiked tail instead. Their short snouts could have been cute if they weren't purple and waxed coated.

"Here to check on the crystal progress, ma'am?" a dwarf asked.

Orla shook her head, "No, Owna. I'm here to check on the progress of homes and show my daughter around."

"Oh, this is Sage. She looks smarter than you made her out to be." Owna looked confident in her remark.

"What?" I looked at Orla in disbelief.

"She's joking!" Orla panicked.

Owna sighed, "I was not."

She looked me up and down in disappointment before taking the Vinna from Orla and leaving the two of us behind.

"She's quirky." Orla forced her to laugh.

"Yeah, quirky." I rolled my eyes.

"So," Orla stopped herself, and I felt the lecturing was about to start dripping from her lips.

"Spit it out." I sighed.

"How are you and Sahir doing?" Her words were strained.

"Do we have to do this?" I grimaced.

"I just want to check on you. It's my job to make sure you're safe. As much as I want to say you shouldn't hang out with her, I'm not. I'm simply checking to see if you need any advice or to vent." She held her hands up in peace.

I closed my eyes, composing myself before answering her again. I'm sure she did mean well, but I'm not sure what she expected me to say. Did she think I would spill Sahir's secrets?

"There isn't much for me to say. She is better behaved than any of you give her credit for. Just because chaos is in her name, she has a bad reputation." I shook my head in disapproval.

"That's not why at all. She stirs up problems between anyone she is next to when she is bored, and she is always bored."

I couldn't argue that.

"Do you ask Ruri these kinds of things, too?" I asked.

Hurt flickered in her eyes, "There was no reason for you to go so low."

A pit formed in my stomach, and I felt regret. "I'm sorry."

"She hasn't talked to me in quite some time. My information comes from Juniper. I'm trying my best to give her the space she wants."

"You two sound exactly alike," I mumbled to myself. "Maybe you should talk to her sometime. She hasn't been spending as much time with anyone as she used to. You can use it as an excuse to check on her. Maybe she will become your perfectly developed child."

"Does your idea of your sister come from who she really is? Or does it come from Sahir's idea of her?" Orla asked.

"What?" I asked, confused.

"You used to admire her. You two were closer than anyone in the realm until Sahir shifted all her free time to whisper in your ear. Are you truly upset with her? Do you really feel like she steals all of your spotlight, or is it Sahir pouring out of your mouth?" Orla watched me.

She only blinked once; she was soaking up even the smallest reaction I had to her words. She was wrong. My idea of my sister came from my sister's actions. No one else's words were influencing me. I wasn't that weak.

"Are we going to see these homes or not?" I asked.

The same flash of pain from before shimmered through her eyes again before she motioned her hand for me to go first. We moved in silence behind a cave wall that opened up into an area large enough that I didn't find the end. Many more giant mushrooms lined one side of the space. The front had carved-out pathways. Each one was designed differently from the last. It looked like it took them days just to design them. They had to have used a chisel. A door at the front of one of the mushrooms opened, and a small, bearded woman walked out, followed by a man with an even larger beard.

"Goddess Orla!" They called, running to her.

They greeted her with such happiness, taking her hand and questioning her endlessly. I left them for a closer look at their homes. When I ran my hand over the mushrooms, they were smooth. I imagined they would have a slickness to them, but I was wrong.

"Orla!" A familiar voice called.

When I turned around, I was taken aback by the man standing beside Juniper. He was huge. He looked like he was bred from something larger than the rest of us. His hair was the color of apples, and his eyes glowed golden. They were the same color as Kyrells, but he had a softness to them, unlike Kyrells. It was the only bit of softness to his face. His presence, his jawline, and even his arms were rough. He looked like

Juniper's bodyguard, and I was into it. My heart fluttered for a moment before Juniper spoke again.

"Sage! This is my son, Onyx." Juniper smiled, pulling him forward. "He is the God of Pestilence."

Son? Juniper's spawn. The fruit of her loins stood in front of me. Not just standing in front of me, but I was just gushing over him. I was staring at each vein in his arms and lusting over him. Bile rose in my throat. I was disappointed in myself. I was disappointed in her for not speaking faster before I could have those thoughts.

"Sage?" Orla leaned over to look at me under my hair. "Are you blushing?"

"No!" I squeaked.

What the fuck was that? I squeaked. I-

"She does look really flushed." Juniper agreed.

"I need to get to bed; I'm tired." I stuttered.

"Bed?" Onyx laughed, "The sun has hardly been up two hours."

"What's wrong with your daughter?" Juniper thought she was whispering.

"She likes him," Orla responded.

"I am tired!" I demanded.

Orla and Juniper exchanged a glance that called me a liar.

"Well, Onyx came to receive assistance from the Dwarves. He wants to run a shop here." Orla said.

"Why here?" I asked, still stuttering despite my best efforts.

"It just felt right," he said, smirking at me.

"Best of luck. I'm sure with the three of you, you'll figure it all out just fine." I waved.

I did not wait for a response; I turned and walked to the cave entrance as quickly as I could. I felt a looming presence following me, but I was too scared to look behind me. I only did my best to walk faster.

A hand gripped my shoulder, and from the sight out of the

corner of my eye, I was sure my bones would be crumpled to dust.

"I surrender!" I cried.

"I come in peace?" Onyx held both hands up.

"What do you want!" I was on the verge of sobbing.

"You aren't exactly what I expected." He said.

Instantly, a wave of anger washed over me, "What is that supposed to mean, huh!"

"Easy, now. I only followed you because I need to give you this." He said. He held a folded piece of paper up for me to take.

I reluctantly took it but didn't open it. "What is it"

He looked down at the paper instead of at me when he spoke. "When I was created, my memories were all for you. I know that sounds intense, but it felt important. I wrote down as much as I could, but I was starting to forget while I was writing."

I opened it, and his writing was awful. The note read like a riddle on its own. It talked about seasonal deities that were murdered. It spoke of needing to find them for a completed ascension. That we needed to remember who we were in our first lifetime.

"What is this supposed to mean?" I asked.

"I was hoping you would know." He said.

I shook my head, "It doesn't mean anything to me. I'm not sure how I would find out, either. There were only a few before me, and I don't recall any deities being in charge of seasons."

"Maybe it'll mean something later." He tried to comfort me.

I folded it and put it in the pocket of my dress that sat on my hip. "Thanks, but unless you know a way to pull memories out by force, I don't think this will be useful anytime soon."

"It will be when Daddy gets here," Sahir said from behind me.

"Starlight, Sahir. You scared me!" I pushed her.

"I'll excuse myself," Onyx spoke as he turned to leave.

He looked at Sahir as if he had seen her before and had already decided that he was not fond of her. It was good to know that he was just like everyone else before I allowed myself to get too close to him."

"He's cute? He reminds me of my dad; who is he?" she asked, sniffing the air.

I shivered in disgust, "Sometimes you remind me of Helia." I said.

She shrugged, "Fine. Don't tell me who he is. I'll find out for myself. Let's go. I've been waiting too long. We have things to do still."

"What are we doing?" I asked, following her out.

"We are going to the river Sin. My daddy told me a story before I came here. It was a story about how to take a deity's place. I'll make it simple," She giggled. "If you eat the heart of a god, you absorb their power. So, we are going to find a heart for me to eat for more power." She skipped ahead of me.

"How many crazy deities do they have to be around here?" I screamed.

Sahir twirled herself around to give me a smile before continuing on as if I would obey her path like a good dog. She was right that I followed. When she stopped in front of the crimson water, I stopped her from diving in.

"What are you really doing?" I asked.

"I told you. My daddy told me to do this, and so I am." Sahir said.

"You can't really think this will work." I scoffed.

"I know it works. I've already eaten Dysis's heart, see." She blinked, and her eyes shifted to resemble a snake. "My daddy was right. I have to keep doing it to get ready for his return." She nodded.

"His return? Kyrell is already here. You sound insane, Sahir!" I yelled.

"You're not being very funny. It's not too late to kill you and eat yours for my daddy, too!" She shoved her finger into my chest.

"You don't make any sense." I shrugged.

"I'll tell you a secret." She leaned into my ear, "My daddy is Yumi's husband. She's kept him a secret, but he's looking for her and us."

"Okay," I pretended to understand.

She turned around and dived into the water; I didn't stop her. I was beginning to doubt if I could do anything for her for the first time. Maybe she really was losing it. Her father was Kyrell, and her mother was Minna. We all knew it, so where was the rest coming from?

Did she truly expect me to take her seriously? There were so many flaws in her words, like Yumi and the fact that she did not have a husband. The only thing that I could take seriously was the fact that she had done something terrifying to her eyes.

I watched her hyperventilate as she tried to adjust to the freezing temperature of the water before she grabbed her nose and disappeared. It felt like she had been gone a while, which made me move closer to the water to try and see anything. The water may have been red, but it was still easy to see through. I finally saw her wiggling her body back to the surface. When she broke the top layer and pulled in the air, she did have a heart in her hand. Perfectly preserved in ice. I couldn't begin to understand how it was possible.

I watched her bite into it as if it were any other piece of fruit.

"It's chewy." She said through chomps.

It was only seconds before her entire body started shaking and glowing. She dipped underwater during her convulsions. But she recovered before I could weigh the pros and cons of jumping in after her. Part of me said it was the right thing to do, but the other half of me wrestled with the idea that her death would mean I didn't have to keep her company anymore. She broke the surface again and shook her hair out.

"Do you want a bite? It's intoxicating!" She held up the other half of the heart.

I shook my head.

"It's a rush, a surge of power, unlike anything you can experience otherwise." She called out.

I only shook my head again. There was a part of me starting to be scared of her. A part of me became convinced that she was broken in a way that had to have happened at creation.

Sahir sat on the edge of the river and took another bite. As she chewed, all of her veins bulged in a wave throughout her body. Her eyes had shifted back to looking as if they were those of a snake, but they filled in with black before they were hidden again.

She threw what was left of the heart back into the river, and we both watched it get lost all over again in the current.

"What is the goal in this?" I asked her. "You take their power, and then what?"

"I open a rift." Sahir answered, "So my daddy can come home because my father is not someone as weak as Kyrell."

"Where is he?" I asked again.

"You don't need anything else yet," Sahir said as she squeezed her hair out.

"Then what now?" I shrugged.

"We go back to Semper." She answered.

I used my leaf to open the portal to the chamber of starlight, and we both entered together.

I wasn't happy that she refused to give me all of the answers I deserved, and even more frustrated that I had to press and pull and plead for the little bits she had given me. It didn't make sense why she wouldn't lay it all out if she were my friend.

On the other side of the vines, the Chamber of Starlight

was busy. Yumi sat on her throne and looked around between everyone in the room before landing eyes on Sahir and I.

Yumi was back to carrying the same sticky, sweet expression that was usually on her face, but I still hadn't moved past the image of her and the Goddess she killed for simply speaking a truth outside of her own.

"Why are we here?" Ruri asked.

"I have noticed that a Goddess is missing from Cylla. She was supposed to be building up a land, but during my checks, I could not find her. I was hoping someone might know something." Yumi answered, ignoring any hint of ill intent in Ruri's voice.

"Maybe she annoyed you, so you killed her too." Ruri's tone was flat.

I didn't miss the extra moment Yumi let linger between the two of them, and my thoughts flashed back to the stories Sahir told of the two.

"She was with Sage last." Sahir inserted.

Yumi's eyes were still darkened on Ruri before moving to Sahir.

Why did she just lie using my name?

"Excuse me?" I scoffed.

"I recall her last with Sahir, actually," Astra said.

I didn't speak; I was too in shock. I spent so much time defending her; why was she doing it? Was it payback for not diving in the river after her? Was she trying to get me killed?

"You haven't been around enough to say, have you, Astra?" Sahir answered.

Astra smirked. "Maybe you're right, or maybe you're lying to cover your own actions."

"I really wouldn't know anything," Sahir answered, her voice calm.

"Since I cannot feel her, I fear she is dead. If you know something, please say so. Whoever did it should serve their punishment in the sunlight garden." Yumi said. "This bickering will get us no closer as a family."

"That's it?" Vespera, the new Goddess of Plague, asked.

"Do whatever you'd like. Nothing comes with real consequences as long as you are weak." Astra said, turning to leave, "Maybe split the punishment between Sahir and Minna."

"Forgive her; she's still mourning," Sahir said with a smile.

"Maybe we need another dinner together to reconnect as a family," Minna said, her voice wavering.

"That's a lovely idea," Yumi said, her tone saying she clearly considered the matter over with.

Yumi lifted herself from the throne and made her way to Minna. Taking her hand, the two left. The relief on Minna's face was evident. Planning voices could be heard even after their exit.

I looked at Ruri with confusion, but she did not speak. My name was dropped and moved over so fast that I didn't know how to approach it.

Ruri turned back to Sahir and asked, "Why did you throw her name out?"

"Isn't that what you told me?" Sahir asked.

Ruri's eyes widened. "I told you?"

Sahir nodded. "I remember you saying that you thought Sage was being a bit suspicious, and you last saw her with Ivory. Did you not say maybe the two were connected?"

Ruri scoffed; her mouth only opened slightly.

"I don't mean to cause any problems; I just don't like keeping secrets," Sahir said, looking at Sage.

"I hope you believe that, and I hope it's all worth it when it's me that rips your tongue from behind your lips," Ruri spoke with an unshakeable calm.

Sahir laughed. "I'm only trying to get to the bottom of things." She lifted her hands in the air, a signal of peace. "The things I hear you say about your sister aren't my business, but—"

Ruri's teeth ground against each other before she lifted a hand, and a string of white webbed itself through Sahir's lips as if sowing them closed. Ruri slung her hand down, and Sahir's body followed, bringing her to a knee against her will.

"You look better like this," Ruri said, walking closer to her. "We didn't set our boundaries well enough. So, let me try again. I'm willing to burn if it means watching you burn, too. I'm willing to hurt you in ways you don't have the power to imagine and eat the consequence like its fucking desert if that's how you want to have it." She lowered herself so she was face to face with Sahir. "I don't care what games you want to play here. Do as you please, with anyone but them."

I had both arms on Ruri before she could continue any further and lifted her to her feet. "Ruri, undo her, and let's go." I pleaded with her.

Ruri shifted her eyes between mine. She was searching for something that I wasn't sure how to let her find. I didn't know if the bond between us was still there at all. If the two shy girls who used to sneak into each other's room to avoid the big compound were ever even real. I wasn't sure they could ever be real again. If we could be as close or as honest as we once had been.

"Please." I pleaded again.

Ruri slammed Sahir onto the ground hard enough that her cheek was pressed flat. She undid the binding on Sahir's lips, taking care to tug at it until every hole she unstrung bled. She left Sahir on the ground and made her way to Merripen's vines. I was overwhelmed with fear at that moment because the only thing that replayed in my mind was the fact that Sahir had been eating hearts.

She had to have eaten the missing Goddess, too. Who knew how strong she was? I didn't want Ruri hurt, but I wasn't ready to give up on Sahir, not truly. She just needed a little extra understanding. She didn't actually mean any harm. She needed me to help her heal from the injuries on her lips, and I could convince her that Ruri was just temporarily out of her mind.

I took Sahir with me, away from the Chamber of Starlight.

Sahir and I spent some time in my quarters, and I healed her wounds. There wasn't a mark left to know it had ever happened to her, and then we went together to the dining hall. We spent the afternoon in silence. It wasn't uncomfortable; she was beyond happy. She just, for once, had nothing to say to me. I took us to dinner early because of it. It wasn't uncomfortable for her, but it was for me.

The room was filled with deities I hadn't gotten the chance to get to know yet before the ones I knew followed. After the first few entrances, I knew tonight would be less peaceful than the day had. It may even be the breaking point in our realm. Certain members were entering with a clear message. They ditched the white colors of our family in their entirety. They wore pure crimson silk. Yumi sat at the head of the table, watching them enter one by one. There were only two seats left and two missing members. Astra came in first, adjusting the belt that held up her pants. Head to toe, she was covered in the same crimson colors as the rest of the small group.

Yumi dropped her glass, shattering it on the ground, when Ruri entered in a lavish crimson dress.

"Emon, please bring another glass for our ruler." Astra gave him a pat before placing herself in one of the open seats.

"I can't stay," Ruri said. "My apologies. I have such a long list of things I have to tend to that this dinner just can't fit anywhere in my schedule. I did bring a gift to make up for my absence, though."

Ruri casually walked in front of the table where her clothing could be seen and gave a bow.

"Are you trying to upset me on purpose?" Yumi yelled as she slammed her fist on the table. "Are you trying to start a war?"

"I am simply trying to keep to the orders and tasks you gave me," Ruri said.

Yumi's nostrils flared in response.

If Sahir were right, we would all know of it.

The entire room blared with voices when Ruri marched past the angels guarding the exit and left, and I zoned out. Everything became a blur for me. I knew that Yumi would have many things to say to her in private.

CHAPTER TWELVE

THE GREAT LIBRARY AND THE TIMEKEEPERS

The Teachings of Starlight
The rules for the realm of the gods are as
follows: Your duty is your contribution to the realm.
It is your purpose, your design. It must be done
to keep order. You can not fail. If you can not do
your duty, you have no purpose. If it is deter-
mined you can not keep up with your tasks, you
will await trial by starlight, and if she should so
choose, be stripped of the title deity and your life-
black ink form over the page, slowly erasing the
words.

SAGE

I was out of ideas entirely until it hit me that we had a deity that enjoyed knowledge. Her hobby was collecting books and scrolls to open her own library. I had already wasted half of my day fighting myself to speak to her. She hadn't set any friendships in stone since her creation. The concept made it seem like a good idea to befriend her myself, but it also left too many questions. More deities had a reputation for being untrustworthy, and if she refused to get close to anyone, it meant she was highly untrustworthy, or she was the only one to trust.

I had been pacing the entrance to her library in Erebus for too long. I grabbed the door handle and pulled the door open with force. The girl inside jumped and then threw her hand on her chest. She let out a terrified sigh before she laughed.

"Is something on fire?" Vespera asked.

"Yes," I responded. "My need for a book."

The side of her lip lifted before she stood. "I think you've come to the right place, then. Romance? History? Maybe horror?"

"History," I said. "Really, old history. Like maybe something from even before Yumi?"

I tried to form my words so that they could be taken as a joke, but she looked at me without a hint of humor.

"So, you want fairy tales," she asked.

"No." I moved further inside and closed the door behind me. "I want to know if you may have something Yumi does not know you have?"

"That seems like a loaded question. If I did, I likely wouldn't admit it to you." Vespera crossed her arms.

"I swear I'm not here to turn you over to Yumi." I sat in the chair next to her. "I was, well, I heard that maybe Yumi had a husband. I heard that maybe he was locked away. That there was a possibility a few lies were going around our realm."

She looked lost in thought as if I had not quite won her over yet. I took her hand in mine, hoping to comfort her and convince her that we could form some sort of trust, but our hands sent a shock wave through them and up our arms.

"Ow!" I yelled and pulled back.

She cradled her hand for a moment, and as if to avoid that conversation, she stood up and immediately agreed to help me. I wasn't sure why we needed to act so strangely about it. It wasn't that big of a deal; I hadn't done it on purpose.

"Let's go to the Great Library of Sunlight. The time-keepers there pride themselves on having the biggest collection of relics. They claim that some of them are from a time before ours." Vespera said.

"There isn't supposed to be a time before ours," I said.

I used my magic to teleport us to the island that I only knew of in passing. Giant waves crashed upon stone that had been worn away erratically from the motion. The water that was slamming the island was as clear as the windows ahead of us. Golden rose bushes lined the pathway carved from stone. The pathway led us up the island and to the black building carved into the grey and brownstone.

The outer library walls were built black, but windows were the main focus; even the glass was outlined in black designs. I could already see case after case of books inside. She did not talk about the size of the library enough.

At the entrance, Vespera held something up and then pointed to me while she whispered. The man, dressed in a golden robe, lowered his hood and pointed at me with her. Their whispers were too low for me to hear. What I did notice was the tattoo of the moon on his palm when he pointed.

"Follow me." Vespera waved.

I was too curious to deny, no matter what they whispered. It was strange to be in a place not decorated with stars. I entered the library, and from the entrance, floor to ceiling, were books. The room was lit by the natural light coming through the windowed walls and chandeliers from the roof. They were so high that I did not understand how they lit anything from where we stood.

I followed the man and Vespera until we reached a

balcony built over the water. Golden accents filled every piece of the black room down to the rug. I felt tiny inside.

"I should lecture you over the deal we made, but I'll wait." The man inside said.

The other golden-cloaked mortal stood at the entrance.

"Maybe I should lecture you." Vespera retorted.

"Mhm. You know she needs to be tested before we allow her to look at anything." He said.

He also had the moons on his palms.

Vespera turned to me. "He's going to test your blood. It won't hurt. It's only to show your lineage."

"My lineage?" I chuckled. I felt like it became a game they played with me.

"I'll explain after," Vespera said.

I held out my hand to the man in the robe, and he pricked my fingertip with a tiny needle. He opened a jar of red powder and dipped his fingers into it before he wrote something in the air. He pressed the powdered fingers into my blood, and it glowed golden immediately.

"I told you," Vespera said.

"Care to fill me in?" I was aggravated.

"You're a daughter of the sun and moon, not starlight; as such, you are welcome here anytime. There is much I wish I could say, but I can not." He bowed in front of me before moving back to Vespera. "Anything she wants, it's hers."

Their feet hit the ground in sync until both of the men were out of sight, and only Vespera and I left.

"Explain?" I pointed to my still-red finger.

"It pains me to tell you that I can only explain a fraction of what I wish I could." She said.

That was why I stuck to Sahir. She was the only one in the entire realm that didn't speak that way. She didn't lie to me. Sure, she played harmless games with others here and there, but not with me. I never doubted what side she stood on. Even if I didn't agree with her disgusting habit of playing with warts, at least she was open about it. Everyone else only spoke to me of riddles and half-truths.

Vespera watched me as if she heard my thoughts turning. I hadn't noticed before that her eyes were such a deep blue. I held regret for the ramble I had gone on, even though I knew she couldn't hear it. She brought me here to help; I could at least give her the chance to explain.

"Why?" I asked.

"There's a curse. A spell? It keeps us from speaking freely. It unwrites words that have already been written. It erases memories that come back. It feels hard for any of us to find information because it is." She said.

"Who did it?" It was a question I didn't need to ask.

"The only one who wants ultimate control over information." She said.

"So if Yumi is—" I gripped my throat because the rest of my sentence wouldn't leave my lips.

"You won't get any further. I brought you here because the library holds the timekeepers on the surface and the order of the sun and moon in secret. They the teachings of moonlight and the journal of the sun God. Things here are kept as secret and in Semper. We are all trusting you to keep this secret." Vespera said.

The softness I saw in her face while she discussed it was something I had not seen before from nearly anyone. She was beautiful. I reached for her face and moved the strand of pastel blue hair that had been dangling over her eyelashes while she spoke and tucked it back in place.

She raised her hand and placed it where mine had just left.

"Sorry," I cleared my throat. "I didn't want it to get in your eye." I walked forward to leave the room and enter back into the open walls of information. "How many people know about this order? If we can't talk about anything they know, how will it help?"

She took a few breaths to start moving, and the space between us grew. I don't know why I did it. I couldn't explain what possessed me to touch her; I shouldn't have done it. I was going to apologize again, but she started moving back to me.

"I brought you because even though we can't openly discuss everything, the order has been working in ways to learn without speaking. There are two scrolls here that have been sealed with something we don't have the ability to do. The words never disappear. Your blood has been tested; you can read it." Vespera said.

The two of us looked at each other in silence, and I felt the need to explain myself again. Instead, she took my hand and led me down a hall with the same impossibly high ceilings.

Her fingers laced around mine, and I felt that same zap as before. She didn't mention it or let go. I found it hard to consider what we were going to look at with the fluttering in my chest and the knots in my stomach.

We stopped inside a small room made of the natural stone around us. A table sat in the middle with the two scrolls she spoke of.

Her fingers loosened from mine, but mine refused to listen. It was only out of the growing embarrassment under her gaze that I could finally tell them to let go. I moved to the scrolls without making eye contact again. I felt my cheeks were flushed. That needed to stay private.

I grabbed the scroll quickly and opened it, using it as a shield over my face.

The moon and the stars sat in an empty, endless sky. The two sisters could not speak, but they could dance. They fluttered and twirled around each other through the black abyss until, one day, the star grew tired of how brightly the moon glowed in comparison. The moon thought about it, and she found it saddening. The moon grew the star bigger in size, but it did not have the effect the moon was sure it would. The star grew hungry for what more the moon could do for her.

By the end of the first phase, the moon had created an entire universe for her sister. A second moon hung in the sky beside a sun. Planets revolved around each other in the same dance the two used to spin. Thousands of stars decorated the sky, and the moon gifted them full forms. They walked the planet instead of watching endless darkness.

The moon could not keep meeting demands, tired, she created others to keep them company. They were assigned tasks, and soon, there were gods to look after all of the things that made their world function. The moon created her partner, the sun god, and the stars did not approve of her sister's attention being taken by love.

I put the scroll down and turned to Vespera. "This is why you think Yumi isn't—" There it was again, the silent squeeze at my throat stopping my words.

"Read the next scroll, too." She pointed.

I sighed and lifted the second scroll. The only regret I had was entertaining any of it. A fairytale that could have and probably was written by someone with an active imagination, and I was supposed to change my life because of it?

We ran out of time. There was no reasoning with her. She lost her mind entirely. I tried my best to make sure my girls held onto what they could of their memories. Repeat after me: by the sun and moon, by love and truth, your dreams will reach you where we cannot.

"Oh." Was all I could say.

"You don't believe yet, but when you go to sleep, you will." She said.

"Okay. Well, I'll get going now." I said. I walked to the exit.

The man in the golden robe that tested my blood was blocking my exit. He flicked my nose with a powder, and I couldn't stop myself from breathing it in.

"Good night." He smiled.

"What was that?" I wiped my face.

"Enjoy your nap." Was all I heard before I felt my body drop.

I woke up in a city of gold. Every building and pathway was golden and marbled. Voices happily carried throughout the town, and in one of the crowds was my sister. Ruri walked with a woman I had never seen before. Caym was behind the two. Onyx ran up to me and grabbed my hand. He held it as if we had been together for years. He pulled me into him and connected his lips with mine before I had the chance to process what was happening.

"Are you ready? The festival of moonlight will start soon." He spoke while he pulled at me.

My reflection in the golden buildings was no different. I looked as I always had. Dark blue hair, ebony skin, teal eyes, and horns. Horns? I grew horns!

The shock was enough that I woke myself up. Vespera and the robed man were standing around me.

"What did you see?" He asked.

"I grew horns!" I ran my hands over my head.

"That scroll held the ability to give you a glimpse into another life, in another realm. A life much older than ours." Vespera said.

"I need to go," I responded.

I had no idea I could run as fast as I did. That place was filled with insanity. I didn't want to know how they could have messed with my head like that. I should not have wasted my entire day listening to nonsense.

CHAPTER THIRTEEN

EXPERIMENTING IN THE SHADOWS

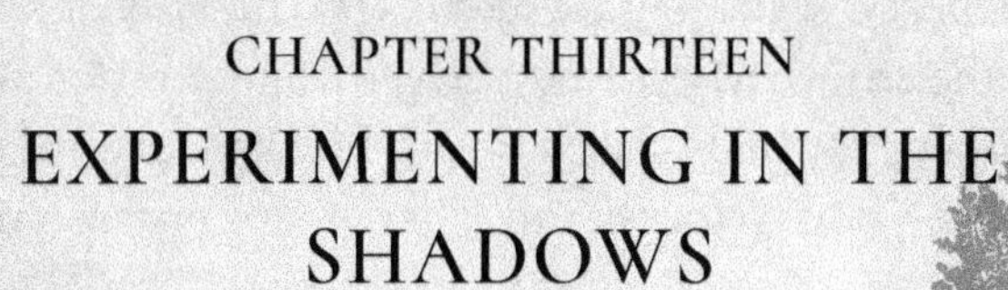

The Teachings of Starlight
In order to obtain and keep perfect order and balance, deity lines will be kept sorted according to virtue. Pride, envy, lust, and the like must keep from interfering with the lines of love, purity, and so on. There will be no exceptions and no excuses— 'this is not the way things were meant to be' was hardly legible under the written words.

SAGE

I was doing my best today to watch my back and avoid Sahir and Vespera. The mortals of several kingdoms planned a ceremony that we were all supposed to attend. They sent our invitations by prayer, and we all heard them. They wanted to give thanks to the Goddess of Storms in the hope that they'd receive good rainfall for their crops.

They tempted us with food and dancing. Our food in Semper was a bland mixture of fruits. The crops we had given them to grow turned into so many things that most of us refused to eat our own food anymore. The taste was beyond anything from the sunlight garden.

Onyx told me about the desserts the mortals made with the strawberry seeds I gave them. He described how they crushed the strawberries with a sweet white powder and used it as a topping for fluffy, cakey bread. I looked forward to it the most. 'Just don't touch any of the mushrooms.' He warned me.

Apparently, the Dwarves of Erebus had learned they could do more than make warm homes and soft lights. I told him I'd take his warning to heart, but I was a little curious. He sought me out and asked if I would accompany him. I agreed, partly out of curiosity for the supposed dream I was given.

Were we like Ruri and Caym? Meant to be together and bonded by souls? I had hoped that a day with him would help convince me one way or the other because I was conflicted. If I took Vespera seriously, the dream was my past, and that meant my past was with Onyx, but my thoughts were with Vespera.

My thoughts sat strictly on the way her hand felt in mine. The way her eyes were so much lighter than her hair. The way she felt easy to be around, even in silence, she was easy to sit with.

I went through the vines to Cylla and came out by the river Sin. It was the only sure way to avoid Sahir; she'd refuse the walk. She would grumble about how it was outrageous to use her legs when she could come through wherever she wanted.

The second upper hand I hoped to have was illusion. We discovered that when the mortals became more abundant, we were much larger in size than they were. Even their biggest men were incomparable in size to us.

It drew too much attention too often. Most deities created a bond with a specific set of mortals in their land; beyond that, the barrage of people hunting us down when they knew who we were was overwhelming. We would blend ourselves in, pick a style, and cast it on ourselves.

When I walked up the river path, Vespera sat by the edge of the water. The Goddess of Plague hadn't sought me out since I ran out on her. I didn't know what to say to her. I didn't want to make her feel bad, but I didn't believe as hard as she did that what they had was real.

"Sage! Come look at this!" She called, hectically getting to her feet. "The mortals started writing these things called books, and in this one, they say they hate each other, but then they share a room with only one bed! One!" Her fingers pointed to the pages in demand.

She acted as if what happened never did.

"One? Why wouldn't they get another room?" I asked. I joined in the pretending so that we could speak, "That makes the most sense?"

"It's not about sense, Sage." Vespera's voice extended, and she lifted her brows much higher than they should have been before she flipped a few pages and directed me to look.

I turned my eyes down and read the words she pointed out, "Oh." I felt my jaw drop open the longer I read. "Oh," was all I could come up with.

"That is a good reason for only one bed at an inn," Onyx said, towering over my shoulder.

Both of us jumped at his words, and Vespera shoved the book into the bag she wore over her shoulder. We both turned in sync and pretended to be in a hurry to the festival in Edur.

"Don't be shy now!" Onyx called from behind.

"When you're free, come to my bookstore, and I'll show you things better than that," Vespera said.

Her comment made my skin heat and my cheeks flush because it only brought thoughts of her and I at an inn and how it could be made better.

There had to be something wrong with me. I was in Cylla

to try to form a relationship with Onyx, and yet here I was, imagining Vespera underneath me.

She broke away from us after giving me a smirk and entered the crowd of mortals devouring a table of treats.

I started counting to five before walking forward. It was enough time that I wouldn't look like I was following her, but I feared it wasn't long enough to wipe the flush from my cheeks before Onyx could see my face.

"Want to sneak off before everyone else shows up?" He asked.

"Sure!" I answered with too much excitement.

"Let's do something you've never done before." He urged. "It needs to be something so unlike you that no one would believe you did it."

If Sahir were around, she would have lived the moment to its fullest while talking about her 'daddy.' She wouldn't have even had to think about it. She was the chaos in our creation. I needed to channel her.

What would she do?

I grabbed a stool that was left empty in the middle of the crowd and stood on it. I ran a hand over my clothes and changed into the robes that Ruri gave out to the priestesses in Ashbell before I drew attention to myself. Onyx watched me with a grin I didn't know he was capable of. It made my heart skip a beat.

Why was my heart acting up for two different people?

"Mortals!" I called.

The crowd silenced and turned to face me. They mumbled in low voices about my clothing, checking amongst each other before giving me full attention. Once they agreed amongst each other, I was a priestess. They begged for word from the gods.

"Don't fear; I have a word for you," I lifted both hands to the sky, giving my best performance. "The Goddess of Magic demanded tribute!"

The voices around got louder again. They talked amongst each other, and a few whispers broke through of me being a crook, but they stayed low.

"She wants virgin men in exchange for the blessing of magic. She wants to have an army of the strongest virgin warriors by her side. She demands the best be sent to the coliseum to battle for the right to guard her in Semper." I called.

Onyx had a hand over his face; he shook his head in defeat and disbelief. I agreed with him for once in the sentiment that it was a foolish idea and would get nowhere.

"Send word to the general!" A man called.

"The army is useless; they aren't virgins!" A woman said from the back.

I waved my hands in the air as if I were a ghost haunting them before stepping off the stool and positioning myself back beside Onyx. His arms were crossed, but he was beaming the first smile I had seen from him.

"This was your idea? You shocked even me." He laughed.

"Let's just keep it to ourselves," I said.

"You think Ruri won't hear about this?" His lips parted, and his eyes widened.

"Why would she?" I shrugged.

"Sage," Onyx pointed me to a group of men, "They are already taking you seriously."

I watched them, trying to read their lips and take in what they were discussing. Some were getting more aggressive in their tone the longer their talks went on. Some had already left to spread the words she left with them.

"You spend too much time with Sahir; you've missed a lot in this realm." He said. "They worship us as if we were the picture of perfection. If you spent a little more time with them, you may have known this was a poor choice." He said.

"Did you come here today just to give me what you think are subtle reprimands?" I furrowed my brows.

"I didn't mean it like that." His lips turned down.

"What do you want then? Huh? Sahir is none of your business." I pointed. "I keep her under control."

"I didn't mean to upset you," Onyx said.

"I don't need another lecture. My mom has done it. Ruri has done it. Enough." I groaned.

"I have no interest in lecturing you." He said. "I was only trying to speak to you as a friend."

His face had to have been made of stone because every bit of his expressions were hardened.

"I just thought you could use a gift. You seem to be struggling." He lifted his hand and offered me a book. "It's an empty book, spelled to keep track of anything you create. It'll track how to use your special portals and the Fiia. I just thought it could be something nice for you."

"Struggling?" I scoffed. "You have some nerve."

"Sage, I truly didn't mean to offend you. I only wanted to show you that there are others around who care about you. That most of us want to be there for you."

"Stop, I'm not a charity case." I shoved the book back in his chest. "Thanks, but no thanks."

I turned to leave, and Sahir was standing, watching with her arms crossed.

"I don't want to hear anything from you," I said, pushing past her.

"Clearly. You left me behind so you could spend time with a boy." She frowned.

"Take him!" I yelled, "You can spend the day with him." I pushed the rest of the way out of the crowd.

I used my leaf to enter back into the Chamber of Starlight, giving them one last chance to take a hint and leave me alone. I wouldn't be treated like a child. I refused to be told what I could and couldn't do, as if I didn't understand right and wrong. I would not let Ruri send others to lecture me when she was too scared to do it herself.

I stopped my stomping and silenced my breath when Yumi

came into my line of sight. She was checking doorways and more on edge than I had ever seen her. It didn't occur to me to take note of who went to Cylla and who didn't. She was leaving the Sunlight Garden and doing her best to be as quiet as I was. Her quarters were connected to the Chamber of Starlight and the Sunlight Garden. Maybe she was just leaving her bed from a late nap.

A part of Sahir had to have rubbed off on me because my curiosity got the better of me, and I slid myself into the entrance of the garden and to her bedroom doorway. She was the ruler; she didn't have quarters like the rest of us. The entire realm was hers. So, she kept only a bedroom. It was too large, in my opinion, but no one cared about that anyway.

I knew I shouldn't be sneaking around. I knew it would be trouble if I were caught, but something about how Yumi snuck out as if she didn't want to be seen wasn't right.

My visit to the timekeepers was something I wanted to ignore. To forget and treat it as a fairy tale. That's exactly what it sounded like. There was a part of me that couldn't stop from connecting the dots between the scrolls and Yumi. I only heard Sahir's voice discussing her daddy when I thought about it all.

If Yumi was starlight, and I were to take it all seriously, then her sister was the moon and her husband the sun. It meant that whoever Yumi's husband was remained a mystery.

I closed the door behind me to draw less attention. Her door was made of heavy stone and had a lock. Much different than ours, as well. There was a drawer on her silver-coated dresser that had not been closed all the way. My eyes spotted it the moment I turned around to scan the room. I moved slowly, sure Yumi had to have traps of some kind. Someone who needed so much privacy had to have those kinds of fall-backs set up.

Nothing happened, so I pulled the drawer out and took the journal that was inside with no consequence. It had me positive the pages were laced with something that would cause my death. If that were the case, it would be too late to turn back. I moved closer to the candle and opened it to a middle page.

Day 14

Things have remained peaceful. There's no sign of abilities yet. One of them arrived against my will, but she seemed to have no memory, so I haven't spoken yet. There isn't much to take note of yet.

I flipped to another section.

Day 24

Helia has grown far too obsessed with Thann; other than that, she shows promising signs of being able to wield her magic type. I haven't said anything to anyone for fear of interrupting the natural process.

Day 25

Astra has become the first to use her abilities with ease. I'm not surprised, but displeased all the same. Even with my main focus being on Kyrell, he's a failure.

I used a finger to hold my page and listened to ensure no one was near. I had never heard Yumi be so blunt about anyone, and it sent my stomach spiraling even lower.

Year 100

My mistake was focusing on only one more than the other. Today, Kyrell finally created a God, but only with the help of the Sunlight Garden. He's still a failure, and it's too late to focus on anyone else. I can not wait another hundred years for things to progress. It's some sort of cruel joke that this is the result of all my efforts.

Year 104

Orla created two daughters, and I sniffed them out instantly. Repugnant little brats. They sealed my time as a failure. I wanted to save the headache and kill them, but they seemed memoryless as well. I'm keeping a close watch.

Year 104, Day 34

Ruri has succeeded in every test I've given her. Kyrell grows weaker with every success she has. I've been injecting Kyrell with the blood I have left from Nikola to keep him held together, but my supply is running low.

Year 104, Day 42

I've been mixing the last of Nikola's blood with mine, and although Kyrell is held together, he is completely unstable. No one is ever sure if he will be okay or lose his grip on reality. The other hasn't been affected. It seems only one pair is in a struggle. I don't know why, but I won't dig into the subject yet. I feel I'm losing my own grip on myself with every day that passes.

Year 104, Day 47

I've been taking Ruri's blood and mixing it with the other ingredients for the tree, and I've never felt better. I killed a Goddess before I learned it would work, and It's caused a rift to grow between some of us, but they can't understand how it feels to be torn apart like I was. They will eventually have to forgive me or die. Ruri has succeeded in making mortals, and I have hope again that things will become stable and my plans will get back on track.

I closed the book; there was no more to read; all the pages were filled. There had to be more. I felt sick and sweaty. My heart was beating so fast I could feel it in my throat. She was bleeding my sister out, just like Sahir said, for the tree? Nikola had to be her husband. My world felt like it was spinning, and I was going to crash. I couldn't do it here. I couldn't be found in her room. I knew that much for sure.

I had a fear of Yumi that I had not felt before.

I put the book back and closed the drawer. I lifted her lock slowly and crept out of the door. I wanted to see the tree. I wanted to look for signs of blood. I needed something real in front of my face to tell me it wasn't a joke. I stumbled over my feet. They felt as if they weren't a real part of me anymore. The tree wasn't far, and when I reached it, I let myself fall. Ungraceful as it was, I felt outside of myself.

I moved the dirt around, but there was nothing. No droplets of red in any direction. I put my palm on the tree to help lift myself up. I was still trying to compose myself. When I tried to stand, the bark under my fingers set me on fire, and I was enveloped in darkness.

I could see nothing moving in any direction. It was as if my eyes were closed, and I couldn't open them. My body felt light and empty. There was a warmth around me that put me at ease.

It was brief before my body was pulled and drug at a speed I could never have moved, with an urgency beyond any I had felt before. The warmth turned to fear and panic.

A bright, blinding light took over everything, and my eyes burned. It was too painful to look at. I tried to lift my arm in protection, but images started playing in quick succession.

I was only a tiny spec of nothing floating over the sight of Yumi placed on bloodied knees, arms chained too high for her to resist. Helia moved in front of her; next, she lifted a chalice and drank from it, laughing as blood stained her lips. It felt too real, and I tried to move away.

No part of me was within my control. I was feeling something that wasn't mine. Hearing a voice that wasn't my own.

I was shoved back in place in a heartbeat, watching myself in Sahir's arms, dying. My heart pounded at the sight of my own body. Sahir was trying to use her feet to shove me into the river Sin. My only trusted friend was hiding my body.

I was grabbed and thrown into the next set of pictures. My breath was gone; I couldn't catch it. Ruri was on her knees over her dragons, and they were all burnt, and souls were leaving them to join the stars.

"What is this?" I screamed into nothing.

The next image was all of Semper on fire, covered in blood. I tried to run. My body listened, but I hit a door. I slammed into it with all my weight and lost my breath. The door swung open, and the outline of a body stood in front of me. I couldn't see her face, but I could see her body.

She lifted her hand and ran it across my cheek. "The markings are the first step to regaining who you are. It's all I can do for you."

She shoved me back into my body with such force I thought my chest had caved in.

I was slung backward and hit the ground. I was heaving for air and glowing. I knew what the glow was; I had seen it before on Ruri. When the light dissipated, I had dark blue markings on my skin like bare tree branches.

"Creator, creator." The Fiia started screeching and fluttering around me, and it sent me into a panic.

I could hardly get to my feet before I started running. I felt the sweat dripping off of my nose. I could not be seen by Yumi. I needed to go somewhere that no one would look for me.

I kept my head out of her way enough that I wouldn't be suspected if she figured out someone was snooping.

I went through the vines to Cylla and inside of Erebus' cave. I dodged the sight of the Dwarves and slammed through the door to Onyx's blacksmith shop. I wiped the sweat off of my forehead and tucked myself into a back corner wall. Gasping for breath, I dropped my legs down.

"What the fuck was that." I almost started sobbing but attempted to breathe instead. Slowly in and out, like Ruri taught me.

"I don't know, you tell me?" Onyx came around the corner, putting a blade into a barrel of water.

An extended scream of terror left me.

Onyx lowered himself down, rested an arm on his knee, and handed me a cup of water. "You came here, and yet you're shocked to see me?"

I tried my best to resist, but tears poured from my eyes.

He lowered himself the rest of the way and sat down beside me. "Do you want to talk about it?"

"No!" I rubbed snot from my nose. "I already look foolish; I don't want to sound crazy, too!"

"I swear you won't sound crazy. Nothing will leave these walls." He said.

"I was sucked into a fucking tree; it showed me my death, spat me out, and now I glow blue." Saying it out loud didn't offer me any relief; it only made me sob harder.

Onyx nodded and held back a small smirk. "You don't sound crazy; You are blue."

"Don't make fun of me." I buried my head into my knees.

"I'm not, I'm not." He lifted his hands. "I had a vision of your sister dying. I still haven't sorted it out, really."

"What?" I peered out of the crack in my arms.

He nodded. "You should talk to her about this kind of thing. She may be more helpful than you think."

"I can't!" I yelled through more tears.

"Why not? The two of you would be better working together than apart like this." He said.

"I can't talk to her until I'm ready to give up on Sahir." I buried my head back.

"That's foolish, not anything else. Your sister is constantly looking for you, but you're always gone. Why are you so ready to give up on Ruri but not Sahir?" He asked.

"It's not that. I just." I pushed my hair back and let all the air in my chest out. "I just need to prove to her that I'm good enough. That I'm worth something before I can walk by her side."

"Do you really believe that? You're only in competition with your imagination. You don't have to prove that you can heal the enemy to be worthy of your sister. If anything, this path is what will end your life." He lingered on my eyes, and I knew he was right.

"You just wouldn't understand," I said. "I came here for safety, and you're lecturing me again."

He handed me a handkerchief and sat beside me in silence.

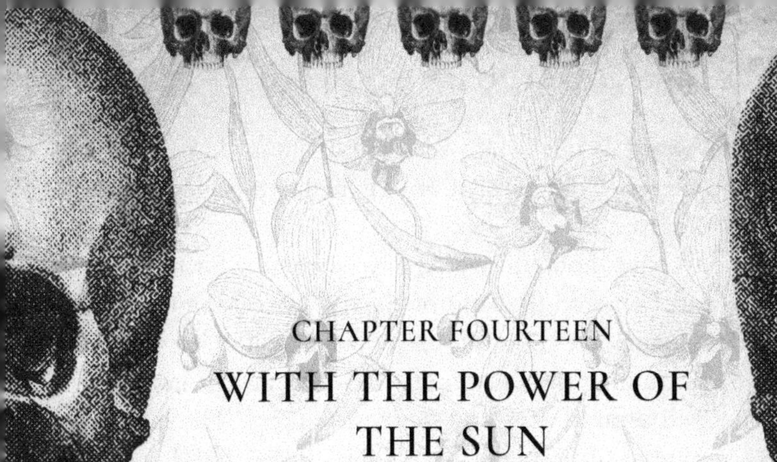

CHAPTER FOURTEEN
WITH THE POWER OF THE SUN

The Teachings of Starlight
The writing on the page was unable to be read.
It was shifting and shuttering into new words in
new handwriting. Someone or something was making
itself known through the pages. It wanted to be
heard, to be seen. It wanted to be free.

CAYM

Kyrell demanded a meeting. He ordered that Koa, the God of War, and I arrive together. It was easy enough to show up together; we were always together. It wasn't as easy to adjust to the idea that he wanted us to meet outside of Merripen. There was even less ease in how erratic he was becoming.

Some days, he showed up unannounced, with black eyes, and only wanted to yell and throw punches. On other days, he showed up sobbing, rambling on about the future and what it would look like. I knew that seeing him cry was supposed to make me feel bad for him, but it had the opposite effect. It made me angry. It filled me with rage to think that he must have seen things so differently from my reality that he thought I would comfort him.

He must have thought I would have sympathy for him.

Koa and I entered the land of Solaris. Kyrells kingdom. I had little information about the area outside of the knowledge that he was training the inhabitants as warriors. His land and laws revolved around breeding the best fighters. The land so closely resembled our realm and Yumi's likes that I wasn't convinced we had left Semper.

Everything was white and silver. The castle and the stairs were white marble. Even the leaves on the trees were shades of white.

Koa and I looked at each other, and his face told me that we were thinking the same things.

We climbed the stairs but only made it halfway before rows of angels came out of the castle, armed and ready to fight. The flash of a thought that I could have called The Nola and taken Kyrell's land was tempting. He wasn't actually my focus anymore. I was arriving on time for his meeting and keeping my mouth shut because, as in charge as he thought he was, there were more important things than him brewing.

Whispers of Sahir eating hearts were growing louder. Yumi was unconcerned, which made me all the more interested. Kyrells sudden shifts seemed to align with Ruri succeeding in something, and with every day that Ruri did not do something with the tree, Yumi grew erratic.

I was ready to make Kyrell feel whatever he needed. I was ready to say whatever he wanted if it meant that I was free to find out what Yumi was doing to Ruri and what Sahir's end goal was. I knew without a doubt that they would all lead me to the answers of the realm in the end.

"We are here on orders from Kyrell," I called with my hands up.

"Hands up, too." One of the angels called to Koa.

He listened but with less enthusiasm than I had. He didn't understand how to put on a mask and ignore your own feelings because he hadn't needed to develop such a skill to survive. I was envious of that.

The angels surrounded us and marched us inside the castle. The walls were lined with silver scone lights. Yumi decorated with starlight. Everything shimmered in her realm. Kyrell shocked me because even though his kingdom was similar to hers, he decorated it with vines and bushes. They wrapped around pillars and hung from the ceiling. The floor looked as if we were walking on water.

They lead us inside of a room bigger than it needed to be. The table was set to hold more people than I could imagine sitting together. The angels pushed me to a chair and shoved me into it by my shoulder.

Did they know I was the God of death? That if I wanted to take his soul with me when I left, all I needed to do was use one finger?

"Sorry about that, boys," Kyrell said as he entered the room.

He motioned for the angels to leave and sat at the head of the table.

"I'm sure you want to get straight to it, so I will. Hopefully, it never comes to this, but in case there is a day that I'm not here, you will need to know how to run Solaris. There's an army here that will be at your command. You know how to run the land of the dead, but here, you'll need to worry about things like food and children." Kyrell paused to look at us.

"He already has an army in The Nola," Koa said.

"That brings me to you. Since the two of you are so close now, I assume he will put you in charge of his army." Kyrell didn't acknowledge Koa, and that was the glimpse of him that I recognized. "There are a few strict rules here. One, If the children can hold a weapon and walk, they start training. Two, women who are pregnant or who are raising children that are too small to train, receive anything they may need from the court. There is a group designed only to supply them with their needs."

"You're serious?" I asked.

Kyrell looked at me as if I were the dumb one. "Why would I joke about this."

"I know how to run a kingdom. Making a change like crops won't make a difficult difference." I said.

"You don't need to fight me on this, son. I want to teach you, and I know you want to bond and learn from a man who has the wisdom you don't." He spoke with a straight face.

Those words made my blood boil. There was nothing I considered him wise in. Even in the land, he looked at everyone as a tool to train. His biggest compassion was free food. Something that was a main point of life. Something that they should have had for free regardless of being with a child.

I wanted to stand up and deny him. I wanted to yell all of my thoughts in his face, but the thought of Ruri and how exhausted she looked when I saw her earlier kept me together enough to swallow my words down again.

"When would we start?" Koa asked. "I have a training session with him today as well that can't be moved. I have my own tasks to attend to for Yumi as well."

Kyrell nodded. "I will see you both when your tasks are handled. Making Yumi happy is important, and we will pick it up from there."

The three of us stood and moved out of the room together.

I walked behind both of them, squeezing my fists over and over so that I could focus on the feeling instead of my thoughts. Kyrell joined the angels as if he had already forgotten about us.

"When she made Ruri create the angels for protection, I didn't expect to see her share them with Kyrell," Koa said.

"Ruri made them?" She never said anything to me about it.

"I assumed you knew?" He said.

"To be honest, I don't know much of anything. She avoids me most days." I said. "Kyrell doesn't exactly send a messenger with updates, either. I depend on what I hear from the vines and what The Nola picks up."

"Then, I assume he hasn't let you in on his newest goal?" Koa asked.

"Does it have anything to do with this?" I asked.

Kyrell telling me he wanted me to take over Solaris did not make sense.

"He wants to be the keeper of the Sunlight Garden and to have Astra banished. So, I think it makes sense for him to hand this place over. He will want his main focus on impressing Yumi." Koa said.

"Astra keeps to herself and does her job. She hasn't even retaliated over her son's death," I said. "Even I wouldn't be able to push down something like that."

"Kyrell thinks she's buying her time. He also thinks heads are gonna roll soon from us splitting family colors, but nothing has moved forward with that yet either." Koa said.

"You know what I think? I think there are a lot of deities making plans in the dark because I can't bring myself to believe there are this many passive deities around. When it breaks, and we see how many different moves are plaid, I don't think it's going to end well."

A portal from the vines opened, and Ruri stepped out.

"I was looking for you!" She said, grabbing the collar of my shirt. "Sorry to interrupt; I only have a small window of time." She yelled back to Koa.

I let Ruri pull me the rest of the way through the vines without a struggle. I helped her feel like she was in control of my steps, and when she slowed, I pretended to crash into her. It left her with no choice but to wrap her arms around me or fall. My body filled with sparks when the choice she made was to wrap around my waist.

"You did that on purpose," she remarked.

Of course, I did. She felt so far away from me these days. She felt so far gone from the girl whose hair I would wash and brush every day. She was so quiet in comparison to the girl who used to say every thought that entered her mind. The one who used to constantly gossip in my ear.

I slung my arms around her and feigned a stumble. "You pulled me so hard; what else would have happened?"

"Mm," She nodded when she let go of me.

It was like a knife had sliced us apart. She was so close to me. My hands were on her. I saw a glimpse of her smile, but it was so small. The moment was so small that I was nearly convinced I was imagining it.

She pulled my arm to turn me around. We were over-looking the view of the volcano that sat in the middle of the land of fire. Tree after tree stood around the bottom of the volcano. The wood held flame leaves but never burnt up. The stump was surrounded by a special kind of ash the Seere would collect and use for healing. I watched the Seere collecting it in baskets. They were shaped like mortal men, maybe a bit taller, but their black-scaled skin shined like obsidian, and between every scale, there was the outline of magma glow. Even their eyes shimmered like what flowed from the volcano.

"It's one of my favorite views in Cylla," Ruri fawned. "When the sunsets, the sky turns into hundreds of shades of red and orange."

I watched her more than I watched the sight she brought me here to see. She thought it was the best view, but I thought there was no better view in Cylla, Semper, or Merripen than her. I had yet to see anything that outshined her. That made my heart thump as rapidly as her smile.

"I wanted to bring you here for just a minute. I know you

are busy. I just needed you to see what I've been working the hardest on." She pointed behind us.

"I'm never too busy to talk to you," I said.

She pointed me to turn around again, but I didn't want her to keep avoiding the empty air between us until it was so big we couldn't come back from it.

"I haven't been too busy to see that you've hardly slept or that you've been using illusion on your hand." I pressed my words harder.

"Please don't ruin this." She said before she pointed me to turn around again.

"You can't decide not to let me in and expect me to be okay with it. This is the only chance you've given me in weeks." I pleaded.

She used her hands and turned me around herself; there was a small obsidian home surrounded by fire flower bushes. It was much smaller than the castle. The home was covered in ash and clearly had thought put into its every detail.

"I know you can't stay away from Merripen. You have duties, and so do I, but I thought this could be our home away from that—a home for just us when all the dust settles down and gets into its rhythm; we should be needed less and less eventually," she said, motioning me inside.

I listened to her this time, and I opened the door to go inside. I was met with a second, almost identical to what I used in Merripen, set of paints.

"If it's missing anything I didn't think of, we have time to take care of it still, and I put crystals--"

I grabbed her by the arm and pulled her into my chest. "As long as you're here, it's filled with everything I need."

"So, will you accept it as my wedding gift to you, then?" she asked.

"What?" My words felt like vomit with how quickly they came out.

"The mortals have been taking part in the ceremony of

marriage. They exchange gifts and then rings." She said, looking at me confused.

I frowned. "I know, I had planned to ask you," I said, pulling out a journal from inside my vest. "I've been writing in this for you as my engagement gift." I took her wrist and turned it to face up. With a black mist, I drew two symbols over her veins. They dissipated and left behind the design of two stars over the top of each other. "The symbol means Jeb is now yours. He's always been yours, but this means it's now his official duty to protect you when I cannot."

She wrapped her arms around my throat tight enough that I thought my head might pop. "Thank you!" She squealed. "So, is that a yes?"

I waited for her to pull back and look at my eyes before I used both of my hands to squish her cheeks together, "Of course it is, wife."

She laid a kiss on every open spot of my cheek she could reach before letting go of me. I only felt truly whole when we were side by side, and as much as I wanted to be truly happy, I knew she was nearing the time when the next word out of her mouth was that she was going to leave me again.

"I'm sorry that I've been avoiding you. I'm sorry that I haven't been telling you everything that's been going on. I will, just not right now, and I need you and everyone around to understand that all I want is to protect you." She searched my eyes before she squeezed my hand.

It was worse than my imagination had been leading me to believe because she left without warning, or goodbyes, or any other words. She only left.

I went back through the vines and into Merripen, where the group of men were talking and laughing amongst each other. I stood and watched them for a moment. I wanted to take in the sight of someone being truly happy because I knew that as soon as I joined them, I would only be giving them fake laughter. I didn't want to do it. I wanted to follow her, to see where she was going. I wanted to know what was going on with her.

She wanted me to understand, but I didn't. I couldn't.

"Could you imagine? Aero cried with laughter. "Some mortal man trying to lift Onyx's blade?"

I took a deep breath before walking the rest of the way into the group and put my mask back on.

Koa was wiping away tears. "Pull out this blade from the stone, and you can be king!"

"I'm convinced," Onyx said, scribbling words on a miniature notepad. "I'm gonna add a little extra weight to the blade, too."

I shook my head at them. "Make sure you hammer it down into the stone, too."

The group erupted in laughter, holding their stomachs.

"That was a quick trip," Onyx said.

"It's never long enough," I responded.

"Onyx is going to make the sword in the stone for the mortals. Anything you think we should add?" Koa asked.

"Actually, I think you guys have it under control. I have something else I need to do." I said.

"You're leaving?" Onyx asked.

"Yea, Sorry," I called back from the vines.

I stepped into Semper, and I slammed my head right into Sage's face.

"Ah," I groaned, "I didn't see you there."

"I can't see anything now! Since you hurt me, you owe me." She said, still holding her head.

"Wait, what?" I asked.

She sighed and looked at the ground. "Okay, I was actually looking for you. I can't talk to Ruri or my mom. I thought about Onyx, but I'm too ashamed of that, too. No one else cares, besides maybe in some way you feel sorry for me enough to hear me out."

"I was coming to find you, so maybe we can skip the pity and offer a trade," I said.

"What do you want from me?" she asked.

"Information on Ruri and Yumi." I said. "What do you need?"

She rubbed her arm with her opposite hand and spoke low. "I want someone to help me tell Sahir we can't talk anymore. I know it sounds stupid, but--"

"She wouldn't hesitate to kill you; that's what we've all been trying to tell you. Count me in, let's go." I said.

She sounded a sigh of relief so heavy it blew the blue hair from her face. She walked ahead of me, and I followed close behind. I didn't know where we were going, but I was sure she did.

"What do you want to know about them?" she asked.

"What is it that Yumi is doing to her? The two of them have so many secrets I don't know where to begin asking." I said.

"You won't like the information you get. On second thought, I don't want any part in this trade anymore." She halted her movements.

I shoved her in step again anyway. "Even if we don't trade, I wouldn't miss this chance to get you away from her," I said. "Why are you breaking up with her?"

"It has to do with you." She said. "She eats hearts, and I thought it was just nonsense, but right now she is—" She turned to face me. "Right now, she is getting a gift ready for me. She says she can breathe this mist into other deities that take over their mind. She said she's going to send them to you. She said that she's doing it because Ruri clearly thinks she's better than us, and so killing you will show her what suffering looks like. When I told her not to do it, she told me that since she's such a good friend, this kind of thing was simple enough. That I didn't need to worry about getting her anything in return." She was out of breath by the time she stopped talking.

"That is a lot to take in," I said.

"I have a lot more information." Sage rolled her eyes.

I followed her, still happy she was making the choice that she was. I couldn't ignore the fact that she didn't come to tell me about the attack before anything else. Was she confident that I'd win? Or did she think Sahir wasn't strong enough to do it?

Wait, her skin was blue now?

"Sage, I didn't know you got markings, too," I questioned.

"I've been trying to keep it quiet." She answered.

"Scared of ending up like your sister?" I asked.

"No, I just--" She went quiet.

"I think what I'm trying to say is that you seem to be withholding a lot from those of us who don't want to be stuck like this. It feels like you may have enough pieces, and if you shared them, maybe we could move more than one step forward." I shrugged.

Sage stopped walking when we arrived at the entrance to Sahir's chambers.

"I'm sorry. I messed up; at a later time, we can discuss all of these things, but right now, there's a bloodthirsty, daddy-obsessed, power-crazed Goddess behind those doors!" She pointed.

We didn't have to step inside for me to see and smell that it was her dwelling. Even from the entrance, it was nothing but filth and chaos. I felt Sage's eyes tilt to me, but I didn't return the glance. I knew she knew we were both thinking the same thing, and I had the feeling she was feeling ashamed enough without my help. I simply motioned her inside.

A part of me knew that I was walking into trouble. The same part of me was excited about the idea. It was easy to say that I was a strong God of Death and that I could do anything, but believing it was different. I had yet to get a win against Koa. It was hard for me to believe that I could against anything.

"Sahir!" She called.

The pond had a few dead fish rotting away in the water, and inside her bedroom was an entire wall covered with drawings of a man with black eyes and short white hair. Sahir lay on her stomach, lavender hair a mess, clearly not expecting company.

"So, you remember who I am then?" She glared up through her lashes.

"Actually, I came because I can't keep avoiding you like this. You need to know, to your face, that we can't be friends anymore after what you said your plans were." Sage held her breath, anticipating what was to come.

"I'll give you one chance to take it back, and only one," Sahir spoke, sitting up. Her usual giggly drawl gone.

Sage shook her head, "look, I thought I could help you. I thought I could show you that what you were doing was wrong. That the things you keep doing are wrong. I clearly can't. You don't think any of it is wrong, so everything I try to tell you is a waste of breath."

Sahir stood up and walked closer to Sage. "You'll come crawling back. No one wants to look into a broken mirror every day, and all you are is a reflection of failures." Sahir's finger was deep in Sage's chest.

Sage opened her mouth to speak, but Sahir cut her off.

"Take," She dug her finger harder. "It, back!" She screamed.

The sound startled me, but it only took me a heartbeat to recover before I grabbed Sage's arm and moved her behind me.

"That's enough," I said.

"So, you're a bodyguard now? Or you can't pick which sister you want the most?" Sahir ran her tongue across her front teeth, "Fine. So be it. If this is how you want things, then

I'll make sure you're miserable every day until I kill you, and then I'll keep your soul with me. If I can't have you this way, then I'll keep you in a necklace."

I was tired of hearing her talk already; There was no way Sage wasn't, too. I grabbed her arm and turned to leave with her.

"Oh, no. You don't get to walk out as if I'm nothing!" Sahir screamed.

She turned and pulled open the door beside her bed, which I assumed was a closet. Behind it were the rotted bodies of deities. Their chests were ripped open, and hearts were missing, but as Sage said she promised, a black mist came from her mouth and into theirs.

The reanimated bodies came at me with no mercy. The sight made me think that I should walk around with more weapons.

I pulled from the only source that I had: the sun magic that Ruri gifted me. I closed my eyes and imagined its warmth and did my best to form a spear out of it that I threw into the head of the one in front. The light turned it into dust, less than dust; not even ash was left behind. The spear didn't stop; it went through all three of them, and I stood with my jaw wide open.

All of our eyes searched each other in as much shock as the next.

Sahir sent another rotted deity in my direction, and I should have called The Nola because there was no way my luck could have kept being that good. There was no way that I was going to do something like that again with a power that I hardly understood.

The corpse charged at me, and I focused on my fist. I closed my eyes and imagined that it was glowing with the same light. When I opened my eyes, I opened my palm and gripped the creature's face until it burnt up the same as the last.

The toll it was taking on my body was unexpected. I wasn't even sure if I was standing straight anymore.

"Who gave you that?" Sahir demanded.

"What?" I asked.

I took her speaking as hope that she was out of bodies.

"Who gave you Olexei's magic!" She screamed. "Daddy didn't say anything about this! Who did it? Who did it!"

I grabbed Sage by the arm; she wasn't going to stop us from leaving.

"Do not go back on this," I said.

Sage shook her head and looked at me like I was her parent reprimanding her.

"I mean it. She won't ever change, and you know it. There are several deities here who want your friendship. Go spend time with them instead." I looked her over with my best impression of Kyrell before turning and going back to Merripen.

I didn't know if it would work, but it was worth a shot. He kept me locked away with that look, after all.

I needed her to listen because whatever I had just done, Whoever Olexei was, I didn't think I could do it again. She still owed me information, but I was sure I couldn't take it in while my adrenaline was so high. My body was still on fire, and there was no way that I was doing anything other than resting.

CHAPTER FIFTEEN

THE CURSE OF SIGHT

The Teachings of Moonlight

Darkness had a beautiful mystery to it. I longed to be wrapped in it for a time. Saddened by the idea that I was too big and too bright to fully appreciate it. That was at the beginning of time. That was hundreds of years before I had sat in it. My sister, small as she was, had big dreams. None of them included darkness. I made it my goal to brighten the world for her, to wrap her in warmth.

RURI

I imbued the dragon eggs with more magic. I was confident that today would be the day a big batch of them would arrive. Their soil was still moist, and there was not a single wilted leaf or petal. As beautiful as the sight of them was, I couldn't wait to meet them. Dragons that would breathe poison sat in purple eggs that shimmered green in the light, their flowers matched in color, and their petals large enough to hold more than one egg. The fire dragons were the opposite; small black leaves with yellow tips and tiny red petals held up their eggs.

Usha, the stone dragon, was already a guardian at the caves of Erebus. A soul in the stars was looking for Caym. The soul was nearly done growing in an egg that sat on golden petals. Sage's dragon egg had me the most curious. Her dragon grew on a pink flower closer to the ground. It had no stem and was notably bigger in size than most others.

At first, I had no intention of making Sage a dragon, but the soul called himself a season and pleaded that I reunite the two. I was still hesitant after. I was afraid that I would make something with so much power, and she would just let it fall to Sahir.

I was hopeful that one of the souls would have information about her. I took advantage of every moment I found to take a soul from the stars. If I was only going to get a small bit of information for every creation, the more dragons, the better. So far, I learned the only true death a deity has is after the complete destruction of their heart. If that doesn't happen, their soul floats until there's something strong enough for it to go into. My dragons were strong enough.

When I moved to the other side of Juniper's garden, there was a tiny emerald dragon lying limp and cold, only half out of its egg. I pulled a blanket out from their pile next to their patch in the garden. We had an ample supply of everything needed in case one hatched. I wrapped the infant dragon in the blanket in preparation for its burial and then waved away the illusion cast on it. It was only a calf.

I held my hand out for a Fiia, and one didn't hesitate to connect with my mind and pull me into its own.

The Fiia showed me Sahir replacing the dragon's heart

with a fake. The little fluttering creature showed me Sahir's mouth covered in blood and the dragon's heart in her hands.

I pulled myself from the Fiia and let it go back to the others.

It was unusual for me to congratulate myself on anything. Only once would I allow myself a moment to smile. My smile turned into a laugh, and before I knew it, I had to cover my mouth with my own hands to keep calm. I pretended to roll the joy into a ball and swallow it down. I allowed myself enough of a win. I wouldn't allow myself to get too cocky. I wouldn't allow myself to get washed away in a single win when I wanted all of them. I wanted to play a long game. To hold the ultimate knowledge in the end.

I leaned down and untucked Sage's still unhatched dragon from the protection of its petals. He was still safe. What she ate was a cow's heart laced with poison. First, her skin would start shedding off, and then she'd itch so badly that she'd help it along. She'd be resistant to pain relief, and her mind would go. It would take time. I wanted it to take time. I caught myself smirking again and pushed it away.

That was the first moment I believed in the dreams the tree was giving me. It showed me the outcome; otherwise, I wouldn't have been able to stop it.

Unexpectedly, an egg began to shake and then crack. It showed a blue-scaled dragon that was medium in size. I lifted her from the leftover egg, and it revealed all of her spikes. They started at the top of her tail and ran down the entire length of her. I sat her beside me, and while all four of her feet stood, her wings opened to their full length. They changed from blue to green with every uncoordinated attempt at flapping. She was not a soul from the stars but a gift of protection to a friend.

Vespera's egg shook next and dropped out of the flower it was sitting in. It broke into a dozen pieces. He thrashed his head at me, showing off his single horn. He realized very quickly he had large black wings and used them to make an escape. He didn't stop until he met Onyx. I hadn't noticed him lurking. The dragon landed in his arms and nuzzled in.

"He protests his ownership." I laughed.

I didn't want to let on that; it made me uncomfortable to consider how long he was watching me in silence.

"I'm not going to deny him." He said as he lifted the dragon.

"He'd be disappointed if you did," I said.

I was shifting from uncomfortable to anxious. I wanted him to leave. I avoided everyone for the last several weeks and isolated myself with only Yumi and Astra. I poured everything I had into growing these dragons. They were to help Cylla and protect my friends, yes, but they were also my only source of unaltered information, and suddenly, he was here when I had my chance to get answers.

I hadn't noticed the dozen other eggs that hatched. An entire patch of Brontide, the land of thunder, was causing chaos while they shot sparks from their mouths. The thought of how much was slipping away while Onyx stood and looked down at me made me want to cry. I wanted to sob and scream.

The smallest dragon yet took its time to crawl its way out of the flowers and scurried up my lap. Burgundy fur covered her, and she flapped her wings open. They were longer than her length, and it was clear she had to grow into them. She only stopped moving when she found her way inside of my dress to lay by my chest. I had her name picked since she was a seedling. Her name was to be Belladonna.

Onyx looked distracted, and I took the chance to whisper. "What do you remember?"

"You look just as you did before. You died. We all died." She spoke low.

"Who are you?" I asked.

"I think you need to know who you are first." She said.

"Then who am I?" I asked.

"You are the daughter of creation. A sister of fate. You are the beginning of life. There are four of you." Belladonna whispered.

"When will the others hatch?" Onyx leaned himself down to my level.

"I'm not sure. Each type is different." I answered. I tried not to sound startled.

"I actually wanted to find you while we could talk alone." He said.

"Oh?" I lifted my brows.

Belladonna curled herself inside of my dress, and I cradled her. Was she scared of him?

"I keep having visions, and you need to know about them." He stated.

"I don't need to know. I'm plagued by my own nightmares showing me the future." I got to my feet so we could continue the conversation.

"In mine," He paused. "Well, they are violent."

"In my own, I die; every choice that I change, I still die. It's either me or every single one of you." I pointed.

He looked at his own feet before meeting my eyes again.

"It's why I had the God of Justice working with the dragon eggs so often. He passed them his sense of justice and judgment. They can help be a sense of right and wrong if all other sources fail." I said.

"In theory, right?" He pressed.

"Of course." I lied. "We will have to pick this up later, though. I need to meet with Yumi."

He nodded at me in understanding and moved out of my way. I was happy to get away from the conversation. I didn't want to hear about his dreams. It didn't matter to me what they were. I had my own focus. The dragons weren't my only plan. I was watering down the mixture I was told to put on the tree.

The less that the tree received, the more it communicated. That tree seemed to hold unending knowledge. I wanted it.

I entered the Sunlight Garden and stood beside the Tree of Life like I was instructed to do every single evening since my markings glowed. It would be just her and I for the next several hours. I felt my heart race against my control.

The panic scattered its way through my body, and every part of me said to leave. To fight. To resist. It always lost. I ate the panic down and turned myself off.

It was a mixture of emotions I didn't think that I could ever get used to. When she was away, I felt stupid, like I was a disappointment for letting these things happen. I felt foolish for acting as if I were a weak babe. I ran over a list of things that I could do or try. I always came back to the idea that it was a small sacrifice to keep everyone else safe until I could be sure, with no room for error, that anything I did would work. I couldn't risk my sister or my friends. Even if they hated me in the end for pushing them away.

When Yumi stood in front of me, her presence alone showed me why I didn't try to act out against her in a bolder way. She made me feel small, insignificant, useless. She had to be sure that she was more powerful than I could imagine if she was willing to act the way she did.

Yumi came in with rage in her eyes and used her fingers to motion me to my knees. I listened, already numb. I had no idea why she was upset today, but it didn't matter. I couldn't talk my way out of anything.

Instead, I was already in my home at Ashbell with Caym. We were surrounded by dragons, and his paintings hung on every wall. The smell of freshly baked cake and strawberries filled the air. He was trimming fresh flowers for our table.

"You should have already known to be in position after what you've been doing." She yelled. "When you decided it was your place to alter the mixture for the tree, you didn't think I would know? You thought you could go unnoticed?" Yumi grabbed her favorite whip from the table.

Three pieces of fabric were attached to it. Triple the pain.

I lowered the back of my dress and let all the scars bathe in the light. I took the time to stabilize myself before she could start. The number of times I hit my face during these punishments were too many; I didn't want another bruise that sat in the open.

I was back home, and Caym was cutting dessert for all of us. Our friends were visiting. His smile was beautiful.

"You get twenty-five to start with. Every whimper is another set." Yumi stated. "I want you to repeat that you will not be like your mother for every whip, or I'll start again, got it?"

"Understood," I said.

I didn't understand why. Orla never stepped a toe out of line. She minded her own, always.

The first crack hit my flesh. It was always the second most painful. The last crack would be the worst.

"I will not be like my mother." I whimpered.

I was with Sage. We were redecorating our Ashbell home. We were making room for a baby.

"I will not be like my mother." I squeezed my eyes shut tighter.

We were laughing together again. Truly enjoying our time together.

"I will not be like my mother."

At least she wouldn't need to cut me, too. Blood was sure to be on the tree.

"I will not be like my mother."

We would need to extend our home in Ashbell soon. It would grow to be filled with the sounds of little feet. I absorbed myself into the dream I was creating.

"I will not be like my mother."

She left me on the ground to pick myself back up. I tucked

a hand under my face to lift it from the dirt and closed my eyes until her footsteps were far enough away that she couldn't change her mind and come back.

I lifted my other hand and pressed it to the base of the tree. I allowed it to pull me inside again. I had allowed it to pull me in so many times that it was no longer an adjustment. My pain was gone, and inside the world, the tree created had a shape like ours. She was no longer a tree, and she let me lay in her lap. She stroked my hair and comforted me, but the end was always the same.

She plagued me with visions of my death. At first, I was afraid. The less of my blood that I gave her, the more she explained to me that my death would create an opening for some sort of awakening.

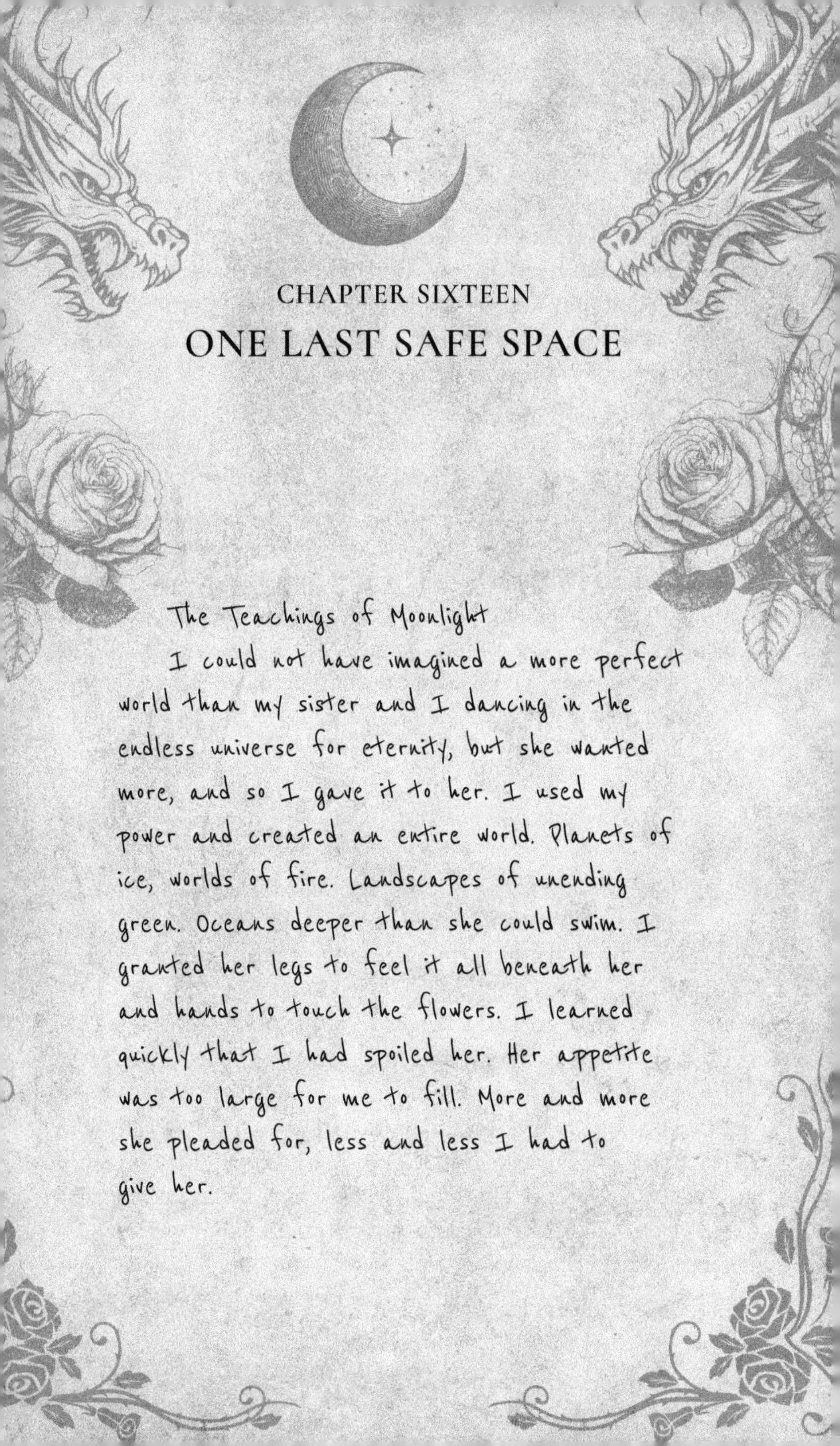

CHAPTER SIXTEEN

ONE LAST SAFE SPACE

The Teachings of Moonlight

I could not have imagined a more perfect world than my sister and I dancing in the endless universe for eternity, but she wanted more, and so I gave it to her. I used my power and created an entire world. Planets of ice, worlds of fire. Landscapes of unending green. Oceans deeper than she could swim. I granted her legs to feel it all beneath her and hands to touch the flowers. I learned quickly that I had spoiled her. Her appetite was too large for me to fill. More and more she pleaded for, less and less I had to give her.

RURI

I was walking the streets of Golden City. Girls danced on a stage; they were surrounded by many clapping hands. The sounds of their jewelry sounded with their movements. A white-haired girl walked beside me. She looked at me with a smile, and her eyes were just as white. Baren tree branches covered her skin the same as my lighting streaks.

"What are these?" I asked her.

She wrapped her arm around mine while we walked, as if she had always known me, as if I were the only one aware it was a dream.

"They're the symbol Mother gave. They are a sign of your magic, your position. The sign of your guardian, as well. They will have the matching marks." Her smile was as kind as her words.

I opened my mouth to speak, but she lifted a hand and signaled me to stop.

"I do hope to see you again, but for now, he's coming. I need you to allow Sahir to do what she's going to do in the Sunlight Garden. Do not stop her." She disappeared in a flash.

I blinked, and my dreams were changed.

I laid in my bed. Wrapped in white silk sheets and velvet blankets. Mesh curtains hung from the posters on all four corners of my bed frame. They were designed with swirls and shapes made of line work. Their color was a bit darker than I liked, but it was a small complaint.

My door slid open at a slow, quiet pace. I didn't lift my head; I kept my eyes on the fabric. I knew who it would be. My breath quickened, and I felt my heart thump in my throat. The blankets at my feet lifted, and I felt the body of a man crawl over my legs. A kiss was laid on my knee before he moved further up. Every time that I dreamt, he made an appearance. The next kiss was on my hip, the next on my stomach. The only thing between us soon was a sheet. I could feel his breath on my face through the fabric. It didn't smell like the mint I was used to, but it smelled of mildew. He always smelled of something left in the dark, wet, for too long.

He leaned down to leave one last kiss on my neck before I pulled the sheet off of his face. When I was facing to face with the man who entered my room, he put his hand over my mouth, anticipating my scream. I saw him every night. He gripped me too tightly, and I thrashed my body. It did nothing against him, but I did not stop.

"Shh." Deimos, God of Dreams, hushed me. "Someone may hear us. We've been so careful. Now is no time to get caught." He leaned down, and I felt his nose run through my hair. He took in my scent until he could no longer breathe in. "You smell as sweet as always." He whispered in my ear.

I opened my mouth to take a bite out of any piece of his hand near enough to latch on to, but he lifted his hand and gave me one last look, running his eyes over me as If they were his fingers before he snapped.

I flung myself up in bed, sitting straight as a board and screaming. I reached up to push the hair, wet and stuck to my face, out of view. A hand reached up and rubbed my back, but it only startled me more, and I screamed again. The pain from the lashings hurt more than the dream had startled me.

"Another dream?" Caym asked, sitting up with me.

He came to discuss with me the magic I gave him, but I was far too exhausted. I tried to convince him to come back another time, but I did not have the energy to press it.

I felt my lip quiver when he searched my eyes. The concern and pain he showed hurt me. I dug my nail into my palm until it was all I could focus on. I could not slip. I absolutely could not allow myself to slip when he was about to leave. He deserved a good time, to think there was peace left behind him. He needed to focus.

"What is it?" He asked.

My day is filled with Yumi, and my dreams are filled with nightmares, and in between that, I'm shown that I need to hurry up and die. Outside of that, everything is great!

I'd never say it out loud, but it felt good to pretend that I had. I pulled my clothes tighter around me. I wanted to ensure nothing slipped and showed too much. I would hold in everything I could, but my skin did not.

"It's nothing, really." My lip shook again, betraying me. "I'm just not used to dreams still, I think. They're something I don't think I'll ever get used to." I smiled.

He gave me a look of understanding that made me feel like an awful deity for lying to him, but there was also a comfort in knowing he was near. He pulled me in and embraced me. I sighed with relief when he put his arms around my neck instead. I would rather he pull my hair than have to explain why my back looked the way it did. I could hear the beating of his heart, calm and slow the longer I let him stay. I would miss him.

I would miss him when he left and when I died. I knew that there was a before. That it was not our first life together. I didn't have proof outside of a tree and my dreams, but it didn't matter to me. I knew that I had known him before, and with that, I knew that if I told him what was happening, I wouldn't be able to control the spiral that came with the information.

He turned me around and motioned me to sit at my vanity before he grabbed my brush and started gliding it through the strands of emerald hair. Every single time the brush ran through my hair, it ran over my back. I wanted to enjoy the moment, but it was a second round of torture.

He pulled it all into a braid and tied it off with a ribbon before he set the brush back down.

"It's been a while since you let me do this." He said.

"Things are just busy." I smiled.

"We could set aside more evenings. We could visit the hot spring, or—"

"No!" I stood. "It's just that we will be together forever, so this time apart is just a small sacrifice."

He searched my eyes, unconvinced. "Are you sure that you have nothing else to tell me?"

"What would there be? I'm simply helping Yumi keep the realm moving forward so that we are needed less. The mortals are advancing, and so are we." I said.

"I won't press you any harder, but I will say before we drop it that if you feel the need to lie to me, I want to know. I want to be able to fix whatever it is that you see in me that tells you I can't be trusted," he said.

There was a pleading in his eyes that broke me. My eyelashes managed to hold back a lake of tears. I hardly understood I had been holding back in such a high amount. Eventually, I would be able to share with him again, but that day was not today.

He would do what he could to stop me. He would never accept the idea that I had to die. I couldn't take the chance.

He rummaged through his pocket. "I learned of a stone called citrine. The way it drank up the light to give back rainbows, I knew you had to have the most perfect piece. It's the closest thing I've ever seen to your beauty." He clipped the chain around my neck and ensured it was sitting as perfectly as it could be. "I know that you will avoid me again after I leave here, and so I will wait. You can keep this as a reminder of that."

"Thank you," I said.

There was nothing else I could say to the rest of his words.

He and I walked, fingers entwined, to the dining hall.

My back ached with my heart. Even with his warmth, his comfort. Even he started to fail at overriding the intense sadness I felt these days.

Caym pulled a chair out for me to sit in, and I followed his lead. I let him pour my cup of tea without complaint as well. It was something I normally liked to do because what I needed to do next was easier if I poured the tea. I pretended to sneeze, and Caym turned to grab a tissue. I used those precious seconds to pour brown powder into my drink.

"Here," He said, holding a handkerchief.

I kissed his cheek and sat it in my lap. I pretended to pour sugar and stir my tea while he was already drinking his. I took bigger gulps. Hopeful that the pain reliever would work faster if I got it all in together. When I sat the cup down, he was already holding a small cake up to my mouth. I greedily took the bite.

"Mm. Orange." I said through food, offering him a much larger piece.

Could he tell how fake my tone was?

"It is good." He was hardly forming real words from all the food.

Even though it was taking him much longer to chew, he grabbed the cloth and dabbed at my face with it. Cleaning crumbs left around my lips.

"I meant to leave it there," I mumbled.

Was that joke funny enough to convince him?

He gave a small nod, and a smile formed, ear to ear, on his face.

Yes, I must have been doing a good job pretending not to be empty inside.

"We should make a date to try those mushrooms I hear so much about in Erebus." He offered.

I shook my head, "No way. Vespera says you enter a made-up land filled with characters, and you hallucinate yourself and drag everyone along for the ride with you. She said sometimes the hallucinations in your head are fluffy and filled with love. Other times, they only make you cry, and everyone dies. Only sometimes there is a happy ending, and it's nearly never the kind of happiness you wanted. She said when it's over, you wonder why you even tried it at all."

I had enough things speaking to me, I did not need aid from any other source.

"The way Onyx put it made it sound better." Caym frowned briefly before holding out his hand, "May I have this dance?"

I shook my head in disagreement but gave in on his second attempt when he flashed me his puppy eyes. He pulled me up quickly and gave me no time to second-guess what we were doing. There was no music, only the sound of our feet and breath. He pulled me into him until I was flush with his chest and laid a hand on my lower back. I was glad to have drank that tea because I didn't feel the lashings when he did. He glided as if he had been dancing for years.

"How do you know what you're doing?" I asked.

"The dead in Merripen taught me a thing or two for you." He said. "They taught me how to make that broccoli soup you like from Edur, too."

I had nothing to say in return. I could tell him that he would have to make it for someone else, but why ruin his thoughts?

We enjoyed a few more uninterrupted moments together, dancing to nothing but our own heartbeats before he had to leave.

I sat back down to drink another cup of tea for my back before I left for Brontide. I was to set up a barrier for them today. I asked Kyra what she thought of it, and she agreed that if it wasn't too much on me, she would not deny a layer of protection on her land. The Goddess of Storms did exactly what I hoped she would. She stabilized the environment in Cylla for the mortals.

If I was going to die, and I would not be able to help anyone again, I had to turn my thoughts to what it was I could do before then. What could I get done that would give the biggest advantage to anyone who was left to oppose whatever would come next?

My answer was to pick a piece of land that could be used to protect those who may need it. Kyra was one of the few deities that I had never witnessed giving in to anything she considered wrong. I would leave a barrier around her lands that kept anyone out that she did not allow in. Then, I would move onto my own land and lay another layer of assistance.

Deimos entered and took a seat next to me; before I could get to my feet, he put a cloth in his lap and grabbed his own plate of cakes.

"I wasn't sure I'd see you here today; you come so little," he said.

"I make it a goal to never be here when you are," I replied.

He smiled from ear to ear, refusing to pretend he wasn't enjoying himself. "it's why I come to you."

My hands started to shake more with every word he said.

"If the Goddess of Love didn't force the bonds on the two of you. If she didn't use her position to decide who was forced together. Would you still pick him?" He raised a brow when he was finished asking the question.

"I have never considered it a forced decision," I said.

Deimos ran his eyes over me, ensuring he went slow enough that I felt every piece of my body his eyes touched. I didn't let him finish before I took my leave. Yumi could force me to sit through punishments. The tree could force me into death. But he could not force me to stay outside of my dreams.

I took the vines to Brontide, the land of thunder.

No one suspected that I was planning for my own death, and I meant to keep it that way.

Kyra was doing well to turn Brontide into one of the most beautiful parts of Cylla. The kingdom was built into rock pillars that went so high that you could touch the clouds.

Waterfalls fell from streams that etched themselves through the biggest formations. The palace rested in the middle of it— a sight to see made entirely of marble and surrounded by shrubbery. I hesitated for a moment so I could take in the mortals living their lives unaffected by anything at all outside of their borders.

Kyra and I worked together to create the Mita. They were beautiful mortals with nearly transparent skin. Golden veins were visible through their bodies, pulsing with lightning magic. Their eyes matched the gold tint. It became a breath-taking contrast when it all sat against their black hair.

Kyra was in the distance, and I pulled myself from spying on mortals who didn't notice me so I could meet her. She was accompanied by a lot more faces than I had expected. Everyone was present, even the men who were supposed to be busy.

"Who's ready to play with magic?" Aero, the God of Justice, pointed at himself.

Onyx looked him up and down, "Do you even have magic? I can't recall a time I've seen you use it."

"Hu," Caym thought, "Me either. Have you been holding out on us?"

Aero caught my eye, "Little help, Ru?"

"I'm just here to put up a barrier; don't put me in the middle of your relationship problems," I answered, lifting my hands.

The two did not hesitate to continue their barrage of questions.

"Are you sure about this?" Kyra asked.

"Did you scatter the crystals around where I told you?" I asked.

"We did." Kyra nodded.

"Then I'm positive," I said.

I was sure that killing another part of myself was worth the comfort I'd have in death.

I moved myself to the edge of the pillar we were standing on, looking for the open space. The rest of the group backed away and gave me distance without my asking.

Part of me smirked, hardly recognizing the feeling when they moved because they may fear the accidental impregnation memories.

I took a deep breath and, pulled two crystals from the small pocket I had inside of my dress, and signaled to Kyra. The sky darkened. It was a rapid change around us. Lighting came first, and I pulled the darkened cloud that was producing it to me, surrounding myself with it. I squeezed the two crystals tighter in my hands. I become a purple glow inside of a black cloud. Two strikes came down, and I pulled them into the crystals. I was pulling from the purest source of the element I could obtain.

The purple glow grew until it encompassed the entire landscape in it. It lifted itself up into a dome and blocked out the sky. I took notice of the townspeople gathering around, but only for a moment. The dome dissolved as quickly as it grew, and it was done. The sky cleared, and the crystals turned to ash in my fingers.

I did my best to choke down the blood that was filling my mouth. I thought I might drown in it. I fought to get rid of it and clean my nose before anyone could take notice. I couldn't allow any of them to see the price I was paying for existing these days. Things needed to be done at any cost. I was willing to pay it because when I left, I needed the peace of knowing they had somewhere safe.

"That was crazy!" Aero yelled.

I paid close attention to the looks being passed around, and Aero was the only one who was as excited as he was.

"Are you all right?" Caym asked.

"I'm fine. I can guarantee it's safe. Brontide will remain untouched." I said.

He kept his look the same. Hardened and unconvinced.

"This is what I was created for. I'm fine! I'll go rest a bit to be safe." I urged.

I didn't give him the time to protest before I opened the vine portal and entered Semper. I did need to rest. I knew I couldn't handle anymore today. My limit was reached.

I only made it two steps in before Astra was behind me, hurrying her steps to be at my side. I only glanced at her from the side of my eyes.

"You may be a good liar, but you aren't a great one." She said.

"I will be fine after a break," I said.

She nodded, "I'm here to ensure you take that break. Take me to Ashbell. Show me around. I have things to tell you."

I sucked in both my lips with my breath and sighed, "All right, fine, Let's go." I pulled her through the vines we hadn't walked far from yet. "But you better start spilling now, not later."

"I'm in love with Kyra. I know we couldn't be together like that. At least no one has yet. It seems sudden, but she has a way of grounding me every time I'm on the edge." Astra sighed with joy. Her eyes looked as if they were filled with hearts.

"Does she feel the same way?" I asked.

A small part of my sadness cleared being on her presence. She had been through what I was dealing with a lot longer, and she had found a way to work past it all. Not just work past it but she was the first to have a smart mouth with Yumi almost always. She had decided if she was going to face the same consequences, that she may as well end up deserving it.

I had not yet reached the point where I could be torn apart and then gossip the next day.

"I'm not sure. I'm too afraid to tell her." Astra admitted.

I nodded but kept silent.

"I'm also sorry that Yumi seems to be rougher with you." She was searching my face for what I was feeling.

"It's not you that needs to apologize. She just hates me." I said.

"You won't get an apology from her," Astra said.

I guided us into the courtyard of Ashbell. Burning flower bushes and gold-trimmed benches decorated the entrance of a garden maze. The other end would put us at the back of the obsidian castle. I pointed her to it.

"Do you think it's strange Sage and Caym have markings but don't receive the same treatment?" Astra asked.

"I did. I don't anymore." I admitted. I checked our surroundings before I spoke any further. A girl with white markings visited me in my dreams, and she has been giving me little bits of information. Caym's markings mean that he's my guardian and Sage is a sister of fate. I don't exactly understand it, but I can understand how I put myself in the spotlight by showing off so much." I said.

"You're blaming yourself?" Astra shook her head. "You could have shown off one hundred times more or never done a single thing and acted powerless. If Yumi was going to do something, there was nothing you were going to do about it."

I whistled, and several three-headed hounds charged us. I lowered myself down and welcomed their licks. "Whose good boys? You are! These are hounds, the pet of Ashbell," I said, directing them to her.

I appreciated what she was doing more than she could have known. More than I could have expressed with words. She wanted to distract me and help me relax, and during our walk, I forgot for a moment that there was a special kind of hell waiting for me back in Semper. It didn't mean that I knew how to handle it any better. It didn't bring me comfort to hear her say those things. It made me uncomfortable because no matter how many times she said it wasn't my fault, I could not pretend to believe it.

"I was curious if you knew anything about this?" I asked,

holding up my palm. "I touched the tree on accident, and now I have this sun and moon on my palm that I can't get off."

"I've never seen that symbol before. If the tree goes too long without Yumi's mixture, things get strange, though. I swear it starts whispering to me." Astra shivered. "Once, it whispered to me about seasonal deities. I haven't made sense of it yet. I know we were the first made. I've never met any such thing."

"Doesn't this ever make you feel like Yumi is lying about something?" I asked.

"What reason would she have to lie?" She shrugged. "If we disagree, we die."

"I can't explain it in a way that makes sense, but I know she's lying," I said.

I watched her play with the necklace I gave her that held the shattered bits of Sin's soul. That was a part of my list that I wasn't sure I could complete. I could not put him inside of a dragon because he was incomplete.

Several large groups of guards came running out of the garden we had entered. They were shouting and grabbing buckets. I grabbed one by the arm, and he looked petrified when he saw me.

"What's going on here?" I asked.

"Ma'am, someone set fire to the Goddess cottage home. It is burning as we speak. We're doing the best we can, but it's like a magical blaze. It's burning so hot, we're making no progress." He rushed past me as fast as his words poured out.

Our home was gone. The home I built for us to stay in. The one I used as my peace when Yumi had me in her hands. The home I was going to hang Cayms paintings in. The home I was going to leave for him when I was gone.

I knew it had to be Sahir's doing.

CHAPTER SEVENTEEN

WHERE DID THE TIME GO

The Teachings of Moonlight

I created the universe, the world, the waters for my sister. I created the mortals to try and give her something the rest could not give her. It was my hope that watching them would show her emotions she had not felt. That they would show her how to care for someone besides herself. I created Olexei, the Sun God, for myself. He was my selfish wish come true. I loved him, and she gave me what I asked her for. She felt emotions that she had never held before.

RURI

I sat on the edge of Merripen, feet hung over the water. I was so close to the sky that both moons were visible behind the sun. I plucked another blade of grass and tossed it to the side.

I felt myself breaking. I was trying my best to keep myself focused and calm, but it became harder for me to find reasons to stay quiet.

I picked another blade of grass and tossed it.

If I tried to kill Yumi and then took Sahir next, the world I would be leaving behind would be safer for them all. It would be safer than leaving them in it.

I plucked a handful of grass and threw it in the water.

I could ask Jeb for his help. I could ask Belladonna for her help, too.

I reached up and tucked my hand inside of my blouse and felt where she slept. The three of us could take on the two of them, couldn't we?

I plucked another blade of grass and tossed it.

Vespera! She collected relics and books. She would like to know if there is a way to get information about Yumi.

"If you keep going, I won't have any grass left at all."

I nearly leaped off the edge of the cliff.

"Don't sneak up on people like that!" I yelled.

"I'd hardly say I snuck up. I've been sitting here for quite a while." Caym said.

"For how long?" I asked, nervous I was mumbling.

"You were pretty locked into your thoughts. I didn't hear anything." He said. "Do you want to talk about it?"

"No," I said too quickly.

He thought for a moment before responding to me. "You don't cure a sickness by avoiding it. If left untreated, it will spread to every corner it can touch. You cure it by getting rid of the illness, and that usually takes outside help." He moved my hair away from my face, "Are you sure you don't need to talk?"

I smiled at him so he could feel a sense of relief from me. His eyes started to tell me that it worked less and less.

"I'm just ready to move on to another phase of life. Semper is not the realm for me." I said.

He opened his mouth to speak, but I stopped him.

"I actually plan to take today away as a break." I stood, "Don't worry about me. Focus on what you have going on."

I opened the vine portal and left Merripen.

What was he doing these days? Time for me felt so hard to keep a grasp on. How long had it been since I asked him that? Weeks? A month?

I stood outside of Vespera's bookstore; inside, I could see her with Sage. They were standing over a pile of open books, comparing pages.

I shouldn't be standing in front of her shop, to begin with. The two of us hardly knew each other; she had no reason to help me. I turned to leave, but the door opened.

"Ruri! What are you doing here?" Vespera asked.

"It's not important." I waved her off.

"I've been waiting for you to show up. I wanted to take you to the Great Library of Sunlight if you will let me." Vespera said.

"If you insist, I'll go. If I'm interrupting something, it's okay to tell me that I need to go." I said.

"You aren't interrupting. I really do want to take you." She said.

I nodded, and she opened the vines for us to go through.

We stood in front of the island, and I needed to ask a question that would sound foolish.

"How long has it been? Since the death of Sin and Yumi, have you taken me to the Sunlight Garden to help the realm?" I asked. I was too afraid to look at her while she answered.

"Ruri, it's been months that she kept you going between the Sunlight Garden and Ashbel. There was some time when you and Kyrell were both there, and we weren't allowed to disturb you." She said.

The confirmation lit something inside of me that I was

sure died. I left Vespera behind and marched to the steps. I took them with a purpose. It had to be the place with answers.

I shoved the doors open, and the men who were scattered around the room in golden robes stopped what they were doing to look at me.

"Who runs this place?" I asked.

"I can help you." A man moved forward. "You can call me Lui."

"Hi, Lui. I'm Ruri. Can you tell me what this is?" I asked as I threw a ball of sun magic out of the library bay window and into the sea. "Maybe you can answer what this means?" I asked and held up my palm to show him the moon and sun etched into my skin. "If you can't answer those questions, maybe you can tell me how to put a soul back together? Can you explain why someone would want to eat hearts?" I was out of breath from yelling, but I still felt so much rage.

"I can answer your questions, but I need to ask that you take a few breaths first. I know that you are surrounded by many enemies, but we aren't one of them." He said.

"Prove it," I responded.

"That magic belongs to the sun God Olexei. He gifted the ability to use it to his daughters." Lui said.

"Then why do I have it?" I asked.

"Come in and sit down." He pointed me to a large cutout balcony that sat over the sea.

I looked back to Vespera, and she motioned for me to follow. I listened only because I wanted the information he seemed to have.

The both of us sat at the table, and he took his hood off.

"Don't offer me anything. I don't want anything but answers." I demanded.

He nodded. "First, I'm on your side. Normally, we test blood before you can walk past the doors, but I can see from your markings—"

"You want blood? I pulled out the dagger from my foot

covers and sliced my hand, which was already all scars. "Take all of it you want. It's not new to me." I allowed the blood to pour onto the table.

The look he gave me was only horror. When I glanced at Vespera, she matched his gaze.

I was the one acting foolish. I closed my hand and hid it under the table.

"I apologize," I spoke, but kept my eye down. "I came to you, and I was out of line. I'd like to know what you can answer for me."

"It's quite all right," Lui assured me. "I think we should start by telling you of the curse that has been placed on all of us. We can only discuss so much. Not all subjects are on the table. It is not because I don't want to answer you but because I simply can not."

He paused and waited for me to speak, but I had nothing to say. I was a Goddess, asking a mortal for assistance, and I made a fool of myself while asking for it. I only nodded.

"The easiest thing I can tell you is that magic belongs to Olexei. You can guess why you have it if it was a gift to his daughters. I cannot explain it to you in a different way. Second, that symbol is part of an awakening ritual. Placed by the moon. Between the symbol and your markings, I'd say you are pretty close to your ascension. Do you understand what I'm saying?" Lui asked.

"Hardly. You're trying to tell me that the moon marked me?" I asked.

"I can not say her name. Starlight has cursed it." He said.

"Then, can you explain this awakening? What are the next steps?" I asked.

"I have no confirmation that it must be in a specific order, but you require your markings, the blessing on your palm, your seasonal deity, and—" He stopped and grabbed his throat. "I apologize. I can't continue."

I ran my hand across my face. "Okay, what is it for?"

"To restore you to your true form," Lui said.

"So, I have lived before?" I asked.

He nodded.

"As for your next two questions, no, I do not know how to repair a soul. Your sister would."

"Why would Sage know that?" I didn't understand.

"Not that sister. There are four of you." He said.

"Where are they?"

He shook his head again. "I can't answer that either."

"What's the purpose of eating hearts?" I wanted him to give me the information faster.

"Power. You eat them for more power. Are you eating hearts?" He asked.

"No," I answered.

"The act will corrupt you. There will be consequences, and whoever told you that you should do it did so because they want to see you—"

"I am not eating them," I said again.

It was becoming too difficult to ignore how many golden-robed mortals were standing in his doorway, staring at me. Still, I tried not to look.

"Can you explain to me why they're watching us?" I asked.

"Our lives are devoted to you and your sisters. To your mother and father. Seeing you here, with your markings. Some of them will mark this as the day their lives were complete. To you, time is different than it is for us. Some of them will die before you ever consider us again." He looked at them while he spoke to me.

His words made me realize that It wasn't just time that I was losing, but myself as well.

I wanted to help them when all of it began. I wanted to live in their world and keep watch over them. All I wanted these days was for everything to end. I didn't want to die like the tree showed me because I couldn't protect my sister from Yumi if I were gone. I couldn't keep Caym from the spotlight either. I wouldn't be able to repair Astra's son from a grave.

If I removed all of that noise and was left with only myself as a reason. I didn't want to stay. I didn't want to spend another day with Yumi. I only felt more lifeless, trying to make sense of how my days blended together so hard.

Once, I was so excited to meet the mortals and spend time with them, and here in front of them, I was closer to Yumi than myself.

I stood, and it wasn't lost on me that Lui sat forward. I did not blame him. I held out my hand to the group, but they only looked at it.

"Do you know how to shake?"

They looked at me as if they felt as foolish as I did. We were two sides trying our best. One man moved forward and took my hand, shaking with all the force he could.

"What is your goal here?" I asked them.

"To preserve the correct telling of history." One of them said.

"To protect the sister's fate." Another spoke.

"So, If I needed you, you would answer?" I asked.

"Of course," Lui interjected.

"You're only mortal men? Not elven or something else with extended lives?" I asked.

"No," Lui answered for them.

"That seems like a bit of a problem. You may be dead by the time I need you again." I sighed. "I'll think of something. Thank you for your answers, Lui."

He gave me a small bow before lifting his golden hood back and allowing me to pass.

Vespera was waiting for me, but she didn't speak first. I locked my arm in hers while we walked, but still, she did not speak.

"Thank you for bringing me here. I want to apologize to you, too, for the way I acted. There's no excuse for it." I said.

"You don't need to apologize to me. I don't plan to hold it against you. You scared me, but only because I didn't think I could stop you if you wanted to sink the entire island." She said.

Once, I would have considered myself strong enough to have done something like that.

"The loudest voice in my head hasn't even been my own for what feels like an eternity," I admitted.

"Are you ready to change that yet?" Vespera asked.

"I am," I answered.

The two of us entered the portals back to Semper, and I squeezed her arm before I let it go and left her behind.

I had one other thing to do today before I had to meet Astra in the garden for our duties. Thann asked that I meet with him. I was set on denying him. I was determined to pretend that I never got word. After today, I wanted to go. I wanted to ride the renewed feeling I was carrying. I wanted to hear what he had to say and use it as another check mark on why I needed to get further away from Yumi.

I entered the dining hall, where they requested I meet them. Orla was outside, checking the halls. No doubt looking for me.

"I'm early, still," I said as I neared her.

"Sure, I just wanted to talk to you before you went in." She said.

"So, it's three of you against me, then?" I remarked.

Orla shook her head, "The opposite; I showed up so you wouldn't be outnumbered."

"You and I have hardly spoken to each other since Yumi moved me out of your quarters," I said.

"We don't have to be enemies. I support your stance on the situation with Thann. What he did was wrong, but he paid." She pleaded.

"Do you? How has he paid?" I pressed, "To me, it looks like you enable him to think he's a good man. You have the position to convince him to give Astra the soul back, but you do not."

"I don't wish to argue; I only wanted to tell you that if you need to be angry, be angry at me. I still love and support you." Orla's eyes searched between mine before she turned and walked inside.

I did not wish to argue, either. She was not my mother. I did not come from someone who would allow someone like Thann to act; however, he wanted to be excused as if he were a child.

I walked in behind her, but I did not sit down. They already had teacups filled and ready. If they thought I'd honestly drink from anything they brought, they were wrong.

"Speak," I said.

"Don't you think this would go better if you had an ounce of positivity in your voice?" Helia asked, lips already turned down.

"Don't you think this would go better if you let him speak instead," I asked.

"Ru, I only--"

I stopped Thann by holding up my hand, "That nickname is reserved for deities I'm close to."

Thann adjusted himself, clearly uncomfortable, before starting again. "I only want to try and start again. Even if it takes time to do."

"Agree to release Astra's son," I said.

"I don't--"

"Agree to it," I demanded.

"It's not that simple," Thann said.

"You're supposed to be the God of Rebirth. I think it would be simple for you." I said.

He looked at me, and he sighed. It was an exaggerated sound, as if it were supposed to make me sad for him.

"Is that a no, then?" I asked.

He looked at me through his lashes. "Will you give me the chance to speak?"

"Speak." I motioned my hand to silently hurry him along.

"I can't take back what happened, but you can't hold it against me forever. I can't change the past, but we can change the future." He said.

"We can change the future. In fact, I showed up today to tell you that in my future, you die. I intend for my visions for the future to be the ones that become a reality."

Helia stood, but I lifted my hand and flicked two fingers at her, using a purple string of magic to pull her feet out from under her and slam her back into her seat.

"I'm going to go back to my duties, and you're going to leave me alone. We are not to speak until you are ready to restore Astra's son."

I walked out of the room with a restored sense of confidence.

CHAPTER EIGHTEEN

FOR EVERY ANSWER, THERE IS MORE PAIN

The Teachings of Moonlight

My sister and her jealousy were beyond anything I could have imagined. She wanted her own companion, and I agreed that it was for the best. If he experienced love, maybe she would also learn to love me. What she created was an abomination. It caused chaos and brought destruction to the world. It was beyond her control. The seasonal deities fought beside Olexei and I, but we still lost so much of ourselves fighting it. I didn't believe we could accomplish our goal, and when we did, none of us believed it. I sealed my sister and her power away. I left her with nothing, and together, we took her memories of the age when she almost ended everything.

RURI

My feet ached, and the only warmth I felt was from the heat of blood dripping out of them. The bottoms were cut in every spot I could feel. I don't know what I thought Cosima, the realm of spirits, looked like, but that wasn't it. I spent so much time in Merripen, where the dead were cared for with a land lusher than even Cylla, that I assumed Cosima would have the same kind of care put into it.

The ground was rough and covered in sharp rocks. The sky was filled with the same pointed, rough terrain on floating islands. The sky was dark, and the air thick. I felt as if I were inside a fire with how much sweat poured off of me, which didn't make sense since I was only in my sleep silk. There was no reason for me to sweat more than I did near my own volcano. I knew I was in a dream. Why was I feeling heat or pain?

I hid behind rocks, hoping to give my feet a break and stay out of sight. I only needed to make it till I figured out how to wake myself. It would have been nice to have foot covers in my sleep, too.

The scream I was following sounded again, so I put my feet back into motion. Every jump I made onto the next floating island stone sent spikes of pain up my legs when I added a new slice to my feet. The screaming girl was finally in front of me. Whatever she was, whoever she had been, was hardly recognizable. She was just scars and dirt.

"Can you hear me?" I asked, leaning in closer.

The girl's eyes opened, and she immediately started screaming and flailing.

"I won't hurt you," I whispered.

She looked at me through bloodshot eyes.

"Who are you?" I asked.

"Nesrin." She was hardly audible.

"Nesrin?" I had to think for a moment, then another, before it hit me. "Koa's sister?"

The girl's lips were sealed before she could answer, as if they had been zipped shut and locked in place. I didn't have proper time to truly take in what it meant before a familiar arm was wrapped around my waist.

"You smell as sweet as always," Deimos whispered.

"It's not hard when this is what you have to compare it to." I retorted.

"You don't like it here?" he asked. He held his grip on me tight.

"She hates it as much as I do." I nodded in Nesrin's direction.

"You can pick the rock with the fae chained to it if you'd like that better. Maybe the one with the dwarf? There's another with a mortal man. What's mine is yours. Take your pick." He waved a hand.

I removed his hand from my waist and backed up, "I'll pass and wake up now."

He watched me but didn't move.

"Let me wake up." I persisted. "I don't understand why you keep coming to my dreams."

"I wasn't interested in you until I could smell you. You smell like your mother now that you've gotten good with your magic. It's how I know you're worth something." He said. "When I brought the girl here, she was so clean. Porcelain skin. Not a single scratch on her. She looks pitiful, doesn't she? If she were more responsive to orders, she'd still have that same skin. However, if I took the time to feel this bad for every worthless life that crossed my path, I'd never get anywhere. You understand her position, don't you?"

He took his hand and lifted it to Nesrin's face. The action made her fling her body around like a worm. Nesrin was terrified; it made me hesitate for a moment and wonder if I should start taking him a little more seriously. I considered him a joke.

A good for nothing, just trying to gain some attention. He spent a lot of time trying to be alone with Yumi.

He touched each of the girl's eyes and put her back inside whatever nightmare he had for her. "I need someone who can talk. Someone who can tell me what it's like to be in the nightmares I've been creating and if my hard work has been paying off or not. That's why she's here."

Deimos moved closer to me; his eyes made me feel as if he was gazing inside my soul. "You and I both know the rules in Semper are weak. That there's too much mercy for the ones who don't deserve it and not enough for those who do." He paused and ran a finger over my collarbone. "I'm smarter than Yumi, and you're stronger than her. That's why she keeps you close to her, and that's why I want you closer to me."

I shook my head, but he covered my mouth with his finger.

"I want to offer you the chance to stand as the Queen of nightmares by my side." He lowered his fingers from my mouth to allow me to respond.

"Why would I ever agree to this?" I asked.

"Because I'll punish the ones you want to be punished. I can give you all the things you've been dreaming about. The things you want to do to them. The things you want done to you. You lend me your power, and I'll serve you the world." He ran his thumb across my bottom lip, and I bit down.

I was met with a slap across my face, and I cupped my cheek.

He lifted his hand and used his pointer finger to cut a line in the sky. When he was finished, he moved to the side. He opened a rift. Through it flew beasts unlike anything I had ever seen before. They were winged, but their wings were shredded. They shouldn't have been able to fly. Some had bodies of fire. Some had eyes that bulged from their skulls.

They lunged at me. They took turns biting down. They ripped my flesh, tearing at the muscle. I felt it all as if it were really happening until I woke up; I shot up, covered in cold sweat for another night of restless sleep. Belladonna slept on my pillow, and Jeb slept on his own bed on the other side of the room. He taught himself to sleep. The rest of the Nola did not.

I left my bed behind to apply the salve from Ashbell to my back, which was nearly healed thanks to it. Today's application didn't burn, which was good news. Jeb roused from my movement.

"Can you do me a favor, Jeb?" I asked.

"Yh- He grunted.

"Yuh." I turned to show him the shape of my mouth.

He mimicked it.

"Es. Ess." I sounded out.

"Yuhess." He grunted again.

He was smarter than the other Nola since he spent so much time with us. He would be the first Nola I taught to speak.

"Can you find out where Koa's sister is? I want to know that she is alright." I said.

His bony fingers gave me a thumbs up, and he nodded in agreement. He was gone in a haze.

I expected Jeb to tell me that Deimos was trying to keep me busy with things that didn't matter. Maybe he was working with Sahir, too. I couldn't talk to Koa directly. It would be a strange thing to say to someone that I really only knew through Caym.

I told myself I would do my best to keep it together today. That I would stick to the confidence that I was carrying. I considered things all night to avoid sleep as long as possible. I would push as much magic as I could into crystals. I would ensure my temple in Ashbel was guarded well. I would go back to looking at the mortals as something I wanted to be involved in. If I helped them, they could help us, too.

Juniper and I were planning to meet in the Sunlight

Garden today, and I would stick to that plan. I needed that to stay on track. I needed to talk to her. I slipped my foot covers on, picked Belladonna up, and made my way. She was growing quickly. Faster than even I anticipated. She was so tiny when she hatched, but I already had to grant her the gift of size manipulation. She had to stay shrunk to lay on my chest.

I slipped into the garden to the table and chairs beside the tree. I took Belladonna out and sat her on the table. She found a spot in the sun to lay. She was growing in size, but she was still only a baby.

"Ruri!" Juniper called, moving faster.

She tucked her red dress in and sat, folding her fingers together and setting her hands on the table. "Onyx came to visit me before he left and told me to stay put no matter what happens. He told me things were going to start falling soon and that I should not leave my place beside the garden no matter what happened."

I wanted to be cautious about how I approached that kind of conversation. No matter what, nothing changed the fact that I wanted it to stay a secret that I was going to die. Having the confidence to move under Yumi's thumb didn't change that. Nothing was changing it. The tree showed me hundreds of ways the future would play out. My death was unchanging.

"I admit, even I feel uneasy lately. Most of us know something is coming. I agree with him. We need you with the garden. It's the most important thing we have." I said. "Your doorway has a barrier for you to come and go, but no one will be allowed to enter unless you agree to it. It's the same as what I did in Cylla."

"I'm sure you want me to say thank you, but you sound just as vague as he did!" She scoffed.

I allowed myself a chuckle, but not more than that. "Ya know, sometimes I'm sure it would be better if I just challenged Yumi. If I could kill her."

I was testing my boundaries. I was curious to see what her reaction would be. I wanted to sort out who would join in the idea of pushing back in a real way.

"You better be sure you can beat her before you start having those kinds of thoughts," She cautioned. "She's the creator."

"I don't think she is," I said simply.

"You went from sounding vague to sounding like you've lost your entire mind." Juniper's eyes were wide, and she looked at me with a raised brow.

"I don't think she is as powerful as she wants us to think she is. If she were, then why doesn't she fix the problems she says I'm needed for?" I asked.

"We won't ever be set up without you, so settle in," Juniper said.

I must have looked at her without blinking for too long because her expression dropped, and I watched the wave of realization wash over her.

"You can't seriously be thinking of that nonsense?" Her mouth never closed after her words were done sounding. "Is that what the barrier is for? The garden? So that you can leave us?"

"It may be the only way we have peace, killing everyone in one swoop." I shrugged.

My heart was racing. I was sure it was going to beat out of my chest.

"You know Caym would never be the same, right? If you don't think that plan is foolish because of the harm it will cause you. If the rest of us also aren't good enough reasons not to do it, consider him." She crossed her arms.

I have been thinking of him and the rest of them. It's why I've done everything I have and everything I still have to do.

"If something were to happen to me, I've created a system of magic that uses crystals. I will leave a book to explain what each one can do. I've filled the caves of Erebus and Merripen with enough to last lifetimes." I said, unblinking.

"I don't want to hear another word about it." She said.

"I just want you to know if something were to happen to me," She held her hand up to stop me from speaking.

"If you think you can't succeed, then any plan you have is not worth it." She said.

"Even if there was only one plan that would bring any peace?" I asked.

"I'd rather live in war with you than a single peaceful day without you." She pressed her lips together.

I made an odd noise. Something between a cry and a laugh. It was a strained sound that I didn't know I was capable of making.

"I do love you, Juniper," I said.

She waved her hands. "You're not ending the talk with that. You need to tell me why this is a thought to you."

"If I said I was shown a vision, would that be good enough?" I said.

"No. I want a reason." She pressed.

"Yumi is not what's strong. It's the tree. She is having a hard time controlling it on her own. Without my blood, the tree starts doing things. Things a tree shouldn't do. My blood only worked once I had markings and the ability to use my magic. If I die, even if I'm reborn, I have to start from scratch again."

She looked at me as if I had grown a second head.

"If I were to say I believe you, even though I think you've been messing with Erebus mushrooms, There are still other paths than your death." She said.

I wish she were right. I said something similar to the tree. I was shown everything that would happen with every other choice we made. I die one way or another; the only difference is who I take with me. Only one way ends with just my death.

My attention was pulled to the back corner of the

Sunlight Garden, where Sahir was walking as quietly as she could. The cherry blossoms of the tree tucked us away from sight, at least from hers. She did not act as if she saw us. She moved vines from the wall they were growing on and bit her thumb open. She used the blood to write something.

That was what I was told about in the dream.

Sahir sliced through the wall as if it were water, and the words written in blood disappeared. She opened some sort of portal like the vines and tucked it away.

Sage entered after her and looked as disappointed as I felt.

"What are you doing now?" Sage demanded.

"I'm helping my daddy. He will need a way back." Sahir said.

"I don't have time for this; you need to get out." Sage pointed to the door.

Sahir shrugged. "We aren't friends, according to you, so I don't see why you care what I'm up to."

"I don't. I only care that you bring it in here. Go." Sage pointed again.

Sahir exited through the Chamber of Starlight, but Sage walked to us.

Juniper cleared her throat, and Sage stopped walking.

"What?" Sage snapped.

"Trouble in paradise?" Juniper asked.

"Of course not, it's paradise." Sage rolled her eyes.

"Don't you have anything else to say?" I asked.

"No?" Sage said.

"You don't want to explain what that was?" I asked again.

"Why don't you go ask her yourself." She shook her head.

"Should I ask her if she's eating hearts, too? It's something else I think you would know the answer to." I said.

"Are you trying to say I'm hiding things?" Sage yelled.

"Girls!" Juniper called. "What do you think you're accomplishing?"

"I was just trying to say that maybe we would have fewer

problems with someone being honest with the people she claimed to care about once," I said.

"Look who is a hypocrite now." Sage drew her words out. "Is that why you hide your palm? Or your nose bleeds? Because you're so open and honest with everyone?"

"I have other things to do," I said.

I went to my quarters and gathered the Fiia. I wanted them to send a message to the Timekeepers. I wanted a list of what mortals would be willing to fight a Goddess if given the magic to do so.

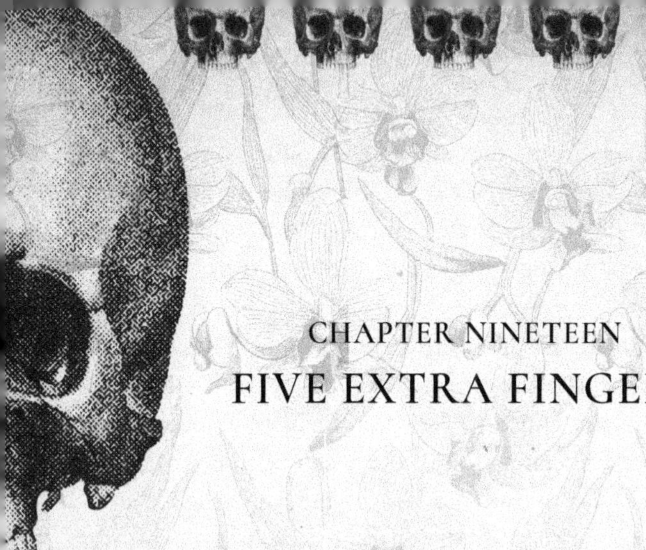

CHAPTER NINETEEN

FIVE EXTRA FINGERS

The Teachings of Moonlight

We rebuilt our world together. My sister watched from the side, barking orders. It was as if I were doing it for the first time again. The seasons asked me why I allowed her to keep her life after what she had done. My answer was not pleasing to even my ear. I loved her. I forgave her. I did not trust her, and so I intended to plan for our future with her in it. I could love her and understand that, despite my desire for it, she did not want to change.

CAYM

The Nola that stayed by my side these days stopped me, rolling its eyes back and showing me a death event. Sahir straddled Morticia's body, digging a blade into her rib cage and ripping at it as if it weren't bone. She ripped and pulled, pried piece by piece until the ribcage was open. Sahir removed the heart waiting inside and dug her teeth into the unprotected flesh.

I sent Nola to assess the situation for me. That would count as my business. She killed someone. My truth was that these situations didn't cause me an emotional reaction in the sense that I was sad seeing them. They caused me irritation that such a thing was allowed to run unchecked when every detail for most of us was cataloged daily. That some of us would be stripped of our duties, and others were free.

My first priority was the man lurking in my room. A second one since arriving in Kyrell's kingdom. They were sent to kill me. I opened a single eye and watched him move closer to me. I wrapped my fingers around the dagger under my pillow and my other hand on my claymore, which I always kept by my side.

The man lowered himself to me and showed his fangs. The same type the last one had. They were called Vampires. The curse of the blood Goddess. She had no official name, but I knew it was Helia. Ruri was kept in the realm of the gods so tightly that she hardly had time to focus on matters in Cylla.

Sage didn't stop thinking of Sahir, even when she wasn't with her. I was being pulled into the realm of the mortals so often that I quickly realized how much was happening there that Yumi kept under the rug.

Thann was running an entire school where he was training mortals for various things. Fighting, magic, if I could think of it, there was a class. Helia was running a temple with the vampires, who were focused on blood magic. Sahir spent her time in Cylla as well. She had Aero, the God of Justice busy enough that he was hiring mortals to aid him in cleaning up her mess. Several times, Onyx was sent to give Yumi a report of these things, and every time, he came back with the same answer: she would look into it.

When the glint of his fangs was close enough to feel the heat of his breath, I lifted my dagger into the underside of his jaw and pushed until his mouth was held tightly shut. I used my other hand to slice my claymore through his neck. His body dropped, but his head was left stuck on my blade. I learned it was the only way to stop them. Headless or nothing.

I left my tent and entered the open camp. Dragons rested on the outskirts, snoozing without a care. Others filled the sky above us, restless and waiting for a reason to leave. Mortals from different realms joined the camp. Everywhere you looked was a different kind of face. They were equally restless. Ready to do what we needed to and get back home to their families or lives. I shared that sentiment. Kyrell was not any family to me. I wanted to get back to Merripen and Ru.

Today, we waited on old men with no connection to reality to discuss what they wanted in exchange for the lives of men and women that they didn't care about. When Yumi discussed the mortals with us, she left out the part where they were as corrupt as gods, with less power. It made them worse. They all felt they had to make up for the lack of magical power in other ways.

Kyrell told Koa and I that joining the mortals at their camp and watching them on the brink of war would help us. He said getting to see them like that would open our eyes to how things worked in the realm. He acted as if we weren't already used to taking orders that didn't make sense and having our freedom stripped because one man thought he had the right to do so.

Most of the hungriest ones never truly lifted a finger. Some took a passive approach and let whatever was to happen. Others considered blood their currency. They'd pay with as many lives as were needed. No power was enough power for some of them. No land big enough under their name to stop killing.

One thing I never lost count of was how many of the men who started conflicts never set foot in the fighting. In the end, both sides would be screaming to the tune of agony that their rulers would never feel. Just like them, we let our self-proclaimed leaders tell us it was what we really wanted in the end.

I entered the biggest tent, where only select men feasted. Koa's eyes met mine before he pushed his damp hair out of his face and took a deep breath. He did his best to pull together every dip of composure he could manage before making his way to me. Through bites of chicken legs and drinks of mushroom wine, the men talked about deals and demands. In true nature, it was only deals that would benefit themselves; never once had he heard an uttering of something that would help the people they called their own.

"Have they made any real progress yet?" I asked, leaning into Koa.

He shook his head.

"Have they officially decided what they're fighting about?" I asked.

He shook his head again.

"If we just took the head of one of them—only one—this would move along much faster," I whispered.

"No," Aero said.

"Yeah, yeah. In the name of justice and all of that. I'd keep it a secret from you if it helped. You'd never have to know it was me who did it." I said.

"I already know it would be you." Aero stared him down.

"So, we find another way?" Onyx asked.

The three of us nodded in agreement while Aero judged us with downturned lips. His idea of serving justice wasn't mine. I respected his ideals, and I loved him like a brother. If I was going to have to do it for an eternity, I wouldn't want to do it with any other group. However, although I disliked the mortals more than I found any I liked, I didn't want to be any different from them. I was beginning to realize the longer I lived around them, the more I wanted to take justice into my own hands, the way it should have always been, and pay with blood the same as they did.

We all silently turned and left the tent. Equally sick of hearing old men rage on about what they were owed or entitled to by their own accidental circumstances. On our exit, there were several more faces standing around than we had left behind.

Sahir was draped over the god of destruction's arms. If I didn't know her, maybe she could have looked like a love-sick girl, but I did know her, and the image brought nothing but disgust.

"I'm glad to see you here," I said.

"Caym, Have you changed your mind?" Sahir lulled.

"I did change my mind. I thought about it, and I decided that Yumi can't be in her right mind if she wants to continue to let you act the way you are without consequences." I shook my finger at her.

"I think Kyrell would have a different opinion." She smiled.

"Would you be scared if I told you that I didn't care?" I questioned.

"Would you be scared if I told you that you couldn't hurt me?" She mocked back.

"That's the thing, actually. I think I can. I seem to have a power you were scared of before. I was thinking if I used it on you, then no one would have to worry about their hearts." I said.

Her eyes widened, but she stayed silent.

"Do you want to explain what you're doing with them?" I asked.

"It's none of your business." She crossed her arms.

"This is me letting you know that I'm going to make it my business now," I said.

She snapped her fingers and opened the vines to Semper. She was going to talk to Yumi, no doubt.

"Follow her," I commanded one of the Nola.

"You know that Kyrell is going to hear about this," Koa warned.

"I know. This can't keep going on. I need to at least understand why Yumi is doing nothing about it." I said, "Can we agree to keep all of this quiet from Ru? She had enough on her plate, and it wasn't getting lighter when we left. I can only imagine how much she's holding up. We can handle it discreetly, yeah?"

Aero nodded in agreement. "Yumi is enough on her own, but with everything else going on." He shook his head. "She's been to the Timekeepers; then there's Deimos making his own moves; I don't know how she's holding on as it is. The less she needs to be involved in, the better for her."

"Excuse me?" I stood back on my feet, even though I had just sat down.

Every bit of color drained from Aero's face. Koa was the one to stand between us.

"She asked us not to worry about it, the same way you just asked us to spare her." He held his hands up in submission.

I didn't care. I didn't take in anything he said. I turned to shadow and entered the Chamber of Starlight. I stopped at the exit. The sight I was looking for was already in front of me.

He already had her pinned against the hallway wall. His disgusting hand was in her hair and then gliding across her cheek. Rage was boiling in my chest.

"I'd say I'm sorry for hurting you, but from the dreams you keep having of me, I'd say you don't hate it that much," Deimos whispered.

"I prefer to call them nightmares." Ruri was clearly stunned from hitting her head on the wall.

"If you're ready for them to become real, we have time here." He ran his nose through her hair.

"I'd rather sow the hole closed myself so I could never use it again than let you in." She was preparing magic in her fists.

The magic was sparking, but it was mine. Deimos was mine to handle.

I learned myself down to whisper in his ear, "I didn't consider you a fool. Looks like I was wrong."

I grabbed him by the hair and threw him onto his back on the stone flooring before I climbed on top of him.

"Which hand was it you just had on her face?" I asked.

He lifted his right hand and mockingly responded, "It's the one I plan on using to make her drip for me when you leave again."

I used the sun magic she gave me to form a golden glowing dagger; the heat from it could be felt all around us. It was a split second. So small it was hardly a heartbeat of time. I didn't look at him; I looked at her. I looked into her eyes when I sliced it through his flesh. I looked into her eyes when his hand hit the ground and when he screamed.

I only looked down at him when I shoved the blade into his open wrist to the hilt. "Would you like me to show you what an eternity with me in Merripen would look like?" he only answered me with a guttural howl. "Use your words," I demanded.

I was dissatisfied when he fainted. Ruri's hands were on my back, and I dissipated the blade before standing up. I put her face in my hands, checking her over for any signs of injury.

"Are you okay?" I asked.

She nodded, "You're glowing," she whispered.

I grabbed her hand and pulled her into the shadow with me and out of the other side. I sat her on the bed inside of our home in Merripen before I pulled a chair and placed it in front of her.

"This has to end," I said, sitting down. "You can not expect me to be okay with learning of something like this from someone else. How long has this been happening?"

She only looked down.

"Why do you keep doing this? What did I do to make it so that you don't trust me?" I lifted her chin until she looked me in the eyes.

"It's not that I don't trust you. It's that I know you'll do something like this." She said.

"What am I supposed to do instead? Be satisfied that you're pulling so far away from me that I hardly know what's going on with you. Do you want me to watch something like that and pretend it didn't happen? Would you want to be around me again if you saw me turn a blind eye? Do you want the hand as a gift? I'll go back and get it right now. I'll take the other for you, too." I said.

"Stop!" She pushed the hair away from her face and let out a breath. "I was dealing with it."

"Ru."

"You may have defended me this time, but you signed your future, too. What good is your defense if, in the end, I only have to worry about what you're going through because of it?" Her lips quivered.

"I'm going to change that," I said. "I'm tired of living this way. Kyrell can give me my freedom, or I'll take his head."

"Don't do anything more foolish than you already have." She stood and looked at me with displeasure.

I hadn't seen that kind of look from her before. Not directed at me. She took a piece of my heart with her when she left without another word. The thought of losing her made me sick. I didn't think it was possible, but every time she walked away from me, I felt us inch closer. It made me doubt myself and my actions.

I knew neither of us could keep going. There would be no part of us left to live in Cylla. I had to do what she wasn't, for her sake. If she used her freedom without me, at least she would still be free.

The Nola I sent to watch Sahir came back. He rolled his eyes to show me what he had seen.

It was Sahir standing with Yumi inside of her room.

"I have given you so much grace, daughter, but now you abuse it," Yumi yelled.

"That guardian bullies me, and you yell at me for it, not him!" Sahir yelled back.

"If you were so obsessed with bringing him back, that guardian wouldn't be bullying you!" Yumi screamed.

"Even if you don't, I miss Daddy!" Sahir matched her volume.

"He doesn't miss you!" Yumi was in Sahir's face.

"That's hurtful mommy." Sahir sat herself on Yumi's bed.

The Nola stopped the images. I was glad to still be sitting in my chair.

Suddenly, so much made sense. The lies went deeper than I understood. We were all so separated, so unwilling to share what we knew, that something like that, something so clear, passed us by.

We would never get ahead of them because they were making sure of it. Sahir would never be stopped because her mother had the ultimate say in the end.

CHAPTER TWENTY

SO MUCH FOR A SECRET ORDER

The Teachings of Moonlight

I planned for balance. I planned for peace in life. In the world. I planned to make sure that if my sister ever unsealed herself, she would still have to face something stronger than her abominations. My daughters would share the power of the universe. I would pass on all that I was to them. They would be the sisters of fate, and through them, all things would have to pass. Creation would reside with one daughter, and she would harness elemental magic. She would bless the universe with the seed. She would be paired with death as her guardian.

CAYM

I was called to the Chamber of Starlight, but I did not have the patience to wait for Yumi or Kyrell to show up before I left. I had waited long enough. I didn't have a single fiber of my being that cared what their opinion was, either. If Deimos wanted to keep his hand, he should have kept it off of my girl. If he touched her with the other one, I'd take it, too. Kyrell would hear the same thing from me. He was lucky; it was all I took.

My blood was boiling again at the thought of it.

I didn't know exactly what the glow on my skin was, but I knew anytime I felt her panic, it glowed. If I felt her too scared or having a nightmare, it glowed. I didn't know if she could feel me the same way I felt her, but I always felt her. Even thinking too hard on yesterday's events, my skin glowed again.

It seemed like she didn't know it, but I felt her joy as if it were my own, her sorrow as if it were my own. I knew she was trying to carry more weight than her shoulders should have had to lift. She just wouldn't talk to me. She wasn't letting me in anymore like she had. At the start of our year together, she gave me every thought that came to her head. She told me about every event she witnessed.

Over time, she just started talking less and less out loud. She had to have forgotten that she was the only thing that mattered to me. I spent more time sitting with her while she was zoned out and clearly somewhere else in her mind than anything else.

Even with her body thrown over my shoulder while I marched us both back to the camp so that I could keep an eye on her, she wasn't struggling. She was just accepting and following anything that happened in front of her. She didn't see what I saw.

She wasn't seeing how tired she looked. How even when

she smiled, it never met her eyes anymore. I felt like I was playing a game with her. One, she thought she was winning while I was dying inside.

I didn't know how to help her, and it seemed anytime I tried, it caused her more pain. If the answer to her problems was cutting off Yumi's hand, too. I'd turn around and do it right. She didn't even need to say the words out loud. I'd understand a nod, a blink from her.

I threw open the cloth to my tent before putting her back on her own feet in front of me.

"You know I can't be here, and everyone just saw it." She said.

"Who's going to stop me?" I asked.

"Do I really need to start listing everyone who is waiting for a chance?" She mocked me.

"Yes. I'll call it my hit list and start as soon as your breath stops. Name them." I said.

She shook her head at me and sat on the edge of my bed without a word.

"I can't protect you if you're there and I'm here. Since you refuse to talk to me, here you will stay." I said.

"I was doing just fine!" She yelled.

"Were you?" I asked.

"You need more protection right now than I do!" She was refusing to make eye contact with me. "Kyrell is going to have your hand, too! You should have just let me leave."

"Stop." I lowered myself to my knees in front of her so our faces were level. "Why are you trying so hard to shut me down? You don't even want to discuss a single bit of what just happened?"

The only sound she made was the sound of her breath while her eyes moved back and forth between my own.

"Talk to me," I whispered.

She whispered in response, "I can't."

I didn't know what piece to move next. To push her or to

tell her that what she was trying to do, the way she was trying to do it all alone, was clearly breaking her. Maybe I should stick to the plan I made and let her be so that I could handle it on my own, for her. I didn't want us to be like that. Moving around each other in secret instead of trusting that we could do it all together.

"Tell me what to do?" I said.

She only shook her head and stood up to move past me.

"I'm glad to see you, actually. I made you a gift." She said, rummaging through her inner skirt.

"How long has Deimos been harassing you like that? Has it gone further?" I asked, standing too.

She loudly cleared her throat, "Ah. Here." She held up a pair of gloves. "It took me longer than I had hoped it would. They'll allow you to do anything you want without harm."

I took them from her and tossed them to the oak bedside table beside us. "Does anyone know? Astra, Yumi?"

"Is Onyx here? I made Sage a mirror of sight. It's best someone else gives it to her, though." She said before she sat it on the table with the gloves. "No one needs to tell her that it's from me. Just see that she gets it."

"Ru," I said again. "If you don't give me an answer, I'm leaving to go kill him now. I won't hurt him and leave. I won't claim another small trophy. I will kill him and give him his own personal prison. I will assign a Nola to look after him so that he never knows a moment's rest." I lifted her face until she had no choice but to look at me while I spoke. "I'm asking you one last time."

"I will make sure it's dealt with." She said.

Defeat was the only word fitting enough to describe the moment we were in. She was hard as a rock, and I didn't think I could crack it with a pickaxe.

"Caym!" Aero called, rushing through the tent. "Kyrell is marching here in a rage. What did you do?!"

Koa and Onyx came crashing in after him.

"Why is she here? It's not even dark. I thought we agreed that if we were going to sneak anyone in, it would be at night?" Koa spoke with dissatisfaction.

"Hide her." I pointed.

The three of them looked at each other as if they didn't have a single brain cell to share with each other. It didn't matter; it was too late for me to help. Kyrell was pushing the tent open with action in his movements. Koa pushed Ruri backward onto the bed, and Aero helped give her a second push until she had fallen off the back and was wedged between the wall and the bed. The three of them threw themselves on the bed, coughing in unison with an obnoxious volume.

Onyx pretended to show Koa his nails, and Aero pretended to flip through a book laid on his stomach across my pillows.

Kyrell stopped at the doorway, uncomfortable with what he was seeing.

"What are the four of you doing in here?" His tone was angered, as usual.

"Where else should we be?" I asked.

"Learning anything at all from the mortals!" Kyrell pointed outside.

The sigh I let out was larger than any before. It was all maddening.

"If you and the self-proclaimed rulers of Semper didn't decide to cut our powers down so far while we were in the mortal realm, this wouldn't be an issue, would it?" I retorted. "We could actually solve any problem the mortals had quickly, and we could do it simply because we are Gods."

"You know why we did it. Could you image Sahir in Cylla, unchecked?" Kyrell asked.

"I can, actually. That's the way that things are! If you know she is enough of a problem to need restrictions, why not do something about her?" I asked.

"It's none of our business. That's why. Pay attention to what tasks fall under your position. I don't want to argue about her. I want to know what you think you were doing in Semper?" Kyrell yelled.

"In Semper? Is there something we don't know?" Koa asked.

That was an understatement.

"I thought he had come to talk about the incident in Ashbell," Aero said.

"Incident?" I asked.

"You didn't tell him yet?" Aero looked around, confused.

"We agreed to wait until we were done here," Onyx said.

"We thought it best you focus on one thing at a time," Koa said.

"What, incident." My teeth ground against each other when I spoke.

"You need to answer me first, boy," Kyrell interjected himself.

"I did what needed to be done, Kyrell, and I'll tell you just like I told him, I'll do it again." I couldn't stop the way my teeth ground together.

"We will see about that." Kyrell narrowed his eyes before he left the tent.

I grabbed Ruri and pulled her up from the side of the bed and onto her feet. Tears filled her eyes for the first time in a long time.

"The home in Ashbell was burnt down," Aero said. "We just didn't want you to act rashly,"

"Anything else?" I was enraged again.

"A lot more than you want to know," Aero mumbled.

In unison, voices yelled at him to stop speaking.

"You lied to me, Ruri. We promised we wouldn't do that to each other, and here you are doing it over and over." My voice cracked in a way I hadn't expected from myself.

"We knew you'd act rashly; I just thought it best to wait until there was less going on." She answered.

"There's always something going on around here!" I scoffed with disbelief.

"You lied to me, too." She called. "You've been asking Jeb to tell you what I've been doing. I've heard about your plans to kill Sahir. So, if we're pointing things out, then why don't we talk about what's going on with you, too?"

"There's nothing going on with me. I'm picking my side." I answered.

"What side is that? Following in Sahir's footsteps?" Her voice was filled with venom.

My mouth was suddenly too dry for comfort. "That comparison is not fair. I love you, Ru, but I can't watch you kill yourself for them. I've tried to respect your choices as much as I can, but how long do you plan to be a puppet?"

"So, you'll keep acting out, even if the price is me?" she asked.

I knew what my answer was. I knew, beyond a doubt, where my lines lay. I knew I did not and would not regret them. Having to give such an answer out loud while she looked at me the way she was, that was pain. Having to push her away or respect a choice that was wrong for the sake of maintaining peace wasn't where I expected us to be.

"Even if the price is protecting you from a distance while you hate me for it. Yes, Ru, I'll pay it. I will keep paying until you feel like you can trust me to be at your side instead of lying to me." I choked out.

She was biting the inside of her cheek, and I could see it. Tears formed in her eyes. I heard the crack in her voice when she tried to speak and had to stop and finish choking back her cries. The oil lamps in my tent did a good job of showing me every negative emotion that ran through her face.

"Maybe we should reconsider our future." She said.

Her feet carried her around me and out of the room in

haste. She could have taken her time; I had no words for her. There was nothing for me to say in response. I would always agree with what she wanted, and she knew it. She was right. Maybe we did need space so I could do what needed to be done. Even if I was shattering at the thought of not being next to her, she needed help; she was screaming for it and refusing to move her lips and simply ask for it.

"Is there anything else I should know?" I asked the men still in the room.

"She keeps a lot close to her chest. If the fire didn't have so many witnesses, I don't think we would know about it, either." Koa said.

"She went to the Timekeepers twice," Onyx said.

I shot myself through shadow and mist to the island of the Timekeepers. I didn't bring anyone, and I didn't walk slowly. If Ruri wouldn't give me the answers to what was going on with her, they would.

I slammed the door of the library built into the mountain-side open.

"Who's in charge here?" I called. I kept my hand on my claymore.

"I never expected an entrance like this to happen once, so the fact that it's happening twice makes me think we need guards." The man in the golden robe lowered his hood and put his hands up. "My name is Lui, and I promise we will help you without this kind of show. Come, sit."

I wasn't expecting to go so easily. I took a seat across from him, brows furrowed, but he started speaking before I could.

"We are the order of the Sun and Moon. We collect the true answers to history and creation. Following along? Yes, we can answer many things, but a bad lady put a bad curse on tongues, so we can only say so many things. It's not to offend you. It's against our will and out of our control. Even if you take our head, it won't change that. We want to help; we like to help. We don't need force or violence. In fact, it's against our rules. Understand?" He paused

I nodded. I was unsure how to respond to him.

"You see those markings? They mean you're a guardian. You're connected to a sister of fate. You protect her or else. No, I can not tell you more than that." Lui stopped to take a drink from his cup before he started again. "Your sister of fate already sent word that she would like us to start organizing an army on our side. The angels were the first to respond. They want to help. Is there anything else?"

There was another lie from her.

"What's next, then?" I asked.

"I thought you were here to tell me that?" Lui looked puzzled.

"How do I kill a god? So that they can not come back?" I asked.

"Their heart. It has to be the entire thing. It's important that you remember that." He stressed.

"Are guardians strong enough to do it?" I asked.

"Of course. All four of you are stronger together, though." He said.

"Four?" I sighed. "There are not four of us."

"Well, there's four of you and a fake." Lui tilted his head back and forth. "No, I can't say anything else."

"Thanks, Lui. You've been a lot of help." I said with a sigh.

CHAPTER TWENTY-ONE

THE NIGHT THE MOUNTAIN FELL

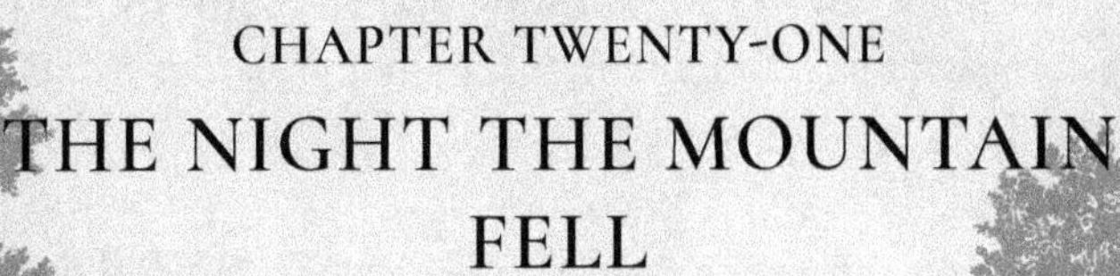

The Teachings of Moonlight

My second daughter would hold the water of life. Through her, all life would grow. She would bless the world with nature magic, and all creatures would be connected to her. She would be paired with pestilence as her guardian.

SAGE

Ruri and I walked the halls with enough space between us that it felt as if we were strangers and not sisters. Sometimes, I thought back to when we spent our days with a small group living in Semper, and we had the freedom to run all over our floating island and never meet anyone. It seemed like another lifetime ago, but it hadn't even been a full year since everyone had been together.

"Have you found out anything new?" I asked, trying to cut the silence.

"No," Ruri answered.

Her tone was as short as her words, and I felt the space between us widen further. She was always so set in her thoughts that it was nearly impossible to change them. She was black and white, right and wrong, with no room in between. Sahir was irredeemable in her eyes, and because I spent so long by her side, so was I. The silence between us didn't change how well I knew her.

"Have you got other things to do today?" I tried a second time.

"I have to go to Cylla and help plant the dragon flower seeds." She answered.

"How many will there be? When they hatch, I mean." I asked.

"As long as things go according to plan, they will hatch once a year." She said.

Once in a while, I thought it would make things between us better if we sat down and talked about what I knew and what she knew, but then I knew she would only get upset because I hid things. I failed to help Sahir, but if I could put all the pieces of Semper together, it would make things better.

We could start new when I could present her with the answer to all the secrets of Semper.

We were sent a request to meet Minna and Orla today. I had to beg Ruri to come with me. She proclaimed to have no interest in anything the Goddess of Fate had to say on any subject. That if it involved Minna, then it didn't need to involve her.

She only relented for my sake. It gave me hope we didn't have to remain in the rut we were in. It fed my need to do something to prove myself to her. To be worth forgiving in her eyes.

When we were at the threshold of our meeting place, Ruri hesitated. She flinched at the idea of stepping a single foot further. I lifted my hand to her back and shoved her into the library.

The clothes on her back were uncomfortably lumpy. It was as if she had thick pieces of cloth under her dress. I don't know how she could have been comfortable dressed like that, but I succeeded in getting her inside.

She didn't look at me or offer thanks for the helping hand. She only sat on a white padded chair across from Orla, still sulking. A table sat between the chairs decorated with clear heated glass. The rainbows it gave were stunning but less stunning than the stained-glass windows that covered every panel of the room. The windows told the story of our creation.

Yumi, a giant glowing star, was the beginning of everything. Her dreams of us grew so intense that the tree of Life grew, and so we became real. It's a story not just written in the windows but in so many books in our library, too. The Teachings of Starlight are the first things we are all taught at creation. We read it until we've memorized it.

I was happy to see Minna enter the room. I was sick of the silence. Minna sat beside Ruri and smoothed out her white velvet dress. The lace pattern looked awful bunched up.

"Hello, ladies," Minna smirked.

"Get to it," Ruri demanded.

"Don't worry. I already presumed you would be in this kind of mood. That's why I decided that now was the time to chat. I heard through the vine that you and Caym are over. You can imagine news like that would spread quickly. Kyrell is overjoyed by it." Minna put one leg over the other and leaned back into her chair.

"I'm sure. If you only came to gossip, I'll go." Ruri glared.

"Ruri, you--" She shot daggers at me with her glare.

"It's fine. I take no offense, Sage. These things are hard. I thought on it, and it seems if you and Caym are over, then you'd have no attachments left to many things or deities. I thought you may need someone on your side. I thought maybe we could form an alliance." Minna waved her lashes in our direction.

"I'd rather pick off each one of my toenails myself than do one single thing hand in hand with you, Minna," Ruri spoke, but she never looked up from her own dress.

"You truly do have quite the attitude when Yumi isn't around. We all saw your creation going a lot differently, you know." Minna sighed. "Let me sweeten the deal, then."

"What do you need an alliance for?" Ruri interrupted her.

"When you've decided what side everyone is on, we can talk about it. I will offer you a slice of information in exchange for trust." Minna said. "Neither of you are Orla's daughters. You aren't even Yumi's daughter. You're so far from being her daughter that the only thing she holds for you is hatred. Think about the alliance, and if the curiosity is enough to convince you we could be a good team, come find me."

Minna stood and met me with a smile on her way out. I was already convinced before she gave me the information; I was eager and curious. Ruri looked less than convinced.

"What do you think she means?" I asked.

Ruri only kept her stare on Orla, "I don't know. Why don't you explain it, Orla."

Ruri's voice told me that she already knew something more than she had shared. As if that were far from a surprise to her.

"I'm unsure what kind of response would make you happy. Who else would you belong to? I admit that before you were born, I had a dream that showed me how to create you. A woman's voice came to me and told me if I made you both from pure intentions and a piece of myself, you would be good and just that the two of you would fix a realm that was broken into pieces. She whispered to me that the pieces needed to be put back together, and you two were the first move to play. I've never doubted for a second that the two of you are stronger than you think and even stronger together." Orla said.

"Everyone here enjoys talking out of their asses, don't they? We aren't your daughters." Ruri rolled her eyes.

"I guess it's better than lying all of the time or hurting the ones I say I love," I remarked. "Orla has never been anything but a mother to me."

When Ruri's eyes met Orla's, my stomach sank. I didn't know why I did it other than the jealousy that was forming inside of me. The distress that was growing in my chest listening to another deity talk so highly of her made me start throwing out things to make her look bad, just hoping something would stick and alter the subject.

"You have no right to be in my business. Maybe if you were helping with anything at all, instead of shoving your nose up everyone's rear end so they'll tell you something nice, I wouldn't need to do both our jobs." Ruri was in my face by the time she was done speaking.

She hit the arms of my chair with both of her hands before she stormed out of the room. The pounding of her feet matched my chest.

"Why do you always insist on these things?" Orla sighed, rubbing the bridge of her nose.

I could only look down and count the lines on the marble floor. I didn't know how to answer her because nothing I gave her would be right to say out loud. I was awful and jealous. I was incapable of being as good as Ruri.

Orla stood and laid her hand on mine. "Come with me to Erebus. Spend a little time with me."

I gave in, weak to her pleas, and followed her. Without the giant shadow of Ruri around, I felt more comfortable talking to Orla.

"Do you think what Minna said is true?" I asked.

Orla's hands rested inside of her sleeves, and she watched her feet while we stepped through the vines to Cylla.

"It could be true that she wants the two of you on her side because she knows, like the rest of us know, what the two of you could do if you were together. If she heals the two of you, and you're in debt to her. It would be the biggest benefit she could have. It could also be true there are many deities trying to make sure you stay separated and at each other's throats. What I know for a fact is that you and your sister came from a piece of my heart and a piece of my soul, and no matter what supreme being claims you. you both will always be a part of me." She answered.

We agreed on that. No matter what turned out to be a fact, Orla was the only mother I knew, and I loved her regardless.

It was more likely to me that Ruri and I were just incompatible than others were conspiring to keep us apart. She didn't need me to be great. She was the center of Yumi's attention all the same. A place I could never be.

Owna and Usha greeted us on arrival at the cave mouth. They had already been waiting for us. She guided us to a hall bigger than anything I had imagined could fit inside of a cave. The cave rocks were so high up that I couldn't begin to consider how they did it. They were covered in chandleries of clear quartz and lit by some kind of magic I hadn't seen before. A table of the same quartz, as thick as it was long, sat in the middle of the room. The contrast of the dark rock and the clear, shimmering decorations was breathtaking.

I took a seat beside Orla, who sat at the head of the table. Erebus didn't run on a royalty system. Orla led, and everyone openly expressed their opinions to her. She took them all equally.

"We have successfully signed a treaty with Ashbell. We will trade healing pots and salves for mushroom wine and protection crystals." Owna said.

"We have also entered into terms with Midori. They will give us grain and meats monthly in exchange for weapons." A dwarf I did not know spoke.

"You were right that they would accept our trade offers,

Miss Orla." Owna said, "We have so much coin between wine and weapons from Onyx's shop that we've run out of ideas on where to put it."

"If I may, I'd like to invest some into the tavern at Edur. We do visit it often, and Investing in the growth of other kingdoms would help us form long-term alliances." Orla said. "I'd also like to donate to the temples placed around the land."

A sound so loud that I thought my ears would bust cried out in the background of the talks. Every single attendant at the table stood and took off in a sprint. Orla stood and grabbed me by the arm, pulling me with them.

"What is that," I screamed.

"It's the horn of the abyss," Orla spoke as if I was supposed to know what that meant.

We were stopped at the exit, only a step or two outside of it, by spiders so big we could slide underneath them. They were hissing, and green was oozing from their mouths. Dwarves had axes and claymores in their hands, but the liquid the spiders were spraying melted the blades without mercy.

Orla didn't hesitate like I did. She acted as if she had seen not just what happened but worse. For a moment, while she was pulling me with unwavering eyes of steel, I thought she must have had a whole life I didn't know about.

"Go!" she yelled, propelling my body ahead of hers.

I knew what she wanted, but I watched her. I watched her while she grabbed a bow and used it as if it were a part of her. I watched the quiet woman I had known my entire life shoot one, then two, then three of them in the head. Not a single shot missed its mark. She was astonishing.

What did she do while I was not with her? How did she develop such a skill? The rest of us just failed constantly. I couldn't think of a single thing the rest of us tried to do that went half as smoothly as her arrows flew to their aimed mark.

My thoughts shifted back to Sahir when she told me that she had plans to give birth to spiders.

I was so transfixed that my mouth grew dry, and I didn't notice the spider charging for me until it had used its fur-covered leg to slam me into a rock. I hit my head before I hit the ground and hit my back.

Ringing filled my ears, and grey filled my vision. I only had time for a split-second thought that I stood where I would die before my vision came slowly into view, just enough for me to make out Sahir driving her blade into one of the dwarves from the meeting. Her feet were surrounded by dead Vinna.

I wanted to get to my feet, but it was not going to happen yet. My back screamed, and my head ached. There was no ease in the spider's intentions. It had to have been convinced I was dead, just like I was convinced that I was dying because it left me behind.

My vision was the only thing in stable shape. Orla raised her bow again and shot her arrow right into Sahir's calf.

My first instinct was to get up and help her. Even while Sahir was holding a blade in the chest of a dwarf, her cry of pain made me scramble to my feet. It did not work. I was hardly able to sit up, let alone get to my feet to help her. A spider created cover for her long enough for her to break the arrow in half and try to make an escape.

She didn't need my help. She didn't notice I was there. If she had, she had no desire to help me like I cared to help her.

"Let's go," Onyx said, pulling me to my feet.

"What are you doing here?" I groaned.

He pulled me up without concern for what injuries could have been there.

"I was gathering information. My dragon and I witnessed the commotion and thought it was in our best interest to help. My shop is here, after all." He said.

"For a moment, I thought you were here for me," I remarked.

Onyx shook his head. "Kaida wanted to eat. He already got the top cleared."

He had pride in his voice when he spoke of his dragon.

"Your timing makes you look like you're spying on me," I said.

I was a fool. A fool desperate for anyone to say that they came only for me. That they did anything only for me.

His smirk grew slowly in front of my eyes. "Would you like me to stalk you, Sage?"

I felt conflicted about how to respond to him. The words I wanted to call out would only make me sound as desperate as I felt. He saved me from having to stutter anything out like a fool when he grabbed my arm and moved me behind him to guide me out.

He was equally as impressive as Orla with the way he wielded his blade. It was too big for me to consider lifting, and yet he threw it around as if it were air.

Watching the two of them made me feel smaller than I did on an average day, and I didn't know that was possible.

On the surface, it was still just as loud. Crys and screams were echoing from all around. There was no sign of Sahir, but I did see the dwarf on her knees with a blanket cuddled to her chest. Footsteps hastened around me as teams of two carried Dwarves from inside to lay in rows on one corner of the caves while slower-moving dwarfs laid the quiet ones on another side.

Onyx didn't relent in his speed. He was pulling me as if he were trying to keep me from seeing anything going on around us.

Orla had her arms around me before I knew she was there. Her bow was pressed between us, and she had her hands in my hair, kissing the side of my face.

"Thank Starlight, you're okay." She cried.

"I'm alright," I said. "I was never truly in danger."

I tried my best to comfort her, but she pulled back and looked at me with a face I didn't know how to interpret.

"Don't worry about me, really. There's more going on." I urged.

A spark of joy filled me with the attention falling on me.

She grabbed my hand for a moment before she turned and left me. When I looked to my side, Onyx was looking at me with the same eyes. Somewhere between shock and disappointment, maybe?

"Why are you both looking at me like that?" I asked.

"Do you understand what just happened here?" He asked.

I nodded. "Spiders attacked."

"Wrong. An angry goddess sent an attack on your home in Cylla. She sent an attack to tear down everything you and your mother built and aimed to have you and her dead, too." He said.

"Sahir wouldn't actually hurt me." I was shaking my head too many times and started to make myself dizzy. "You don't understand her. She likes to stir some pots, but she wouldn't ever truly hurt anyone."

"Sage. She has done more than hurt. She has killed. She has killed deities, and she killed that dwarf's baby." He pointed in one direction, "That dwarf just lost his entire family, and that one is home. You're mother almost lost you, and she did lose members of her lands that she cared about. Wake up."

He left me behind and didn't hesitate to start helping with the efforts happening in front of me, but my world crumbled around me.

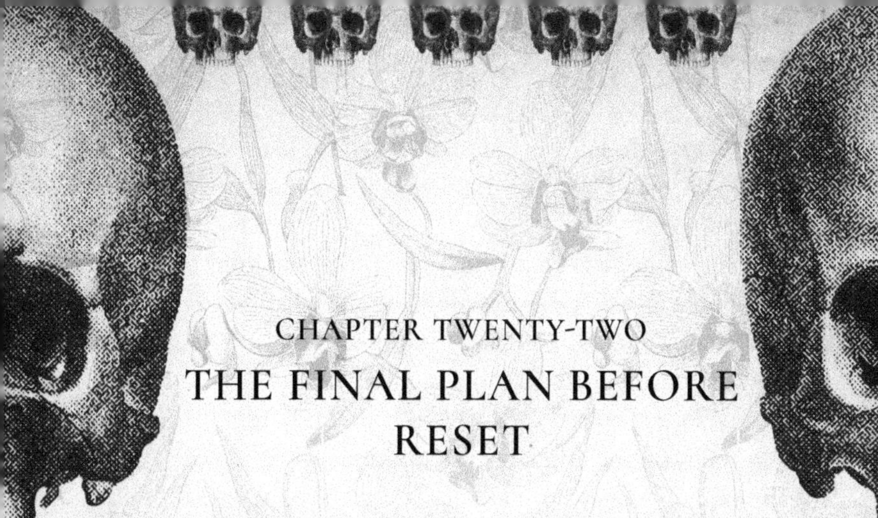

CHAPTER TWENTY-TWO

THE FINAL PLAN BEFORE RESET

The Teachings of Moonlight
My third daughter was to be the clock.
She was to be the keeper of lifetimes. It
would be in her hands to decide how long something lingered in the land of the living. She
would be blessed with blood magic and her
guardian was to be war.

CAYM

I tapped my foot against the ground, and my leg shook; I was eager to move things along. I was anxious to start what preparations we may need. Koa entered first. We would use my castle for the first real time since I built it. I never felt right residing inside of it.

It wasn't right to consider myself the ruler of Merripen, the only leader, when I knew that I'd step aside and allow Kyrell to enter and tumble it down the way he did. That wasn't behavior a ruler presented.

The only thing that kept me grounded. That stood between me and cleaning up Semper, no longer sat by my side.

My role changed. I was to be her protector from far away. It meant that it was time for me to use the skills Koa helped me develop. Someone was false. Someone was lying. Someone was helping Yumi and didn't belong in our circle.

I pulled the gloves that Ruri left for me off, finger by finger, and sat them on the table in front of me.

Onyx and Aero entered next, side by side. They sat beside Koa. My weakness was going to be Koa. I would never suspect him of anything. I was ashamed to admit that he could tell me to my face he was the traitor, and I would try my best to convince him to change sides.

Vespera came in last, and it caught my attention the most. She was not someone often in our circle. We exchanged greetings at gatherings, but she never bonded with the group of us.

"I heard from the Timekeepers that you had been to see them. That led me to hear about a meeting here. I want to help." Vespera said.

"Help what, specifically," I asked.

She looked between us all and pulled out a chair. Her voice was confident. She didn't act as if we hardly knew each other.

"I want to help kill them." She sat down. "Sage is my friend. I admire Ruri. I think she and I could be friends too, one day. I'm tired of being kept in the dark, too. The events in Semper don't only affect your small group. They affect all of us in one way or another."

"Kill who?" Aero's face scrunched with disapproval.

"Yumi, Sahir, Deimos. Kyrell. Point me in a direction. It's all the same to me." She said.

"Is this why you called us here?" Onyx asked.

I called them to meet so that I could get an idea of who was willing to go how far because the one who resisted had to be the traitor. I knew the other Guardians had to be in the room. Koa, Aero, Onyx, and I made four. My hope was that by the end of the meeting, I could confirm that we were all guardians and that the traitor was still outside of us.

"I called everyone here because I want to move forward with my plan. Things have to change, and I'm confident that we can make it happen together. I think that with how hard we've trained and with everything Kyrell has unknowingly taught us, we can remove the deities that need to be removed." I said.

Silence filled the room.

Was I wrong? Were they not going to end up being guardians? Lui said that I would know because they would feel an intense need to be close to the girls to protect them.

"I'm in," Koa said.

"It's been too long since justice was last in Semper." Aero agreed.

"My forge is always open for use. Count me in." Onyx said.

"If we don't succeed, you understand we are likely to lose our lives?" I asked.

All heads nodded.

"It can't be worse than being under Yumi's thumb," Vespera said.

"What is the plan then?" Onyx asked.

I found myself suddenly hesitant to share. I opened my mouth to speak, but my mind told me that if I gave too much to the wrong one, it was Ruri who would pay the price for my carelessness.

Was that what Koa counted on? The idea that I was careless for him?

Is that why Onyx wanted me to lay it all out for him? So he could report back?

How did Vespera hear of the meeting? A spy in the Time-keepers?

"Caym?" Aero asked. "Are you all right?"

"Yes." I shook my head.

These were my friends. They were on my side. The traitor had to be outside of us. They had to be.

"My plan is to start with Deimos. Then move to Sahir." I said. "When they are out of the way, I plan to kill Yumi."

"What do you need from us?" Koa asked.

"The angels that guard Yumi have asked to join us. They say her treatment of them is unspeakable. I intend to use them to help us. They can restrain Yumi without raising suspicion, which will make things safer for us in the end." I said.

"The angels? Her personal guards have turned against her?" Vespera looked shocked.

"I don't find it that shocking," Aero said.

"They put on such a good show. I never would have guessed." She said.

"It's why the plan won't fail on their end," I said.

"You're going to kill Deimos. The angels will capture Yumi. What of the rest of us?" Onyx asked.

"Sahir has been eating hearts. I've sent the Nola to look into it, and I met with." I paused. I did not want to risk the Timekeeper's entire order. "Some who had information about the effects. She's going to be stronger than we are. She's been absorbing power from the hearts. It will take more than just one of us. The rest of you should focus on her."

"Sage is never going to forgive us," Aero said.

"I don't foresee Ruri forgiving you, either," Deimos said as he entered the room.

All of us stood from our seats, but only a few of us were armed.

"My ears started ringing, and I thought to myself, who is it that would be filling their day with thoughts of me? I knew it had to be you." He said. He took a seat at the other end of the table.

"I'll only warn you once," I demanded.

"Calm down. Let's chit-chat for a minute. I think you owe me that." He said, lifting his stump and waving it.

Onyx tossed me his oversized claymore, and I caught it.

"You can't spare me two minutes?" Deimos gave a disappointed click of his tongue. "You'll want to hear it."

"Hurry up," Aero growled.

"I had a Nola in my realm just a bit ago. He was snooping around and looking for information on a missing girl. It was amusing to know that it was Ruri who sent the Nola, but she didn't tell anyone else." He sighed; he was in no rush to say what he needed to say. "Do you know what I've been doing with my time? I've been working on nightmares and how I can better use them. It's been going so well that even I had a hard time believing it. I managed to convince Koa that his sister was off living a peaceful life. He hardly even remembers who she is. I was able to have an entire relationship with Ruri in her dreams. The possibilities have been endless." He got back to his feet and pushed the chair back in. "I came today to give Koa his sister back and to show you what nightmares are like."

Deimos used his finger to open a portal into his realm, and a girl emerged. Her clothes were torn, and her skin was dirty. She looked as if she hadn't seen light in ages. She was so frail that it was impressive that she could walk. Koa moved to her, and I reached to grab him, but I was too slow.

The girl held a crystal from the caves in each hand.

"Nesrin?" Koa moved himself to her at a faster pace,

"You shameful disappointment of a brother. This is where you've been? While I've been locked away and used as an experiment, you were living a life of luxury in a castle?" Her voice scratched and cut out as if she hadn't drunk water in just as long as she was in darkness.

Koa didn't stop until both hands were on her shoulders. "You told me that you've been in Sephtis. That you didn't want me there."

She resisted his touch with what little strength she had.

"I've never set foot in Sephtis. I was taken the moment we were created, and I've done things you couldn't imagine for a hint at freedom. I only did it for you." Her pleas turned to laughter. "I did it all for you because I could not believe it when Deimos told me you had forgotten me. While he tortured me, I clung to a falsehood of you. I held on to the idea that you'd come for me. That you'd save me. That you were searching for me, and I only had to hold on a little longer!"

Deimos wore a smile from ear to ear.

"You're going to die. You and your friend, but before you do, he promised me that I could have my revenge. My justice. You'll spend what little time you have left cursed to change into the creature that haunted my nightmares every night." She took the crystal in her left hand and shoved it down Koa's throat. She took the one in her right hand and chanted a few words into it before shattering it on the ground.

None of us could move fast enough to stop it before it was too late.

Koa was on his knees, choking blood and screaming around a crystal shard that glowed orange. His screams of pain turned into echoes of fear as he shifted into a wolf in front of us.

Deimos reached his hand up and cut another slice into the sky. Creatures with shredded wings and bodies of fire rushed through and into Merripen. Vespera was all right fighting them.

Deimos tossed the girl back into the portal and walked through after her.

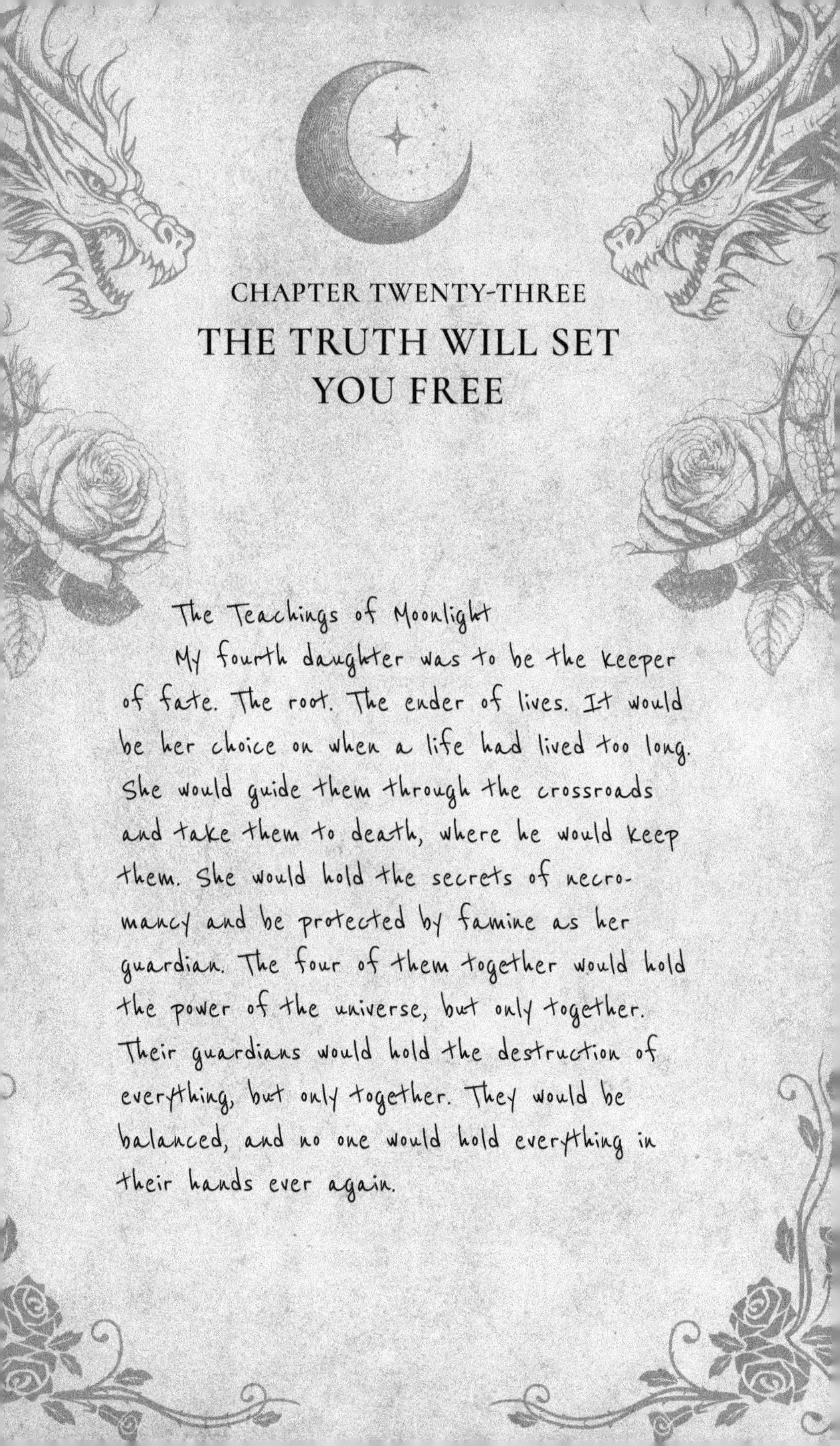

CHAPTER TWENTY-THREE

THE TRUTH WILL SET YOU FREE

The Teachings of Moonlight

My fourth daughter was to be the keeper of fate. The root. The ender of lives. It would be her choice on when a life had lived too long. She would guide them through the crossroads and take them to death, where he would keep them. She would hold the secrets of necromancy and be protected by famine as her guardian. The four of them together would hold the power of the universe, but only together. Their guardians would hold the destruction of everything, but only together. They would be balanced, and no one would hold everything in their hands ever again.

RURI

I leaned my back against the tree. I wished she could have told me her name. She was talking to me less and less the closer my death got to becoming a reality. I didn't think it was because she didn't want to talk to me, but because she couldn't.

At least, I had to believe that was true.

If I was putting the puzzle together correctly, the tree was connected to me.

The silence that was filling in was making me uncomfortable. No more dragons hatched with old souls, only new ones. The Timekeepers had nothing else that they could share with me. I was at the end of what I could do.

I prepared a safe space in Cylla. An entire land that no one would be able to enter after my death. The caves of Erebus were overflowing with crystals for magic. I was going to Ashbel soon to leave them with what I could.

There was one last thing that I had not done, and it was to read the journal Caym gave me when I showed him our home in Ashbel. I hadn't seen it since our home was burnt away.

Part of me did not want to read the journal still, but it was all I had left of him. I couldn't seek him out for comfort and allow him to think we could find our way back to the old days when I knew I only had a sliver of time left.

When I opened the pages, his smell hit me.

Entry-

I wanted to tell her how beautiful she was, but I knew she had to be growing tired of hearing it. I wanted to tell her I loved her, but I knew she would grow tired of hearing it, too. I wanted to tell her how much she glowed when she was helping in Merripen. How cute she was sneaking around Semper to find a way in to see me. I wanted to tell her how she was the best thing ever created, but all of those words felt too simple. They were all too plain for her. She was worth more than any single thing I could think of to give her. I wanted to follow her on every adventure she wanted to go on, and she had planned many. I spent hours trying to find a way to tell her that without her, my heart wouldn't beat. That she was the moon, the stars, the air. I couldn't find a way to express to her that I felt worthy of her explaining that I loved her mind and the way it worked just as much. The way she viewed life, and friendships, and love. It was all a part of her glow. Jeb was helping me find something that could be a worthy gift. We went through flowers and animals; we dug deep into caves. We watched weddings between mortals to try and learn common gifts, but none of them felt like enough.

I closed his journal and sat it beside the tree. I didn't have the strength to keep going. It was already too much for me to try and read it clearly through the tears pouring down my cheeks. I would miss him.

I already missed having him next to me.

Astra sat down beside me, throwing her legs out. She was always in trousers these days. I hadn't noticed she was in the garden at all. Her lips drooped, and she played with her fingernails. She picked at things not even visible.

"I heard what happened." She said.

It was the last string holding back my river. I sobbed like I hadn't in a long time. I leaned on her shoulder and let myself cry until it was pouring from my nose as well. I hadn't allowed myself to truly break. I forgot how good it felt just to let it go. She didn't move me; she only held my hand until I felt like I was done.

She pulled a cloth tissue from the top under her vest and held it in front of my face. I laughed only because she was prepared even when she didn't realize she had prepared, or maybe I was just always a blubbering mess around her. Either choice deserved a laugh. I deserved to laugh, even just once.

"Thank you for being the best friend I have." I choked out.

"I couldn't have made it without you, either." She said.

I was still crying, but I couldn't stop myself from talking about plans and acting as if I were fine. I only felt okay anymore if I was moving forward, as if things outside of my current bubble weren't real. Too much reality too fast made me feel like glued together glass.

"We need to discuss Thann," I said as I wiped my face.

"Do we need to do it now?" she asked.

"Yes. He's the last big plan to wrap up before I die." I said.

"Are you sure it has to be this way?"

"Yes. The tree was clear. She showed me so many things, Astra. She showed me exactly how things have to go. I have to die." I sat up with a smile. "It's the smallest of things I could do for you all."

I did my best to comfort her every time we had to discuss it. I knew it must have felt so heavy on her. She was the only one I knew I could trust to carry it, though, as cruel as it was to ask of her. The tree's visions were clear on what I had to do. My blood needed to be reset.

If I died, I would be unaware of my abilities, my magic. I would be useless to Yumi.

The Tree could be free. They could be free.

"So, what is the plan then?" she asked.

"I need you to check in on Kyra and make sure her barrier is still problem-free, then see Caym. Say anything you need to keep him from acting out again. I am going to give Thann a poison. It will make him sick, and Helia will need help. I'll pretend to cure him, but what he's going to take will render him unconscious, and you'll take that time to capture Thann. Take him to Orest. I've already placed fate chains in the dungeon and illusion crystals with them so you can disguise yourself as him."

She looked at me as if she hardly heard anything I had said.

"Are you sure? There's no other way?" She asked again.

I placed both of my hands on her head and met my forehead to hers.

"I'm not scared," I whispered. "You shouldn't be either.

I've spent all of this time letting things slide so I could prepare for the day it has to happen."

I stood from our place under the tree and held out my hand to her. She clicked her tongue at me and stood up on her own.

"Save it for the maidens." She shot.

I grabbed the basket of fruit for Emon and nudged her. "How is your maiden?"

Her cheeks instantly flushed. They were redder than any apple I carried.

"She is delightful, ravishing, elegant, brilliant, wise."

"Astra, you have hearts growing in your eyes." I laughed.

"Whatever," She mumbled. "How about you? Do you plan to make up with Sage?"

"I do not. If she hates me, my death will be easier for her. It's the same for Caym. He can move on, too."

She was looking at me with disagreement, but I couldn't take hearing it.

"Caym's dragon did hatch, though," I said.

It was my attempt to change the subject and move far, far away from it. The closer it got to my last day, the harder it became for me to have such a tight hold on myself. We had too many tasks to get done for me to be crying.

"I wanted to ask Kyra if she would marry me. It seems too soon, though, if I really consider it. She says she wants to help me get my son back, too. We've been talking about what we would do as a family."

She didn't look at me; she cleaned out the pond of flower petals and leaves, but her face was still glowing. She was hard to imagine as someone in love. She had the presence of someone who should be a general, not someone playing dress up and baking goods in a little cottage.

"Why not? Take her on a picnic and ask her then." I said. "You have my blessing."

We both laughed, but she was still blushing.

Jeb came to tell me a dragon egg was hatching, and I left to go to the garden. There was one last hope I was waiting for. One small glint of possibility that I could find a path the tree could not see.

Amari, the goddess of truth, was doing her best to crack the egg open. I assisted when I could. It was hard to tell which areas were safe to puncture when I couldn't see inside. She was my first attempt at piecing a soul back together after a heart was partially eaten.

Her head finally pushed through the bottom, and she gasped for air. I did my best to turn the egg around without shaking her too much. Maybe I was being too gentle. I lowered her a little further and dropped the egg.

"Ow!" She yelped.

"Sorry, but it did work." I tried to offer comfort.

She lifted each of her brown paws and shook them individually until they were clean.

"What am I?" She was somewhere between a scream and a cry.

"It's the only way I could bring you back. You may be a dragon, but you have a jaw again." I tried to smile at her.

She stared at me, unimpressed.

"Okay, we're starting off on the wrong foot, but that's alright. I needed information that could only be trusted from you." I pleaded.

She was still glaring at me as if imagining tearing me apart.

"Do you know anything about Yumi? Our realm? Anything at all?" I asked.

She sighed. "I'm not a fortune teller; I can only keep deities honest. This means I can only tell you what I have witnessed or what deities lie about. Yumi is interested in guardians; there is a fake one, and she knows who it is. She is worried he will slip up because he knows more than he should."

"Is there any way this gets resolved without death," I asked.

Her expression fell, and she looked at me with pity; she shook her head no.

I had to laugh. It was the only thing to keep me from crying. My last flicker of hope was in her answers. In the hope that the truth would be a little bit different from the visions. I would have happily given a million apologies for everything that I've done to everyone I've pushed away if there was a single other way it could end.

I told myself I was ready to die. That it would be fine, but it was easy to think when there were still options left. I would die to keep everyone alive. I would do it without saying a single word to them about it. I wouldn't burden them with knowing that I truly was afraid, but in the dark, I would cry for the loss of my future. My single life for theirs was worth it, but the ache was heavy.

I swallowed hard; everything I had to choke down was thick. "Thank you, Amari. Go find Juniper and tell her I sent you. Tell her that you need a place in her residence. She will keep you safe."

I pulled two boxes from under my table. It was nothing special. Just simple wood from the Tree of Life held together. They were small and would be discreet when placed.

I inhaled and held my breath as tightly as I could before I reached inside my own chest; I ripped a part of my heart and pulled it out. It was only a piece, but It was the worst pain I had to endure. Silence helped her enjoy punishments better.

"What are you doing?" Amari's voice was filled with disgust.

"I'm moving forward with what has to happen now. If you eat the heart of a deity, you get their power; eat the whole heart, you take their position, too. This is how I can ensure my time and safety when I cannot remember who I am. We are unlike mortals, a small cut to their heart, and it's over. A piece of our heart is hardly enough to move us to death, but it is enough to steal from us."

"What are you planning?" she asked.

"Thank you for your help, Amari," I said, leaving the room without an answer.

I needed to meet Sage. She and I needed to see each other one last time.

I passed many deities in the halls, but they didn't pay me any attention. I even passed Deimos, which gave me pause. It was rare to pass anyone, let alone Deimos. He did not leave his realm. I would notice. If I weren't pressed for time, I would investigate. So much activity let me know I had to move my feet faster.

My end was nearing.

I closed Sage's doors behind me. They were huge and took more effort than the normal ones, but they were necessary. I rushed into her bedroom and closed that door behind me, too. She was writing, which I did not expect to see. I hadn't known she had learned to write. I hadn't gotten time to keep up with much. I had to keep pushing it down.

"Ruri?" She was confused, but I wouldn't explain. "I was thinking about you. I should have already come to see you, but I didn't know if you would want to see me. I can start by telling you that I'm sorry—"

"Stop,' I said, holding my hands up.

I couldn't stand here and listen. I could not take in what could be the last thing she said to me and have it be an apology. I couldn't carry that. I couldn't handle making the sacrifice while knowing that she did her best to make things right between us, and then had to live thinking I left her anyway.

I needed her to think we weren't on good terms. I needed her to have that to hold on to.

"I know I don't have a good excuse, but-"

"Don't," I pleaded.

I couldn't tell her anything, and I couldn't apologize for

any of my own deeds, either. I could only leave with more pain to keep me company in whatever afterlife I'd end up in. She would move past things and create a beautiful life for herself; I knew she would.

"Please, let me explain."

"Sage," I yelled. "Just stop. It doesn't matter. It doesn't matter if she used a spell or fed you herbs. It doesn't matter if Yumi herself unbound the two of you, and now you can see clearly. Nothing you could come up with would change anything. It is too late. You kept your secrets, and I kept mine. It's too late for anything beyond finding peace in them."

I wiped my hand across her face before she could speak again, and she hit the bed. She would wake up soon. I watched her for a moment. She was growing, changing. I wouldn't be around to tell her I was proud of her or that it was my fault for being a bad sister.

I wouldn't be around to apologize for treating her badly or tell her how I wished I had tried harder to understand why she felt so outcasted. There was nothing I could do, though, and no time left to tell her everything was my fault. I would die the bad sister and be remembered that way.

I reached into her chest and took a piece of her heart, too. I put it in the other box. I tucked them both into my dress.

I took every precaution I could to get back to my own room without being seen again. I closed and locked every door on the way back into my own room and wasted no time pulling out my journal. I wrote a note to Caym and a separate note to Astra. I put each of them under the boxes with instructions on what temple to take them to. I wrapped my citrine necklace around Caym's note and tucked them in the drawer of my vanity.

My preparations were done.

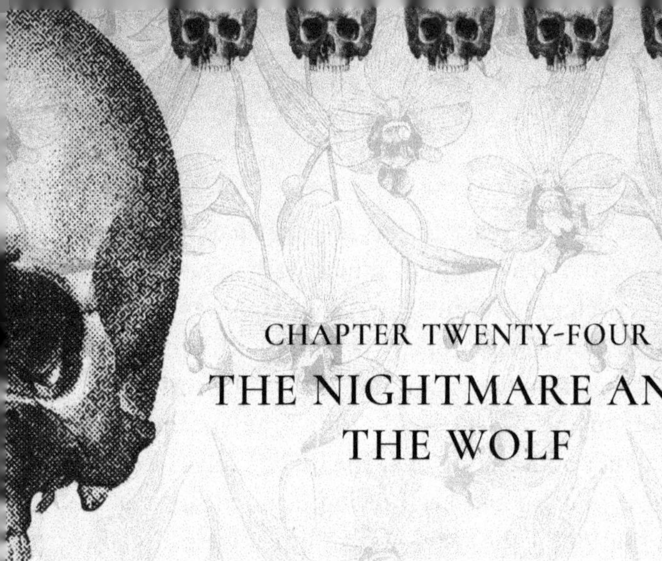

CHAPTER TWENTY-FOUR
THE NIGHTMARE AND THE WOLF

The Teachings of Moonlight

Our second age of peace was nearly as brief. He was back. We spent so much time fighting, only for him to come back. He seems to have no memory, the same as my sister. She calls him Nikola. She thinks they are in love. He watches me but never speaks. Signs that it truly is him have started showing. Creatures that mimic his true form have been appearing. Grotesque, rotted things. The girls do not understand why I've started pushing them so hard to work with the seasons and get a better understanding.

CAYM

None of us knew how to react to the situation happening in front of us. We were under a kind of attack we had never seen before, by things we had never imagined, and Koa was a wolf.

I didn't know how to approach the situation. I thought, when I watched the crystal enter his mouth, that he was dead. That I was losing my best friend, and I didn't understand how he was alive. I didn't understand what she had done.

I didn't know that I could keep trying to understand it. I saw The Nola outside of the windows, and they were already fighting the creatures pouring out of the rift. Onyx tried to go through it, but after Deimos, the rift sparked and tossed him across the room.

Vespera did not stay to check on Koa or Onyx. She left immediately to join the Nola and fight. Maybe I was wrong about her. Maybe she was on our side.

I bent down to put my hand on the crimson and black wolf. The contact made it feel real. He looked at me and shook his head. I couldn't understand him. He took off out of the castle to join the others; I understood that.

I followed him until I reached the doorway that Onyx was resting in.

"Are you all right?" I asked.

"I'm fine. Go on without me. I need a few more minutes, and I'll be there. You don't need to waste time here with me." He said.

I did not argue. I had to protect my realm.

I ran through the halls of my castle and down the stairs. Merripen was on fire. The souls that were under my care were in horror. They ran to find protection. The difference between the dead and the living was that no matter how much you hurt the dead, they had to endure it because they couldn't die again.

I formed balls of sun magic in my hands. One after

another, I flung them at creatures flying in my sky. The Nola and I would have a lot of work to do when everything ended. The ground around us was unrecognizable.

A creature lunged down at me and took a piece of flesh from my arm, and I slapped my hand against it with the sun magic until it was ash.

There were so many, and I didn't know how we would clear them all out. Every one of them that I saw die brought a handful more. Koa was lunging in the air to bite at them. Vespera was doing her best to cut down as many as she could with her axe.

I took a hit to the chest with a bolt of fire that one of the creatures shot out of his mouth. I wanted to end things. I gathered the sun magic that I could in the core of my stomach and pulled it out with my hands. I grew the round shape to be as large as I could imagine it to be. All of my inspiration came from Ruri and the way she used her.

I let my breath out and unleashed it into a swarm. The beam was too bright for even my eyes.

When I had no more to let out of myself, smoke and dirt filled the air. My own lungs pulled in the air too quickly and took dirt with it. Sweat dripped from my nose, and I shook it away.

The ground under my feet shook and quaked. A rumble like the ground was going to break open underneath us. The roar of a dragon was next. The air settled, and a golden dragon lowered its head to eat the remaining swarm.

Aero ran into another crowd of the creatures screaming. "I brought help!" Several more dragons followed him in.

I turned to the dragon sitting beside me. "Thanks."

"Thank me properly with my name. It is Ryujin; it's the least you can do after I choked down such an awful meal."

"Thanks, Ryujin." I corrected. "I don't recognize you, Ryujin. Where do you belong?" I asked.

"I broke the chains of the egg that held me hostage and

sniffed you out for where I belong." He stretched and shook his floppy golden jowls too casually, all things considered. "I should like my reward."

"You did just eat," I offered.

"Then you are my next meal?" He showed his teeth.

"I'll take you to the mortal realm and show you cows."

"Will you continue to endlessly move your jaw, or do you intend to help clear out the land?" He asked.

I looked at him in disbelief. What did he think I had been doing?

"Olexei would not be pleased to see that you have his magic, but do not use it to end this. End it!" He yelled at me again.

I was being reprimanded by a strange dragon that I had only known for a few heartbeats. He had only done a single thing since leaving his egg.

He lowered his head and shot hot air into my face before repeating his words. "End it."

Fine. I'd show him that I could. I would solve it.

I took my gloves off and shoved them into the pocket of my trousers. I closed my eyes again and pulled from somewhere deep inside of me. Some place untouched, a place I didn't recognize or remember. A place that felt like me.

I opened my eyes and pulled my arm back before punching it forward and opening my palm. Out of my hand came a burst of shadow. The sky darkened until there was nearly no light left, and the shadow turned itself into wraiths.

I tried again, but the lions, which were made of tree roots and leaves, stood large enough to take a bite out of the creatures while they flew. Their paws left behind rough ditches in their path.

Ryujin clamped down one of the creatures as it flew past. He didn't chew; he just chomped and swallowed.

The sky was clear; they were gone.

"It would have been best if you had done that sooner," Ryujin said.

"I would have if I had known I could!" I yelled.

"How many times did you try it, I wonder?" He said.

Koa ran to my side and sat, still a wolf. The only thing he could do was whimper.

Vespera and Aero walked up behind him, they both wore looks of sadness.

"What do we do?" Vespera asked.

"I don't know," I answered honestly.

"We should ask Juniper," Aero said.

"I'm going to go take more than Deimos hand. The two of you can see Koa to Juniper." I said.

Ryujin was the one to stop me. He used his teeth to pick me up by my clothes and hung me off of the ground.

"What are you doing!" I yelled.

"One thing at a time. He is not yet your next step." He sat me down. "Help your friend."

I didn't feel as if I had an option on the next move.

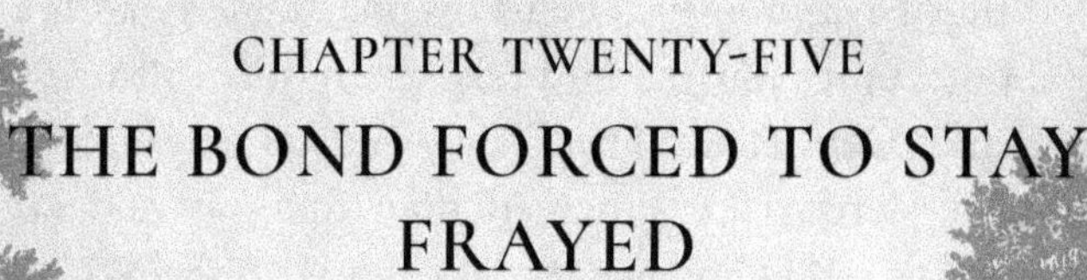

CHAPTER TWENTY-FIVE

THE BOND FORCED TO STAY FRAYED

The Teachings of Moonlight

The creatures, the two of them have been calling their children, have started to destroy crops and give illness to the mortals. The Goddess of Space has created a cage for them. She formed a planet that they can be moved to. I tried to reason with my sister that this was the best we could do for her. She screamed that I was jealous and cruel. That I had my Goddess send them to be tortured and murdered. That her children were equal to mine. She blamed the Goddess of Space for hurting her children.

SAGE

Things around me were beginning to feel too close, too tight. I was starting to lose touch with what peace felt like. Today, I decided that I was going to focus on one single goal: find out more about Yumi's journal and take the results to Ruri. Many of the deities were at Erebus. They were still investigating the events of yesterday. Orla helped plan funerals and lay out blueprints for rebuilding what was ruined. She told me she wanted my help, that they hadn't planned for any deaths anytime soon, so they had nowhere to put the dead.

I declined their meeting and her plea for help. I didn't want to discuss what happened. I didn't want to hear the cries again. It was too much for me when there was nothing I could do about it.

I had to use my time wisely. I needed to get into Yumi's room, copy what I found, and get out. If I could solve the mystery of Semper, if I could clear Sahir's reputation while I was at it. If I could show everyone that she and I were both misunderstood, then both of us could have a new start.

We may be able to heal our friendship, too. The idea was invigorating. If I could show Ruri something to be proud of, maybe she would want me next to her again, too. If I could just do something right, I could redeem myself.

I made it into the Sunlight Garden unseen. I passed the tea table and the Tree of Life. My feet were already wet from the dew along the ground. It even smelled like freshly cut wet grass everywhere. I rounded the corner and ran my hand through the soft green bushes lining everything. They were wet, too. I was so close to her room that I started to feel excited before I ran face-first into someone.

"Why are you here?"

Astra stared into my eyes with unrelenting anger.

"I'm exploring, like I'm free to do." I crossed my arms and leaned to the side. She wouldn't bully me into leaving.

"The only thing past me is Yumi's room." She held up the journal, "Looking for this? Some of us weren't distracted by Sahir or some fake redemption and already went snooping."

My heart sank, "I don't know anything about that."

"That's good." Every word Astra spoke was filled with more venom and sarcasm than the last. "If you did, it would mean you've been lying, not just to your sister, but to all of us."

She pushed herself closer to me, forcing me to drop my arms and stumble backward. Astra was intimidating. Anyone who said otherwise was lying. Even the sounds of her breath sent a silent shiver through me. I was positive Yumi kept Astra where she did and under her thumb because she was scared, like I was scared, that Astra could be nearly unstoppable if she wanted to be.

"You and Sahir not being friends is an act. You're pretending so you can spy on your sister for Sahir." Astra shoved me with both of her hands.

"Of course not!" I stumbled.

"I don't trust you, and if you were anyone else, I'd send you to a cold, lonely planet to rot by yourself for an eternity." She shoved me again, and I fell on my rump. "Get up and get out."

"I believe it," I uttered in what I hoped to be an undetectable whisper.

There it was again, that feeling that all of the walls were closing in on me. The sweat that formed on my palms. The beating in my throat. I got to my feet after a second attempt. Astra's presence watching me was making it harder for me to function in the normal way I knew I could. I hurried my steps; I wanted to leave quickly before she changed her mind and decided that answering to Ruri was worth being rid of me. I wanted to be clear of the garden before she decided being a silent face behind Yumi's footsteps wasn't what she wanted any longer.

"Sage."

No, please.

"There you are. I heard from Sahir you showed up with markings like your sister, too. Why didn't you come to tell me?" Yumi asked.

She was blocking my exit. I didn't tell you because I wanted to remain forgotten. Deep down, I knew there was more going on than I didn't know. Because a part of me knew what she did to Astra had to also be happening to Ruri. She used to be so headstrong. She was a beaten-down shell. I was afraid to have the truth placed in front of me and be able to do nothing about it, too.

"I didn't know It would matter. They showed up, but they didn't do anything." I said.

"Why are you shaking and stuttering?" she asked as she grabbed my hand.

Was I?

She used a white light to cut my palm open; I felt the heat but not the cut. My hand started pouring blood onto a root she held in her hand. She cut too deep, and my knees buckled. It resulted in only a whimper. Nothing happened to the root, and Yumi clicked her tongue in disappointment. No one was more disappointed in me than myself.

Yumi turned me around and marched me back to the tree as if I were a mortal child being punished. She was shoving me faster than my feet could carry, and I thought I'd trip onto my face.

She had a rage about her that was beyond something normal. It was beyond upset; it wasn't the kind of rage you felt when your favorite vase was broken. No, she pulled me with an irrational fury. The kind that told me I was a whisper away from death.

"Make the tree do something," she demanded, her voice grew increasingly irritated with me.

I don't recall ever seeing her that way. I didn't know what she wanted me to do. I could only look at her, lost and confused. She took my hand and slammed it against the bark. She slid it down without mercy, pulling and ripping at the bare, already-cut flesh. Again, nothing happened. The only result was my quivering lip attempting to hide my crying.

"Yumi, please." I whimpered.

"Try again!" She yelled. She relentlessly shoved me.

"I can't!" I begged

Her hand made contact against my face with a force that pushed the air out of me and filled my ears with a clap. My first instinct was to lift my hand to meet the burning. My second was to cry. Both won. The sound that exited me was an indescribable, embarrassing mess, and I felt the snot start to run from my nose.

"Make it walk, talk, dance. It doesn't matter. Try again!" Yumi pointed.

My mind raced, but the best I could come up with was to wave my hand in front of it.

"I told you she was useless," Sahir said, moving from behind Yumi. "Daddy would have killed her by now."

"Don't you dare mention that man in front of me again, or you'll be sent back to him, do you understand me? You're both failures." Yumi didn't give me a second glance before leaving.

I wanted to collapse as if the sting of Yumi wasn't enough; the one deity that was supposed to be loyal to me was the one that sent her to me.

Sahir let out a scream. She was loud and unbothered by the pitch. She lunged at me like an animal, and I was on the ground underneath her.

"You couldn't do one thing for me, could you? I'm gonna rip your heart out and eat it, too!" Sahir screamed.

She was clawing at me, already ripping fabric. I lifted my hands to protect my face, but she wasn't concerned about it. She was absolutely serious when she said she wanted my heart. Her only focus was on it.

"Sahir, stop!" I tried to push her, but she shoved my arms back down.

She was so sure of what she was doing it was like she had done it before. I tried to push her off of me, but it was a failed attempt. She was stronger than I thought for someone who never did anything on her own. I considered calling for Astra, who I was sure was still near, but I knew deep down she wouldn't help me. She was more likely to be watching with laughter.

I reached up to touch her face. I thought maybe if she could calm down and come to her senses, she would stop on her own, but she was still screaming and grunting. I didn't want to die. I wasn't ready to go yet; even if my existence was a waste, I still wanted it. Alive, I had the chance to redeem myself. I couldn't die yet. I didn't want my lingering memory to be Sahir's puppet.

When my hands made contact with her face, roots started sprouting from her eyes. They slowly grew from her mouth, too, as if forming a plant inside of her. She started gasping and choking. I could see the power coming from my hands. My scream replaced hers, and I let go. She dropped off of me to her back next to me on the ground. We were both panting.

"I thought you'd never do anything cool. Of course, you finally do when I'm set on killing you." Sahir said through panted breaths.

"You're insane!" I yelled.

She only laughed.

I pulled myself to my feet, realizing my hand was still bleeding, and I ran. I ran to Ruri's room. I thought maybe she would understand. Even if we weren't getting along, she was sure not to turn me away if I were injured.

When I threw myself into her room, she was unmoving. She lifted her eyes, but not a singular twitch of anything else happened. I dropped myself to her floor, back against her bed. Still panting.

"I need to confess." I was still cradling my hand. "I found a journal; Yumi has been writing in it. She's using your blood on the tree; it didn't say why. She wrote about how Kyrell is unstable and needs some guy named Nikola's blood." I stopped to catch my breath and inhale again, "The tree gave me visions, too. It showed me more deaths. So much death, and--" I thought harder. "I've been to the Timekeepers, too. They have knowledge, scrolls!"

"Stop." She said, "I already know. I knew you were lying to me, so we lied to you, too. You could have saved us so many problems if you had just spoken up sooner. Sahir was more important to you. Go tell her this. You waited too long to decide you wanted to be a team player. Now, there is only one team left for you."

I was exhausted already by how quickly and drastically my emotions were changing. I was sure my body wouldn't be able to handle much more trembling. I felt like I was freefalling, and there was no end in sight, only more rocks to slap me. Maybe my life really was ending.

"You're so full of yourself, aren't you?" I laughed, shaking my head. "I can't believe I picked to come here. I should have known." My heart was thumping in my throat again.

"you're always the victim, aren't you? Always concerned about what you can't do, but it's only because you won't even try. You'd rather cry than put any effort into anything else. You've got your nose shoved so far up your own ass that you won't even see what's going on around you. I had every bone in my body broken just for Yumi to see if I could put myself back together again while she watched. Do you know why? Because it was me or you, and I made the sacrifice. You wouldn't know it, though, would you? What did you come here for? Comfort? Forgiveness? Healing?" She was screaming, too.

Everyone was screaming at me today. Today was supposed to be a good day. I was supposed to make her proud. To make myself proud. Instead, I ruined everything again.

"It doesn't matter. Forget it; I won't give you any of those today. I've been keeping secrets, too. A dragon hatched for you. His name is Cyrus. He's the God of summer. He is from the Age of Moonlight. The one that Yumi says there never was. He's been looking for you." She stood to walk past me. "It's the last thing I'll do for you. Go back to Sahir and leave me be."

She left me behind, bleeding, on my knees in her room with a dragon staring at me. I didn't need to speak to him to already see that he would be the same. His lips were turned in disgust, and his eyes yelled loud and clear that he knew he was better than me.

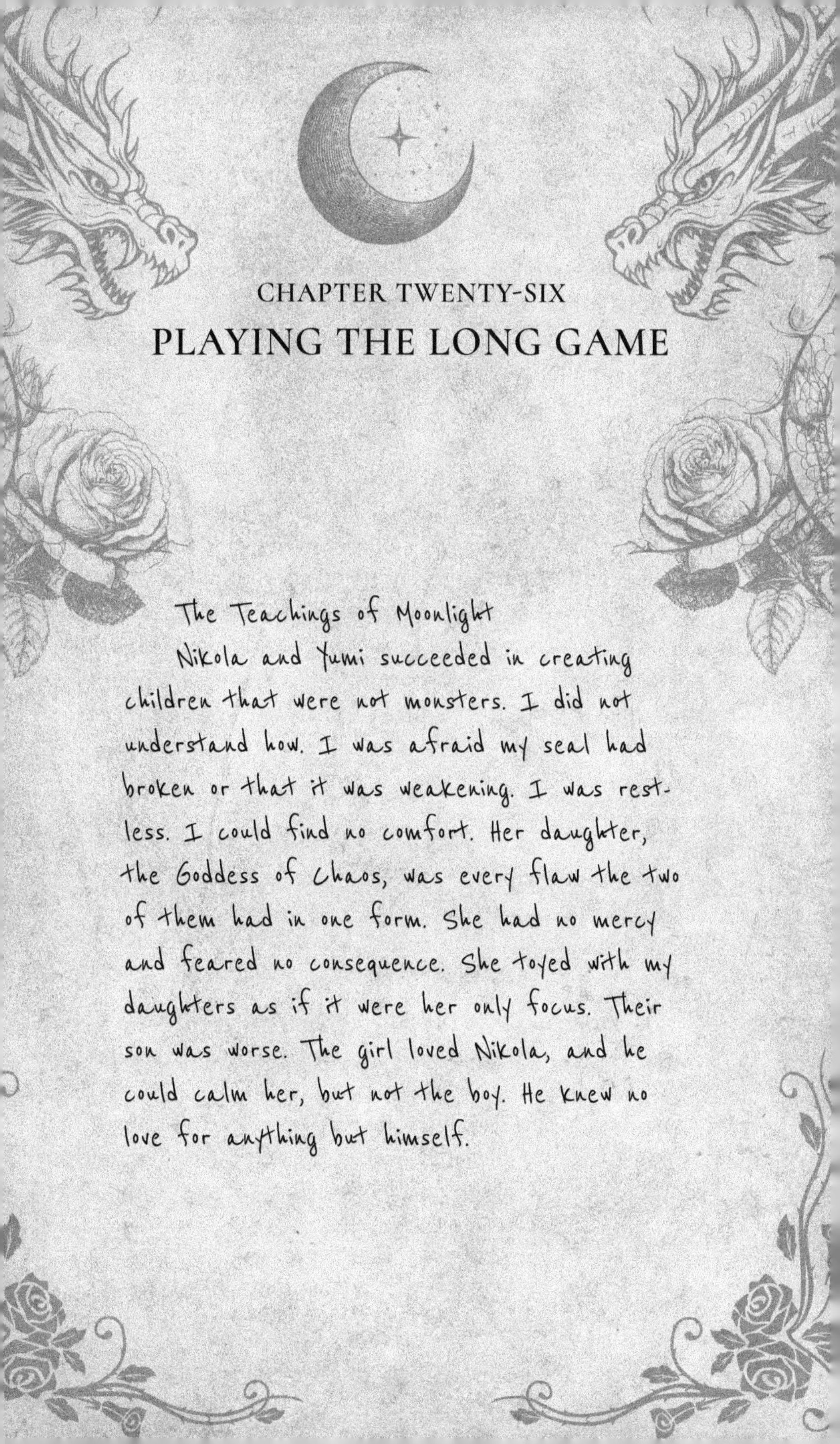

CHAPTER TWENTY-SIX

PLAYING THE LONG GAME

The Teachings of Moonlight

Nikola and Yumi succeeded in creating children that were not monsters. I did not understand how. I was afraid my seal had broken or that it was weakening. I was restless. I could find no comfort. Her daughter, the Goddess of Chaos, was every flaw the two of them had in one form. She had no mercy and feared no consequence. She toyed with my daughters as if it were her only focus. Their son was worse. The girl loved Nikola, and he could calm her, but not the boy. He knew no love for anything but himself.

RURI

I waited outside of Helia's quarters for her invitation to come inside. She sent word to every resident of Semper that Thann was sick. I believed he was ill because I had done it. I had happily made him sick enough that he was on the brink of death. She was pleading for something to heal him. I knew I could. I knew that it was within the range of things I would succeed in, but I wouldn't. I only came to set the rest of the plan for Astra in motion.

She would take over his entire life; she would be able to go unnoticed. She would have an advantage with any information that she may have needed. She would be able to kill him if she chose and take revenge if she wanted.

It was going to be within her grasp to take charge of soul sorting and rebirth. I wanted someone I could trust in charge of my soul after I died. If I had any hope of one day coming back, if it was at all the slightest chance, she was the one I could trust to be level-headed in my place.

"Ruri, come in." Helia motioned, and I followed. "I'm sure you understand why I'm apprehensive to accept your help."

"Mhm," I responded.

"It would be fitting for you to use this chance to kill him instead." She said again.

"Mhm."

She glared at me from the side of her eyes.

"If I wanted him dead, why would I wait outside peacefully? Do you think you could stop me?"

Her smile was wide enough for me to see all of her teeth. We both knew the challenge would be welcomed. I didn't need proof to know she helped convince Thann to hurt Astra's son. I didn't need to see it with my own eyes to know she had a hand in it. I held just as much resentment for her as I did for him. Even if I was wrong, which I wasn't, and she didn't convince him he was right in his choices, she didn't stop him when she knew she could have. That made her just as guilty as him. She held herself on some sort of pedestal, but I had yet to figure out why.

"Besides, you're desperate. You'll accept my help." I said.

She took me into her bedroom, where Thann lay. He was reminiscent of a shriveled grape that hadn't seen the sun in days. It was a good look for him. Being so close to death, so weak and useless. It was exactly what he deserved to be feeling. I wanted him to stay the way he was. I didn't feel wrong about it, either. He made his choices and never paid a cost.

I watched the other side pay, though. I watched Astra rock an empty cradle with tear-soaked blankets in front of her. I knew the cries for her son that came out in her sleep. Anyone around her could feel the pain radiating from her in the wrong conversation.

It wasn't my place, though. His last breath was not mine to take. As much as I wanted it, I knew she needed it.

"Can you do something?" Helia asked, her hand was on her hip.

She was doing her best to keep her voice calm, but I heard the shake in it.

"I can," I handed her a vial. "Have him drink this; he'll be fine by tomorrow."

"Or dead." She phrased it as a question.

"He's clearly near that without me. Do you want to toss a coin and test it?"

"What do you want for this?"

"I want you to teach me how to use time magic," I said.

"What will you use it for?"

"Do I need to tell you such a typical love story? I'll use it to sneak around and see the man I'm forbidden from going near." I said.

She used her thin golden spoon to stir the tea she poured into her cup. She was thinking it over as if she had other options. I knew she didn't. There was no one else in Semper that could do the things I could except Sage, and she didn't have the garden that I did.

"If he survives the week, I'll teach it to you." She said.

I bit my smile before it could finish forming. I held out my hand instead. "Deal."

She took it, and we shook on the deal.

I only needed the interaction to be trustworthy enough for her to make him drink. I didn't need her help. I didn't want any kind of ability she possessed. I wouldn't be with them soon enough.

"Do you know how he got sick? He is a god, so it's a bit strange." I asked

"I have the potion; you have your deal. We can part ways." She said before she stood.

"Okay. I can take the hints." I smiled on my way to my feet. "I have more to do today, too."

She didn't bother to see me out, and I didn't bother to say goodbye.

I went to Cylla instead of spending any more time or thoughts on her. I told the King of Ashbel to bring the important members of the council and have them meet me for lunch. I found the mortals at their happiest with food. Ashbel did not have a tea house, but they did have a meat shop. The shop sold mushroom wine and any meat you could think of in any way you wanted it. Smoked Bear was one of my personal favorites.

I arrived in the realm, standing in front of Sorcery Slicers, and I knew I was late today. Royal guards stood outside, still as stone. I went inside, and the whole place was cleared out as I had requested. The room was covered in lush red carpets and smelled of hickory. Wooden framed windows covered the building, and between each was a mounted head. I never was fond of it, but they reasoned with me that it was a way to advertise what kind of meat they sold and that they truly could catch it on their own. The owners were proud that their products were all fresh. I couldn't argue their points.

I took my seat at the opposite end of the table from the king that I hand-picked to rule. Food already lined the table, and although I didn't need it, it smelled delicious. The man I placed as king looked more comfortable in his role than when I gave it to him. He was growing quickly, and it was always a reminder of how small their lifeline was.

"Today, I'll give you the last set of orders before I hand the entire kingdom over to you," I said, clearing my throat.

"You're leaving?" King Em asked.

I nodded. "You've done better than I could have imagined when I decided it was you that would rule. You don't need my help anymore."

His once-happy face started to drop. I knew it was hard for him; he thought I would be with him for his entire lifetime. I was happy not to endure his passing. It would have been a difficult time, but I also thought I would have been around for his entire lifetime once, too.

It's why I came to say goodbye. I wanted to have one last, small moment to watch the mortals that I once thought I would live eternity with.

"I'd like you to create the temple guardians. You should send them to Orest to be trained. It should be a requirement that your line picks the guardians that get sent to Orest. I will be putting something of unimaginable importance in the temple of magic here. I'm also going to be sending out the last of the dragons. I've assigned the dragon guardians for each land, and should you need them, they are there, but." I held up my finger. "It's still important you stay out of the wars that will eventually come. It will serve you better to make peace deals in exchange for healing. I entrusted you and the land as the place where anyone could come for aid. Trust in the dragon's opinions. They won't be wrong."

My mind was racing to ensure I left them with all the important information they would need.

"We have been discussing the need to trade something more than healing salves." King Em said.

I nodded. "If you find a resource you consider valuable, do it. This is your kingdom. I have handed you the tools; you must use them."

He nodded. "Will you be back for what you leave in the temple?"

"I'm not sure. The Goddess of space and the Goddess of storms are allowed inside at any time, for any reason. Outside of that, all access should be denied." I said.

He cleared his throat and sat a bit straighter, "Are you saying we should prepare to fight against other gods? Specifically, the God of death?"

"If he comes here, he won't be in his right mind. Trust in the crystals I've left behind. The magic I've put in them is as strong as what I can use from my fingers." I assured him.

"Will you stay for a meal one last time?" he asked.

"It smells too good to leave behind." I smiled while I grabbed a napkin.

It was such a different world in Ashbel than in Semper. Even the sky was peaceful. The events that transpired during their wedding would have sent other places spiraling, but they were still doing their best to talk things out and keep level-headed.

"How have things been here, in general?" I asked.

"The new queen is trying to settle in, and I'm doing my best to make her comfortable. Neither of us have had much time together since the marriage was arranged."

I gave a soft chuckle at the sarcasm as well.

"I do hope that you two can find peace and happiness once this is handled. I know the love isn't there, but it may yet come, and I will ensure whoever put those plans in motion pays."

"I do believe you," he said. "Can I ask you something else?"

"Mhm," I mumbled while taking another bite.

"Why haven't you brought Caym lately?"

His question hit me so hard that I didn't want to look up from my food. I comforted myself with the thought that the mortal realm wouldn't know anything, and maybe we would be written about somewhere. That we would have a place for the rest of forever, that would remain untouched, and in some way, we could live out the dreams we had. I didn't want to lie to him, either.

I looked at him and his questioning and sighed.

"Sometimes we have to do things we don't want because bigger things are needed."

"So, you left him? For someone else?"

"There would never be anyone else for me."

I sat my clothes down on the table, and Em took the hint. I was thankful I didn't need to elaborate any further. Words out louder felt heavier than the ones only uttered inside.

CHAPTER TWENTY-SEVEN

THE BEGINNING OF THE END

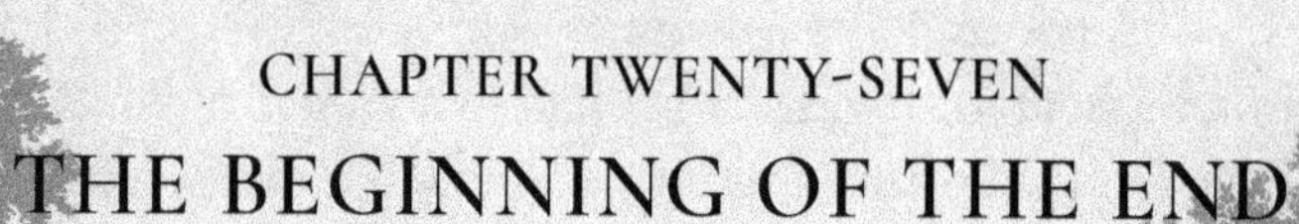

The Teachings of Moonlight

We learned that the creation of their children was deeper than we thought. There were two boys and two girls. They had done it much sooner than I understood. A false guardian was placed inside of the ones I made to protect my girls. I tried everything that I could, but I could not find a way to guarantee that the one that I was to kill was their child and not my own guardian. Cyrus, the God of summer, and I went over every piece of knowledge he had ever recorded to find any idea that we could consider.

SAGE

I took Cyrus into the Sunlight Garden. I thought if he had something in front of him to keep him busy, I could leave, and he wouldn't notice that I was gone.

I had a plan for the day. I wanted to seek out Sahir.

The room had the opposite effect. He looked even more upset than usual, and I hadn't seen a single smelly tooth during a smile since his arrival in my presence.

Even in the most beautiful room on our floating rock. Even in the presence of fresh scents. Even with the crystal-clear pond, he could still be testy. I could not take him with me to see her.

"The shimmer of stolen souls," Cyrus murmured.

I wasn't used to talking dragons yet. His voice still caught me off guard.

"We call those twinkles stars. Our creator, the Goddess of Starlight--"

"Do not speak to me of that deceiver, that ingrate. That ender of worlds!" He growled.

"I'm sorry?" I questioned what I was even apologizing for.

"In a world long since lost, summer and the flower fell in love. They were close enough to become one. The flower was plucked of its every petal, and Summer swore it would be back to help it recover what was lost. Summer has mourned every day that it had to wait for something strong enough to hold its soul. Summer could bloom many flowers with many petals, but none would come close to the original. To Summer's dismay, its ability to keep its promise depends on a good-for-nothing that refuses to get its marbles in one bag." He grunted at me.

For the first time since our introduction, he left my side to sit under the Tree of Life and watch the sky. It felt wrong to try and remove him. I could have sworn that one of the lower branches moved to the dragon's back and gave it a pet before it moved back.

I had to look around and see if there was anyone else around to confirm it or not. Of course, there wasn't. Why would there be? As if I needed more evidence of my mental state.

I took my chance to leave him while I had it. I couldn't focus on what my imagination was doing. I had a goal, and I wanted to stick to it. I sent a message to Sahir with the Fiia. She did not respond, but I knew she would show up.

I entered the bathing chamber, and there she was. She was lowered into the bath in the same way she always waited for me.

I spent hours beside Sahir on more than one occasion, passing her supply after supply. She needed a brush. The soap bar was the wrong soap bar; find the other. Wash my back; that was the wrong motion, and start again.

She was grated my patience like the mortals grate their cheeses, but there I was, still by her side. Searching for her soaps.

Part of me did miss her friendship.

She threw her head back and fully submerged in the water. I removed my foot covers and sat on the edge of the water. I put my feet in and kicked around until she came up. When she came to the surface, her skin looked like it was melting off of her around her midsection. Her forearms were covered in a rash that looked equally as painful. I recognized it because I helped come up with it. It was a type of poison from Juniper's Garden.

"What's wrong with your body?" I asked.

"A gift from your sister." She answered. It was clear she didn't understand it. "It itches in a way you would not believe."

I would believe it because I wanted it that way.

"Why did you ask to meet me here?" She questioned.

"Why did you turn me over to Yumi?" I asked.

"Why did you hide it from her? You could have been with your sister." She answered.

"Do you think that we have the ability to be friends again?" I asked.

"You can be my loyal maid." She smiled.

I rolled my eyes, and my head shook with the motion.

"Really. I want to know why you put me through that with Yumi and why you were eating hearts."

"You didn't take an interest in anything I did before; why are you now?" Sahir dunked her head back in the water again.

"I didn't take you as seriously as I should have," I said.

"So, if you did, you wouldn't want me?"

"Sahir."

"Fine. It's going to take a lot of power to get my daddy back from the prison she locked him in. It's a sealed cage, a galaxy away. I never lied. I said what I was doing. I gave you to Yumi because you deserved it. You shouldn't have left me behind like you did." She turned away from me to grab her soap bar.

The way she could just toss a coin and change emotions before it could land was truly a talent reserved for her insanity.

"If you want to make up and be friends again, then you have to promise not to help me in anything I ask. No questions." She said.

Sahir lifted herself out of the water and grabbed her clothes. It was unfortunate that she didn't have a different set of priorities. If I were her, I would be begging the people of Ashbel to heal me. It must have been embarrassing to walk around with Ruri's handprints as scars across her face. I found it more amusing than I should have. It was a glimpse of the sister I remembered. The one that had fight flaring in her eyes. The one that was long gone. Beaten into submission by Yumi's side.

Paradise had a way of beating us all down until we were different versions of ourselves. Ruri would have been a fierce deity if she could have just held on to that fire. It took me too long to admit to myself that my admiration rotted to jealousy. It would be longer still before I said any such thing out loud.

"What is it you want me to agree to do?" I asked.

"Killing your sister." She said.

"Why?" I asked.

"It's nothing personal, but your sister is important. Don't fret. It's her magic, not really her. It's just that you're only the goddess of nature. You can't really use elemental magic in its raw form like she can."

I made sure my face was cold as ice and unrelenting. I wanted it to match the way I was feeling. I wanted her to see that Things between us were shifting. I needed her to know that I wasn't going to be a puppet for her anymore.

"I won't kill her if you don't want me to, but imagine all of the power we could have and everything we could rule with that in our hands." She said. "Imagine your sister crying in my hands while I give her worse than a scar."

"You can't honestly expect me to agree to this? You're a monster, and I don't think I can ever change you." I shook my head.

I couldn't believe that I had spent so long with her and put so much hope into her for this to be what she wanted from me.

"Me? Take a look at yourself. You've been by my side, growing into one, too. You've absorbed so much of my knowledge that if I'm a monster, you're only a step behind." She pointed at me.

I wanted it to be our end. I wanted today to go the way it was. I wanted Sahir to be the one to help me break free of her. I needed her to look me in the eyes and tell me that she never cared about me or our friendship, and she did.

A fire lit inside of me, and while she was fixing the little white dress that she had just put on, I hit her. I used every bit of force I could to hit the side of her head. I watched Sahir's eyes roll before she hit the ground.

I wasted no time and climbed on top of her. I didn't want to be her toy any longer. I didn't want to allow her to keep causing problems.

I wanted to kill her. I was going to kill her.

The two of us changed positions quickly, but it was easy to see that she was still stunned and just doing her best. Sahir still landed a hit to my nose. Blood streamed from it immediately.

I rolled off of her and cradled my nose. I let out a slow, deep breath. A snap came next, ringing through my skull.

Sahir didn't give me any chance to recover. She was on top of me with both of her hands around my neck. I couldn't take a breath in, but my hands were free.

She always thought less of me because she always compared me. She never considered me an individual, so she never thought of me as a deity who had their own magic.

I let her tighten her grip on me, and I shut my eyes. I couldn't stop choking, and I couldn't take in any more air, but I could still call nature. I placed my palms on the ground, and the trees around us came to life. They marched on their roots to where she was, and a thick branch came down into her side, throwing her across the room and into the wall.

The oak tree followed to the spot where Sahir landed, and while I struggled to catch my breath. While I choked and gasped and tried to collect myself, the tree hit her with its branches over and over.

The tree I gave life to turned her into something unrecognizable. It helped me spare the world from her plans. From the things that I could not stop by simply offering her friendship.

I slowly got to my feet and hugged the tree. It wrapped its branches around me, and we stayed like that for a moment. It saved my life. It saved many lives.

I left the tree to go where it wanted. It was free to make

that choice. I wouldn't take what I had given it so that it was stuck in place again. I rushed back to my quarters. I needed to clean myself up. I was glad that Sahir was gone. I was happy that it was me who did it. I would not take it back, but I did not want to be in the center of Yumi's attention after our last meeting.

When I closed my oversized doors and looked at the bridge over the pond, my fish were dead. The door to my bedroom had been left open.

My stomach sank. I was covered in blood, my nose was swollen, and someone was here. Everything I did not want.

I took my time to walk to the bridge, and I moved even slower over it.

"Who's in my room?" I called. "You need to come out."

"Your wish is my command," Deimos said.

He left my room and met me on the small bridge before I could process that it was him. He had his hand on my throat in the same way Sahir just had, and I relented under the pressure. I was already sore, sensitive, broken. I needed time to recover. Time he was not allowing me. He drug me by my throat, and the tips of my toes scrapped across the ground.

"What are you doing." I hardly managed to get the words out.

He pressed his finger to his lip to hush me before he shoved my head into the pond with my dead fish, and I inhaled the water.

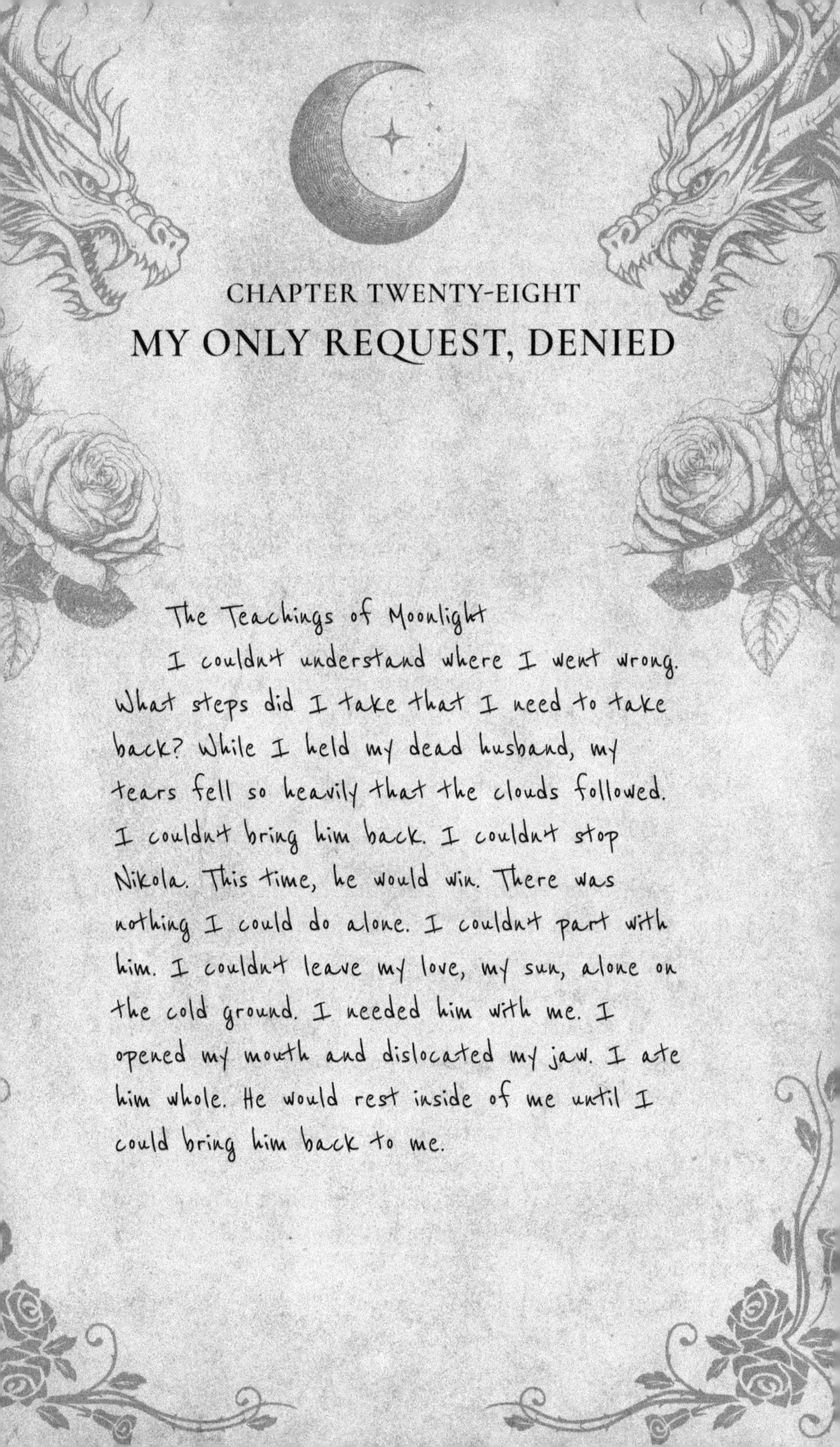

CHAPTER TWENTY-EIGHT

MY ONLY REQUEST, DENIED

The Teachings of Moonlight

I couldn't understand where I went wrong. What steps did I take that I need to take back? While I held my dead husband, my tears fell so heavily that the clouds followed. I couldn't bring him back. I couldn't stop Nikola. This time, he would win. There was nothing I could do alone. I couldn't part with him. I couldn't leave my love, my sun, alone on the cold ground. I needed him with me. I opened my mouth and dislocated my jaw. I ate him whole. He would rest inside of me until I could bring him back to me.

RURI

I was finding it harder and harder to sleep the closer my time came. I knew it was coming because the visions always warned me of the increase in activity that would happen in the realm.

I spent my night in the library instead of my room. I had hoped to find anything that spoke about the Age of Moonlight or any other deities there may have been. I would have accepted anything, but there was next to nothing. A lot of blank books to make it look like a full library. There were books that detailed our lives in Semper, but most of them were false. Most of the books were about Yumi.

I couldn't help but notice while I sat under glass chandeliers and admired stained glass windows; in every saying of our creation, the Tree of Life is what truly did everything. I couldn't help but wander onto the thoughts of how she came up with ideas to build our home after not knowing anything but darkness. Maybe she had been creative in her dreams before we were solid forms, but where was it? Where was it when the mortals needed to be made so desperately? Over one hundred years of waiting for them didn't feel very creative.

I opened my eighth book about creation. The eighth book that made Yumi sound magical and caring. I opened book number eight and scribbled on every page I could flip open. 'Fraud'. If I was going to die, what consequence would I pay? The book of teaching could be torn to shreds for all I cared.

They were simply a history written by someone with bias and no proof. Mortals would read them and praise her. Being surrounded by so many copies of her lies, I was disappointed that I couldn't bring the kind of order that should have been brought to Semper. I wanted to be the one to find out what was going on and to give Yumi a taste of what she had put me through.

Being surrounded by so many lies made me sure that

when I was nothing but a soul, I would do what I had to do to get back to a body. To hold onto these memories. I would come back. I would find Yumi again. I would use my bare hands to show her that her time was up.

I left the library and made my way into the Sunlight Garden. I wanted to make sure Astra was set, and Thann was in the dungeon of his school in Cylla.

"Astra!" I yelled. "Astra!"

There was no answer, but when I finished walking inside, I knew why. Deimos stood with Orla. He had her on her knees.

"What is going on?" I asked.

"It seems Orla has been sneaking around to help you girls create lies about Yumi." Deimos accused.

"What?"

"I found proof of Orla trying to say Yumi is not the creator. She was trying to start a revolt so she could rule over Semper." He answered.

"Orla stayed out of everyone's way; there is no way you have that kind of proof," I said.

"It turns out she was only resting in the shadows so she could get away with snooping," Deimos smirked.

"Do you truly expect this to sound believable? Maybe if we said it about you!" I pointed.

He pulled out fate chains and snapped them around Orla like a snake. They coiled tightly, and Orla begged louder for her innocence.

"You see, the thing is, when you're in a certain position, you don't need proof of anything." He gripped Orla's tongue and pulled it from her mouth. "I only need to say that I think she's a problem, and I do. I think that she will spend her time in Semper trying to look for a way to bring you back when I kill you."

He held up a small box with an orange glow. "The Goddess of Fate made this box specifically for Orla. It'll shrink down and sit anywhere I put it so she can watch but not move."

He tossed it in the air and caught it before shoving Orla's body inside of it and shrinking it even smaller. The only thing on the side of the box was an eye. It searched around, pleading for help.

That wasn't how any of the visions the tree showed me went. It never said that anyone else would be hurt.

"I will give you one last chance to accept my offer. Being my queen can't be worse than death." He held out his hand to me, but I slapped it away.

"Spare me having to listen to you before I die," I begged.

"So be it." He said.

He snapped a set of fate chains around my wrist and used them to lift me to my feet. He pulled me to the Chamber of Starlight.

"Why are we going here? You could have killed me in the garden." I said.

"I need you to see one more thing before you die." He said.

He pulled me the vines so that I could see into Cylla and used the chains to pull me back to my knees. The force he used sent pain radiating through my legs.

"I learned of a few meetings that were going on. Something about needing an army in the mortal realm. Angels betraying their master and a secret order hiding away on an island." He waved his fingers in the reflection of the vines until it showed the island the Timekeepers were on.

That isn't how things were supposed to end. I was careful. I took precautions. I planned every detail I could think of. I listened. I kept my head down. I took the beatings.

I did it so no one was hurt but me.

No one was supposed to be hurt but me.

"Stop. Leave them alone, and I'll offer you a gift. I'll give you magic like I did, Caym." I pleaded.

He lifted his fingers to the watery image and flicked the image. I watched as a fiery rock crashed into the library and sent half of it tumbling into the water. The other half that was on fire received a second hit, and the entire rock crumbled into the ocean.

He turned to look at me and gave a short laugh of pity.

"We could have done great things." He said.

He lifted a sword he had to have stolen from Onyx and plunged it into my stomach. I dropped to my knees, but I didn't feel them. I felt the pain from him moving the blade. I choked out blood, and he pulled the sword out. He sliced my arms with the movement, and I dropped to my hands and knees.

"I'm glad I get to see two fate sisters die." He whispered, lifting the sword a second time. "She struggled, too. She pleaded for you before I held her head under dirty water."

Two? What did he mean by two? I was supposed to be the only one.

Me, it was only supposed to be me. I sacrificed, so it was only me.

I felt the cold steel make contact with my skin.

CHAPTER TWENTY-NINE
THE UNBREAKABLE CHAINS

The Teachings of Moonlight

She ripped apart all of the deities that I gave life to. She was shoving their souls into the stars and throwing them into the sky. She held up my daughter, my little waterdrop, and tore her soul from her body. I heard the screams of the stars from the ground. I gave her everything, and she took even more from me. I did the last thing I could do. The Goddess of space and I tore the realm in half before my sister took Astra from me, too.

CAYM

We all sat around an egg that just kept shaking and rattling like all the other eggs had done, but this egg had already taken over an hour with no luck. I didn't want to hurt it. Ruri never left instructions for what we should do if the dragon couldn't get out. They had all just done it when I was around. No one else wanted to explain that they hurt a dragon if they touched the egg, either.

I couldn't leave. Koa was recovering, and he asked that I stay. Juniper was positive that he would make a full recovery. He was talking, which made me think he would as well. It was strange to see someone I considered the strongest among us so knocked down. Mentally and physically. He said he wasn't ready to talk about it, and I wanted to respect it.

We decided to send Astra to try to find Ruri so she could help with the egg. I was nervous to see her, but I swore that the next time I laid eyes on her, I was going to apologize. I vowed that I would do anything she needed me to do to be close to her again.

I'd stop pressuring her to let me in. I'd let her know that I was satisfied to sit beside her in silence again if that's what she wanted.

Ryujin made quick movements and dug his fang into the egg. He ripped it and spit the shell. He moved without allowing a chance to be denied. I disapproved of what he did, but at least someone had done something.

"No! bad boy!" I pointed.

"Would you like my fang in your anus, too?" Ryujin huffed air into my face.

"Do you want to be jerky?" I mumbled.

The egg rolled around, and out came a powder blue dragon with a shell over its head. Ryujin lowered himself back down and nudged the shell off. The dragon was in full view. Powder blue with antlers that resembled white oak.

"Sina!" Ryujin rumbled.

My head shot in his direction, "How do you know her? How can you tell if she's anyone?"

"I would know her anywhere, in any form, by her scent. She is the Goddess of Winter." Ryujin said.

"Mi Amore!"

"Where did you come from?" I asked while I shifted between the two.

"The tree. Ryujin, what is wrong with him?" Sina asked.

"It appears she was successful." He answered.

"Less riddles," I said, rubbing my temples.

She pranced on all four of her chubby paws to the Nola I kept by my side.

"You look dead, yes?" Sina asked.

The Nola squealed in response.

"Oh, and loud. We will try this. You are dead and not from our past; in theory, I can tell you anything I'd like. We are sealed to silence, a curse on our tongues. The stars here are souls. They are waiting to be born again. Yumi is playing a roulette game with creation. She is hoping to get as many deities as possible back while keeping the guardians locked away. Only guardians get markings, and they glow when met with their match. There are four of you and a fifth who is false." Sina said. "We have to move quickly before any information can fade." She urged.

"Why is this happening?" I asked.

She opened her mouth to speak but growled and roared in response instead.

"I cannot answer. The pain if I try, even with the dead, is too much. Ask something else." She whimpered. "Do not ask me about how we got here. Ask me about how we move forward."

"Why can you answer these things, but Ryujin can't?" Aero asked.

"He Is much stronger than I am, but I am much older and smarter than he is."

Ryujin gave a huff in the backdrop.

"Then how do we move forward?" I asked.

"You find the sisters of fate." She was still discussing this with Nola. "Four seasons, four guardians, four sisters of fate. One is in charge of the seed, where all life outside of the deities comes from. One is in charge of the stem, where all growth and nurturing come from. One is the clock, where the span of breath exists. The last is the scythe, the one who decides when to cut the root. Together, they unlock the secret kept too long." Sina said. "All that Yumi has here is stolen. She wants memories and voices to stay locked until her own children can take the place of the fate sisters."

"Well, if we are looking for markings, then we know Ruri and Sage are two? Right?" Aero asked.

"Correct." She nodded.

"So then, who exactly are you two? Why do you know more than the others?" I asked.

"Yumi is sealing memories before being reborn, but we were not reborn. We were placed inside dragon eggs. She was arrogant and didn't consider these things. It's a small accidental slip on her part. Great luck on ours." She said.

"So, then you should know who the fake guardian is?" I narrowed my eyes on her.

"No. We didn't figure it out before," Her voice trailed off.

"You said she's trying to get rid of the fate sisters for her own children?" I asked.

"You will want to find the ones that are double. Ruri is life, Sage is rebirth, Shivani is blood, and Hesperia is fate." Sina answered.

"Then its Kyrell, Helia, Thann and Minna." Aero said. "Right?"

"The girls must be the ones to kill them in order to be whole again," Sina said.

I didn't have anything else to ask because it was already so much to take in. It was starting to make sense why none of them could ever do the same things the rest of us could. Why they never felt right.

"I will also need a place to stay. I cannot be near Yumi." Sina said.

"You can stay in Merripen. It is my realm, with many different inhabitants. You won't stick out." I said.

"I'll take her!" Aero jumped up, holding his arm high. "I can do it!"

He didn't wait for any of us to respond; he rushed her out without us.

"So, there really is a before time then? Is Yumi the creator? Truly? Was I there? What did I do? I was strong, huh." Aero's words turned to a ramble before they were out of sight.

Ryujin stalked his way out after them, and I didn't stop him. I felt a wave of sadness wash over me at the sight of another happy couple enjoying what I was no longer allowed to do. I was slapped with the knowledge that I couldn't kill Kyrell. If what the dragon said was true, I would have to endure Kyrell until Ruri could kill him.

I spent too long waiting for Ruri to show me where my pawn sat when I was all too happy to be on her board. To be a piece placed in her presence.

I crossed my arms and looked to the only deity left beside me.

"Koa, what do you think about all of this?" I asked.

He reached up and moved the red hairs from his face, "I teach aggression, not defense. You already know what I think. Give away your position, give too much time, and then you may as well surrender. If you're going to strike, the sooner, the better."

"You need to keep resting," I said.

"Who put you in charge?" He looked me up and down.

I truly did admire him.

We parted ways, and I went to the Chamber of Starlight. I asked the Nola to request a meeting with Yumi. I told her it needed to be private as well. Things were all lined up for me to do what had to be done.

If I was a guardian, I needed to do something bigger.

Something other than watching the things around us all unfold.

Yumi was already waiting for me when I entered. I stopped at the bottom of her throne. It sat only a few steps up from the rest of us. Far enough that she was above us but not far enough to be called arrogant like she should be.

"What the matter, Caym? It's not like you to be so secretive and restless." She asked.

"I have some questions I wanted to ask you," I said, snapping my fingers.

More Nola than I could count rushed her from the shadows. I had stolen my own set of fate chains. They clasped them around Yumi's wrists before she had the chance to understand what was going on around her. One of the Nola handed me the ends of the chains, and I threw them to the roof, whipping them around a beam to pull her up.

She struggled, but it was for nothing. "What are you doing!"

"I want answers. I said it already. What did you do? Did you allow Kyrell to lock me up because you knew I was a guardian? Is it why you kept me from the Sunlight Garden? You didn't want me to infect your tree?" I asked.

My words were demanding, but she didn't answer me. I signaled the Nola to whip her with the same whip she used on Ru and Astra.

"He's going to start with five and go up from there every time you refuse to answer me," I yelled.

"We will start easy. Did you keep me from the Sunlight Garden because I'm a Guardian?" I asked again.

She looked at me as if I were a joke, so I pointed to the Nola, and he didn't hesitate. The sound of the crack on flesh filled the room. He wasn't loyal to her; he didn't care who she was. He only cared about what I told him to do. He showed her the same mercy she showed others.

"Yes," She cried.

I almost hoped she would lie to me again so I could have him give her another set of lashings.

"Did you know Ru was special when you trapped her with the tasks in the garden?"

She looked at me through her lashes with rage.

"What did you do to her in there?" I asked again.

"You wouldn't like the answer." She said.

I lifted my hand for the Nola to give ten more. It only took her two to try to answer my question.

"No, no. You heard the rules. You can finish with what you have earned already, and we will try again. He's going to continue." I crossed my arms and enjoyed the scene.

It was unfortunate that Astra had not come back with Ru yet. It was for her.

"Why can't I touch the tree?" I asked.

"You still don't understand the tree, do you?" Her voice was weak, but I enjoyed it.

"Then explain it to me," I said.

"No." She groaned.

I motioned to the Nola to start again, and he listened. She deserved that sooner.

Several sets of feet came into the chamber, but before I could turn around, I was on my stomach, with my face pressed against the cold floor. The collar around my neck was shooting spikes through me so hard I only saw grey.

"Those are good questions," Deimos said.

"This is too perfect." Helia laughed. "We planned to put Yumi in chains, and here you are, doing the hardest part for us, just like Deimos said you would." She clapped her hands, "Thank you. Truly."

"It's a shame, too. The only one of you that saw it coming is gone." Minna interjected.

Deimos made his way to Yumi's throne and sat on it as if it were his own. My body was still radiating too much pain for me to focus on what was happening.

"You know what I didn't want?" Helia sighed and grabbed Minna's hand, drawing a symbol on it I could not see before she dropped it again, "I did not want someone speaking over my speech."

Minna looked down at her hands and looked back to Helia. She started to struggle, clearly in pain, but from my view of the floor, I couldn't see why.

"What are you doing?" Minna's voice was filled with horror.

"No one paid any attention to me; they were too busy with dear Ruri. The girl with all the magic. No one took the time to see what was going on with anyone else. It wasn't until Deimos came to me and made me an offer. We would rule together, and I would keep Thann by my side. It wasn't until that deal that I realized my blood magic was worth something, even if everyone hadn't seen it yet."

Minna was watching her body turn from flesh to bleeding muscles. There was no skin in sight.

"I have, indeed, gotten really good at it." Helia smiled. "I made a list when Deimos and I decided to rule together of who was the most useless. Minna, you truly are the top. I'm going to keep you as a quiet pet. So be quiet so we can finish what we came here to do."

Helia moved to the throne and took her seat on Deimos's lap. The dark colors of her dress against the shimmer of the throne room were a large contrast to what was expected.

Minna finished her transformation, and she was nothing more than a grotesque, fleshless dog with no jaw. Helia called her over to sit by her side and watched with a smile as every step she took caused her visible pain.

Men with the same kind of muscled skin and deformations entered the room wearing golden armor and positioned themselves near every column in the room.

"Meet my blood guards." Helia tapped her chin and

released the hold on the fate chains enough that I could get to my knees. "It's no fun if I can't see your face for the rest."

The grin Deimos grew sent a pit to my stomach.

"There are a few more things to consider before we accept your apology, and you behave like a good boy. The Time-keepers were sent to the bottom of the ocean, and your lover got to watch it while we chatted about how I killed her sister." Deimos tapped the arm of the throne as if he were thinking.

"Where is Ruri?" I struggled against the collar.

"Kyrell is feeling better. It's not completely better if we're being honest. I don't know when she did it, but Ruri took a piece of him before she left." Helia pointed to the spot between her legs. "He's not too happy about losing the appendage she took, but I do admire her for it."

I couldn't allow myself to admit I understood what she was saying. My Ru. My Ru was not dead.

I tried to use my sun magic to break the collar. The move backfired and knocked down three columns in the room before she gave me another shock and dropped me to the ground again.

"Come now, destroying my pretty room won't bring her body back to life. I'll give you two choices now: kill yourself and rid me of another problem, or go quietly collect her corpse and stay out of my way." Deimos smirked.

Teachings of Moonlight

Nikola trapped me inside bark and took away my voice. He hardened my bark to stone so that I could not move, and he covered me in a seal. He whispered to me about our future, but he did not see my sister watching him. She locked him in the shattered realm that I created and sealed him there. She took me and the stars to the other half of the broken realm. She vowed to me that I would spend eternity watching her hurt the ones I loved the most. That she would bring them to sit in front of my tree and receive all the pain she could inflict. It was to be my punishment for failing to give her the future she wanted. She took everything I created from me and gave it her name instead.

Chapter Thirty—In Another Life, In Another Time—Caym

He knew I wouldn't hesitate. If what he said was true, I would be coming back for him. He could have Semper. He could take the throne and kill Yumi. He could have Merripen. He could not have my wife.

He was not allowed to touch the other half of my soul. I stumbled to get to her room. I could hardly stay upright with how light-headed the thought of her being gone made me. My body felt heavy as if we were separate, and I pulled it against its will.

When I entered the Sunlight Garden, it was empty. There was nobody, only blood. Enough of it to tell me she was gone, and it hadn't been peaceful. Strands of her hair were matted into the blood in several spots on the ground, and I lost control of my legs. The hair was the only sign there was any truth to what I was told happened.

Her emerald hair that I brushed. That I braided. Matted into blood.

I was going to save her. I was hours away from making the realm safe for her.

I was minutes away from being able to see her again and tell her I was sorry.

I was on the edge of making things right between us so that we could stop avoiding each other.

I was waiting for Astra to bring her to me.

Cold rushed over my body, and I couldn't form a coherent

thought. I felt the rush of moisture from my eyes, but I didn't feel I was crying. I felt my body lighten, and I was falling, but I didn't feel myself hit the ground.

I knew I was alive, but I didn't feel like living. My ears only took in ringing.

A Fiia was sitting on the ground in front of me, fluttering its wings, calling my name.

I didn't want to breathe the air that held her death. I didn't want to disturb the evidence I would use to justify my actions when I killed each deity in Semper that allowed things to go so far with my own hands.

I struggled to get to my feet, to leave the sight in front of me. To use my body the way it was meant to be used.

The Fiia led me to her room and pointed me to the drawer of the vanity to reveal her necklace; I had no thoughts. It was all that was left of her, and if it was here, it meant she had to have known. She had to have prepared. She had to have suffered in silence with the thought.

My poor, sweet Ru had no one to lean on, and I didn't even shove my pride far enough down to be there for her.

I should have been there for her. It was all over her face. She needed someone. I should have never left her side when Deimos started harassing her. I should have known what was going on.

I grabbed both pieces of paper up and opened the first one.

Astra,

The garden is growing everything you'll need for Thann and Orest. Collect the amethyst crystals from Owna; they hold the magic of illusion. She also knows the magic system I set up for the crystals. With me gone, there's no way to know for sure how the magic will react, but they won't fail you. Sage will be crushed to learn what had to happen. Give her time to come to terms with it. Help her to understand that she couldn't have made a difference no matter what she did. She did the best she could, and I'm proud of her. I've left two boxes. The Fiia should have taken them by now, but if not, they know what to do. You don't have to hold any more secrets for me now. Thank you for being the best friend I could have had. Give Emon his extra fish for me so he's not sad, either.

If I can ask you one more thing, please look after my daughter for me. Please keep Kyra safe and love her in the way I never openly could.

I couldn't stop myself from stumbling backward and hitting the ground. I should have read the name on the pages first. I couldn't handle it. She was saying Kyra was our daughter? Is that why she picked her land to give a barrier to?

Caym,

I am sorry for lying to you. It's okay to hate me and move forward. I give you permission. You were right when you said we had to pick sides. I listened to you. I picked the one that would guarantee your safety. There are new paints in your home. I put them in your favorite box. I'm sorry I couldn't do more for you. Please remember me as I was in the beginning and then put me away, and don't look back. I love you, husband, and I give you a clean future to start over without any guilt.

Koa was behind me. He grabbed my arms and pulled me backward away from the room. I didn't have it in me to struggle. He didn't speak to me, and I didn't speak to him. He got me to my feet and took me to Cylla.

When he finally let go of me, I tumbled into the grass and let go of anything that was inside of me onto the ground.

I sat next to my bile, and my eyes felt heavy. They felt as heavy as the rest of me did.

Things were hazy after when they told me Sage had died, too. I was hardly involved in any funeral preparations. Koa and Vespera prepared them. They tried to make me feel better by telling me they already knew that both of them would be reborn as mortals until we could find something else to do for them.

It didn't make me feel any better. It made my heart ache even more to consider that she may form an entire life, maybe multiple lifetimes, without me to help.

That I could fail her over and over again.

I would find her; I would see both of them. I would make it my mission even if it took centuries.

They filled me in on their plans with Thann and how they took him and locked him in the depths of Orest. They kept him before she could die so that they had control over rebirth. So that they could find her after she died. She went through so much alone.

She carried so much without anything from me. I only helped add to her burden. I spent time upset because she wanted to leave me. I was mad at her because she didn't say goodbye to me. In truth, it was my fault she had to carry it all alone. I should have been able to read her. I should have known what was happening.

We were standing in front of the burning coffins when I next had full recollection. Koa went to Ru's body before me so that I didn't have to see it. He told me not to open the coffin. That Deimos had taken her head.

Even while we burned them, he stood close enough to me that he could stop me if I tried to move for her. He pleaded with me that my last memory of her should not be the way she looked. I didn't have the strength to fight him. Even after what he had just been through, he was by my side.

He was an example of what I should have been for her.

Onyx wanted Sage to have her funeral with Ru, and I agreed. Deimos killed Sage before she sought out Ru. They died back-to-back, and even if they didn't get to say it one last time, they loved each other. Their funeral should have been together.

We were going to rebuild our home in Ashbell once they were laid to rest. Cyrus was the only one to speak to me like I knew I should have been. The dragon of summer berated me with his words. He lectured me about my failures. He told me I should have been stripped of being a guardian when I let them die the first time so that I couldn't have failed a second time, and he was right.

"I know this is a bad time, but two girls just landed in the Sunlight Garden. One of them is a sister, and she's not doing well. I don't know if we can save her." Sina said.

"Koa?"

I didn't have to finish; he left with the goddess of winter to see what was going on, and I knew I owed him more than I could ever have repaid him. I needed time to gather myself to stop the ringing in my ears.

I need to be with her until the last ember burnt out. I couldn't leave her side until I was sure every last ash of hope was gone. I could not help anyone with any other problems swirling around us until I saw with my own eyes that my heart, my soul, was burnt up in front of me and lost.

REFERENCE GUIDE

Dragons
Ryujin—Second in Command of the Armies from the Age of
Moonlight, in dragon form.
Sina—Winter Goddess in dragon form
Vero—Fall Goddess in dragon form
Cyrus—Summer God in dragon form
Belladonna—Ruri Dragon
Usha—Erebus Guardian
Divala—Brontide Guardian
Kaida—Onyx Dragon

Realms
Semper—Realm of the Gods
Cylla—Realm of the Mortals
Cosima—Realm of Dreaming Souls
Merripen—Realm of the Dead

Deity-led kingdoms
Ruri—Ashbell
Kyrell—Solaris
Thann—Orest

Astra—Edur
Kyra—Brontide
Orla/Sage—Erebus
Izaria—Daxon

Other notable inhabitants.
Fiia—A small fluttering creature made of starlight that helps send messages back and forth.
Lui—Leader of the Timekeepers.
Jeb—Commander of the Nola.
Nola—Keepers of the underworld, helpers to the God of Death.
Vina—Cave protectors
Seere—Clerics of Ashbell, created by Ruri. They are covered in black scales with magma-colored veins, orange eyes, and black hair. They commonly wear masks to avoid breathing in the excess ash on their land.
Mita—Nearly transparent skin. Golden eyes and tinted skin. Black hair. Their golden veins pulse with the thunder magic they wield.
Angels—Guardians created to protect Yumi and the realm of the Gods.
Timekeepers—Collectors and protectors of knowledge from the Age of Moonlight.
Blood Guards—Second created guardians of Semper. Made by blood from Helia, the Goddess of Time.
False deities—Deities created in the likeness of powerful originals to take their place.

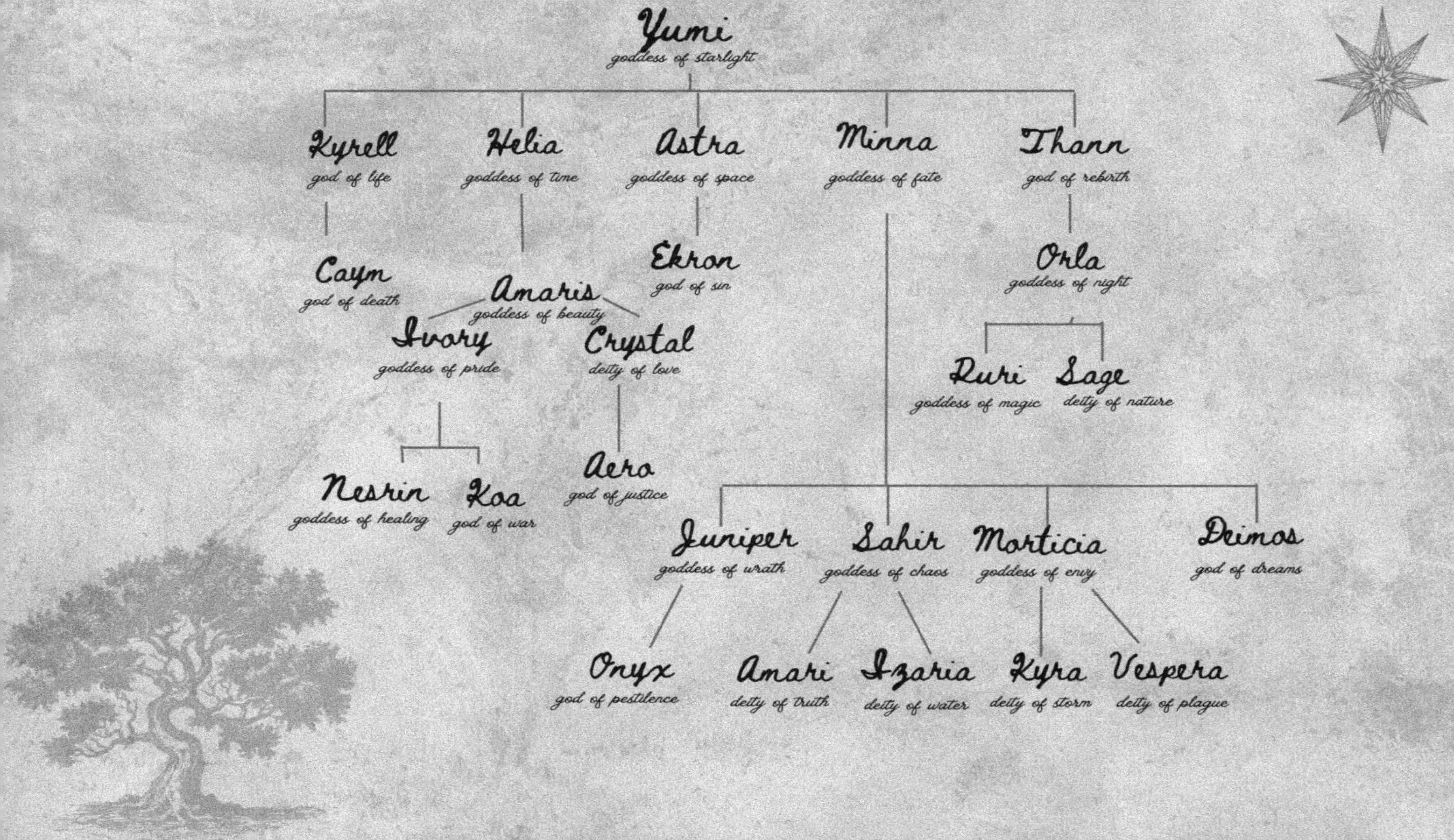

Yumi
goddess of starlight

Kyrell
god of life

Helia
goddess of time

Astra
goddess of space

Minna
goddess of fate

Thann
god of rebirth

Caym
god of death

Amaris
goddess of beauty

Ekron
god of sin

Orla
goddess of night

Ivory
goddess of pride

Crystal
deity of love

Ruri
goddess of magic

Sage
deity of nature

Nesrin
goddess of healing

Koa
god of war

Aera
god of justice

Juniper
goddess of wrath

Sahir
goddess of chaos

Morticia
goddess of envy

Drimos
god of dreams

Onyx
god of pestilence

Amari
deity of truth

Izaria
deity of water

Kyra
deity of storm

Vespera
deity of plague

ALSO BY HARLEIGH ROSE KNIGHT

Coming soon…

Viper and the Gods, Book two

Sunlight and Shadow, Book three

Rage of Gods and Dragons, Book four

Keep up to date with the latest news and release dates for the rest of the series by following them on social media.

Harleigh Rose Knight on all platforms.